Thorns of the Eternal Rose

Destinies Entwined in Shadows

Book 1

By

Everett Vale

Dedication

For those who walk the line between light and shadow, who fight battles unseen and carry burdens untold. May you find strength in the thorns and beauty in the darkness.

Table of Contents

Prologue:

The Rose's Shadow

The air in the throne room hung heavy, steeped in a gloom that neither candlelight nor the brilliance of the gilded columns could dispel. Shadows clung to the edges of the vast chamber like restless spirits, whispering secrets to those who dared listen. Queen Lysenna Lysoria sat at the head of the long, polished table, her slender fingers tracing the rim of a crystal goblet. She stared at the dark red wine swirling within, her expression a mask of icy serenity.

Her beauty was a weapon, sharp and deliberate. High cheekbones caught the dim light like the edges of a blade, and her pale skin glowed with an almost unnatural luster. Her emerald eyes, as piercing as the jewels they resembled, seemed to see far beyond the walls of the palace—to some distant horizon where fate itself trembled.

"You've come far for this," she said, her voice a low murmur that resonated through the silent hall.

Across from her, a figure stepped forward from the darkness. He moved with a predator's grace, his cloak a tattered shadow billowing around him. Varyn Morryn's smile gleamed in the dim light, a wicked curve that seemed to cut deeper than any blade. He flicked a silver coin between his fingers, the metallic clink echoing faintly.

"I came because you summoned me, Your Majesty," he replied, his voice as smooth as silk soaked in venom. "Few possess the audacity—or the desperation—to call upon the Shadowborn."

Lysenna's lips twitched into the barest hint of a smile. "Desperation is a weapon when wielded correctly, Varyn. You of all people should know that."

Varyn leaned forward, resting his palms on the table. The candlelight carved sharp hollows into his angular face, making him look like a creature born of shadows. "You want the Eternal Rose. But you know its cost."

The queen's fingers tightened around the goblet. "What is the survival of a kingdom worth if not blood? If not pain?"

Varyn's laugh was low, almost intimate. "And yet you would offer another's pain before your own. How... predictable."

Lysenna rose to her feet, her gown whispering against the marble floor. Her gaze burned as she stared him down. "Do not mistake me, Varyn. I will see this kingdom endure—whatever the cost. Even if it means shattering the lives of those I hold dear."

The coin stopped spinning in Varyn's fingers. For a moment, he studied her, as though weighing the worth of her words. Then he nodded, his expression coldly approving.

"So be it," he said. "But remember, Your Majesty, the Eternal Rose is no mere relic. It chooses its bearers, and it thrives on suffering. You cannot control it—only survive it."

Lysenna's lips curved into a grim smile. "Survival will suffice."

A Bride's Farewell

The morning was an uneasy blend of beauty and sorrow. The palace gardens, normally a riot of color and vitality, seemed subdued beneath a sky streaked with gray. Dew clung to the roses and lilacs as though reluctant to let them go, their petals heavy with the weight of the day. Somewhere beyond the hedges, the faint hum of preparations carried through the air: carts creaking, horses stamping, the murmur of voices.

In her chambers, Anira Lysoria stood before a gilded mirror, unmoving as the maids fluttered around her like anxious moths. Her gown—a masterpiece of silver silk and pale blue embroidery—was a marvel of craftsmanship, but it felt like a shroud draped over her slender frame. Her raven-black hair, braided and coiled in intricate patterns, framed a face that was too pale, too still.

"You look beautiful, Your Highness," said Wyn, her maid and closest confidante, though her voice lacked its usual warmth.

Anira's reflection offered no response. Her emerald eyes, so vibrant in better moments, were dulled by resignation. The soft line of her mouth barely moved as she finally spoke.

"Do I?" she asked, her tone brittle. "Or do I look like a lamb trussed up for slaughter?"

Wyn rolled her eyes, tugging at the final braid with slightly more force than necessary. "Slaughter is such a strong word, my lady. I prefer 'sacrificial offering.' It has a nicer ring to it, don't you think?"

A faint smile flickered across Anira's lips. Wyn always had a way of cutting through the tension, but even her humor couldn't fully banish the ache gnawing at Anira's chest.

"They'll send me off with flowers and praise," Anira murmured, her voice barely audible. "And I'll never return. That's what my mother believes. That's what she wants."

Wyn stepped back, her sharp eyes softening. "And what do you want?"

For a long moment, Anira stared at her reflection. The woman in the mirror was a stranger—a porcelain doll dressed in finery, her sharp edges dulled by duty.

"I want…" she began, but the words faltered, lost somewhere between her heart and her lips. What did it matter? Her wants had never been a part of the equation.

Wyn sighed and began packing a satchel with her usual brisk efficiency. "Well, if you're going to brood, at least do it dramatically. Maybe lean against the window and sigh wistfully. That's what princesses do, isn't it?"

Anira couldn't help the small laugh that escaped her. "You're incorrigible."

"And you're hopeless," Wyn shot back, flashing a grin. "But lucky for you, I'm coming with you. Someone has to make sure you don't start quoting poetry at your new husband."

"Isn't he a scholar?" Anira asked dryly. "Perhaps he'll enjoy my dramatic sighs."

The sound of boots on stone drew their attention. The door opened to reveal Ashric, dressed in the plain armor of a low-ranking guard. His broad shoulders filled the doorway, his presence commanding despite his unassuming role. His sharp blue eyes flicked briefly to Anira, then away, as though he found her finery too bright to look at for long.

"Your Highness," he said, his tone curt. "The caravan is ready."

Anira met his gaze in the mirror, her pulse quickening at the intensity she saw there. There was something in his eyes—a depth that hinted at pain, secrets, and a storm he had long since learned to weather.

"Thank you," she replied, her voice steadier than she felt.

Wyn snorted softly. "Oh, good. Another brooder. Just what we need."

Ashric's lips quirked, barely perceptible. "I'll take that as a compliment."

And with that, the moment was broken. Anira turned away from the mirror, the weight of the day settling over her shoulders like a mantle she could never remove.

The palace courtyard bustled with energy, but it was not the sort that inspired joy. The clamor of preparations—the stamping of horses, the loading of luggage onto carriages, the crisp bark of orders from guards—echoed off the cold stone walls. The air was thick with unease, as though even the bricks and mortar understood that this day marked an end.

Anira descended the wide marble steps slowly, her gown sweeping behind her like a silver wave. She held her head high, her features composed, but inside, her heart beat with the steady thrum of impending finality. Wyn trailed close behind, muttering under her breath as she adjusted the hem of Anira's cloak.

"Honestly, you'd think they could have made this lighter," Wyn grumbled. "Are they hoping the sheer weight of it keeps you from running away?"

"Perhaps that's the plan," Anira replied, her voice soft but edged with bitterness. "No bride can flee if she's tethered to half a kingdom's treasury."

Ashric stood near the lead carriage, his armor catching glints of the pale morning sun. He was speaking quietly with another guard, his expression inscrutable, though his posture was tense—coiled, like a predator ready to strike. The contrast between him and the other men was stark. Where they stood with the stiff, polished arrogance of those who had never seen true battle, Ashric carried the weight of experience. His scars were not just etched into his skin but also woven into his very presence.

He glanced up as Anira approached, his piercing blue eyes locking on her. For a fleeting moment, something flickered in his gaze—pity, perhaps, or understanding. Then it was gone, replaced by his usual stoic mask.

"My lady," he said with a slight bow, his voice low and steady. "The carriage is ready. We'll be riding through the eastern forest by midmorning."

Anira hesitated, her gaze flicking to the carriages lined up in a neat row. The wheels, freshly oiled and shining, looked as though they were ready to carry her to the edge of the world.

"Will you be riding ahead?" she asked, surprising herself with the question.

Ashric's brow furrowed slightly, as though he hadn't expected her to speak directly to him. "No, Your Highness. I'll be riding alongside your carriage. The eastern routes can be... unpredictable."

"Unpredictable," Wyn repeated, her tone dripping with sarcasm. "That's comforting."

Ashric's lips twitched, almost imperceptibly. "Don't worry, Miss Garrow. I've encountered bandits before. They're not terribly creative."

"Oh, good," Wyn shot back. "As long as we're only being attacked by uncreative bandits, I'm sure we'll be fine."

The faintest shadow of a smirk passed across Ashric's face before he inclined his head. "Your Highness," he said, addressing Anira again, "we should leave soon."

She nodded, though the weight of the moment pressed against her chest like a stone. As she stepped toward the carriage, her gaze wandered to the palace gates. They loomed tall and unyielding, flanked by guards who stood as still as statues. Beyond them lay the world she had only seen in stories—the world that now demanded her submission.

The interior of the carriage was lavish, yet suffocating. Plush velvet cushions in deep crimson lined the seats, and the faint scent of lavender lingered in the air. Anira settled onto one side, smoothing her gown absently while Wyn fussed with the small satchel she had insisted on bringing.

"You could pretend to be excited, you know," Wyn said, her tone light but probing. "It might make the trip less miserable."

Anira leaned her head against the cool glass of the window, her green eyes fixed on the passing courtyard. "Excited," she murmured. "To be sold off to a prince I've never met? To a kingdom where I'll be little more than a decorative token?"

"You're more than that," Wyn said firmly. "You always have been."

"And yet here I am," Anira whispered, her voice almost drowned by the sound of the carriage wheels creaking into motion.

Ashric rode alongside the carriage, his horse keeping a steady pace despite the uneven cobblestones of the palace road. He kept his head tilted slightly forward, his sharp eyes scanning the crowd that had gathered to watch the royal procession. Faces blurred together: some curious, others disinterested, and a few openly resentful. He could feel their eyes on him, their judgment sharp and unrelenting.

It didn't bother him. He was used to judgment.

The real threat lay not in the crowd but in the forest beyond the city walls. He'd seen the way the trees grew there, their branches twisted and gnarled like skeletal fingers. He'd heard the stories, too—of bandits, beasts, and darker things that moved in the shadows. Ashric didn't put much stock in stories, but he trusted his instincts, and his instincts told him that this journey would not be as simple as the queen wanted it to be.

As they passed through the gates, leaving the sprawling city behind, Ashric allowed himself a brief glance at the carriage. Through the small window, he caught a glimpse of Anira's pale face, her expression distant. There was a hardness to her features now, something that hadn't been there when he first saw her in the throne room. He wondered how much of that was because of her mother—and how much was because of him.

The eastern forest loomed ahead, its edges shrouded in mist. The trees rose like silent sentinels, their blackened trunks gnarled and ancient. The air grew cooler as the caravan entered the forest, the sounds of the city fading into an eerie stillness.

Inside the carriage, Anira shivered, though she wasn't sure if it was from the chill or the sense of foreboding that crept over her. Wyn had fallen quiet, her usual chatter replaced by a nervous fidgeting as she adjusted the straps of her satchel.

"Does it always feel like this?" Anira asked softly.

Wyn glanced up. "Like what?"

"Like the world is holding its breath."

Wyn hesitated before answering. "Maybe it's the trees," she said, attempting a small smile. "They look like they've been waiting for something. Or someone."

Outside, Ashric tightened his grip on the reins. His eyes scanned the shadows beneath the trees, searching for movement. He couldn't shake the feeling that they were being watched. The forest was too quiet, the kind of quiet that wasn't natural.

He slowed his horse slightly, falling back to ride closer to the carriage. The flicker of tension in his chest had become an ache, a gnawing certainty that something was coming. Something inevitable.

He leaned slightly toward the nearest guard. "Keep your hand on your blade," he murmured. "We're not alone."

The guard's eyes widened, but before he could respond, the stillness of the forest was shattered by the sound of an arrow slicing through the air.

The arrow struck one of the lead guards with a sickening thud, embedding itself deep into his shoulder. He let out a strangled cry before toppling from his horse, the thump of his body hitting the forest floor reverberating like a drumbeat.

"Ambush!" Ashric barked, his voice slicing through the chaos as a second arrow whizzed past his head, narrowly missing its mark. He yanked his horse to a stop, drawing his sword in one fluid motion. The polished steel gleamed in the dim light of the forest, catching what little sun broke through the dense canopy.

Inside the carriage, Anira froze, her breath catching in her throat. The shout, the thud of bodies falling, and the metallic ring of swords being drawn shattered the fragile bubble of detachment she had wrapped herself in. Wyn's hands gripped the edge of the seat, her knuckles white as her sharp eyes darted toward the small window.

"What's happening?" Anira demanded, her voice trembling despite her effort to sound calm.

Wyn peered out, her expression tightening as she took in the sight of guards scrambling to form a defensive line. "Something bad. Stay here."

Before Anira could argue, the carriage door was wrenched open. Ashric stood there, his sword slick with blood, his blue eyes blazing with a fire that seemed to hold the world at bay.

"Out. Now," he ordered, his voice sharp enough to cut through Anira's hesitation.

"What? Why—" she began, but he grabbed her arm, not unkindly, and pulled her from the carriage. His grip was firm and unyielding, his movements efficient as he pushed her behind him.

"They're targeting you," he said without looking back. His words were a weapon, blunt and irrefutable. "The carriage is a coffin. Stay close to me."

The smell of blood and iron filled the air, mingling with the earthy scent of the forest. Anira's heart thundered in her chest as she tried to process the scene around her. Shadowed figures darted between the trees, their movements quick and purposeful. The guards were holding their ground, but for how long? The attackers were too coordinated, too focused.

And then she saw him—Varyn Morryn.

He emerged from the shadows as though he had always belonged to them, his silver coin spinning lazily between his fingers. His smile was a jagged thing, sharp and mocking, his dark cloak billowing around him like a phantom's shroud. There was something both regal and monstrous about him, a charisma that drew the eye even as it repelled the soul.

"Well, well," he said, his voice carrying effortlessly over the clash of steel and the cries of the wounded. "A royal procession in the middle of nowhere. How quaint."

Ashric stepped forward, positioning himself squarely between Anira and Varyn. His stance was that of a man prepared to kill, his sword steady despite the chaos around him.

"Varyn," he said, his voice low and laced with venom. "I should have known this was your handiwork."

Varyn's smile widened, his sharp features catching the faint light in a way that made him look more wolf than man. "Brother," he drawled, the word dripping with mockery. "It's been far too long."

Brother. The word slammed into Anira like a physical blow. She stared at Ashric, her mind reeling. He didn't deny it, didn't even flinch. Instead, he tightened his grip on his sword, his expression darkening into something fierce and unyielding.

"This isn't your fight," Ashric said through gritted teeth. "Leave. Now."

"Oh, but it is," Varyn replied, his tone almost playful. "You know as well as I do that the Eternal Rose has chosen her. You've seen it, haven't you? The way it burns. It's why you've stayed by her side."

Anira's stomach twisted as Varyn's gaze shifted to her. His eyes, pale and predatory, lingered on her with an intensity that made her skin crawl.

"You feel it too, don't you, Princess?" he said, his voice softer now, coaxing. "The pull of something greater. The weight of destiny."

Anira's mouth went dry. "I don't know what you're talking about."

"Oh, but you will," Varyn said, his smile returning. "Sooner than you think."

Before Ashric could react, Varyn flicked his hand, and the shadows seemed to come alive. Figures surged forward, their weapons gleaming as they closed in on the caravan. Ashric moved with lethal precision, his sword cutting through the attackers with the fluidity of a man who had spent his life in battle.

"Stay close to me!" he barked at Anira, his voice breaking through her daze.

She obeyed, her body moving on instinct as Ashric fought to keep the attackers at bay. Every clang of steel, every cry of pain, felt like it reverberated inside her skull. The world was a blur of blood and chaos, and yet her focus remained locked on Ashric.

He moved like a storm—relentless, devastating, and impossible to look away from. And yet, there was a desperation to his movements, a fury that seemed to burn brighter with every swing of his blade.

"Anira!" Wyn's voice cut through the din, sharp and panicked. She had ducked behind the overturned carriage, clutching a small dagger that looked absurdly inadequate in her trembling hands. "What are you doing? Run!"

Run. The word seemed foreign, almost absurd. Where could she go? The forest was alive with enemies, and Ashric—Ashric was...

Her thoughts fractured as another shadow lunged toward her. Before she could react, Ashric was there, his blade slicing through the air with a deadly hiss. The attacker fell at her feet, lifeless.

Ashric turned to her, his face streaked with blood, his eyes burning with fury. "I told you to stay close."

"I—" Her voice faltered. She didn't know what to say. Didn't know how to explain the storm of fear and defiance raging inside her.

"Your Highness!" A guard's shout rang out, and Ashric turned just in time to block another attack. The clash of steel rang out as he pushed the attacker back, but the effort left him exposed. Another shadow moved in, blade raised.

This time, it was Anira who acted.

Without thinking, she snatched a fallen dagger from the ground and drove it into the side of the attacker's neck. The blade sank deep, the shock of it jolting through her arm as blood sprayed across her gown. The attacker crumpled, his weapon slipping from his fingers.

For a moment, everything went still. Anira stared at the body, her chest heaving, her mind struggling to comprehend what she had done.

Ashric's voice pulled her back. "Anira." It wasn't a shout, wasn't even loud, but the way he said her name—sharp, urgent, almost reverent—cut through the haze.

She turned to him, her hand still clutching the bloodied dagger. His eyes met hers, and for a brief moment, the battle around them seemed to fade. There was something in his gaze that she couldn't name—something raw and unguarded.

Then the world surged back into motion, and Ashric grabbed her arm, pulling her close. "You're not safe here," he said, his voice hard but not unkind. "We need to move."

And with that, he led her deeper into the forest, away from the carnage, away from Varyn's mocking laughter that lingered like a promise in the air.

The forest closed around them, its shadows deepening as Ashric pulled Anira through the undergrowth. The air was damp, heavy with the scent of moss and earth, and every breath

Anira took felt thick with the weight of what had just happened. Her legs ached from the uneven terrain, her gown snagging on brambles as she stumbled after him, the bloodied dagger still clutched in her hand.

Ashric didn't speak, his focus sharp as his eyes scanned their surroundings. The way he moved—silent, deliberate—was both reassuring and unsettling, as though he belonged more to the forest than to the world she knew. His sword was still drawn, the blade streaked with blood that gleamed faintly in the dim light filtering through the canopy.

Finally, after what felt like hours, they reached a small clearing. A jagged rock formation jutted up from the earth like the bones of some ancient beast, casting long shadows that curled into the trees. Ashric stopped abruptly, turning to face her, his broad shoulders rising and falling with each measured breath.

"Are you hurt?" he asked, his voice low but urgent.

Anira shook her head, though her hands trembled as the adrenaline began to fade.

"No," she managed, though her voice was thin and unsteady. "Not physically."

He studied her for a moment, his piercing blue eyes searching hers. There was a depth to his gaze that she couldn't quite place, something that hinted at an understanding she didn't expect.

"You did well," he said finally, his tone softer than she'd heard it before. "Back there."

Her grip tightened on the dagger, her knuckles white against its worn hilt. "I killed a man."

"You saved your life," he corrected. "And mine."

The weight of his words settled over her like a shroud, and she looked down at the dagger, at the blood that had begun to dry on its blade. "I never... I didn't think..." She trailed off, shaking her head as her thoughts tangled.

Ashric stepped closer, his presence grounding despite the tension crackling between them. "The first time you take a life, it feels like the world shifts beneath your feet," he said quietly. "You'll never forget it, but you'll learn to carry it. And that burden doesn't make you weak."

Anira glanced up at him, startled by the raw honesty in his voice. For a moment, she saw past the grim, battle-hardened exterior to the man beneath—the man who had seen too much, lost too much, and still stood tall.

"Thank you," she said softly, unsure if she meant for his words, his protection, or both.

His jaw tightened slightly, and he turned away, scanning the tree line. "We can't stay here long," he said, his voice shifting back to the cool practicality she had come to expect. "Varyn's men will be hunting us."

"Varyn," she murmured, the name heavy on her tongue. "He called you his brother."

Ashric's shoulders stiffened, and for a moment, he didn't answer. When he finally spoke, his voice was edged with something bitter and sharp. "We share blood," he said. "That's where our connection ends."

Anira wanted to press him, to ask about the history that clearly haunted him, but the look on his face—the tightness in his jaw, the flicker of pain in his eyes—kept her silent.

Whatever had passed between them, it was a wound that hadn't healed.

"What does he want from me?" she asked instead, her voice steady despite the storm of questions swirling in her mind.

Ashric turned back to her, his gaze intense. "It's not you he wants," he said. "It's the Eternal Rose."

The words sent a chill down her spine. She had heard whispers of the Rose before, stories of its beauty and power, of the lives it had touched—and destroyed. But those stories had always felt distant, like something out of a dream. Now, they loomed over her like a shadow, too real to ignore.

"What is it?" she asked, her voice barely above a whisper.

Ashric hesitated, his expression unreadable. "It's a relic," he said finally. "An artifact older than the kingdoms themselves. It's said to hold the power to bind life, death, and... love."

His voice caught slightly on the last word, and Anira's breath hitched. "Why would he think it has anything to do with me?"

"Because the Rose doesn't just exist," Ashric said, his tone grim. "It chooses. And from the moment I saw the glow in your hands back in the forest... I knew it had chosen you."

Anira's heart clenched, her mind racing as she tried to process his words. The Rose had chosen her? What did that mean? What was expected of her? And why did she feel an invisible weight settle over her shoulders, as though the world itself had shifted?

Ashric's voice cut through her spiraling thoughts. "You don't have to understand it now," he said. "But know this: Varyn won't stop. He'll hunt you to the ends of the earth if it means getting to the Rose."

"And you?" she asked, meeting his gaze. "Why are you still here?"

Something flickered in his eyes, something raw and unspoken. He didn't answer immediately, and when he did, his voice was low, almost reluctant. "Because I've made enough mistakes to know when it's time to make things right."

Before she could respond, the distant sound of hooves echoed through the forest. Ashric's head snapped toward the noise, his expression hardening.

"Move," he said sharply, motioning for her to follow. "They're coming."

Without another word, he led her deeper into the shadows of the forest, his presence steady and unwavering. Anira clutched the dagger to her chest, her mind racing with questions and fears that had no answers.

The forest closed around them, the trees whispering secrets she couldn't understand. But one thing was clear: her life would never be the same again.

Into the Shadows

The forest seemed alive. The trees whispered in voices too faint to hear but too persistent to ignore, their skeletal branches weaving a canopy so dense that only thin beams of pale light managed to pierce through. Shadows shifted across the ground, stretching and curling like the grasping hands of something unseen. Every step Anira took felt like an intrusion, her soft footfalls swallowed by the damp earth beneath her boots.

Ashric moved ahead of her, his presence a grim reassurance. His broad frame was a dark silhouette against the muted backdrop of the forest, his sword still unsheathed and held low at his side. He didn't speak, but every motion of his body radiated tension—his gaze darting to every shadow, his shoulders coiled as if expecting an attack at any moment.

Anira's breath was shallow, her chest tight as she struggled to keep pace. Her gown, torn and stained from the ambush, clung to her legs with every step. The dagger in her hand felt foreign and heavy, its weight a constant reminder of what she had done.

"What happens if they catch us?" she asked, her voice barely louder than a whisper.

Ashric slowed just enough to glance back at her, his blue eyes cold and sharp. "They won't."

It wasn't the answer she wanted, but the steel in his tone left no room for argument.

The faint sound of hoofbeats echoed behind them, distant but growing louder. Anira's pulse quickened, her grip tightening on the dagger. The Shadowborn were closing in, their presence a shadow that stretched across her mind as much as the forest around her.

"They're gaining," she said, her voice trembling.

"I know," Ashric replied, his pace quickening. "But this isn't their terrain. It's ours now."

Ours. The word struck her as strange. She was no warrior, no survivor of ambushes and bloodshed. She was a princess, raised in the gilded confines of a palace where danger was something whispered about in the distant halls of court intrigue. And yet here she was, following this battle-worn stranger into the depths of a forest that felt more alive than it had any right to be.

They descended into a gully where the air grew cooler, the trees thickening until they formed walls of gnarled wood on either side. Moss clung to the rocks, slick and luminous in the dim light, and the faint trickle of water echoed through the hollow. Anira shivered, though she couldn't tell if it was from the chill or the oppressive atmosphere that seemed to press down on them.

Ashric stopped abruptly, raising a hand for silence. Anira froze, her heart pounding in her ears as she strained to listen. The hoofbeats had stopped, replaced by a silence so deep it felt unnatural.

"What is it?" she whispered.

He didn't answer immediately. Instead, he turned his head slightly, his gaze scanning the ridge above them. The muscles in his jaw tightened.

"They've stopped following us," he said, his voice low and grim.

"That's good, isn't it?" Anira asked, though the knot in her stomach told her otherwise.

"No," Ashric said, his grip tightening on his sword. "It means they're waiting."

"For what?"

His gaze flicked to her, sharp and assessing. "For us to make a mistake."

Anira swallowed hard, her fingers trembling around the hilt of the dagger. "And if we don't?"

Ashric's mouth twitched into something that might have been a smirk if it weren't so laced with bitterness. "Then they'll create one."

The air grew heavier as they pressed on, the silence thick and cloying. Anira's thoughts churned, a chaotic whirl of fear and uncertainty. What was waiting for them in these woods? And why did it feel as though the forest itself was watching, its unseen eyes following their every move?

As they climbed the slope of the gully, Ashric stopped again, his body tense. His head tilted slightly, as though listening to something she couldn't hear. A moment later, his hand shot out, grabbing her arm and pulling her sharply to the side.

"Down," he hissed.

Anira barely had time to react before he pulled her behind a boulder, his body pressing close to hers as he shielded her from view. His warmth and the sharp scent of leather and steel enveloped her, but her attention was fixed on the ridge above them.

Figures moved among the trees, their shapes shifting like shadows come to life. They were humanoid, but their movements were unnaturally fluid, their limbs stretching and bending in ways that defied logic. Anira's breath caught as she watched them, her heart hammering in her chest.

"What are they?" she whispered.

"Not human," Ashric said grimly. "Shadowborn use them when they want to track without being seen. They won't attack unless provoked."

"Unless provoked?" she repeated, her voice rising slightly.

Ashric's eyes narrowed. "That means stay quiet."

She clamped her mouth shut, her pulse thundering in her ears as she watched the shadowed figures move closer. Their movements were unnerving, almost hypnotic, as though they were made of the forest itself. She could feel the weight of their presence, an unnatural pressure that seemed to squeeze the air from her lungs.

Ashric shifted slightly, his hand brushing hers. "They'll pass if we stay still."

Anira nodded, though every fiber of her being screamed at her to run. The seconds stretched into what felt like hours as the figures glided through the trees, their dark forms blending seamlessly with the shadows. One of them paused, its head tilting as though sniffing the air.

Ashric's hand tightened on his sword, the muscles in his arm tensing. Anira held her breath, her eyes locked on the creature as it turned its head toward their hiding spot.

Then, as suddenly as it had stopped, it moved on, disappearing into the dense trees.

Anira let out a shaky breath, her legs trembling beneath her. "What were those things?"

"Shadow wraiths," Ashric said, his voice low. "They're part of the forest now, bound to the magic the Shadowborn use. They don't leave much of you behind if they find you."

Anira shuddered, her mind struggling to grasp the weight of his words. "And you didn't think to mention this earlier?"

"I didn't want to worry you," Ashric replied, his tone dry. "Apparently, I failed."

As they pressed on, Anira couldn't shake the image of the shadow wraiths from her mind. Their movements, their presence, had felt wrong in a way she couldn't describe. And yet, she couldn't help but feel that their appearance was somehow tied to her. To the Rose.

She glanced at Ashric, his face set in a mask of grim determination. His silence was heavy, but she could see the tension in his jaw, the flicker of something raw in his eyes when he thought she wasn't looking.

"What aren't you telling me?" she asked, her voice quieter now, almost hesitant.

He didn't answer immediately. When he finally spoke, his voice was low and weighted with something she couldn't name. "The Rose doesn't just choose randomly. It doesn't just bind itself to anyone."

"What does that mean?"

"It means," he said, his gaze meeting hers with a sharp intensity, "that the Shadowborn aren't just after you because of who you are. They're after you because of what you're becoming."

Her breath caught, the weight of his words sinking deep into her chest. She wanted to ask more, to demand answers, but before she could, a sound cut through the air—a faint, high-pitched hum that seemed to vibrate through the trees.

Ashric's expression darkened. "Run."

The hum grew louder, resonating through the forest like the whisper of a thousand voices speaking just out of reach. Anira's pulse spiked, her instincts screaming to flee even as her legs felt frozen to the ground. Ashric's hand shot out, gripping her wrist, his voice sharp and commanding.

"Move!"

This time, she obeyed without question. They sprinted through the forest, their footsteps muffled by the damp earth but their breathing loud in the still air. The sound followed them, growing in intensity, an eerie chorus that seemed to come from everywhere and nowhere at once.

"What is that?" Anira gasped, struggling to keep up with Ashric's long strides.

"Wraithsong," he said grimly, glancing over his shoulder. "It means they've found us."

The trees blurred past, their gnarled branches reaching like skeletal hands. Anira's heart pounded in her chest, her gown catching on low-hanging thorns as she ran. The sound of the wraithsong was all-encompassing now, filling the air with its haunting melody, each note tugging at her very soul.

Ashric suddenly veered left, pulling her down into a shallow ravine where the earth smelled of moss and decay. He shoved her against the side of a large, craggy boulder, his body pressing close to hers as he peered up the slope.

"Stay quiet," he murmured, his voice barely audible over the ringing in her ears.

Anira pressed herself into the rough surface of the rock, her chest heaving as she fought to control her breathing. The dagger in her hand felt heavy, its bloodied blade trembling with every shaky breath she drew. She tilted her head slightly, trying to listen beyond the hum of the wraithsong.

Then she saw them.

They glided into view, their forms blending seamlessly with the forest. The shadow wraiths were close now, their movements graceful and predatory. Their bodies shimmered faintly, as though made of mist and twilight, and their eyes glowed with an unnatural silver light. Anira's breath hitched as one of them paused, its head tilting toward the ravine.

Ashric's hand closed over hers, the heat of his palm grounding her. She looked up at him, her gaze meeting his. His expression was calm but fierce, his blue eyes sharp and unwavering. He gave the faintest shake of his head, a silent command: Stay still.

The wraith drifted closer, its silver eyes scanning the ground. Anira felt as though it could see through her, as though it could sense her fear and the weight of the Rose burning within her chest. She gripped the dagger tighter, her pulse hammering in her throat.

The wraith's head snapped toward them.

Ashric moved faster than she could process, his sword flashing as he lunged forward. The blade struck the wraith's form, and for a moment, the creature let out a high, keening scream. Its body flickered, the mist-like substance unraveling, but not before it lashed out. A shadowed tendril struck Ashric across the chest, sending him staggering back with a sharp grunt of pain.

Anira didn't think—she acted. Her body surged forward, the dagger in her hand slashing wildly at the wraith. The blade connected, the resistance strange and ethereal, as though cutting through water. The wraith's scream rose to a deafening pitch before it dissolved into nothingness, leaving behind only a faint shimmer in the air.

Ashric was already on his feet, his movements quick despite the gash across his chest. "Come on," he said, his voice rough. "That won't keep them off us for long."

She wanted to argue, to demand answers, but there was no time. The hum was rising again, the wraithsong swelling like a storm about to break. Anira forced herself to follow as Ashric led her deeper into the forest, his movements precise and purposeful despite the growing darkness.

They stumbled into a hollow where a massive tree rose from the earth, its twisted roots forming a natural archway. The air here felt different, heavier, as though the forest itself had drawn its breath and was holding it.

Ashric turned to her, his face pale but determined. "Through there," he said, nodding toward the archway.

"What is it?" she asked, her voice trembling.

"A threshold," he replied. "The wraiths won't follow. It's old magic—they can't cross it."

Anira hesitated, her gaze flicking between him and the strange archway. The space beyond the roots was dark, the shadows within almost liquid in their depth. She didn't trust it, but the sound of the wraithsong closing in left her no choice.

She stepped forward, the shadows enveloping her like a cold, silken veil. The air seemed to hum around her, heavy with power, and she felt a strange pull in her chest—a sensation that was both comforting and unnerving. She turned back to see Ashric stumble through the archway behind her, his movements slower now.

The hum of the wraithsong cut off abruptly. The silence that followed was almost deafening.

Ashric slumped against one of the massive roots, his sword falling from his hand as he pressed a hand to his chest. Blood seeped through his fingers, dark and viscous. Anira's heart clenched at the sight, the sharp edges of her fear replaced by something softer, more fragile.

"You're hurt," she said, dropping to her knees beside him.

"It's not the first time," he muttered, his lips curving into a faint, humorless smile.

"Stop trying to be noble," she snapped, her hands fumbling to pull a strip of fabric from the remains of her gown. "You're bleeding."

"And you're bossy," he replied, his tone dry despite the pain that laced his words. "We all have our burdens to bear."

Anira glared at him, but her hands were steady as she pressed the fabric to his wound. He flinched slightly but didn't pull away, his blue eyes watching her with an intensity that made her stomach flutter.

"You didn't have to do that back there," she said quietly. "You could have left me."

Ashric's gaze softened, the sharp edges of his expression easing for just a moment. "You're the one who didn't leave me," he said. "Seems fair to return the favor."

Anira didn't know how to respond to that. Instead, she focused on tying the makeshift bandage, her fingers brushing against his skin as she worked. His warmth was a stark contrast to the cold air around them, grounding her in a way she hadn't expected.

When she finished, she sat back, her hands still trembling slightly. "What now?"

Ashric leaned his head back against the root, his eyes slipping closed for a moment. "Now," he said, his voice low, "we rest. And then we figure out how to stay alive."

Anira nodded, her gaze drifting to the shadows beyond the threshold. They weren't safe—not yet. But for now, they had a moment of quiet, a fleeting reprieve from the storm that still loomed on the horizon.

She clutched the dagger in her lap, its weight a strange comfort. The forest around them was still, but she knew better than to trust the silence. Whatever lay ahead, she was certain of one thing: this was only the beginning.

Anira sat back on her heels, her hands resting in her lap as she stared at Ashric. The makeshift bandage she'd tied around his chest was already darkening with blood, and yet he still exuded a quiet strength that made her chest tighten. She couldn't decide what unsettled her more—the way he carried himself, like a storm that had learned to walk on two legs, or the way her gaze kept finding its way back to the sharp lines of his face, the curve of his jaw, the faint stubble that softened the otherwise chiseled edges.

He shifted, his eyes opening to meet hers, and the intensity in that gaze nearly stole her breath. It wasn't just the color—though the deep, crystalline blue seemed almost inhuman—it was the weight of it, as if he saw everything she tried to hide.

"Are you going to keep staring, or do I need to start charging for it?" he asked, his voice low and rough, with just the faintest edge of humor.

Heat rushed to her cheeks, and she quickly looked away, embarrassed at being caught. "I wasn't staring," she said defensively, though the lie sounded weak even to her.

"Hmm." He tilted his head, that faint smirk tugging at the corner of his mouth. "If you say so."

Anira scowled at him, but there was no real venom behind it. She hated how effortlessly he seemed to disarm her, how his presence alone unsettled something deep within her. It wasn't fair, the way he could make her feel both safe and on edge at the same time.

"You're awfully smug for someone who's bleeding all over the place," she muttered, trying to focus on something other than the inexplicable pull between them.

Ashric chuckled, a sound that was deep and rich, though it carried the faintest rasp of exhaustion. "Smug is better than dead."

She rolled her eyes but couldn't stop the corner of her mouth from twitching into a reluctant smile. His humor, dry as it was, had a way of cutting through the tension. It reminded her that he wasn't just some hardened warrior; there was a man beneath the scars, one who could still find something to laugh about even in the face of danger.

Her gaze flicked back to his face, studying him more openly this time. The flickering light from the archway cast shadows across his features, emphasizing the strong lines of his cheekbones and the faint crease between his brows. His hair, dark and streaked with silver at the temples, fell messily across his forehead, and she had the sudden, ridiculous urge to reach out and brush it back.

"What?" he asked, his voice softening as he caught her staring again.

Anira hesitated, caught between the desire to retreat and the pull to move closer. "You're different than I expected," she said finally.

Ashric raised an eyebrow, his smirk fading into something more thoughtful. "What did you expect?"

"I'm not sure," she admitted, her fingers curling into the fabric of her skirt. "You're gruff, and infuriating, and you barely talk unless you're giving orders. But you saved me. Twice now. I didn't expect that."

His expression shifted, a flicker of something unreadable crossing his face. "Don't mistake practicality for kindness," he said quietly. "Protecting you... it's not just about you."

The words stung more than they should have, though she couldn't say why. "Because of the Rose," she said, her tone flatter than she intended.

Ashric nodded, his gaze holding hers. "You're tied to it, whether you want to be or not. That makes you important."

Important. The word felt hollow, stripped of its usual weight. She didn't want to be important to some ancient relic or a prophecy she didn't understand. She wanted to be important for reasons that were her own, for something that wasn't tied to the shadow of her family or the expectations of others.

Still, she couldn't deny the way her heart twisted when he looked at her like that—like she was more than just another burden to carry. She wondered if he realized how much of himself he revealed in those unguarded moments, how the hardness in his eyes softened just slightly when his gaze lingered on her.

"You're not like anyone I've ever met," she said, her voice quieter now, almost hesitant.

His lips quirked, though the smile didn't quite reach his eyes. "That's probably a good thing."

She shook her head, frowning. "That's not what I meant. I just... you're not what I expected, Ashric. And that surprises me."

He studied her for a moment, his expression unreadable. Then he leaned back against the root, letting out a slow breath. "You're not what I expected either."

Her chest tightened at his words, at the raw honesty in his tone. "Is that a good thing?"

"Ask me when we're not running for our lives," he replied, his smirk returning, though it lacked its usual sharpness.

Anira let out a soft laugh despite herself, shaking her head. "You're impossible."

"And you're stubborn," he countered, his voice carrying a faint warmth that sent a shiver down her spine.

The silence that followed was thick but not uncomfortable. She found herself watching him again, the rise and fall of his chest, the way the tension in his jaw seemed to ease as his eyes drifted closed. He looked younger like this, more vulnerable, though she knew that vulnerability was an illusion. Even in rest, he was dangerous.

She didn't know what to make of the feelings stirring inside her—this mix of fascination, frustration, and something far more dangerous. All she knew was that the world felt different with him in it, as though he had stepped out of some story meant to rewrite her own.

And that terrified her more than anything else.

"Get some rest," Ashric murmured, his voice a low rumble that sent another shiver racing down her spine. "We'll need it."

Anira nodded, though she doubted sleep would come easily. Her gaze lingered on him for a moment longer before she finally leaned back against the root, clutching the dagger to her chest. The shadows around them seemed to deepen, the air growing heavier with each passing moment. But for the first time, the darkness didn't feel as suffocating.

Because Ashric was there. And as much as she hated to admit it, that made all the difference.

The air in the hollow grew heavier as the minutes stretched into an uneasy silence. Anira couldn't shake the feeling that they were being watched, even though Ashric's assurances about the threshold still rang in her ears. The ancient archway of roots loomed nearby, its presence oddly comforting despite the ominous aura it seemed to exude.

She sat with her back against the rough bark of the massive tree, her gaze drifting over to Ashric as he rested a short distance away.

His breathing had steadied, though his eyes remained closed. The bandage she had hastily tied around his chest was holding for now, but the sight of his blood still lingered in her mind. She traced her fingers along the edge of the dagger in her lap, its weight a strange comfort in the tense stillness.

"You're staring again," Ashric murmured, his voice cutting through the quiet like the faint rumble of distant thunder.

Anira jolted, heat rushing to her face as she tore her gaze away. "I wasn't staring."

A faint smirk tugged at the corner of his mouth, though his eyes remained closed. "You should get better at lying if you're going to make a habit of it."

She huffed, trying to ignore the way her stomach flipped at his teasing. "I was just… thinking."

"About?" he asked, finally opening his eyes. They gleamed faintly in the dim light, sharp and curious.

She hesitated, turning the dagger over in her hands. "About what you said. About the Rose... and why it chose me."

Ashric's smirk faded, his expression darkening. "It's not something I can answer for you," he said after a moment. "The Rose has its own will. Its reasons aren't always clear—not to those it chooses, and not to those who've seen what it can do."

"Have you seen it before?" Anira asked, her voice soft but insistent.

He hesitated, his fingers curling loosely around the hilt of his sword. "Once," he admitted. "Years ago. It was bound to someone else then."

Her heart tightened at his words. "What happened to them?"

His gaze flicked to hers, the storm in his eyes deepening. "They didn't survive," he said bluntly. "The Rose doesn't bind itself to someone without cost. It demands everything. And if you're not strong enough to bear it..." He trailed off, the weight of his words hanging in the air.

Anira shivered, the gravity of what he was telling her sinking in. "And you think I'm strong enough?"

"I think you have to be," he said, his tone softening just slightly. "Because the alternative isn't an option."

Her fingers tightened around the dagger, her chest aching with a mix of fear and determination. She wanted to argue, to protest that she hadn't asked for any of this, but deep down, she knew it wouldn't change anything. The Rose had chosen her, and there was no undoing that.

The sound of rustling leaves pulled her attention to the edge of the hollow. Her heart leapt into her throat as she sat up straighter, her gaze darting to Ashric. He was already on his feet, his sword drawn and his body tense.

"Stay here," he said, his voice low and commanding.

"Like hell I will," she shot back, rising to her feet and gripping the dagger tightly. "If something's out there—"

"Anira." His voice was sharp now, cutting through her protests. "Stay. Here."

She opened her mouth to argue again, but the look in his eyes stopped her. There was no room for negotiation, no space for her defiance. He wasn't just asking—he was pleading, in his own, stubborn way.

"Fine," she muttered, though the tension in her chest didn't ease.

Ashric stepped carefully toward the edge of the hollow, his movements fluid and silent. The rustling grew louder, and Anira held her breath, her fingers tightening around the dagger as she prepared for the worst. She half-expected another wraith to emerge from the shadows, its silver eyes gleaming with malice.

Instead, a figure stumbled into view, their steps unsteady and their clothes torn. It was a young man, his face pale and streaked with dirt, his breathing labored as he clutched his side. He looked as though he had been running for miles, his wide eyes darting nervously as he scanned the hollow.

"Help," he rasped, his voice barely audible. "Please... help me."

Ashric lowered his sword slightly but didn't move from his position. "Who are you?" he asked, his voice steady but cold.

The man staggered forward, his knees buckling as he dropped to the ground. "They're coming," he gasped, his eyes wild. "They're... they're everywhere."

Anira stepped forward instinctively, her concern overriding her caution. "Who's coming?" she asked, her voice trembling.

"The Shadowborn," the man whispered, his words barely more than a breath. "They're hunting anyone who... who resists. Please. You have to—"

His words were cut off by a sharp, wet gasp. Anira froze as she saw the arrow protruding from his back, the shaft quivering as he crumpled to the ground. Her blood turned to ice as her gaze shot to the edge of the hollow, where figures were beginning to emerge from the shadows.

Ashric moved in an instant, his body a blur as he stepped between Anira and the approaching threat. "Get behind me," he barked, his voice sharp and commanding.

Her feet felt rooted to the ground, her heart pounding in her ears as the Shadowborn came into view. Their dark cloaks seemed to blend with the shadows, their faces obscured beneath hoods. Each carried a weapon—blades, bows, and things Anira didn't recognize, all gleaming with an eerie, unnatural light.

Ashric raised his sword, his stance steady as he faced them. "If you want her," he said, his voice like steel, "you'll have to go through me."

One of the Shadowborn stepped forward, their movements unnervingly graceful. "We expected nothing less, Ashric," the figure said, their voice smooth and laced with malice. "But you should know by now—you can't protect her from what's coming."

Anira's breath caught as the figure's hood fell back, revealing a face that was both cruelly beautiful and hauntingly familiar. It was Varyn.

"Brother," he said, his smile sharp enough to cut. "It's good to see you again."

Varyn's smile was a blade, sharp and deliberate, his pale eyes gleaming with an unholy light. He stepped forward slowly, his movements unnervingly calm, as if he had all the time in the world to end them. His dark cloak billowed with each step, blending into the shifting shadows around him, and the coin he always carried flicked lazily between his fingers.

"Stand down, Ashric," he said, his tone smooth and coaxing, like a snake whispering to its prey. "You've bled enough for lost causes. You know how this ends."

Ashric didn't move. His sword was steady, unwavering, though Anira could see the tension in his shoulders, the subtle way his fingers flexed around the hilt. "You've been wrong before, Varyn," he said, his voice as cold and sharp as the steel in his hand. "I'm still here."

"Are you?" Varyn replied, tilting his head with mock curiosity. "Because from where I stand, you're clinging to something that isn't yours to keep."

His gaze shifted to Anira, and the weight of it hit her like a physical blow. There was something about his eyes—cold and calculating, yet searing with a strange intensity—that made her stomach twist. She forced herself to stand taller, gripping the dagger in her hand even though it felt like a child's toy compared to the weapons the Shadowborn carried.

"You don't scare me," she said, though her voice trembled slightly.

Varyn chuckled, a low, chilling sound that echoed through the hollow. "Oh, but I should," he said, taking another step forward. "You have no idea what you're holding, do you? The Rose doesn't just choose anyone. It binds itself to those it deems worthy—those it can break."

"I'm not afraid of being broken," she shot back, her pulse thundering in her ears.

Varyn's smile widened, a wicked curve that made her blood run cold. "Not yet, little princess. But you will be."

Before she could respond, Ashric shifted, his body angling slightly to shield her. "Enough," he growled, his voice low and dangerous. "If you want her, Varyn, you'll have to go through me."

Varyn's gaze flicked back to his brother, and for a moment, something darker crossed his face—a shadow of something that might have once been pain or regret, long since buried. Then it was gone, replaced by a cruel amusement.

"You think you can win, don't you?" he said softly. "You always were stubborn. It's almost admirable, the way you refuse to let go of a fight you can't win."

"Try me," Ashric said, his tone daring.

Varyn's smile sharpened. "As you wish."

He raised his hand, and the shadows around him shifted violently. The other Shadowborn surged forward, their weapons gleaming as they closed the distance with unnerving speed. The hollow erupted into chaos, the clash of steel ringing out as Ashric moved to meet them head-on.

Anira's instincts screamed at her to run, to flee into the safety of the archway's threshold, but she couldn't move. Her feet felt rooted to the ground, her pulse racing as she watched Ashric fight. He was a blur of motion, his sword cutting through the air with precision and force. Every strike was deliberate, every movement calculated, but there were too many of them. For every

Shadowborn he cut down, two more took their place.

"Anira!" he shouted, his voice breaking through the din. "Go! Now!"

Her stomach twisted at the desperation in his tone, but she couldn't leave him. Not like this. Gripping the dagger tighter, she stepped forward, her legs trembling but her resolve firm. She wouldn't be a burden. She wouldn't let him fight alone.

One of the Shadowborn broke from the group, their dark eyes locking on her. They moved quickly, their blade flashing as they closed the gap between them. Anira's breath caught as she raised the dagger, the weight of it unfamiliar in her hand. The Shadowborn lunged, and she twisted at the last moment, the dagger's edge slicing into their side.

The figure hissed in pain, but before she could strike again, they lashed out with a backhanded blow that sent her stumbling to the ground. Her dagger slipped from her grasp, landing just out of reach as the Shadowborn loomed over her, their weapon raised for the killing blow.

Time slowed.

Anira's heart thundered in her chest as the blade descended, the edges glinting like the teeth of a predator. She braced for the impact, her body tensing—

And then Ashric was there, his sword flashing as he cut through the Shadowborn in a single, brutal stroke. The figure crumpled, their body dissolving into mist as Ashric turned to her, his chest heaving and his eyes blazing with fury.

"I told you to run," he snarled, his voice raw.

"I'm not leaving you!" she shouted back, her own anger rising to meet his. "I'm not just some helpless girl you can push aside!"

He stared at her for a moment, his expression torn between frustration and something else—something deeper, almost vulnerable. "This isn't about you being helpless," he said finally, his voice quieter now. "It's about keeping you alive."

Before she could respond, Varyn's voice rang out, cold and commanding. "Enough."

The remaining Shadowborn froze, their movements halting as if controlled by an unseen force. Ashric turned sharply, his sword still raised, as Varyn stepped forward, the shadows parting around him like water. He stopped just at the edge of the archway's threshold, his smile returning as he studied them.

"You've both been entertaining," he said, his tone dripping with mockery. "But this is far from over."

He tilted his head, his gaze locking on Anira with unsettling intensity. "We'll meet again, little princess. And next time, you won't have your knight to protect you."

Anira's jaw tightened, her fear giving way to a defiance that burned in her chest. "Don't count on it," she said, her voice steady despite the tremor in her limbs.

Varyn chuckled softly, a sound that lingered in the air long after he turned and disappeared into the shadows. The remaining Shadowborn followed, their forms dissolving into the darkness until the hollow was silent once more.

Anira sank to the ground, her chest heaving as the tension drained from her body. Ashric stood over her, his sword still in hand, his eyes scanning the tree line as if expecting them to return.

"They'll come back," he said grimly. "They always do."

"Then we'll be ready," Anira said, her voice firmer than she felt.

Ashric glanced down at her, his expression softening just slightly. "You're stubborn," he said, a faint smile tugging at his lips.

"You're infuriating," she shot back, though a small smile of her own crept onto her face.

For a moment, the weight of their situation lifted, the air between them lighter despite the darkness that lingered just beyond the threshold. But the reprieve was fleeting, and Anira knew better than to trust it.

The fight was far from over. And the shadows weren't done with them yet

The silence that followed was heavy, broken only by the faint rustle of leaves in the canopy above. Anira's hands were still trembling as she gripped the dagger, its hilt sticky with blood she didn't want to look at too closely. She glanced at Ashric, who stood like a sentinel at the edge of the hollow, his sword still in his hand and his eyes scanning the shadows.

"They're gone," she said, her voice tentative, almost questioning.

"For now," Ashric replied, his tone hard and distant. He lowered his sword but didn't sheathe it, the tension in his body still coiled as though he expected an attack at any moment. "But Varyn doesn't give up. He's waiting for us to slip, to make a mistake. We'll need to move before he finds a way around the threshold."

Anira's chest tightened at the mention of Varyn. His face, his voice, lingered in her mind like a ghost, his threats still echoing in her ears. She shuddered, shaking off the chill that crept down her spine. "Where can we even go?" she asked. "He seems to know every step we take before we take it."

Ashric turned to her, his sharp blue eyes locking onto hers. There was something in his gaze—resolve, but also a flicker of something more vulnerable, something unspoken. "There's a place," he said after a moment. "Not far from here. It's... not safe, exactly, but it's hidden. Varyn won't find us there easily."

"Not safe?" Anira repeated, arching an eyebrow. "That's comforting."

Ashric's lips quirked into a faint smirk. "It's safer than staying here."

She couldn't argue with that. The hollow, with its protective threshold, felt like a fragile sanctuary at best. The air was thick with the remnants of the wraithsong, and the shadows seemed to press closer now, as though mourning the absence of their masters.

Anira pushed herself to her feet, ignoring the ache in her legs and the sting of bruises she hadn't noticed before. She wiped her hands on her gown, though the blood smeared across the pale fabric only deepened the impression of the violence they'd just escaped. The dagger in her hand felt heavier now, its edge dulled by the weight of her inexperience.

"Can you even walk?" she asked, nodding toward the blood seeping through Ashric's bandage.

He glanced down at the wound, his expression unreadable. "I'll manage."

"That's not an answer," she said, crossing her arms.

"It's the only one you're getting," he replied, his smirk returning briefly before he moved past her to retrieve a satchel hidden near the archway. He slung it over his shoulder with a grimace but didn't falter.

Anira shook her head, muttering under her breath. "Stubborn."

"I heard that," Ashric said without turning around.

"You were supposed to," she shot back, falling into step beside him as they moved toward the edge of the hollow. The air outside the threshold was colder, heavier, and she couldn't help but glance over her shoulder as they left the ancient tree behind.

They walked in silence for a time, the forest around them alive with faint sounds—rustling leaves, distant calls of unseen creatures, the occasional snap of a twig underfoot. The tension in the air was palpable, as though the shadows themselves were waiting for their moment to strike.

Finally, Anira couldn't take the quiet anymore. "This place we're going—what is it?"

Ashric hesitated, his jaw tightening. "An old waystation," he said. "It was used by... people like me. Back when I had something to fight for."

The weight of his words hung between them, and Anira didn't press further. She could hear the bitterness in his voice, the ghosts of whatever past he carried clinging to him like armor. Instead, she focused on the path ahead, the trees closing in around them like the walls of a labyrinth.

"What happens next?" she asked, her voice quieter now.

Ashric glanced at her, his gaze softer than she expected. "We keep moving," he said. "And we figure out what the Rose wants. Why it chose you."

The mention of the Rose sent a pang through her chest, its weight settling like a stone in her stomach. She reached up, her fingers brushing against the pendant hidden beneath her gown. It was cool to the touch, almost comforting, but it pulsed faintly, a reminder of its presence—and its power.

"And if we can't figure it out?" she asked, her voice barely above a whisper.

Ashric didn't answer immediately. His expression darkened, and for a moment, she thought he might brush off the question. But then he looked at her, his gaze steady and unwavering. "We will," he said simply. "Because we don't have a choice."

The conviction in his voice should have comforted her, but it only made the knot in her stomach tighten. The road ahead felt endless, shadowed by dangers she couldn't see and choices she wasn't ready to make. But as she glanced at Ashric, his presence steady and unyielding beside her, a flicker of something resembling hope stirred within her.

Whatever lay ahead, they would face it together.

The shadows deepened as they pressed on, the forest growing darker and more labyrinthine with each step. The air carried a faint hum, a reminder of the danger that still loomed just out of reach. But as the first faint glow of dawn began to filter through the canopy, Anira allowed herself a single, tentative thought.

Maybe they would make it through the night after all.

The Waystation

The first light of dawn bled weakly through the canopy, painting the forest in muted hues of gray and gold. The world felt heavy with the lingering weight of the night, as though the shadows were reluctant to loosen their grip entirely. The forest was quieter now, but it wasn't the peaceful kind of quiet—it was the kind that made Anira's skin prickle with unease, the silence of predators biding their time.

Ashric walked ahead of her, his movements steady despite the injury hidden beneath the bandage she had tied hours ago. His cloak swept the ground behind him, the fabric catching on the occasional root or low-hanging branch, though he barely seemed to notice. His focus was forward, his sharp blue eyes scanning the path as if expecting the forest itself to rise up against them.

Anira followed, her fingers brushing against the hilt of the dagger she had slipped into her belt. She could still feel the phantom weight of the blood on her hands, the memory of the wraith and the Shadowborn burned into her mind. Her body ached, every step a reminder of how far they had traveled, but she refused to complain. She wouldn't let him see her weakness.

"Not much farther," Ashric said, his voice breaking the stillness. He glanced back at her briefly, his expression unreadable. "You holding up?"

"I'm fine," she replied, though her voice carried more bite than she intended. She was tired, cold, and sore, and his calm, measured tone only seemed to highlight how much she was struggling.

Ashric raised an eyebrow but didn't comment on her tone. "You'll need to be. The waystation isn't exactly inviting."

"Why does that not surprise me?" she muttered, tugging her cloak tighter around her shoulders. The chill in the air had seeped into her bones, and no amount of fabric seemed to block the cold.

"Because you're learning," he said, a faint smirk tugging at the corner of his mouth.

Anira rolled her eyes but found herself watching him a moment longer than necessary. He moved like a man used to carrying the weight of the world, his shoulders broad and his stride purposeful. Even in the dim light, his features seemed carved from stone, his jaw set with determination. The lines of exhaustion etched into his face only made him seem more steadfast, as though nothing could break him.

And yet, there was something in the way he held himself that hinted at vulnerability—something she couldn't quite place. It wasn't weakness, exactly. It was the kind of weariness that came from fighting battles no one else could see.

"Are you going to keep staring, or should I just assume you're plotting my demise?"

Ashric asked without looking back, his tone dry.

Anira's cheeks flushed, and she quickly averted her gaze. "I'm trying to decide if you're worth the effort."

He chuckled softly, the sound low and rough, and it sent an unexpected shiver down her spine. "Good luck with that."

The tension between them was a strange thing—sharp and electric, yet laced with something warmer, something unspoken. Anira couldn't decide if she wanted to argue with him or close the distance between them. Both options felt equally dangerous.

The forest began to thin as they continued, the trees growing sparser and the undergrowth less tangled. The air shifted, carrying a faint metallic tang that made Anira's stomach twist. It was the smell of rust and decay, though there was something else beneath it—something she couldn't name but instinctively recoiled from.

"What is that?" she asked, her voice quieter now.

Ashric's expression darkened. "The waystation."

She followed his gaze, her stomach tightening as she saw the structure ahead. It was a crumbling ruin, its stone walls half-swallowed by ivy and moss. The roof sagged in places, and the windows were little more than jagged holes, their frames splintered and warped. The whole place looked like it had been abandoned for centuries, yet the air around it felt... alive.

"Safe, you said," she murmured, her voice tinged with skepticism.

"Safer than the forest," Ashric replied, though the look on his face made her wonder if he even believed his own words.

As they approached, the details of the waystation became clearer. Symbols were etched into the stone, strange markings that seemed to shift and writhe when she looked at them for too long. The doorway was framed by weathered carvings of serpents and roses, their lines barely visible beneath the grime and lichen.

"What is this place?" she asked, her voice barely above a whisper.

"It was built by those who served the old ways," Ashric said, his tone guarded. "People who understood the balance between light and shadow. They're gone now, but their magic lingers."

"Lingers?" Anira repeated, the unease in her chest growing.

"It'll keep the Shadowborn out," he said. "But it might not let us in."

Her eyes widened. "What do you mean it might not—?"

Ashric raised a hand to silence her, his gaze fixed on the doorway. "It reacts to intent," he said. "If it senses a threat, it'll shut us out."

"And what happens if we can't get in?" she asked, though she wasn't sure she wanted to hear the answer.

"We keep running," he said simply. "But let's not plan for failure."

Before she could argue, Ashric stepped forward, his hand resting lightly on the hilt of his sword. The air around the doorway seemed to shift as he approached, a faint shimmer flickering over the threshold like a heat mirage. Anira held her breath as he reached out, his fingers brushing against the worn stone.

The shimmer intensified, rippling outward like a wave. For a moment, nothing happened. Then, slowly, the doorway seemed to breathe, the light fading as the shimmer sank into the stone. Ashric exhaled, his shoulders relaxing slightly as he turned back to her.

"It'll let us through," he said, motioning for her to follow.

Anira hesitated, her gaze flicking to the strange symbols that still seemed to writhe against the stone. She didn't trust this place—not entirely—but the alternative was far worse. Taking a deep breath, she stepped forward, the threshold cold against her skin as she passed through.

The air inside the waystation was heavy, thick with the scent of damp stone and something ancient, like the ghost of incense long since burned away. The light filtering through the broken windows was faint, casting jagged shadows across the floor. The room was bare except for a cracked stone table in the center and a few scattered remnants of what might have once been furniture.

"It's not much," Ashric said, his voice breaking the silence. "But it'll do."

Anira glanced at him, her heart still racing from the strange energy of the threshold. "Do you think we'll be safe here?"

"For now," he said, his gaze scanning the room. "But we can't stay long. This place has its own dangers."

"Dangers like what?" she asked, but he didn't answer. His silence was more unsettling than any explanation he could have given.

Instead, Ashric moved to one of the walls, his fingers brushing over the strange carvings etched into the stone. The tension in his body hadn't eased, and Anira could see the flicker of pain in his expression as he leaned against the wall.

"You should rest," she said, surprising herself with the softness in her voice.

Ashric glanced at her, his lips twitching into a faint smile. "And leave you to watch for trouble? I don't think so."

She rolled her eyes, though her chest ached at the sight of him pushing himself so hard.

"You don't always have to be the hero, you know."

He chuckled, the sound low and tired. "And you don't always have to argue with me."

"Someone has to keep you in line," she said, the faintest smile curving her lips.

Their eyes met, and for a moment, the weight of the world seemed to fade. The shadows around them still lingered, heavy and oppressive, but there was something about the way he looked at her—something steady and unyielding—that made her feel like she could face them.

"Get some rest, Anira," Ashric said softly. "I'll keep watch."

And though she wanted to argue, the exhaustion in her bones won out. As she sank onto the cold stone floor, her gaze lingered on him, his silhouette sharp and steady against the flickering light. The shadows might have been watching, but so was he.

And for now, that was enough.

Anira drifted in and out of uneasy sleep, her body too exhausted to resist but her mind unwilling to surrender completely. The cold stone beneath her was unforgiving, and though her cloak provided a barrier, it did little to shield her from the chill that seeped through. Shadows flickered on the walls, cast by the pale light filtering through the cracked windows. They seemed to move with a life of their own, twisting and curling like restless spirits.

She woke fully at the sound of soft movement. Her eyes snapped open, and for a brief moment, panic surged through her chest. Then she saw him—Ashric, sitting at the edge of the room near the wall, his back against the rough stone. His sword rested across his knees, and his gaze was fixed on the doorway, the tension in his posture making it clear that he hadn't allowed himself to relax.

"You're supposed to rest too, you know," she said, her voice hoarse from disuse.

His head turned toward her, his expression unreadable in the dim light. "I don't sleep much."

"Why not?" she asked, sitting up and wrapping her arms around her knees.

Ashric hesitated, his jaw tightening slightly. "Too many memories," he said finally, his voice low and rough.

It wasn't the answer she'd expected, and for a moment, she wasn't sure how to respond. She watched him carefully, the way his fingers flexed over the hilt of his sword, the faint shadow of weariness in his sharp blue eyes. He always seemed so composed, so unshakable, but now, in this quiet moment, she saw the cracks beneath the surface.

"You talk about the past like it's a ghost that never leaves you," she said softly. "But ghosts only have power if you let them."

Ashric's lips twitched into a faint, humorless smile. "Spoken like someone who's never had to carry one."

Anira frowned, bristling slightly. "You don't know what I've carried."

He studied her for a moment, his gaze sharp and assessing. "Maybe not," he admitted. "But I do know this: the Rose doesn't choose lightly. Whatever burden it's put on you, it's not something you can run from."

"I'm not trying to run," she shot back, her voice firmer than she felt. "But you're so sure it's about strength. What if it's not? What if it's just... cruel?"

Ashric leaned forward slightly, resting his arms on his knees. "Maybe it is," he said. "But cruelty has a way of revealing what we're made of."

She didn't respond immediately, her chest tightening at his words. There was something brutally honest about the way he spoke, as though he'd spent years wrestling with the same questions and had finally accepted that there were no easy answers.

"Is that what it did to you?" she asked quietly. "Revealed what you're made of?"

He let out a soft, bitter laugh, his gaze dropping to the floor. "It showed me what I was willing to lose."

The weight of his words settled heavily in the room, and for a moment, neither of them spoke. Anira wanted to ask what he meant, to press him for the story behind his scars—both the ones she could see and the ones he kept hidden. But there was something in his expression that stopped her, a quiet pain that felt too raw to touch.

Instead, she said, "You're different when you're like this."

Ashric raised an eyebrow, his smirk returning faintly. "Like what?"

"Not brooding," she said, a hint of teasing slipping into her tone. "It's almost like you're human."

He chuckled, the sound low and rich, and it sent an unexpected warmth through her chest. "Don't get used to it."

The moment of levity was brief but grounding, a small reprieve from the tension that still lingered in the air. Anira leaned her head back against the wall, her gaze drifting to the faint glow of the symbols carved into the stone. The waystation felt alive in a way she couldn't explain, its presence both protective and unnerving.

"What happens if it stops working?" she asked, nodding toward the door.

Ashric followed her gaze, his expression darkening. "It won't. Not unless something inside betrays it."

Anira frowned, turning her attention back to him. "What does that mean?"

"It means magic like this isn't perfect," he said. "It's bound by intention. As long as we don't give it a reason to turn on us, it'll hold."

She shivered, pulling her cloak tighter around her shoulders. "That's not exactly reassuring."

"It's not meant to be," he said, his tone matter-of-fact. "Places like this... they don't protect for free. They take something in return."

"What did it take from you?" she asked, her curiosity outweighing her caution.

Ashric hesitated, his jaw tightening as he considered her question. "Trust," he said finally, his voice quieter now. "And a part of me I'll never get back."

Her chest ached at the vulnerability in his words, and she found herself leaning closer, her voice softening. "You don't have to carry it all alone, you know."

His eyes met hers, the storm within them momentarily easing. "And what would you know about carrying my burdens?" he asked, though his tone lacked its usual edge.

"Nothing," she admitted. "But I know what it feels like to be drowning in something bigger than yourself."

The air between them grew heavier, charged with something unspoken. She could see it in the way his gaze lingered on her, in the way his shoulders relaxed slightly as though her presence alone was enough to ease some of the weight he carried.

"Get some rest," he said after a long moment, his voice low. "We've got a long day ahead."

Anira wanted to argue, to press him further, but the exhaustion tugging at her bones was too strong. She nodded, leaning her head against the wall and letting her eyes drift shut.

But sleep didn't come easily. The hum of the waystation's magic buzzed faintly in her ears, and the shadows on the walls seemed to twist and writhe with every flicker of light. Her thoughts churned, filled with questions about the Rose, about Ashric, about what lay ahead.

And then there was Varyn—his voice, his threats, his cruel, knowing smile. He was still out there, waiting for them to make a mistake. The thought of facing him again sent a chill down her spine, but she pushed it aside, focusing instead on the steady presence of Ashric across the room.

As long as he was there, she thought, they might just stand a chance. But deep down, she knew that their fight was far from over.

And the shadows were closing in.

Anira didn't know how long she'd been sitting there, staring at the flickering shadows on the wall, before Ashric's voice broke the stillness. It was low and soft, almost like the rumble of distant thunder.

"You should be sleeping."

She glanced at him, her tired gaze meeting his. He hadn't moved from his place near the wall, though his posture was less rigid now, his sword resting against his knee. The lines of tension in his face were still there, but they had softened, just enough to make him look almost approachable.

"I could say the same to you," she replied, her voice quiet but laced with a hint of defiance.

Ashric smirked faintly, though it didn't quite reach his eyes. "I told you, I don't sleep much."

"Right," she said, shifting slightly to face him more fully. "Too many ghosts."

He raised an eyebrow, his smirk fading as his gaze sharpened. "Careful, Anira. Prying can be dangerous."

"So can shutting everyone out," she shot back, surprising even herself with the boldness of her words.

For a moment, he didn't respond, his expression unreadable. Then he let out a soft laugh, the sound low and rough, like the scrape of steel against stone. "You've got fire," he said, his voice carrying a trace of admiration. "I'll give you that."

She frowned, unsure if he was mocking her or genuinely impressed. "Is that supposed to be a compliment?"

"It's an observation," he replied, his tone even. "You don't scare easily. That's good. You'll need that."

The intensity in his gaze made her stomach twist, but she refused to look away. "I'm scared," she admitted, her voice quieter now. "I'd be a fool not to be."

Ashric leaned forward slightly, his elbows resting on his knees. The flickering light caught the sharp angles of his face, highlighting the faint scar along his jaw and the hollow beneath his cheekbone. He was striking in a way that felt dangerous, like a flame that could burn just as easily as it could illuminate.

"Fear's not the problem," he said, his voice soft but firm. "It's what you do with it that matters."

Anira nodded slowly, her fingers brushing absently against the pendant hidden beneath her gown. She could feel the faint warmth of the Rose against her skin, a constant reminder of the weight she carried. "And what about you?" she asked, tilting her head. "What do you do with your fear?"

His gaze darkened, and for a moment, she thought he might not answer. Then he said, "I keep moving."

"That's not an answer," she said, her brow furrowing.

"It's the only one that works," he replied, his tone carrying a finality that made it clear the subject was closed.

Anira sighed, leaning back against the wall. She studied him out of the corner of her eye, her thoughts swirling with questions she didn't know how to voice. There was a wall around him, solid and unyielding, but every so often, she caught a glimpse of something beneath it—a flicker of vulnerability, a crack in the armor he wore so tightly.

"You act like you've already decided how this ends," she said softly.

Ashric's eyes flicked to hers, and for a moment, the weight of his gaze was almost too much to bear. "Because I've seen what happens to people who think they can control the Rose," he said. "It doesn't care about hope, or love, or happy endings. It's a force, Anira. A storm. And storms don't spare anyone."

His words sent a chill down her spine, but she refused to let him see how much they affected her. Instead, she straightened, her chin lifting slightly. "Maybe storms don't, but people do. You've spared me twice now."

Ashric's jaw tightened, and he looked away, his hand absently tracing the hilt of his sword. "That wasn't about mercy," he said. "It was about duty."

"Is that what you tell yourself?" she asked, her voice tinged with skepticism. "Because I don't think it's that simple."

He didn't respond immediately, his silence heavy with unspoken thoughts. When he finally looked at her again, there was something in his eyes that made her breath catch—something raw and unguarded, like the briefest glimpse of a man who had carried too much for too long.

"Maybe it's not," he said quietly. "But simple or not, it doesn't change the fact that you're tied to something bigger than both of us. And I'm not going to let you throw your life away."

Anira's chest tightened at his words, the intensity in his voice striking a chord deep within her. She didn't know what to say, didn't know how to respond to the weight of what he was telling her. All she knew was that, for the first time in a long while, she didn't feel completely alone.

She glanced down at her hands, her fingers tracing the edge of the dagger resting in her lap. The silence between them stretched, heavy but not uncomfortable, and she found herself leaning into it, letting it settle around them like a fragile truce.

"You know," she said after a moment, her voice softer now, "for someone who says he doesn't care about happy endings, you're doing a terrible job of convincing me."

Ashric let out a soft laugh, shaking his head. "Don't mistake pragmatism for pessimism," he said. "I'm just realistic."

"And realism means no hope?" she asked, her gaze steady.

"It means hope is a luxury," he said, his tone firm but not unkind. "And right now, we can't afford luxuries."

Anira frowned but didn't argue. There was truth in his words, even if it wasn't the truth she wanted to hear. Still, she couldn't shake the feeling that there was more to him than he let on—that beneath the stoicism and sharp edges, there was a man who wanted to believe in something more.

"You don't have to protect me," she said finally, her voice barely above a whisper. "I'm not some fragile thing that needs saving."

Ashric's gaze softened, his expression momentarily unguarded. "I know," he said. "But that doesn't mean I won't try."

Her breath caught at his words, the weight of them settling deep in her chest. There was something about the way he looked at her—steady, unwavering—that made her feel seen in a way she hadn't expected. It wasn't just duty that drove him, she realized. It was something deeper, something unspoken.

And for the first time, she let herself wonder what it might feel like to trust him completely.

The silence between them grew heavier, charged with something that felt fragile yet undeniable. Neither of them moved, neither of them spoke, but the air between them crackled with an unspoken promise—a connection that was as dangerous as it was undeniable.

Whatever lay ahead, Anira knew one thing for certain: she and Ashric were bound together, whether by the Rose, by fate, or by something neither of them fully understood. And the storm they were heading into would test that bond in ways neither of them could imagine.

The silence between them stretched, heavy with meaning neither dared to name. The flickering light cast shadows that seemed to dance across Ashric's face, sharpening the angles of his jaw and softening the guarded lines of his expression. Anira couldn't look away, though she told herself it was only because she was searching for cracks in his armor, some sign of the man beneath the weight he carried so effortlessly.

"I've met knights before," she said quietly, her voice breaking the stillness like a single drop of water in a still pond. "They were... polished, perfect, and hollow. You're not like them."

Ashric tilted his head slightly, a faint smirk tugging at his lips. "You're saying I'm not polished or perfect?"

"I'm saying you're not hollow," she said, her gaze unwavering. "And I don't think you ever were."

His smirk faded, and for a moment, his expression was unreadable. Then he looked away, his hand tightening around the hilt of his sword. "You don't know me, Anira."

"Maybe not," she admitted. "But I see the way you carry yourself. Like someone who's seen too much and lost more than anyone should. And yet, you keep fighting. You keep protecting people who don't even know what it costs you."

Ashric's jaw tightened, his eyes fixed on a distant point in the shadows. "I'm not a hero," he said, his voice low and rough. "I'm just a man trying to do what little good he can before the darkness takes the rest."

"That sounds like something a hero would say," she countered, her tone softer now, almost teasing.

He let out a soft, bitter laugh, shaking his head. "Heroes don't make the mistakes I've made."

"Maybe not," she said, leaning forward slightly. "But they don't keep going the way you do, either. Whatever you've done, it hasn't broken you."

Ashric turned to her then, his gaze sharper than she expected, like he was searching her face for something he couldn't quite name. "And what about you?" he asked, his voice quieter now, almost gentle. "Do you think you're unbroken?"

The question struck her like a physical blow, and for a moment, she couldn't speak. She thought of the life she'd left behind—the weight of her mother's expectations, the constant pressure to be something she didn't want to be, the gnawing fear of a future that had been decided for her. And now, the Rose. Its power, its mystery, and the way it seemed to pull at her very soul.

"No," she said finally, her voice barely above a whisper. "I don't think anyone can go through life untouched."

Ashric nodded, his gaze softening slightly. "Then you understand why I don't believe in heroes."

"Maybe," she said, tilting her head. "But I still believe in you."

The air between them grew heavier, the weight of her words settling like a stone. Ashric's hand twitched, as though he wanted to reach for her but thought better of it. His blue eyes held hers, and for a moment, the world outside the waystation faded into nothing.

"You shouldn't," he said, though his voice lacked conviction. "You don't know what I'm capable of."

Anira leaned forward, her fingers brushing against the cold stone beneath her. "You think I don't see it? The way you put yourself between me and danger? The way you look at me like you've already decided I'm worth saving, even if it costs you everything?"

Ashric's breath hitched, and for the first time, she saw his composure falter. He didn't speak, didn't move, but his silence said more than words ever could.

"You're not as cold as you pretend to be," she said softly. "And you're not as untouchable as you think."

He looked away then, his hand dragging over his face as if to wipe away whatever emotions were threatening to surface. "You're stubborn," he muttered, his voice rough.

"And you're infuriating," she shot back, though there was no heat in her tone. If anything, there was a faint smile tugging at her lips, a warmth that surprised even her.

Ashric let out a soft chuckle, shaking his head. "You have no idea what you're getting yourself into."

"Neither do you," she said, her gaze steady. "But we're in this together, whether you like it or not."

He turned to her again, his eyes catching the faint light and holding her captive in their stormy depths. "Together," he repeated, the word heavy with unspoken promises.

Anira felt her pulse quicken, her chest tightening with a mix of fear and something else—something warm and electric that she couldn't quite name. The space between them felt too small and too vast all at once, the tension crackling like a spark caught between two opposing forces.

Before either of them could speak, the faint hum of the waystation's magic grew louder, vibrating through the air like the low growl of a restless beast. Ashric's expression hardened instantly, the moment between them shattering as he pushed to his feet, his sword already in hand.

"What is it?" Anira asked, rising as well, her own hand instinctively reaching for the dagger at her belt.

Ashric's eyes scanned the room, his body tense. "The magic's shifting," he said, his voice low and grim. "Something's coming."

Anira's heart raced as she turned her gaze to the doorway, the symbols etched into the stone flickering faintly with light. The air felt thicker now, heavier, as though the waystation itself was holding its breath.

"Shadowborn?" she asked, her voice trembling despite her best efforts to stay calm.

"Or worse," Ashric said, his tone clipped.

He moved to stand in front of her, his broad frame blocking her view of the doorway. "Stay close to me," he said, his voice firm but quieter now, almost as if he were speaking only to her. "Whatever happens, don't let go of that dagger. And don't leave my side."

Anira swallowed hard, her fingers tightening around the hilt of her weapon. The tension in the room was palpable, the anticipation pressing down on her chest like a weight. But despite the fear clawing at her throat, she found herself focusing on Ashric—on the steadiness of his presence, the sharpness of his gaze, and the unspoken promise in his words.

Whatever was coming, they would face it together.

And in that moment, she realized that she trusted him completely—more than she had trusted anyone in her entire life.

The hum of the waystation's magic continued to vibrate in the air, faint but insistent, like the ticking of a clock counting down to something neither of them could see. Anira's grip on her dagger tightened as she stood behind Ashric, her eyes flicking toward the flickering symbols on the doorway. They seemed to pulse faintly, as if warning of an impending storm.

Ashric's body was a wall of strength in front of her, his stance protective, his sword steady in his hand. She found herself focusing on the sharp lines of his shoulders, the way his dark hair brushed against the collar of his cloak, the faint tension in his posture that betrayed how attuned he was to their surroundings. There was something almost hypnotic about the way he held himself—powerful and unyielding, yet not without an underlying grace.

The intensity of her thoughts startled her, and she looked away quickly, hoping he hadn't noticed the way her gaze lingered too long.

"Whatever it is," he said softly, his voice breaking through her thoughts, "it's not coming yet."

The sound of his voice—low and rough, like distant thunder—sent a shiver through her that had nothing to do with the chill in the air. She forced herself to focus, nodding even though he wasn't looking at her.

"Do you think it knows we're here?" she asked, her voice steady despite the flicker of nerves in her chest.

Ashric tilted his head slightly, his sharp gaze scanning the room. "If it's anything tied to the Rose, it already knows," he said. "Magic like this doesn't hide easily."

She swallowed hard, her free hand brushing against the pendant beneath her gown. Its faint warmth was a constant reminder of the power she didn't fully understand and the burden it had placed on her shoulders.

"You're too quiet," Ashric said suddenly, glancing back at her. His expression was unreadable, but there was a flicker of something in his eyes that made her stomach twist. "That's not like you."

She bristled at his tone, though there was no real heat in her voice when she replied. "Maybe I'm just trying to survive the night without another lecture."

The corner of his mouth quirked, but the smirk didn't quite reach his eyes. "I'm not lecturing you, Anira. I'm trying to make sure you live long enough to prove me wrong."

"Wrong about what?" she asked, tilting her head slightly.

"That you're stubborn enough to get yourself killed," he said, though there was no bite in his tone.

Her heart did an unexpected flip at the way he said her name—softly, almost reverently, as though it were something precious. She hated the way it made her feel—vulnerable, exposed—and yet she couldn't stop herself from wanting to hear it again.

"You're one to talk about stubbornness," she shot back, trying to mask the warmth rising in her chest with a spark of defiance. "You're the one who refuses to let anyone in."

Ashric stiffened slightly, the faintest flicker of emotion crossing his face before he looked away. "It's not about letting people in," he said quietly. "It's about keeping them alive."

Her breath caught at the rawness in his voice, the hint of pain he tried so hard to hide. "And what about you?" she asked softly. "Who's keeping you alive?"

He didn't answer immediately, his gaze fixed on the flickering symbols as though they held some kind of answer. When he finally spoke, his voice was low, almost a whisper. "I don't need someone to save me, Anira."

Her chest tightened at his words, and she opened her mouth to argue, to tell him he was wrong, but the look in his eyes stopped her. There was a weight there, a depth that made her realize just how much he carried—how much he kept hidden beneath the sharp edges of his wit and the unyielding strength of his presence.

"You're wrong," she said finally, her voice barely above a whisper. "Everyone needs someone."

His gaze flicked back to her, and for a moment, the air between them felt charged, the tension crackling like a storm waiting to break. She could see the conflict in his eyes, the way he seemed to wrestle with himself, as though torn between pushing her away and pulling her closer.

"You don't know what you're asking for," he said, his voice rough, almost strained.

"Maybe not," she said, stepping closer despite herself. "But I know what I see."

"And what do you see?" he asked, his tone low, almost dangerous.

"I see someone who's willing to risk everything for people he barely knows," she said, her gaze steady. "Someone who's stronger than he gives himself credit for. Someone who's worth saving, even if he doesn't believe it."

Ashric's breath hitched, and for a moment, she thought he might look away, might retreat back into the walls he'd built around himself. But he didn't. Instead, he held her gaze, the storm in his eyes softening into something deeper, something raw and unguarded.

"You shouldn't look at me like that," he said finally, his voice quieter now, almost a whisper.

"Like what?" she asked, her heart pounding in her chest.

"Like you see something worth saving," he said, his lips curving into a faint, bittersweet smile. "Because I'm not sure I'll ever believe you."

She reached out then, her hand brushing lightly against his arm. The contact was brief, almost tentative, but it sent a spark through her that she couldn't ignore. She saw the way his body tensed at her touch, the way his jaw tightened as though he were trying to fight something within himself.

"You don't have to believe it," she said softly. "Not yet."

Ashric stared at her for a long moment, his eyes searching hers as though looking for answers to questions he couldn't ask. Then he stepped back, the space between them suddenly feeling colder, emptier.

"We should rest," he said, his voice hardening again. "Whatever's coming, we'll need to be ready."

Anira nodded, though her chest ached at the distance he had put between them. She knew he was trying to protect her—not just from the dangers outside the waystation, but from himself. And yet, she couldn't shake the feeling that he needed her just as much as she needed him.

As she settled back against the wall, her gaze lingered on him. He stood near the doorway, his sword resting at his side, his shoulders tense as he watched the shadows. He looked like a man at war—with the world, with himself, with something she couldn't see.

And though he didn't look at her again, she couldn't help but hope that, in his own way, he felt the pull between them too. Because no matter how much he tried to hide it, there was something undeniable in the way his gaze had lingered, the way his voice had softened when he said her name.

Whatever lay ahead, they were in it together. And that thought, fragile as it was, gave her the strength to close her eyes and let sleep take her.

The waystation's hum grew louder, a low vibration that seemed to resonate through the stone walls and into Anira's chest. It was subtle at first, a faint background noise that barely registered over the soft rustling of the forest outside. But as the minutes ticked by, it deepened, taking on an almost menacing edge, as though the ancient magic was warning of something unseen.

Anira's eyes snapped open. She hadn't meant to fall asleep, and the disorientation left her momentarily breathless. The air was colder now, heavier, and the flickering light from the waystation's symbols cast long, shifting shadows that seemed to crawl across the walls.

Ashric was still near the doorway, standing perfectly still, his sword gripped loosely in one hand. He hadn't noticed her stirring, his gaze fixed on the threshold as though he were listening for something she couldn't hear.

"Ashric," she said softly, her voice breaking the tense silence.

He turned his head slightly, his sharp blue eyes meeting hers. "You're awake."

"There's something wrong," she said, sitting up. "The waystation feels... different."

Ashric nodded, his expression grim. "I noticed. The magic's reacting to something. Something close."

Her stomach twisted at his words, the tension in his voice sending a shiver down her spine. "Shadowborn?"

"Maybe," he said, his gaze shifting back to the doorway. "Or something worse."

The room seemed to grow darker, the light from the symbols dimming as though the waystation itself was retreating into its defenses. Anira pushed herself to her feet, clutching the dagger at her side as she moved to stand next to Ashric. The air around him was warmer, grounding, but it did little to ease the rising fear in her chest.

"What happens if it gets in?" she asked, her voice quieter now.

Ashric glanced at her, his jaw tightening. "Then we fight."

The simplicity of his answer was terrifying, but she refused to let it show. She stood a little taller, gripping the dagger tightly, though her hands trembled faintly. "You make it sound so easy."

"It's not," he admitted, his tone softer now. "But it's what we've got."

The hum grew louder, almost a growl now, and the flickering light from the doorway turned red, pulsing like a heartbeat. Anira felt it deep in her chest, the rhythm too steady, too deliberate, as though something just beyond the threshold was testing the waystation's defenses.

And then it stopped.

The silence that followed was absolute, so profound that it made her ears ring. Anira held her breath, her heart pounding in her chest as she stared at the doorway, half-expecting something to burst through at any moment.

Ashric's voice broke the stillness, low and sharp. "Stay close."

She nodded, moving a fraction closer to him, the faint brush of his cloak against her arm a strange comfort in the growing tension. Her pulse raced, every nerve in her body screaming that something was coming.

The doorway shimmered.

It was subtle at first, a faint ripple that distorted the edges of the threshold like heat rising off stone. Then it spread, the symbols flickering wildly as the shimmer turned into a violent surge of energy. The magic roared to life, the air vibrating with the force of it, and for a moment, the waystation felt alive, its ancient power surging to meet whatever was trying to break through.

A figure stepped into view.

It was cloaked in shadows, its form shifting and indistinct, but its presence was undeniable. The air seemed to warp around it, the edges of its body dissolving and reforming like smoke caught in a storm. Its eyes burned like molten silver, locking onto Ashric and Anira with an intensity that made her blood run cold.

"Wraith," Ashric said under his breath, his grip tightening on his sword.

Anira's chest tightened as the creature took a step forward, its movements unnaturally fluid. The waystation's magic flared again, a blinding flash of light that forced her to shield her eyes, but when she looked back, the creature was still there, pressing against the threshold like a wave against a dam.

"It's testing the magic," Ashric said, his voice tense. "Trying to find a weakness."

"Can it get in?" she asked, though she already feared the answer.

"Not yet," he said, but there was a grimness to his tone that sent a shiver through her.

The wraith tilted its head, as though sensing their conversation. Its silver eyes gleamed, and a faint, inhuman sound escaped its shadowed form—a low, resonant hum that seemed to vibrate in her very bones. The symbols on the threshold flickered again, their light dimming as though the waystation was struggling to hold its ground.

Ashric moved then, stepping forward to stand directly between Anira and the wraith. His sword gleamed in the flickering light, the sharp edge catching the faint glow of the doorway.

"Anira," he said without looking back, his voice low and steady. "If the magic fails, I need you to run."

Her breath caught, her heart hammering in her chest. "I'm not leaving you."

"Yes, you are," he said sharply, his gaze locked on the wraith. "If it gets through, I can hold it off long enough for you to get away. But you have to go."

She stepped closer, the heat of defiance rising in her chest. "I'm not running. Not this time."

"Anira—"

"I said no," she interrupted, her voice firmer now. "We're in this together, remember? Whatever happens, we face it together."

Ashric turned his head slightly, his eyes meeting hers for the briefest moment. There was something raw in his gaze, something that made her chest ache, but he didn't argue. Instead, he nodded once, his jaw tightening as he turned back to the wraith.

"Then stay behind me," he said, his voice quieter now, almost resigned. "And don't do anything stupid."

The wraith surged forward again, its form colliding with the threshold in a burst of energy that lit up the room. The symbols flared brightly, holding the creature at bay, but the strain in the magic was palpable. The waystation wasn't going to hold forever.

The air grew colder, heavier, as the wraith pressed against the barrier. Anira's grip on her dagger tightened, her knuckles white as she braced herself for whatever was coming. Beside her, Ashric stood like a fortress, his presence steady and unyielding even as the shadows closed in.

Whatever happened next, they would face it together. But as the wraith let out a bone-chilling scream and the magic of the waystation flickered again, Anira couldn't help but feel that the true fight was only just beginning.

The Fractured Threshold

The air in the waystation pulsed with a low, resonant vibration, like the deep toll of a bell that never quite faded. The sound seemed to come from the very walls themselves, a warning that the ancient magic protecting them was straining against an overwhelming force. Anira felt it reverberate in her chest, its rhythm uneven, like the faltering heartbeat of a creature too old to keep fighting.

The symbols carved into the stone doorway blazed brighter with each passing moment, their flickering light casting jagged shadows across the room. They shimmered and rippled, as though trying to hold back a tidal wave of energy threatening to crash through. The wraith pressed harder against the threshold, its formless shape shifting and curling like smoke caught in a violent wind. Its silver eyes burned with cruel intelligence, fixed on Anira and Ashric as though it could already taste their fear.

"Anira," Ashric said, his voice sharp and steady despite the tension in his shoulders. "Move back."

She shook her head, her fingers gripping the hilt of her dagger so tightly that her knuckles ached. "I'm not leaving you."

His jaw tightened, but he didn't argue. Instead, he stepped forward, his sword gleaming as he raised it in a defensive stance. The blade caught the flickering light of the symbols, reflecting it back like a promise of defiance. His presence filled the room, grounding her even as the wraith's keening sound—high-pitched and otherworldly—seemed to claw at her mind.

The creature surged forward again, its shadowy form slamming into the barrier. The vibration in the air deepened, a resonant groan that echoed through the room and made the stone beneath Anira's feet tremble. The waystation's magic flared brightly, the light almost blinding, but the strain was clear. Cracks began to appear in the carved symbols, faint lines spidering out across the stone like fractures in ice.

"It's breaking through," she said, her voice tight with fear.

"Not yet," Ashric replied, his tone firm. "It's testing us. Looking for weakness."

"And if it finds one?"

"Then we don't let it," he said, glancing back at her briefly. His blue eyes burned with determination, though there was something else there too—something softer, unspoken.

The wraith let out another scream, its sound splitting the air like a blade. Anira flinched, the vibration of it settling deep in her bones. She could feel the Rose beneath her gown, its warmth growing stronger, almost searing. It pulsed against her chest, a rhythm that matched the faltering beat of the waystation's magic.

The creature seemed to sense it. Its silver eyes narrowed, and for a moment, its shifting form stilled. Then it moved again, faster this time, slamming into the threshold with enough force to send a wave of energy rippling through the room. The walls groaned under the strain, the resonant sound filling the space like the mournful wail of a distant horn.

Ashric braced himself, his sword steady as the light from the doorway dimmed. "Whatever it's after," he said, his voice low, "it's tied to the Rose."

Anira's chest tightened. "You think it's drawn to me."

"I don't think, Anira," he said, his tone clipped but not unkind. "I know."

Her pulse quickened, and she stepped closer to him despite the tremor in her legs. "Then what do we do?"

Ashric's gaze flicked to hers, and for a moment, the steel in his eyes softened. "We stand our ground."

The wraith struck the barrier again, the sound of it like thunder reverberating through the hollow. The cracks in the stone symbols deepened, small fragments crumbling to the ground as the magic faltered. The vibration in the air grew more erratic, the once-steady resonance now a disjointed series of beats that seemed to echo her own fear.

"You've fought these things before," Anira said, her voice rising over the chaos. "How do we stop it?"

Ashric didn't answer immediately. His focus was on the wraith, his body coiled like a predator waiting to strike. "You don't stop a wraith," he said finally. "Not completely. You outlast it."

"That doesn't sound promising."

"It's not," he admitted, his lips twitching into the faintest semblance of a grim smile. "But it's all we've got."

The wraith let out another unearthly wail, and the waystation shuddered violently, the walls trembling as though the entire structure were alive and in pain. The light from the doorway flickered, dimming to a dull red that cast the room in an eerie glow. Anira could feel the energy of the magic waning, its strength bleeding away with every passing moment.

Ashric stepped forward, his sword raised. "Stay behind me," he said, his voice leaving no room for argument.

Anira nodded, though every instinct screamed at her to do more. She gripped her dagger, her hands slick with sweat as she watched the wraith press against the barrier again and again. The cracks in the stone deepened, and the vibration in the air turned into a low, mournful drone, like the last breath of something ancient and dying.

The wraith struck one final time, and the barrier shattered.

The force of the magic breaking sent a shockwave through the room, throwing Anira back against the wall. She cried out as the impact stole the breath from her lungs, her vision swimming as the wraith surged into the waystation. Its form expanded, filling the space with writhing shadows and silver light, its presence overwhelming and suffocating.

Ashric moved instantly, his sword flashing as he charged the creature. The blade sliced through its shadowed form, the impact sending ripples through the air, but the wraith didn't falter. It turned on him, its silver eyes burning with fury as it lashed out with a tendril of darkness. Ashric barely dodged in time, the tendril striking the wall behind him and leaving a scorched mark in the stone.

"Anira!" he shouted, his voice raw. "The Rose—use it!"

Her heart lurched at his words. "I don't know how!"

"Trust it!" he yelled, his sword cutting through another tendril as the wraith closed in on him. "It chose you for a reason—use it!"

The pendant burned against her skin, its heat almost unbearable. Anira reached up, her fingers trembling as she pulled it free from beneath her gown. The Rose glowed faintly, its blood-red petals seeming to shift and pulse with an inner light.

The wraith paused, its silver eyes locking onto the pendant. For a moment, the room fell silent, the oppressive weight of the creature's gaze pressing down on her like a physical force. Anira's breath caught, her chest tightening as the Rose's warmth spread through her, its energy filling her veins like fire.

She didn't know what she was doing, didn't know how to control the power coursing through her. But as the wraith lunged toward her, she raised the pendant instinctively, the light flaring brighter than she thought possible.

The creature let out a deafening scream, its form unraveling as the Rose's light consumed it. The shadows writhed and twisted, dissolving into nothingness as the wraith was torn apart, its silver eyes fading into darkness.

And then, silence.

Anira collapsed to her knees, the pendant slipping from her fingers as the light faded. The room was still, the air heavy with the scent of scorched stone and magic. Ashric was at her side in an instant, his sword falling to the ground as he knelt beside her.

"You did it," he said, his voice low and steady. "You stopped it."

She looked up at him, her vision blurred by tears she hadn't realized were falling. "I didn't know I could."

"You can," he said, his hand brushing against hers. "And you will."

The waystation was quiet now, its magic dim but steady. The threat had passed, but Anira could feel the weight of what had happened pressing down on her. The Rose had chosen her, but at what cost?

As Ashric helped her to her feet, his touch warm and grounding, she realized that this was only the beginning. And the shadows waiting beyond the waystation would not be so easily defeated.

The quiet after the battle was eerie, as though the room itself were holding its breath. The waystation's magic had dimmed, its once-persistent resonance reduced to a faint vibration, like the dying embers of a once-roaring fire. Anira leaned heavily against the stone wall, her knees weak from the surge of power she had wielded, her breath coming in shallow gasps. The pendant of the Rose hung limp against her chest, its glow extinguished, though its warmth still lingered faintly beneath her fingers.

Ashric stood a few feet away, his sword resting tip-down against the ground, his shoulders slumped in exhaustion. His dark hair was damp with sweat, clinging to his forehead, and a faint smear of blood streaked his cheek. He didn't speak, his sharp blue eyes scanning the room as though expecting another attack.

"You don't have to keep looking," Anira said softly, her voice barely above a whisper. "It's gone."

"For now," he said, his tone clipped. But when he turned to her, some of the hardness in his expression softened. "You... did well."

She let out a faint, disbelieving laugh, her fingers still trembling. "I had no idea what I was doing."

"Doesn't matter," he said, stepping closer. "You did it anyway."

Anira tilted her head, studying him through the haze of her exhaustion. He was close now, closer than he usually allowed himself to be, and there was something in his eyes that made her chest tighten. A flicker of something vulnerable, almost gentle, that he seemed to be fighting to keep buried.

"You were right," she said, her voice quieter now. "The Rose... it feels alive. It's like it was guiding me."

Ashric nodded, his gaze lingering on the pendant. "That's what it does. But the question is why."

"What do you mean?" she asked, frowning.

He hesitated, his fingers tightening briefly around the hilt of his sword before letting it fall to the ground with a soft clatter. "The Rose doesn't just give power—it takes. There's always a cost, Anira. And you'll need to be ready for that."

Her stomach twisted at his words, but she refused to look away. "You think I'm not?"

"I think you don't know what you've signed up for," he said, his voice low. "And I don't know if I'm strong enough to help you survive it."

The raw honesty in his voice took her by surprise, and she reached out instinctively, her hand brushing lightly against his arm. "You don't have to do this alone, Ashric," she said softly. "Neither of us does."

For a moment, he didn't move, his gaze locked on hers. There was something fragile in the air between them, a connection that felt as delicate as spun glass. She could feel the tension in his body, the way his muscles coiled as though ready to pull away, but he didn't. Instead, his hand came up, hesitant but deliberate, his fingers brushing against hers.

"You're stubborn," he murmured, his voice softer now, almost teasing.

"You're infuriating," she replied, a faint smile tugging at her lips despite the weight of the moment.

His lips quirked into the barest hint of a smile, but before he could respond, a sharp crack echoed through the room, like a whip snapping against stone.

Anira jerked back, her heart leaping into her throat as her hand flew to her dagger. Ashric was already moving, his sword in his hand before she even registered the sound, his body placing itself squarely between her and the doorway. The faint flicker of warmth between them vanished, replaced by the cold, biting edge of survival.

"What was that?" she asked, her voice trembling despite her best efforts to stay calm.

"I don't know," Ashric said, his tone low and dangerous. His eyes flicked toward the doorway, the faint glow of the cracked symbols casting flickering shadows on the walls. "Stay behind me."

She wanted to argue, but the tension in his voice stopped her. She stepped closer to him, her dagger clutched tightly in her hand as her gaze darted around the room. The waystation had grown impossibly still, the faint vibration in the air replaced by an oppressive silence that made her skin crawl.

Another sound—a faint scuffling, like boots against stone—sent a spike of fear through her chest. Ashric's grip on his sword tightened, his body coiled and ready to strike.

"Whatever it is," he said under his breath, "stay close."

The sound grew louder, closer, and Anira held her breath, her heart hammering in her chest. Then, with a suddenness that made her jump, something burst through the shadows near the far wall—a dark shape moving quickly toward them.

Ashric lunged, his sword slicing through the air with deadly precision. The figure let out a startled yelp and threw up their hands, a small, battered satchel falling to the ground with a loud thud.

"Wait! Wait!" the figure cried, their voice high and panicked. "Don't kill me!"

Ashric froze, his sword inches from the stranger's throat. The figure—small and wiry, with a shock of tangled hair and a face streaked with dirt—stumbled back, their wide eyes darting between Ashric and Anira.

"Who are you?" Ashric demanded, his voice sharp.

"I—I'm no one!" the stranger stammered, their hands trembling. "Just a traveler! I didn't know anyone was here, I swear!"

Anira stepped around Ashric, her eyes narrowing as she studied the stranger. They were young, barely older than she was, their clothes patched and worn as though they'd spent years on the road. There was a desperation in their eyes that made her hesitate.

"What are you doing here?" she asked, her voice firmer than she felt.

"I—" The stranger hesitated, their gaze darting toward the satchel on the ground. "I was looking for shelter. That's all. I didn't mean to scare anyone."

Ashric didn't lower his sword, his gaze cold and unrelenting. "You picked the wrong place to hide."

The stranger swallowed hard, their hands still raised. "Please," they said. "I'm just trying to stay alive. Same as you."

The tension in the room didn't ease, but Anira felt something shift. The stranger's fear was real, tangible, and though she didn't trust them, she couldn't help but feel a flicker of sympathy.

"Ashric," she said softly, her hand brushing against his arm. "Maybe we should hear them out."

He glanced at her, his jaw tight. For a moment, it seemed like he might argue, but then he stepped back, lowering his sword slightly.

"Talk," he said, his voice hard. "And make it quick."

The stranger nodded frantically, their hands still trembling as they bent to pick up the satchel. "Thank you," they said, their voice shaking. "I swear, I won't cause any trouble."

Anira exchanged a glance with Ashric, unease coiling in her chest. Whoever this stranger was, they had just thrown another layer of uncertainty into an already dangerous situation. And as the waystation's magic flickered faintly behind them, she couldn't help but feel that the storm was far from over.

The stranger stood frozen, clutching their satchel like it was the only thing tethering them to the ground. Their wide, darting eyes flicked between Anira and Ashric, lingering on the latter as if deciding whether his sword might come swinging again.

"You've got about ten seconds to start talking," Ashric said, his voice dry but edged with menace. He leaned casually against his sword, as though the weight of the situation were nothing more than an inconvenience. "Nine, now."

"Alright, alright!" the stranger blurted, holding up their free hand in surrender. "My name's Kael. I swear, I didn't mean to scare you—I was just looking for a place to hide. You know, from the things out there."

Ashric raised an eyebrow, his lips twitching faintly in what might have been a smirk. "Things. Very specific. That clears everything up."

Kael shifted nervously, their satchel clinking faintly as they adjusted it. "You know—things. Shadowy things. With claws and glowing eyes that look like they want to eat you."

Ashric's gaze didn't waver. "And you decided to run straight into this waystation, with all its glowing ominous symbols and clear 'do not disturb' vibes?"

Kael hesitated, looking down at their feet. "It... looked safe."

Ashric let out a short, humorless laugh. "Safe. Right. Did the crumbling walls or the impossibly creepy energy field give that away?"

Kael flinched, their face flushing under the layer of dirt. "Look, I didn't have much of a choice, okay? I've been running for miles. I thought I was going to die out there."

Ashric stepped forward, his sword still in hand, though he rested the flat of the blade against his shoulder with an air of nonchalance. "You still might," he said, his tone almost conversational. "Depends on what you're really doing here."

"Ashric," Anira said sharply, her tone a warning. She stepped closer to the stranger, her gaze softening slightly. "Give them a chance to explain."

He glanced at her, one eyebrow arching. "A chance to explain what, exactly? That they're a magnet for trouble? Because we've got plenty of that already."

Kael raised their hands again, their expression panicked. "I swear, I'm not here to cause trouble! I don't even know what this place is—I just stumbled across it trying to get away from the Shadowborn."

At the mention of the Shadowborn, Ashric's smirk disappeared, his jaw tightening. "You saw them?"

Kael nodded fervently, their satchel shaking in their grip. "Yeah. A group of them—five, maybe six. They were scouring the forest. I've seen them before, but they seemed... different this time."

"Different how?" Ashric pressed, his voice hard again.

Kael hesitated, glancing at Anira as if searching for reassurance. "More focused. Like they were looking for someone specific."

The air between them grew heavier, and Anira's stomach twisted. She didn't need to ask who the Shadowborn might be searching for—it wasn't hard to guess. Her hand brushed against the pendant at her chest, the faint warmth of the Rose a constant reminder of the weight she carried.

"And you just happened to stumble into the one place we're hiding?" Ashric asked, his tone laced with skepticism.

"I told you, I didn't know anyone was here!" Kael said, their voice rising in desperation.

"I'm not looking for a fight—I'm just trying to survive!"

Ashric studied them for a long moment, his sharp gaze making Kael squirm. Then he sighed, lowering his sword completely but keeping it within easy reach. "Fine," he said, though his tone made it clear he wasn't entirely convinced. "You can stay. For now. But the first sign you're leading them here—"

"I'm not!" Kael interrupted quickly, shaking their head. "I swear, I'd never—"

Ashric held up a hand, cutting them off. "Save it. You're on thin ice already."

Kael nodded quickly, clutching their satchel to their chest like it might protect them from Ashric's sharp tongue. Anira, watching the exchange, couldn't help the faint smirk that tugged at her lips. For all his gruffness, Ashric had allowed the stranger to stay, and that spoke volumes about the man beneath the sword.

"You don't trust anyone, do you?" she said, her voice teasing as she glanced at him.

Ashric shrugged, leaning back against the wall with an air of practiced indifference.

"Trust gets you killed. Cynicism keeps you alive."

"Charming," she said, arching an eyebrow. "Remind me to embroider that on a pillow for you."

His lips twitched, the faintest hint of a smile breaking through his usual stoicism. "I'll treasure it."

Kael looked between the two of them, their confusion evident. "Are you two always like this?"

Anira exchanged a glance with Ashric, and for a moment, the tension in the room eased, the weight of the earlier battle lifting just slightly. "Pretty much," she said, her voice lighter now.

Kael sighed, shaking their head as they sank onto the ground near the wall. "Great. Stuck with a pair of bickering warriors and no idea what's happening."

"Welcome to the club," Ashric said dryly, crossing his arms. "Meetings are every time the world tries to kill us."

The sarcasm in his voice sent a faint ripple of laughter through the room, and Anira couldn't help but smile, despite the danger still looming over them. The shadows were still waiting outside the waystation, and the cracks in the barrier hadn't gone away. But for now, in this moment, there was a strange comfort in the warmth of shared humor.

Anira settled down beside Kael, her fingers still brushing against the Rose at her chest. Ashric, ever the sentinel, remained standing, his sword within reach as he kept his gaze on the doorway. The quiet stretched again, but it was different now—not oppressive, but oddly companionable.

"Get some rest," Ashric said, his voice softer this time. "I'll keep watch."

Anira glanced at him, her chest tightening faintly at the steadiness in his gaze. There was so much he didn't say, so much he kept locked away, but she was starting to see the cracks in his armor. And she couldn't help but wonder what it would take to break through them completely.

As the waystation settled into silence once more, Anira leaned back against the wall, her thoughts a swirl of exhaustion, curiosity, and the faintest spark of something warmer. Whatever lay ahead, she knew one thing for certain—Ashric would be by her side. And that, for now, was enough.

The waystation seemed to exhale as silence settled once more, though it wasn't the peaceful kind. The tension lingered, like the taut string of a bow, waiting to snap. Anira leaned back against the wall, her body aching from the night's events, but her mind refused to quiet. The faint vibration of the waystation's weakened magic still resonated in the air, a reminder that their refuge was fragile at best.

Kael sat slumped against the opposite wall, clutching their satchel like a lifeline. Their wary eyes darted around the room, lingering on Ashric more than once, though they quickly looked away whenever his sharp gaze flicked in their direction. Anira studied the stranger in the dim light, noting the dirt-smudged lines of their face, the frayed edges of their clothes, and the exhaustion that weighed down their every movement. Whoever they were, they hadn't had an easy time of it.

Ashric, ever the sentinel, remained standing near the doorway, his sword resting against his shoulder. His posture was relaxed, but

Anira wasn't fooled. She could see the way his eyes scanned the room, the way his fingers flexed occasionally around the hilt of his weapon. He was like a coiled spring, ready to strike at the first sign of danger.

"You could sit, you know," Anira said, breaking the quiet. "The floor's not comfortable, but it beats standing all night."

Ashric's lips twitched faintly, though his gaze didn't leave the doorway. "Someone has to keep watch."

"You've been keeping watch since we got here," she countered, her voice softening. "You need rest too."

He glanced at her then, the faintest flicker of something unreadable in his eyes. "I'll rest when I'm sure we're not about to be ambushed."

Kael let out a soft, nervous laugh from their corner. "With the way you're wound up, I'm starting to think the floor is safer."

Ashric raised an eyebrow, his smirk returning faintly. "If you're looking for reassurance, you won't find it here."

"I'm noticing that," Kael muttered, shifting uncomfortably. "Do you always act like the world's about to end?"

Ashric's gaze darkened slightly, though his tone remained dry. "Because it usually is."

Anira sighed, shaking her head. "He's always like this," she said to Kael, her voice tinged with teasing exasperation. "Don't take it personally."

Kael snorted, their tension easing just slightly. "Good to know."

Ashric rolled his eyes, though the faintest hint of amusement lingered in his expression. "You're both welcome, by the way."

"For what?" Anira asked, arching an eyebrow.

"For not letting the wraith tear us apart," he said, his voice laced with sarcasm. "It's exhausting being this indispensable."

Anira couldn't help but smile, the corners of her mouth tugging upward despite herself. "And here I thought you enjoyed being the hero."

Ashric's smirk faded, his expression sobering. "I don't," he said quietly, his gaze returning to the doorway. "But someone has to."

The weight of his words settled over the room, a reminder of the burdens he carried. Anira's chest tightened as she watched him, the way his shoulders bore the weight of not just his own survival, but theirs as well. She wanted to say something, to reach out and ease the tension etched into his face, but the words wouldn't come.

Instead, she shifted closer to him, her voice soft when she spoke. "You don't have to do it alone, you know."

His eyes flicked to hers, and for a moment, something raw and unguarded passed between them. "Maybe not," he said finally, his voice barely above a whisper. "But it's better that way."

"Why?" she asked, her brow furrowing.

"Because it's easier to lose yourself," he said, his gaze hardening. "Than to lose someone else."

The quiet that followed was heavy, the truth in his words cutting deeper than she wanted to admit. Anira's hand brushed against the pendant at her chest, the faint warmth of the Rose grounding her even as the weight of its choice pressed against her heart.

Kael cleared their throat awkwardly, breaking the tension. "So, uh… what's the plan? Do we have one? Because I'm not keen on waiting for something else to crash the party."

Ashric straightened, his expression sharpening as he turned his attention to the stranger. "We move at dawn," he said, his tone all business. "The waystation's magic is holding for now, but it won't last much longer. We can't stay."

Kael frowned, their grip on the satchel tightening. "Move where? The forest is crawling with Shadowborn."

"Which is exactly why we don't stay here," Ashric said firmly. "The longer we stay in one place, the more likely they'll find us."

"Great," Kael muttered, slumping back against the wall. "This just keeps getting better."

"You wanted shelter," Ashric said, his voice dry. "This is what it costs."

Kael opened their mouth to respond, but Anira cut them off with a wave of her hand. "Enough," she said, her voice carrying more authority than she felt. "We're all tired, and arguing isn't going to help."

Ashric glanced at her, his lips twitching faintly in what might have been approval. "She's right," he said, his tone softer now. "Get some rest while you can. Morning will come fast."

Kael muttered something under their breath but didn't argue further, curling up against the wall with their satchel clutched tightly. Anira watched them for a moment before turning back to Ashric.

"You should take your own advice," she said quietly, her gaze steady.

"I will," he said, though the way he stood, sword still in hand, made her doubt it.

Anira sighed, leaning back against the wall as she let her eyes drift shut. The tension in the room lingered, a reminder of the danger waiting outside the waystation, but she let herself hold on to one small comfort.

No matter how heavy the shadows, Ashric was still standing. And somehow, that made the darkness feel just a little less suffocating.

The night dragged on, the oppressive silence broken only by the faint, irregular groan of the waystation's fractured magic. Anira tried to rest, but sleep refused to come. Every time she closed her eyes, she saw the wraith's silver gaze, the way its shadowy tendrils had torn through the threshold like it was nothing more than mist. The fear lingered, coiled in her chest like a serpent.

Across the room, Kael was curled up against the wall, their breathing slow and shallow. For all their earlier nerves, they had managed to fall asleep, their satchel clutched tightly in their arms like a child holding onto a favorite toy. Anira envied them. Sleep felt like an impossibility, the weight of the Rose and the uncertainty of what lay ahead pressing down on her like a stone.

Ashric hadn't moved. He still stood near the doorway, his sword resting loosely at his side, his sharp gaze fixed on the flickering symbols etched into the stone. His presence was a constant, steady and unyielding, like the last pillar holding up a crumbling structure.

"You should sit," she said softly, her voice breaking the stillness.

Ashric glanced at her, his blue eyes catching the faint light from the doorway. "You're persistent," he said, a faint smirk tugging at his lips. "I'll give you that."

"Someone has to be," she replied, shifting to sit cross-legged. "You're too stubborn for your own good."

"And you're too naïve," he shot back, though his tone was devoid of any real heat.

Anira smiled faintly, the corners of her mouth lifting despite the tension in her chest. "Maybe. But I'm still here."

Ashric's smirk faded, and for a moment, something unreadable flickered in his eyes. "For now," he said quietly, almost to himself.

The weight of his words settled heavily between them, and Anira felt her chest tighten. She wanted to say something, to remind him that they were in this together, that she wasn't going anywhere, but the look on his face stopped her. There was something fragile about him in that moment, something raw and unguarded, and she didn't want to shatter it.

Instead, she said, "Morning will come soon."

Ashric nodded, his gaze returning to the doorway. "And with it, more trouble."

"You sound almost excited," she said, her tone lighter now.

His lips twitched into the faintest semblance of a smile. "Excited isn't the word I'd use."

"Terrified?" she offered, raising an eyebrow.

"Prepared," he said, his voice firm.

The quiet that followed was less oppressive this time, the tension between them easing just slightly. Anira leaned her head back against the wall, letting her eyes drift shut. She wasn't sure how long she sat there, her thoughts swirling in the darkness, but when she opened her eyes again, the faintest glow of dawn was beginning to creep through the cracks in the waystation's walls.

Ashric was still standing, his silhouette sharp against the dim light. He turned his head slightly as the light grew stronger, the first rays of sun casting a golden sheen over the fractured threshold.

"It's time," he said, his voice breaking the silence.

Kael stirred in their corner, groaning softly as they sat up. "Already?"

"Move," Ashric said, his tone leaving no room for argument. "The longer we wait, the more likely we'll be found."

Anira pushed herself to her feet, her body protesting with every movement. She tucked the pendant beneath her gown, its faint warmth a reminder of the power she carried—and the danger that came with it.

As they prepared to leave, the waystation seemed to hum faintly again, its magic flickering like the dying embers of a fire. Anira glanced back at the doorway, the etched symbols cracked and faded. The place that had protected them for the night was spent, its strength nearly gone.

Ashric caught her lingering gaze. "It won't hold much longer," he said quietly. "We're lucky it lasted as long as it did."

She nodded, her fingers brushing against the pendant. "Let's hope we don't need it again."

Ashric didn't respond, but his expression darkened, as though he knew better than to believe in luck. He stepped forward, his sword held loosely at his side as he motioned for her and Kael to follow.

The dawn light cast long shadows as they stepped outside, the forest quiet but heavy with a tension that made Anira's skin crawl. Every step felt like a gamble, the faint crunch of leaves underfoot too loud in the stillness.

"We head north," Ashric said, his voice low. "There's a river not far from here. If we can cross it, we'll gain some distance from the Shadowborn."

"And then?" Kael asked, their voice tight.

Ashric glanced back, his sharp gaze cutting through the morning mist. "Then we keep running."

Anira tightened her grip on her dagger, her heart pounding as they moved deeper into the forest. The shadows around them felt too thick, the air too still, as though the world itself was holding its breath.

The waystation was behind them now, its fractured magic nothing more than a memory. But the danger hadn't faded—it was waiting, lingering just out of sight.

And Anira knew, with a certainty that made her chest ache, that the worst was still to come.

A Fragile Light

The morning was crisp, the air carrying the faint scent of dew and pine. Sunlight filtered through the trees, its golden glow breaking through the dense canopy in shards, scattering soft patches of warmth across the forest floor. The faint rustling of leaves in a gentle breeze provided the only sound, and for the first time in what felt like days, Anira could breathe without the weight of the world pressing down on her chest.

She walked a step behind Ashric, her eyes fixed on the dappled light playing over his broad shoulders. His cloak moved with the rhythm of his stride, brushing against the fallen leaves. For all his sharp edges and constant vigilance, there was something almost peaceful about him in this moment, as though the sunlight had found a way to soften even him.

Kael trudged a few paces behind her, their satchel bouncing against their side with every step. They muttered occasionally under their breath, a string of complaints about the early hour, the chill in the air, and the ache in their feet. Anira might have been annoyed, but instead, their grumbling felt strangely grounding—an ordinary complaint in the midst of extraordinary circumstances.

The forest seemed alive, but not in the oppressive, menacing way it had the night before. Here, the trees whispered secrets in soft tones, their branches swaying gently as though welcoming the new day. Birds called to one another in the distance, their melodies weaving a fragile serenity that was almost enough to make Anira forget the dangers lurking just beyond the edges of her awareness.

Almost.

"They're quiet," Ashric said suddenly, breaking the stillness. His voice was low, but it carried easily in the hush of the forest.

Anira glanced at him, her brow furrowing. "Who's quiet?"

"The Shadowborn," he replied, his gaze sweeping the tree line. "I don't like it."

"They don't exactly announce themselves," Kael said, their tone dry.

Ashric cast them a sharp look. "Exactly my point."

Anira's grip on her dagger tightened, her momentary ease evaporating. "You think they're tracking us?"

"They're always tracking us," Ashric said simply, his voice devoid of emotion. "But this silence feels wrong."

Kael let out a soft groan, running a hand through their tangled hair. "Can't we just enjoy the morning for five minutes? The sun's shining, there's no wraith trying to rip us apart, and I haven't tripped over a root yet. Let me have this."

Ashric gave a faint snort, though his expression remained grim. "Enjoy it while you can. It won't last."

Kael muttered something under their breath, but they didn't argue further. Anira, meanwhile, couldn't stop her gaze from darting to the trees, the shadows between the trunks suddenly feeling a little too deep. The sunlight that had seemed so comforting moments ago now felt fragile, as though it could be snuffed out at any moment.

"Do you ever let yourself stop?" she asked Ashric, her voice softer now. "Even for a moment?"

He didn't answer immediately. Instead, he slowed his pace slightly, letting her draw even with him. His gaze remained fixed on the path ahead, his sharp blue eyes scanning the forest with practiced precision.

"Stopping gets you killed," he said finally, his tone low but not unkind.

"You can't run forever," she said, her brow furrowing.

Ashric glanced at her then, his lips quirking into the faintest semblance of a smile. "Maybe not. But I'll die running before I stand still and wait for the end."

Anira's chest tightened at his words, the weight of them settling heavily in her mind. She wanted to argue, to tell him that there had to be more to life than survival, but she knew better. Ashric wasn't the kind of man who believed in hope—not anymore.

Instead, she said, "I think you're wrong."

"Do you?" he asked, his gaze flicking to hers. There was a challenge in his eyes, but it was softened by curiosity.

"I do," she said firmly. "Stopping doesn't mean giving up. It means taking a moment to remember why you're still fighting."

For a moment, he didn't respond, his expression unreadable. Then he let out a soft huff of laughter, shaking his head. "You're relentless."

"And you're stubborn," she shot back, though her tone carried no heat.

A faint smile ghosted across his lips, but it disappeared as quickly as it had come. He turned his attention back to the path, his posture straightening as the tension in his body returned.

The quiet was broken only by the sound of their footsteps crunching over leaves, the occasional rustle of a bird taking flight in the distance. Anira tried to focus on the light, on the warmth of the sun on her skin, but the shadow of Ashric's words lingered, a reminder of the danger that followed them.

"Look," Kael said suddenly, pointing ahead.

Anira's gaze followed their outstretched finger, her breath catching as she saw the faint glimmer of water through the trees. A river wound its way through the forest, its surface sparkling in the sunlight like a ribbon of liquid silver. The sight was almost surreal, a stark contrast to the dark, oppressive places they'd been forced to endure.

Ashric stopped at the edge of the riverbank, his gaze scanning the far side. The water was swift but shallow, its gentle roar filling the air with a sound that felt strangely soothing. He knelt down, dipping his fingers into the cool water before rising again.

"We cross here," he said, his tone practical. "It'll cover our tracks for a while."

Kael groaned, tossing their satchel over one shoulder. "Why does every plan involve getting soaked?"

"Because it works," Ashric said, stepping into the river without hesitation. The water rose to his calves, soaking his boots, but he didn't flinch. "Move."

Anira followed, the chill of the water biting into her legs as she waded into the current. The river's song wrapped around her, its rhythm steady and constant, and for a moment, she felt the tension in her chest ease. It wasn't safety—not really—but it was something close.

As they reached the other side, Ashric turned to her, his gaze lingering for a moment longer than necessary. "Stay close," he said, his voice quieter now.

She nodded, her fingers brushing against the hilt of her dagger. "I will."

Kael, dripping and muttering under their breath, trailed after them as they disappeared back into the shadows of the forest. The river's gentle song faded behind them, replaced once again by the faint rustle of leaves and the unrelenting quiet.

And though the moment of reprieve had passed, Anira held onto it, letting its warmth settle in her chest. Because in the fragile light of the morning, she'd been reminded of something Ashric seemed to have forgotten.

Hope wasn't a luxury. It was a necessity.

The forest beyond the river was darker, the sunlight struggling to pierce through the thick canopy of ancient, gnarled trees. The air felt heavier here, the vibrant hum of nature subdued, as though even the birds were hesitant to break the silence. Moss clung to the trees like a second skin, their trunks twisted and warped as if shaped by unseen hands. The path ahead was little more than a suggestion, a faint trail of broken leaves and disturbed earth that wove between the towering oaks and pines.

Anira adjusted her cloak, the damp fabric clinging uncomfortably to her legs as she followed Ashric's steady pace. The chill of the river had lingered, seeping into her bones, but it was the unease in the air that truly set her on edge. Every snap of a twig, every rustle of leaves, felt magnified in the stillness, her heart leaping at each sound.

Ashric moved ahead like a shadow, his steps sure and deliberate. He seemed impervious to the oppressive atmosphere, his sharp blue eyes scanning the forest with the practiced vigilance of someone who had spent far too long being hunted. The faint glint of his sword, still unsheathed, caught the occasional stray ray of light, a reminder of the danger they carried with them.

Kael trailed a few steps behind, their satchel swinging heavily with each step. They muttered under their breath, the words too soft to catch, but their nervous energy was palpable. They kept glancing over their shoulder, their fingers twitching as if ready to grab the knife tucked into their belt at the first sign of trouble.

"This place feels wrong," Kael said finally, their voice breaking the tense quiet.

Ashric didn't turn around. "It's just a forest."

"It's not just a forest," Kael insisted. "It's too quiet. Too... still."

"They're not wrong," Anira said, her voice low as her gaze darted to the shadows between the trees. "It feels like we're being watched."

Ashric stopped abruptly, holding up a hand. Anira nearly bumped into him, her breath catching as he turned his head slightly, his sharp gaze sweeping the trees around them.

"We are being watched," he said, his voice a low murmur. "Keep moving. Slowly."

Anira's fingers tightened around the hilt of her dagger as they resumed their pace, each step careful and deliberate. Her eyes scanned the forest, searching for movement, for anything that didn't belong. The shadows between the trees seemed to shift, the light playing tricks on her, and she had to force herself to breathe, to stay focused.

"It's not the Shadowborn," Ashric said suddenly, his voice so soft she barely heard it. "Not yet."

"Then what is it?" Kael whispered, their voice trembling.

Ashric didn't answer immediately. Instead, he gestured to a cluster of trees ahead, their thick trunks forming a natural barrier. "There. We'll rest there. Keep your weapons ready."

Anira's stomach tightened at his words, but she followed him without question. The cluster of trees offered some shelter, their roots twisting together to form a hollow that was just large enough for the three of them to crouch within. The air inside was damp and earthy, the faint scent of moss and decay clinging to the space.

Ashric knelt at the edge of the hollow, his sword resting across his knees as he stared out at the forest. "Stay quiet," he said, his voice barely audible. "And stay close."

Anira settled beside him, her heart pounding in her chest. She could feel the tension radiating from him, the sharp edge of his focus, and it only heightened her own sense of unease. Kael huddled on her other side, their hand resting on the hilt of their knife, their wide eyes darting nervously around the hollow.

Minutes passed in silence, each one stretching longer than the last. Anira strained her ears, listening for any sound beyond the faint rustle of leaves, but the forest remained oppressively still. Her grip on her dagger tightened, the cold steel grounding her as her thoughts churned.

"Do you think it's still out there?" she whispered, her voice barely more than a breath.

Ashric didn't look at her. "Yes."

Kael let out a soft, shaky breath. "And what happens when it finds us?"

Ashric's gaze flicked to them, his expression unreadable. "It won't."

"How can you be so sure?" Anira asked, her voice quieter now.

"Because I won't let it," he said simply, his tone carrying a quiet intensity that left no room for doubt.

The weight of his words settled over them, and for a moment, the tension in the hollow eased just slightly. Anira glanced at him, her chest tightening at the sight of his profile—sharp, resolute, and utterly unyielding. He carried himself like a man who had seen too much, endured too much, and yet still refused to break.

"You can't protect everyone, Ashric," she said softly, her voice carrying a note of both defiance and something gentler.

He turned his head slightly, his sharp blue eyes locking onto hers. "Maybe not," he said, his voice quieter now. "But I can protect you."

Her breath hitched at his words, the intensity in his gaze striking something deep within her. She opened her mouth to respond, but before she could speak, a sudden rustling broke the stillness, the sound sharp and jarring in the quiet.

All three of them froze, their weapons raised as they turned toward the noise. The rustling grew louder, closer, and Anira's heart pounded in her chest as her eyes searched the shadows.

A figure stumbled into view, their movements clumsy and frantic. It was a man, his clothes torn and bloodied, his face pale and streaked with dirt. He fell to his knees, gasping for breath, his eyes wide with terror as he looked around wildly.

"Help me," he rasped, his voice barely audible.

Anira's grip on her dagger faltered, her chest tightening at the sight of him. But Ashric didn't lower his weapon. His gaze was sharp, unyielding, as he stepped forward, placing himself between her and the stranger.

"Stay back," Ashric said, his voice hard. "Who are you?"

The man coughed, his body trembling as he tried to speak. "They're coming," he gasped. "They're... coming."

Anira's stomach dropped, dread washing over her like a wave. She looked at Ashric, her eyes wide. "He means the Shadowborn."

Ashric didn't move, his sword steady as he stared at the man. "What are you running from?" he demanded.

"Them," the man whispered, his voice shaking. "They're everywhere."

The forest seemed to close in around them, the shadows deepening as the weight of his words sank in. Anira's chest tightened, her pulse racing as she turned her gaze to the trees beyond.

And then she heard it—the faint, haunting sound of footsteps, growing louder with every passing second.

The faint sound of footsteps echoed through the forest, growing louder and heavier, as though the shadows themselves had come alive. Anira tightened her grip on her dagger, her chest pounding as she tried to keep her breathing steady. The stranger who had stumbled into their hollow lay motionless now, his shallow breaths the only indication he was still alive. Ashric stood at the ready, his sword poised and his gaze sharp, scanning the darkness with the practiced intensity of someone who had been hunted before.

Kael shifted uneasily beside her, their back pressed against the twisted roots of the hollow. Their eyes darted to Ashric, then to Anira, and back again, as though trying to gauge who would break the silence first.

"Do we trust him?" Kael whispered, nodding toward the injured man.

Ashric didn't look back. "We don't trust anyone."

"You two are really winning the optimism award tonight," Kael muttered, their voice tight but tinged with their usual dry sarcasm.

Anira cast them a quick glance, a flicker of curiosity breaking through her fear. Kael's tone was sharp, but there was a flicker of vulnerability beneath it, a note of uncertainty they couldn't quite hide. She'd noticed it before, the way they deflected questions with humor, the way their eyes hardened whenever Ashric's gaze lingered too long. It was like they were building a wall around themselves, and she couldn't help but wonder what lay behind it.

"Kael," she said softly, her voice barely more than a breath. "Why do you—?"

"I know what you're going to ask," Kael interrupted, their tone sharper than she expected. "And the answer's simple: it doesn't matter."

Anira blinked, caught off guard by their sudden shift in tone. "I wasn't trying to—"

"I don't care what people call me," Kael said, their eyes flicking to hers, their expression a mixture of defiance and something softer, almost pleading. "He, she, they—it's all the same to me. I stopped caring about labels a long time ago. When you're running for your life, it's not exactly a priority."

Anira's chest tightened at their words, the weight of them settling like a stone. "I didn't mean to pry," she said quietly. "I was just curious."

Kael let out a soft, bitter laugh, shaking their head. "Curiosity's dangerous, you know. Gets people killed."

"Not always," she countered, her voice gentle but firm. "Sometimes it's how we understand each other."

Kael looked at her for a long moment, their expression unreadable. Then they sighed, their shoulders slumping slightly. "You're not like the others," they muttered, almost to themselves. "Most people just assume what they want and move on. You're... different."

Anira opened her mouth to respond, but Ashric's sharp voice cut through the tension. "Quiet."

The single word snapped them back to the moment, the heavy silence of the forest pressing down on them once more. Anira's heart raced as she turned her attention to the darkness beyond the hollow, her ears straining to catch the faintest sound.

The footsteps had grown louder, closer, the steady rhythm echoing through the trees like a drumbeat. But they weren't alone. There was another sound now, faint but unmistakable—the soft, whispering hum of the Shadowborn. It was like the rustling of leaves in a windless forest, a sound that crawled beneath the skin and set every nerve on edge.

"They're here," Ashric said, his voice low and calm. He stepped forward, his sword gleaming faintly in the dim light. "Stay behind me."

Kael stiffened, their hand clutching the hilt of their knife. "Great," they muttered. "Just what we needed."

Anira's stomach twisted as she glanced at the injured man. He was still breathing, but barely, his face pale and drawn. Whatever had chased him here was close, and she knew they didn't have much time.

"Ashric," she said, her voice trembling slightly. "What do we do?"

He didn't look back, his gaze fixed on the darkness. "We fight," he said simply. "And we don't stop until they're gone."

The words sent a chill through her, but she nodded, her grip on her dagger tightening. The shadows between the trees seemed to shift, the air growing colder as the sound of the Shadowborn's whispers grew louder. Anira's pulse quickened, her breath catching in her throat as she prepared for the inevitable.

And then, they came.

The Shadowborn emerged from the darkness, their forms shifting and curling like smoke, their silver eyes glowing with unholy light. There were three of them, their movements fluid and predatory as they closed in on the hollow.

Ashric moved first, his sword flashing as he stepped forward to meet them. The blade sliced through the nearest Shadowborn, its form unraveling into mist with a shriek that sent shivers down Anira's spine. But the others didn't falter, their silver eyes locking onto her and Kael.

"Stay back!" Ashric barked, his voice sharp as he struck again, driving the creatures away from the hollow.

Anira didn't hesitate. She stepped in front of Kael, her dagger raised, her heart pounding as the nearest Shadowborn lunged toward her. Its form was cold and unnatural, its movements too fast to follow, but she didn't flinch. She lashed out, the blade catching the edge of its shadowed form, and it shrieked, pulling back with a hiss.

Behind her, Kael cursed under their breath, their knife trembling in their hand. "This isn't what I signed up for," they muttered, their voice tight with fear.

"You'll be fine," Anira said, her voice firmer than she felt. "Just stay with me."

The fight was chaos, the hollow filled with the clash of steel and the unearthly screams of the Shadowborn. Anira's chest burned, her muscles aching as she fought, but she didn't stop. She couldn't. The creatures were relentless, their silver eyes gleaming with malice as they attacked again and again.

And through it all, Ashric was a storm. His movements were precise and deadly, his sword flashing as he cut down the creatures with ruthless efficiency. But even he couldn't hold them off forever. The Shadowborn were relentless, their numbers growing as the darkness pressed closer.

"Anira!" Ashric's voice cut through the chaos, sharp and commanding. "The Rose—now!"

Her breath hitched, her fingers brushing against the pendant at her chest. The warmth of it surged through her, the power within it stirring like a waking beast. She didn't know what to do, didn't know how to control it, but she didn't have a choice.

Taking a deep breath, she raised the pendant, its glow flaring to life as the Rose's power erupted from within. The light was blinding, searing through the darkness like a blade, and the Shadowborn shrieked, their forms unraveling as the light consumed them.

When the light faded, the forest was silent once more. The Shadowborn were gone, their presence nothing more than a lingering chill in the air.

Anira fell to her knees, her chest heaving as the power of the Rose receded. Ashric was at her side in an instant, his hand steadying her as she struggled to catch her breath.

"You did it," he said, his voice low and steady. "You stopped them."

She looked up at him, her vision blurred with exhaustion. "For now," she whispered. "But they'll be back."

Ashric nodded, his gaze hardening as he helped her to her feet. "Then we'll be ready."

The air in the forest was thick with the lingering presence of the Shadowborn. Though the creatures had been destroyed, their whispers seemed to hang in the silence like echoes, as if the shadows themselves remembered their passing. Anira leaned heavily against Ashric, her legs still trembling from the rush of power that had surged through her moments before. The warmth of the Rose was gone now, replaced by a cold weight at her chest that felt far heavier than its physical presence.

"We can't stay here," Ashric said, his voice low but firm. His hand rested on her arm, steadying her as he scanned the forest with sharp, unyielding eyes. "If there are more of them nearby, they'll be drawn to the magic. We need to move."

Anira nodded, swallowing hard against the dryness in her throat. "What about him?" she asked, gesturing weakly to the injured man still slumped at the edge of the hollow.

"We take him with us," Ashric said without hesitation. "If they find him here, he's as good as dead."

Kael groaned softly from their corner, their satchel still clutched to their chest. "Great," they muttered. "Just what we need. Another stray to slow us down."

Anira shot them a sharp look, but Ashric didn't acknowledge the comment. Instead, he crouched beside the unconscious man, slipping his arms beneath the stranger's shoulders and knees. The man let out a faint groan as Ashric lifted him with practiced ease, but he didn't wake.

"Let's go," Ashric said, his voice leaving no room for argument. He glanced at Anira, his expression softening just slightly. "Can you walk?"

"I'll manage," she said, straightening despite the ache in her legs.

Kael pushed themselves to their feet with a muttered curse. "Just so we're clear," they said, pointing a finger at Ashric. "If I get killed carrying your new charity case, I'm haunting you."

"Noted," Ashric replied dryly, shifting the unconscious man's weight in his arms. "Now move."

The group slipped into the forest, their steps careful and deliberate as they wove through the dense undergrowth. The trees seemed closer here, their twisted branches reaching out like skeletal hands, and the faint light of dawn barely pierced the thick canopy above. Anira's heart pounded in her chest, every sound in the forest amplified by the oppressive silence that surrounded them.

They moved quickly, but Ashric's sharp gaze darted constantly to the shadows, his body tense and ready to spring into action at the slightest sign of danger. Anira stayed close behind him, her dagger still in hand, while Kael brought up the rear, their knife clutched tightly in their trembling fingers.

The forest grew darker as they pressed on, the sunlight fading behind thick clouds that rolled in overhead. The air was cooler now, damp with the promise of rain, and Anira shivered as the chill seeped through her damp clothes. Her breath came in shallow gasps, the strain of their pace taking its toll, but she didn't dare complain. The memory of the Shadowborn's silver eyes was too fresh, too vivid to allow any thought of slowing down.

A faint rustling sound to their left made her freeze, her heart leaping into her throat. She turned sharply, her eyes scanning the shadows for the source of the noise. Beside her, Ashric tensed, his sword shifting slightly in his grip.

"Keep moving," he said under his breath, his voice barely audible. "Don't stop."

Anira nodded, forcing herself to keep walking even as her gaze lingered on the darkened trees. Kael let out a soft hiss behind her, their tone sharp with unease. "Something's out there."

"I know," Ashric said, his voice tight. "Stay quiet."

They moved faster now, their steps nearly silent as they wove through the undergrowth. The rustling grew louder, closer, the sound accompanied by the faint crunch of twigs snapping underfoot. Anira's pulse raced as she glanced over her shoulder, her stomach twisting at the thought of what might be following them.

Then, the sound stopped.

The sudden silence was deafening, the absence of noise far more unnerving than the rustling had been. Ashric slowed, his steps deliberate as he scanned the forest with careful precision. Anira gripped her dagger tighter, her breath catching as she waited for something—anything—to happen.

But nothing came.

"Is it gone?" Kael whispered, their voice trembling.

Ashric didn't answer immediately. His gaze lingered on the shadows ahead, his body coiled with tension, before he finally spoke. "No," he said, his tone grim. "It's waiting."

Anira's stomach twisted, but before she could speak, Ashric motioned for them to follow him. "Keep moving," he said, his voice low but commanding. "Slowly. No sudden movements."

They obeyed, their pace careful and deliberate as they continued through the forest. Every step felt like a gamble, the oppressive silence pressing down on them as the shadows seemed to close in. Anira's breath came in shallow gasps, her chest tight with anticipation, but she forced herself to stay focused.

Minutes passed like hours, the tension stretching unbearably as they moved deeper into the forest. The rustling sound didn't return, but Anira couldn't shake the feeling of being watched, the weight of unseen eyes crawling over her skin.

Finally, Ashric stopped, glancing back at them with a sharp gesture. "There," he said, nodding toward a break in the trees up ahead. "We'll lose them in the clearing."

Anira squinted, her eyes adjusting to the faint light that filtered through the thinning canopy. The forest opened up ahead, the dense undergrowth giving way to a wide expanse of tall grass swaying gently in the breeze. The openness was both a relief and a risk, but it was their best chance to put distance between themselves and whatever was following them.

They moved quickly now, their steps nearly silent as they slipped through the grass. The cool wind brushed against Anira's face, carrying with it the faint scent of rain, and for a moment, the oppressive weight of the forest lifted.

When they reached the far side of the clearing, Ashric finally slowed, his sharp gaze scanning the tree line behind them. The forest was silent, the shadows still, and Anira let out a shaky breath she hadn't realized she'd been holding.

"Did we lose them?" Kael asked, their voice breaking the quiet.

Ashric nodded, his expression grim. "For now."

Anira's legs trembled as she sank to the ground, her chest heaving with relief. She glanced at Ashric, her heart still racing as she caught the faintest flicker of exhaustion in his eyes. "That was close."

"Too close," he muttered, shifting the unconscious man in his arms. "We need to keep moving."

Kael groaned, collapsing onto the ground beside her. "Can we at least have five minutes? My legs are going to fall off."

Ashric's lips twitched faintly, though he didn't smile. "Five minutes," he said. "No more."

Anira let herself relax for the first time since they'd crossed the river, the cool breeze brushing against her face like a fleeting promise of peace. But even as she closed her eyes, the memory of the shadows lingered, a reminder that their escape was only temporary.

The breeze across the clearing was refreshing, carrying with it the faintest promise of reprieve. Anira tilted her head back, the sunlight warm on her face as she tried to push away the lingering chill of the shadows. Her body ached, her legs trembling from the tension of their flight, but she clung to the momentary stillness.

Ashric, ever vigilant, stood at the edge of the clearing, his sharp gaze scanning the tree line for any sign of movement. The unconscious man rested against a nearby tree, his breathing shallow but steady. Kael sat cross-legged on the ground, their satchel open as they rummaged through its contents with a frustrated mutter.

"Tell me you're finding something useful in there," Ashric said, his voice dry.

Kael shot him a glare, pulling out a piece of dried bread that looked like it had seen better days. "Depends on your definition of 'useful.' If you're looking for a three-course meal, you're out of luck."

"Shocking," Ashric said, his tone deadpan. "I'll try to hide my disappointment."

Anira couldn't help the faint smile that tugged at her lips as she watched their exchange. Despite the tension in the air, there was something almost comforting about their banter, a thread of familiarity woven into the chaos.

Kael tossed the bread back into the satchel with a huff. "What about you, Mr. Always Prepared? Got any secret rations tucked away in that fancy coat of yours?"

Ashric didn't bother to look at them. "You think I'd share if I did?"

"Touché," Kael muttered, leaning back against the grass. "Guess I'll just starve quietly then."

"Good practice for being quiet in general," Ashric said, his lips twitching into the faintest smirk.

Kael groaned dramatically, flopping onto their back. "You're insufferable."

"And you're alive," Ashric replied, his tone turning serious. "So maybe stop complaining for five seconds and appreciate that."

Kael opened their mouth to retort, but before they could speak, Anira's voice cut through the tension. "What's that?"

She had been scanning the clearing absentmindedly, her gaze drifting over the tall grass and scattered stones, but now her attention was fixed on something just beyond the far edge of the trees. It was faint, half-buried beneath the dirt and moss, but unmistakable—a small, weathered carving etched into a fallen tree trunk.

Ashric was beside her in an instant, his sword in hand as he followed her gaze. "What do you see?"

"There," she said, pointing to the marking. "That symbol—it looks like the ones on the waystation."

Kael sat up quickly, their curiosity piqued. "You think it's another one of those magic hideouts?"

"Maybe," Anira said, her brow furrowing as she studied the carving. "But it's old. Faded."

Ashric moved toward the tree cautiously, his eyes scanning the surrounding forest for any sign of danger. When he reached the trunk, he knelt down, brushing away the dirt and moss with careful precision. The symbol came into full view—a spiral intertwined with jagged lines, its edges worn by time.

"It's a guide mark," he said, his tone thoughtful. "The people who built the waystations used these to mark safe paths and sanctuaries."

Kael perked up, their earlier irritation forgotten. "Sanctuary, you say? Like a place where we can sit, eat, and not get murdered by shadow monsters?"

"Potentially," Ashric said, rising to his feet. "But it's also a risk. These marks were meant to be hidden, but if we found it, someone else could have too."

"Do we really have a choice?" Anira asked, her voice steady but tinged with exhaustion. "If we stay out here, we won't last much longer."

Ashric hesitated, his jaw tightening as he considered their options. Then he nodded. "We follow the mark. But stay alert. If anything feels wrong, we leave."

Kael groaned as they got to their feet, slinging their satchel over one shoulder. "Alert and starving. Great."

The group moved quickly, following the faint trail of guide marks etched into trees and stones. The path wound through the forest, the air growing cooler and the shadows deepening as they pressed on. Anira felt her heart quicken with every step, the tension in her chest a constant reminder of how precarious their situation was.

After what felt like hours, the trail opened into a clearing, and Anira let out a small gasp. Nestled against the base of a rocky hill was a crumbling stone structure, its edges worn smooth by time but still standing. Vines and moss clung to the walls, but the faint glow of magic shimmered faintly around the entrance, like an invisible barrier warding off the outside world.

"Another waystation," Ashric murmured, his tone both wary and relieved. He stepped forward cautiously, his hand resting on the hilt of his sword. "Wait here."

Anira watched as he approached the structure, her fingers brushing against the pendant at her chest. She felt the faintest pulse of warmth from the Rose, as though it recognized the magic surrounding the waystation.

When Ashric reached the entrance, he paused, his gaze scanning the shimmering barrier. Then he stepped through, his body disappearing into the faint glow. Moments later, he reappeared, nodding to them.

"It's safe," he said. "For now."

The interior of the waystation was sparse but dry, the air carrying the faint scent of stone and earth. There was a small hearth at the center, its edges blackened from long-extinguished fires, and a few remnants of furniture—wooden stools and a stone bench—scattered along the walls. It wasn't much, but it was enough.

Kael dropped their satchel onto the bench with a sigh of relief. "Finally," they muttered, pulling out the dried bread and tearing off a piece. "Not exactly a feast, but it beats nothing."

Anira settled onto one of the stools, her body sagging with exhaustion as she let out a slow breath. "It's better than being out there," she said, nodding toward the door.

Ashric leaned against the wall, his arms crossed and his gaze sharp as he watched them. "Don't get too comfortable. We're not staying long."

Kael rolled their eyes, tossing a piece of bread in Ashric's direction. "Let us have five minutes of peace, will you? Even you can't scowl forever."

Anira hid a smile as Ashric caught the bread with a quick hand, his lips twitching faintly. "I'll scowl as long as I need to."

"And you're so good at it," Anira teased, her tone lighter now.

Kael snickered, taking a bite of their bread. "It's his natural state. I think if he ever smiled, the world might actually end."

Ashric's smirk deepened, though he shook his head. "You two are unbearable."

"Admit it," Anira said, leaning forward slightly. "You'd miss us if we weren't."

For a moment, the tension in the room lifted, the faint glow of the hearth casting warm light across their faces. The danger was still out there, lurking in the shadows, but here, in this fragile sanctuary, they had found something rare.

A moment of peace.

The waystation offered a quiet reprieve, its walls imbued with the faint hum of protective magic that softened the oppressive weight of the forest beyond. Though the structure was crumbling and weathered, it carried a sense of enduring strength, as though it had been built to withstand more than time.

Kael stretched out on the stone bench, their satchel serving as a makeshift pillow. They had dozed off quickly, their steady breathing filling the quiet space. Anira sat on one of the wooden stools, her eyes half-closed as the last remnants of tension ebbed from her body. She hadn't realized how much her muscles ached until she stopped moving. Even the faint warmth from the long-dead hearth seemed to soothe her.

Across the room, Ashric leaned against the wall near the entrance, his arms crossed and his sword resting at his side. His sharp gaze swept the room, lingering on each of them in turn before flicking to the doorway, where the shimmering barrier pulsed faintly. His posture was relaxed, but Anira could see the tension in the set of his jaw, the faint lines of exhaustion etched into his face.

"You should rest too," she said softly, her voice barely above a whisper so as not to wake Kael.

Ashric glanced at her, his expression unreadable. "Someone has to keep watch."

"We're safe here," she said, gesturing toward the barrier. "That's the whole point of this place, isn't it?"

"Safe is relative," he replied, his tone matter-of-fact. "The barrier will keep out what's already looking for us, but it won't stop something from finding us if we stay too long."

Anira sighed, leaning back against the stool. "You don't let yourself stop, do you?"

He didn't answer right away. Instead, he shifted his weight slightly, his gaze turning toward the faint light of the barrier. "Stopping means letting your guard down," he said finally, his voice quieter now. "And that's how you get killed."

"You don't have to carry it all alone," she said softly, her chest tightening at the weight in his words. "That's what we're here for."

Ashric's lips quirked into the faintest smirk, though it didn't reach his eyes. "You say that now."

"I mean it," she said firmly, her gaze steady. "We've made it this far because we've been together. That counts for something."

He held her gaze for a moment longer, something flickering in his eyes that she couldn't quite name. Then he exhaled, the tension in his shoulders easing just slightly. "Fine," he said, pushing off the wall. "But only for a while."

Anira smiled faintly, watching as he settled against the opposite wall, his sword still within reach. He closed his eyes, though his posture remained tense, as though he was ready to spring into action at a moment's notice. It wasn't much, but it was something.

She let her own eyes drift shut, the faint hum of the waystation's magic lulling her into a light sleep.

When Anira woke, the air in the waystation felt fresher, lighter, as though the magic itself had rejuvenated them during the night. Kael was sitting up, yawning and rubbing their eyes as they rummaged through their satchel. Ashric was already awake, his sword in hand as he stood near the entrance, his gaze sharp and alert.

"You're awake," he said, glancing over his shoulder at her.

Anira stretched, her muscles aching faintly but feeling stronger than before. "What time is it?"

"Early," Ashric replied. "We should leave soon. The longer we stay, the more likely we'll draw attention."

Kael groaned, slinging their satchel over their shoulder. "I was hoping for a few more hours of peace."

"You'll get plenty of rest when we're out of the woods," Ashric said dryly. "Literally."

Anira stood, brushing dust off her cloak as she adjusted the dagger at her belt. "Do we have a plan for where we're going?"

"North," Ashric said. "The guide marks should lead us to another waypoint, but we can't count on finding more magic. We'll need to be careful."

Kael rolled their eyes, though the tension in their voice betrayed their nerves. "Careful. Right. Because that's been working out so well for us so far."

Anira ignored the sarcasm, focusing on the task ahead. She felt steadier now, her thoughts clearer after the night's rest. The Rose at her chest pulsed faintly, its warmth reassuring, though she couldn't help but wonder how much longer it would remain her ally before its cost became too great.

Ashric motioned for them to follow, his steps confident as he led the way out of the waystation. The shimmering barrier rippled faintly as they passed through it, the air growing cooler as they stepped back into the forest. The shadows seemed less oppressive in the early light, though the faint rustle of leaves reminded Anira that they weren't alone.

They moved in silence for a time, their steps careful and deliberate as they wove through the trees. The guide marks were faint but consistent, etched into stones and tree trunks that seemed to watch over their path like silent sentinels. Anira's senses were sharper now, every rustle of the wind and crack of a twig setting her nerves on edge.

Kael broke the silence first, their voice a mixture of curiosity and unease. "So, what's the plan when we find this next waypoint? Sit around and wait for something to attack us again?"

Ashric didn't slow his pace. "The plan is to keep moving. The more distance we put between ourselves and the Shadowborn, the better."

"And if they catch up?" Kael pressed.

"They won't," Ashric said firmly.

Anira glanced at him, her brow furrowing. "You don't know that."

"I know enough," he said, his tone clipped. "We've bought ourselves time. We just need to use it wisely."

Kael muttered something under their breath, but they didn't argue further. The tension in the group was palpable, but it was undercut by the faint sense of unity that had formed during their brief respite. They were different—each carrying their own burdens, their own fears—but they were in this together.

And for now, that was enough.

The forest felt endless, its ancient trees pressing in on them with a suffocating weight. The brief rest at the last waystation had rejuvenated their bodies, but the tension of the journey ahead was unrelenting. Every step felt purposeful yet precarious, the silence around them like a coiled spring, ready to snap.

Ashric moved with sharp precision at the head of the group, his sword at his side, his focus unwavering. Anira followed closely behind, her fingers brushing the dagger at her belt as she scanned the dense undergrowth for signs of danger. The forest was quieter than before, unnervingly so, the usual chirping of birds and rustling of small animals replaced by a heavy stillness.

"Are we sure this is the right way?" Kael asked from the back, their voice carrying a mix of weariness and irritation. "Because it feels like we're walking in circles."

"We're not," Ashric replied without looking back. "The guide marks are clear. We're on the right path."

Anira glanced at him, her brow furrowed. "You're certain the marks lead to another waystation? What if they lead somewhere else?"

"Then we find out when we get there," Ashric said simply, his tone clipped. "There's no point in second-guessing now."

Kael groaned, shifting their satchel as they sidestepped a low-hanging branch. "Great. Blind faith. That always works out so well."

"Better than standing still and waiting to be found," Ashric shot back.

The tension in the group was palpable, the strain of their constant vigilance wearing on them. Anira felt the Rose at her chest, its faint warmth steadying her even as her thoughts churned with unease. She didn't doubt Ashric's ability to lead them, but the unspoken fear that they might be walking into another trap gnawed at her.

Hours passed in silence, the oppressive quiet broken only by the crunch of leaves beneath their boots. The guide marks became more frequent as they moved deeper into the forest, etched into stones and carved into tree trunks with a precision that suggested purpose. Each mark felt like a small victory, a sign that they were headed toward something.

"What do you think we'll find?" Anira asked softly, her voice barely audible in the stillness.

Ashric's gaze didn't waver from the path ahead. "Another waystation, if we're lucky. If not, a place we can fortify until we move again."

Kael sighed, their breath visible in the cool air. "I'll take anything with walls and a roof at this point."

The forest began to change as they pressed on, the trees growing thinner and the ground beneath their feet turning rockier. The air carried a faint chill, a subtle shift that made Anira's skin prickle. The guide marks led them to a narrow path carved into the side of a hill, its edges worn smooth by time and weather.

As they crested the hill, the path opened into a wide clearing, and Anira's breath caught. At the far edge of the clearing stood a structure—stone and weathered, its edges softened by moss and vines. It was larger than the previous waystation, its walls taller and sturdier, with faint carvings etched into the stone that glowed softly in the fading light.

"This is it," Ashric said, his voice low but certain. "Another waystation."

Kael let out a shaky laugh, their relief palpable. "Finally. I was starting to think we'd be sleeping under the stars again."

Anira stepped forward, her gaze fixed on the faint shimmer of light around the structure. The air here felt different—heavier, but not oppressive. It was as though the magic of the place recognized their need and offered its protection willingly.

Ashric moved to the entrance, his hand brushing against the faint glow of the barrier. The air rippled under his touch, the magic flaring briefly before settling again. He nodded to the others, stepping inside and disappearing into the shadows.

Anira followed, her heart pounding as she passed through the barrier. The air inside was cooler, carrying the faint scent of stone and earth. The room was wide and open, its stone walls lined with alcoves that held broken pottery and rusted tools. A hearth sat in the center, its edges blackened from long-forgotten fires, and faint symbols etched into the floor pulsed with a steady rhythm.

Kael entered last, letting out a low whistle as they glanced around. "Alright, this is better. Creepy, but better."

"It's safe," Ashric said, his tone firm. "For now."

They settled into the space cautiously, their movements slow and deliberate as they took in their surroundings. The waystation felt ancient, its magic strong but worn, like an old sentinel standing guard against an unseen threat. Anira let out a slow breath as she sank onto a stone bench, the tension in her shoulders easing just slightly.

"Do you think we can stay here for a while?" she asked, glancing at Ashric.

"Long enough to rest," he said, his gaze sweeping the room. "But not too long. These places are meant for refuge, not permanence."

Kael flopped onto the floor near the hearth, rummaging through their satchel with a faint grumble. "I'll take what I can get. This beats sleeping on roots."

The group fell into a tentative rhythm, their exhaustion dulling the sharp edges of their fear. Anira felt the weight of the journey settle into her bones, but the warmth of the waystation's magic gave her a fragile sense of hope. For now, they were safe. For now, they could breathe.

And though the shadows still waited beyond the stone walls, their next steps would be taken with renewed strength.

The interior of the waystation was a solemn testament to time and magic. The faint glow from the carved symbols on the walls pulsed like a quiet heartbeat, casting a soft, golden light that illuminated the space in uneven waves. The air inside was cool and carried a dampness that hinted at long-forgotten rains seeping through cracks in the stone. It was quieter here, the oppressive weight of the forest replaced by the hum of ancient magic that seemed to whisper through the room.

Anira sat on a wide stone bench built into one of the walls. The surface was smooth from years of wear, but cold against her skin. Above her, a narrow slit in the wall let in a faint sliver of light from the overcast sky, though it did little to brighten the space. Moss crept along the edges of the stonework, its green tendrils weaving intricate patterns that seemed to echo the magic in the air.

The hearth at the center of the room drew her attention. It was larger than the one in the last waystation, its stone edges carved with intricate designs of intertwining vines and spirals. The faint scent of ash lingered, though the fire that had once burned here was long gone. She wondered how many people had gathered around it, seeking the same refuge they now needed.

Kael had sprawled on the floor near the hearth, their satchel acting as a pillow. They'd rummaged through its contents earlier, pulling out a small loaf of bread and a few withered strips of dried meat that were now neatly arranged beside them. Despite the relief on their face, they hadn't let go of their knife, which rested on the ground within easy reach.

"Do you think the people who built these places are still out there?" Anira asked softly, her voice barely breaking the stillness.

Ashric, who stood near the doorway, glanced back at her. His shadow stretched across the room, distorted by the glow of the symbols on the walls. "If they are, they're doing a better job of hiding than we are."

Kael let out a faint chuckle, though it was devoid of humor. "I don't blame them. If I had the magic to build something like this, I'd lock myself inside and never come out."

Anira leaned forward, her elbows resting on her knees as she studied the carvings on the hearth. "It feels... alive," she murmured. "Like it's watching us."

"It is," Ashric said simply, his tone matter-of-fact.

Kael sat up, their brow furrowing as they glanced around the room. "That's not comforting."

"It's not meant to be," Ashric replied, his gaze flicking to the symbols etched into the floor. "These places are powered by intention. They were built to protect, but that protection comes with a cost."

"What kind of cost?" Anira asked, her fingers brushing against the Rose at her chest.

Ashric hesitated, his gaze darkening. "Magic this old doesn't act without purpose. If it's keeping something out, it's also keeping something in."

Kael groaned, falling back onto their makeshift pillow. "You know, you're great at the whole ominous speech thing. Really uplifting."

Ashric's lips twitched into the faintest semblance of a smirk. "Glad to hear it."

Despite the lighthearted exchange, the weight of his words settled heavily in the room. Anira glanced around again, her gaze lingering on the alcoves carved into the walls. Some were empty, their contents long gone, while others held remnants of tools and vessels—shards of pottery, rusted blades, and fragments of glass. It was as though the lives of those who had come before had been left behind, their stories etched into the very stone.

"What do you think happened to them?" she asked, her voice quieter now.

Ashric didn't answer immediately. Instead, he moved toward the hearth, his footsteps echoing faintly on the stone floor. He crouched beside it, his fingers tracing the edge of one of the carvings. "They survived," he said finally. "For a while."

Kael raised an eyebrow, sitting up again. "That's supposed to make us feel better?"

"It should," Ashric said, his tone sharp but not unkind. "Because it means these places work. They did their job then, and they'll do their job now."

Anira nodded, though the unease in her chest didn't entirely fade. She stood, moving toward one of the alcoves, her fingers brushing against a shard of pottery that rested within. The surface was rough, its edges worn smooth, but she could still make out faint markings—symbols similar to those etched into the walls.

"It feels like a tomb," she said softly.

"It's a sanctuary," Ashric corrected, rising to his feet. "But sanctuaries only exist because there's something to hide from."

Kael let out a low sigh, running a hand through their tangled hair. "Fantastic. Can't wait to leave this cozy little deathtrap."

Anira glanced at them, a faint smile tugging at her lips despite the tension in the room. "You're always so cheerful."

"It's my best quality," Kael said with a smirk, though their grip on their knife tightened slightly.

The group fell into silence again, each of them lost in their thoughts as the faint hum of the waystation's magic filled the air. The room felt both alive and eerily empty, as though it had been waiting for them, but offered no promises of safety beyond its walls.

"We leave soon," Ashric said finally, his voice breaking the quiet. "Rest while you can. The next leg won't be easier."

Anira nodded, settling back onto the bench as she let the magic of the waystation wash over her. It wasn't peace, not really, but it was enough.

For now.

The stillness inside the waystation stretched on, though it felt less oppressive now, as though the ancient magic had settled into a quiet vigil. Anira sat on the cold stone bench, her thoughts churning as she watched Ashric pace near the doorway. His sharp gaze never strayed far from the shimmering barrier, his sword resting in an easy grip at his side. Even here, within the protective magic of the waystation, he seemed incapable of letting his guard down.

Kael had finally stopped fidgeting, their legs stretched out as they leaned against the base of the hearth. They were twirling a shard of pottery between their fingers, the dim glow of the symbols on the walls catching the edge of the fragment as it spun. Despite their usual sarcasm, their brow was furrowed in thought, their usual bluster subdued.

Anira felt the weight of the Rose at her chest, the warmth of it pulsing faintly against her skin like a second heartbeat. It was a reminder of the burden she carried, the power she hadn't fully come to understand. She brushed her fingers against the pendant, the sensation grounding her as she stared at the alcoves lining the walls, wondering how many others had sat in this very space, waiting for the courage to take their next step.

"How far do you think the next waypoint is?" she asked softly, breaking the quiet.

Ashric glanced at her, his expression unreadable. "If the guide marks hold steady, maybe half a day's journey."

"And if they don't?"

"Then we improvise," he said simply.

Kael let out a faint groan, tossing the shard of pottery onto the ground. "That's reassuring. Nothing like wandering through a cursed forest with no map."

Ashric shot them a look, his tone dry. "Would you rather stay here and hope the Shadowborn don't figure out how to breach the barrier?"

Kael opened their mouth to respond but seemed to think better of it, letting out a huff instead. "Point taken."

Anira studied Ashric's profile, the sharp lines of his jaw and the faint shadow of stubble along his chin. He carried himself like a man who had long since resigned himself to being the one everyone relied on, no matter the cost to himself. She wondered how many times he had stood in places like this, calculating risks, always one step ahead of the danger trailing behind him.

"You've done this before," she said, her voice gentle but certain.

He met her gaze, his blue eyes narrowing slightly. "What makes you think that?"

"Because you're too good at it," she replied. "Too good at reading the terrain, at keeping us moving, at knowing when to stop and when to push forward. You've survived things like this."

His jaw tightened, and for a moment, she thought he might brush her off with a sarcastic quip. But then he sighed, his shoulders slumping slightly as he leaned against the wall. "A few times," he admitted, his voice quieter now. "Not all of them ended well."

Kael perked up slightly, their curiosity evident despite their exhaustion. "Define 'not well.'"

Ashric's gaze darkened, his lips pressing into a thin line. "Not something you'd want to hear."

Kael raised their hands in mock surrender. "Alright, fair enough. I'll stick to happy ignorance."

Anira watched Ashric carefully, her chest tightening at the faint shadow of pain that crossed his face. He wasn't a man who let others see his vulnerability, but in that moment, it was there—a flicker of something raw and unguarded. She wanted to ask him more, to press for the stories he kept buried, but she knew better than to push.

Instead, she said, "You've kept us alive so far. That counts for something."

His eyes softened slightly, though his expression remained guarded. "It's not enough," he said quietly. "Not yet."

Kael let out a faint snort, shaking their head. "You've got a hell of a standard for 'enough.'"

Ashric didn't respond, his gaze returning to the barrier. The shimmering light rippled faintly, the magic's steady hum a constant reminder of the fragile safety they had found.

"We leave at first light," he said after a long moment, his tone firm. "The longer we stay, the more likely we'll be found."

Kael groaned, rubbing their temples. "I knew you'd say that."

Anira smiled faintly despite the tension in the room. "At least we're rested now."

"Speak for yourself," Kael muttered. "I feel like I've been run over by a very angry troll."

"You're still alive," Ashric pointed out, his smirk faint but visible.

"Barely," Kael grumbled, though the corner of their mouth twitched as they fought back a smile.

The banter eased the weight in the air, if only slightly. Anira leaned back against the stone wall, letting her eyes drift to the glowing carvings on the walls. The symbols pulsed faintly, their rhythm steady and unchanging, like the beat of a distant drum. She wondered if they would hold once they left, or if the waystation would fade again, its magic retreating until the next travelers stumbled upon it.

The thought made her chest tighten. The waystations felt like fleeting promises—temporary sanctuaries in an unforgiving world. But they wouldn't last forever. And neither would their luck.

"We'll make it," Ashric said suddenly, as though reading her thoughts.

Anira glanced at him, her brow furrowing. "You sound sure."

"I have to be," he replied, his tone steady. "Because if I'm not, none of us will be."

The weight of his words settled over her, grounding her even as it reminded her of the danger they faced. She nodded, gripping the pendant at her chest as she drew strength from its faint warmth.

Morning would come soon enough, and with it, the next leg of their journey. But for now, in the dim light of the waystation, they had found a moment of quiet—a fragile reprieve that they would carry with them into the shadows ahead.

The faint glow of the carvings on the walls pulsed steadily, casting uneven shadows that seemed to shift and stretch across the room.

The others had begun to settle in, Kael muttering under their breath as they adjusted their satchel into something resembling a pillow. Ashric still stood near the doorway, his sword at his side, the tension in his posture making it clear that, even here, he wouldn't let his guard down.

Anira couldn't help but watch him. His focus was so singular, so unrelenting, that it was almost mesmerizing. The sharp lines of his face were softened only slightly by the faint light, but his expression remained hard, his jaw set and his gaze distant. He was like a statue carved from stone—beautiful in its severity but untouchable all the same.

"You're going to wear yourself out," she said softly, breaking the quiet.

Ashric turned his head, one dark brow arching as his sharp blue eyes met hers. "I could say the same to you."

She smiled faintly, leaning back against the bench. "I'm not the one standing guard in a place that's already warded by magic."

"That magic won't save us if we're not ready," he replied, his tone even but carrying a hint of something sharper. "Complacency kills."

"And you're never complacent," she said, tilting her head slightly. "Are you?"

"No," he said simply, his gaze lingering on her for a moment longer than necessary.

There was a weight in the air between them, something unspoken but undeniable. Anira felt her pulse quicken, though she told herself it was nothing more than the lingering tension from their journey. Still, she couldn't stop the way her chest tightened when he looked at her like that—like he saw more of her than she was ready to show.

"You act like the whole world rests on your shoulders," she said, her voice softer now. "Like you're the only one who can keep us alive."

Ashric smirked faintly, though it was more bitter than amused. "Someone has to."

"Maybe," she said, her gaze steady. "But that doesn't mean you have to do it alone."

His expression darkened, his jaw tightening as he looked away. "Alone is safer."

"For who?" she asked, leaning forward slightly. "For you? Or for us?"

Ashric didn't answer immediately. Instead, he stepped away from the doorway, his movements deliberate as he crossed the room to where she sat. He stopped in front of her, close enough that she had to tilt her head back to meet his gaze.

"For everyone," he said quietly, his voice low and rough, like distant thunder.

Anira's breath caught at the intensity in his eyes, the storm of emotions he kept buried just beneath the surface. She wanted to argue, to tell him he was wrong, but the words tangled in her throat, caught by the weight of his presence.

"You're wrong," she said finally, her voice barely above a whisper.

"Am I?" he asked, his tone softer now, almost teasing. He leaned down slightly, his sharp features illuminated by the faint glow of the carvings. "Because I think you're starting to see it too."

"See what?" she asked, her pulse pounding in her ears.

"That the closer you get to someone," he said, his voice dropping lower, "the easier it is to lose them."

Her chest tightened at his words, a flicker of pain cutting through her. "And what about the people who are already close?" she asked. "The ones who won't leave, no matter how hard you push them away?"

For a moment, Ashric didn't move. His gaze lingered on hers, the tension in his jaw softening as something unguarded flickered across his face. "Then maybe they're the ones who need to be protected the most."

Anira's breath hitched, her chest tightening as his words sank in. There was a vulnerability in his tone, a rare crack in the armor he wore so tightly, and it made her want to reach for him, to close the distance between them.

But before she could speak, Kael's voice broke the moment like a sharp crack in the stillness.

"If you two are done with your brooding and meaningful stares," Kael said, their tone dripping with sarcasm, "some of us are trying to sleep."

Ashric straightened instantly, the faint flicker of emotion in his eyes vanishing as his smirk returned. "Sleep faster, Kael. You'll need the energy."

Kael muttered something under their breath, rolling over and burying their face in their satchel. Anira let out a faint laugh, the sound breaking the tension in her chest, though her heart was still racing.

Ashric stepped back, his sharp gaze lingering on her for a moment longer before he turned toward the doorway. "Rest while you can," he said over his shoulder. "Morning will come sooner than you think."

Anira watched him as he resumed his post, the weight of his words settling over her like a shroud. Despite the darkness that surrounded them, the danger that loomed just beyond the waystation's walls, there was something about him that made her feel steady, even as it left her completely unmoored.

And though she couldn't explain why, she found herself hoping he felt the same.

The waystation had grown eerily quiet, the faint hum of its protective magic blending into the oppressive stillness of the forest beyond. The carvings on the walls pulsed steadily, but the rhythm felt slower now, as though the ancient magic was tiring. Even Kael, who had been grumbling moments ago, was still, their breathing deep and even as sleep overtook them.

Anira remained awake, her fingers tracing the edge of the Rose pendant at her chest. Its warmth pulsed faintly, a constant presence that both comforted and unnerved her. She glanced toward Ashric, who stood near the doorway, his silhouette sharp against the faint shimmer of the barrier. He hadn't moved since their exchange, his body tense, his gaze locked on the forest outside.

The stillness dragged on, the air heavy with anticipation. Anira closed her eyes, trying to let the faint hum of the waystation's magic lull her into rest. But just as her breathing began to steady, a sound shattered the quiet—a sharp, high-pitched crack that echoed through the room like the snapping of bone.

Her eyes flew open, her heart pounding as she shot to her feet. The sound had come from outside, its source hidden within the dense shadows of the forest. Ashric had already drawn his sword, his body coiled like a spring as he stared into the darkness beyond the barrier.

"What was that?" Anira whispered, her voice barely audible.

"Trouble," Ashric muttered, his tone grim.

Kael stirred, their eyes blinking groggily as they sat up. "What now?" they mumbled, their voice thick with sleep.

Before Ashric could respond, the sound came again—closer this time. It wasn't the snap of a twig or the rustle of leaves; it was something deliberate, something unnatural. A faint scraping noise followed, like claws dragging against stone, and Anira felt a chill crawl down her spine.

"It's testing the barrier," Ashric said, his voice low but steady. He took a step forward, his sword glinting faintly in the dim light. "Get ready."

Kael was on their feet instantly, their knife trembling slightly in their grip. "You're kidding me," they said, their voice rising in panic. "Didn't we just deal with this?"

"Stay quiet," Ashric snapped, his sharp gaze never leaving the doorway.

The scraping stopped abruptly, leaving the air heavy with silence. Anira's pulse pounded in her ears as she gripped her dagger tightly, her knuckles white. She stepped closer to Ashric, her eyes fixed on the shimmering barrier as she tried to pierce the shadows beyond.

And then it came—a low, guttural growl that vibrated through the air, so deep and resonant that it seemed to shake the very stone beneath their feet. It wasn't like the whispers of the Shadowborn or the unnatural keening of the wraith. This was something different. Something worse.

Ashric's jaw tightened, his sword raised and ready. "It knows we're here," he said, his voice barely above a whisper. "And it's not alone."

The growl was joined by another, and then another, the sound multiplying until it surrounded the waystation on all sides. Anira's breath caught in her throat as she realized just how close the creatures were, their guttural snarls growing louder with each passing moment.

"What do we do?" Kael asked, their voice trembling as they pressed their back against the wall.

Ashric didn't respond immediately. He turned to Anira, his blue eyes meeting hers with a fierceness that made her chest tighten. "The Rose," he said, his voice low but urgent. "It's the only thing that can stop them."

Her stomach twisted, the weight of his words settling heavily over her. "I don't know how," she said, her voice shaking. "I don't even know what it's capable of."

"You don't have to know," he said firmly, his hand brushing briefly against her arm. "You just have to trust it."

The growls grew louder, more frantic, as the creatures outside pressed closer to the barrier. The faint shimmer of magic flickered, the carvings on the walls dimming as though the waystation itself was struggling to hold its ground.

Anira swallowed hard, her fingers tightening around the pendant. The warmth of the Rose pulsed against her skin, stronger now, as though it was waiting for her to act.

She could feel the power coursing through it, wild and untamed, like a storm trapped within a single fragile bloom.

"Anira," Ashric said, his voice cutting through the chaos. "Now."

Her breath hitched, her heart pounding as she stepped forward. The growls outside grew deafening, the scraping sound returning with frantic intensity as the barrier flickered again. The creatures were closing in, their presence pressing against the magic like a wave ready to crash.

Anira raised the pendant, the warmth of it flooding her veins as she closed her eyes. She didn't know what she was doing—didn't know if it would work—but she reached for the power within it, letting it surge through her like fire.

The last thing she heard before the room was consumed by blinding light was Ashric's voice, steady and unyielding:

"Don't stop."

Then, the world erupted.

Through the Shattered Barrier

The world was light and sound, a chaos that roared in Anira's ears and seared her vision. She stumbled backward, the pendant's heat radiating through her chest like fire, its power flooding the room in a wave of blinding brilliance. The guttural growls outside the waystation turned to shrieks, high-pitched and inhuman, as the creatures were struck by the force of the magic.

Then, as quickly as it had erupted, the light faded, plunging the room into eerie silence.

Anira blinked rapidly, her breath coming in short gasps as her vision swam. The carvings on the walls were dim now, their pulsing glow reduced to faint flickers like dying embers. The once-steady hum of the waystation's magic had faltered, replaced by an uneasy stillness.

Ashric was the first to move, his sword still in hand as he stepped toward the doorway. The barrier was gone, its protective shimmer reduced to faint tendrils of light that clung to the edges of the entrance like smoke. He glanced back at her, his sharp blue eyes narrowing as he took in her trembling frame.

"Are you alright?" he asked, his voice low but urgent.

Anira nodded, though her legs felt like they might give out beneath her. The Rose was still warm against her chest, but its pulse had slowed, its earlier power receding as if spent. "I think so," she said, her voice barely audible. "What happened?"

"You happened," Kael said, their voice unsteady as they stepped away from the wall, their knife clutched tightly in their hand. "That was... What was that?"

Anira shook her head, her fingers brushing against the pendant. "I don't know. I just—"

"You didn't have a choice," Ashric interrupted, his tone firm. "And it worked."

He turned back toward the doorway, his body tense as he scanned the clearing outside. Anira followed his gaze, her stomach twisting at the sight. The creatures were gone, their forms reduced to smoldering black marks on the ground. The air outside carried the faint scent of ash and something metallic, sharp and unpleasant, that made her stomach churn.

But the danger wasn't over. The forest beyond the clearing felt darker now, its shadows deeper and more menacing. Whatever had been drawn to them wasn't finished, and the faint rustling of leaves in the distance was a grim reminder that they were far from safe.

"We need to move," Ashric said, his voice breaking the tense quiet. "The barrier's gone. This place won't hold if more of them come."

Kael groaned, slinging their satchel over their shoulder. "Of course we do. Because why would we ever get a break?"

"Because the world doesn't care if we're tired," Ashric shot back, his tone clipped. "Get ready."

Anira took a steadying breath, forcing her legs to carry her forward. She felt drained, the energy from the Rose's magic leaving her hollow, but she pushed the fatigue aside. There was no time for weakness now—not when the shadows were closing in again.

They stepped outside, the cold air hitting Anira like a slap. The clearing felt oppressive, the trees towering overhead like silent watchers. The marks on the ground where the creatures had been were still smoldering, faint wisps of smoke curling into the sky. Ashric led the way, his sword held loosely in his hand, though his posture was as sharp as ever.

Kael followed reluctantly, their eyes darting toward every shadow as they muttered under their breath. "Next time, we find a nice quiet cave. Maybe one without ancient magic or monsters trying to eat us."

Ashric ignored them, his focus on the guide marks that continued faintly ahead. Anira stayed close to him, her fingers brushing the hilt of her dagger as she scanned the forest for movement. The tension in the air was palpable, each step a reminder that they were being hunted.

They moved quickly, the forest growing darker and more tangled as they pressed on. The path was narrow, lined with roots that twisted across the ground like veins, and the faint light from the overcast sky barely pierced the canopy above. Anira's breath came in shallow gasps, her chest tight with the weight of the journey.

"How much farther do you think?" she asked, her voice breaking the quiet.

"Not far," Ashric replied, though his tone was grim. "The marks are leading us somewhere. Let's hope it's somewhere we can hold."

"And if it's not?" Kael asked, their voice tinged with sarcasm but underscored by genuine fear.

Ashric glanced back at them, his expression hard. "Then we improvise."

Kael let out a soft groan, muttering something under their breath, but they didn't argue. The group pressed on, their pace steady but cautious. The faint rustling in the distance grew louder, a constant reminder that they weren't alone, and Anira's grip on her dagger tightened.

The guide marks led them down a steep incline, the ground beneath their feet shifting with loose stones and damp leaves. Anira stumbled slightly, her hand brushing against Ashric's arm as she steadied herself. He glanced at her briefly, his gaze softening for just a moment before returning to the path ahead.

"Careful," he said, his voice quieter now.

"I'm fine," she replied, though her legs still felt shaky. "Let's just keep going."

The incline leveled out into another clearing, this one smaller and surrounded by dense, gnarled trees. At the center of the space stood a low stone archway, its edges worn smooth by time and weather. Symbols were etched into the stone, their faint glow pulsing steadily like a heartbeat. It wasn't a waystation, but the magic emanating from it was familiar—protective and strong.

"Another waypoint," Ashric said, his tone cautious as he stepped toward the archway. "Not a refuge, but a step forward."

Kael groaned softly. "Does it at least come with snacks?"

"No," Ashric said flatly, his smirk faint as he motioned for them to follow. "But it might keep us alive a little longer."

Anira stepped through the archway, the magic pulsing around her like a faint breeze. The tension in her chest eased slightly, though the weight of the journey ahead still loomed heavy.

They didn't know what awaited them beyond the next turn, but one thing was certain: they couldn't stop. Not now. Not when the shadows were still so close.

The archway stood like a sentinel in the clearing, ancient and unmoving, its weathered stone worn smooth by time and touched by the weight of centuries. The symbols etched into its surface glowed faintly, pulsing with a rhythm so subtle it felt almost like breathing. The air around it carried a strange charge, a faint hum that was just barely audible, as though the magic within it waited, watching, deciding.

Ashric stepped forward, his boots crunching softly against the moss and loose stones beneath his feet. He paused at the base of the archway, his hand brushing over the edge of the stone. His sword was still in his other hand, though he held it loosely, the blade glinting faintly in the dim light. His face was set, every line of it carved with focus, his sharp blue eyes scanning the clearing with the precision of a man who had learned never to trust stillness.

Anira lingered just behind him, her breath shallow as she took in the sight before her. The archway was unlike the waystations they had found before—less a place of refuge and more an entryway, a door to something unseen. Vines twisted up its base like veins, their dark green leaves dotted with tiny white flowers that seemed out of place in the oppressive gloom of the forest. She could feel the Rose at her chest stirring, its warmth growing faintly stronger as though it, too, recognized the power of the arch.

Kael hung back, their arms crossed tightly over their chest as their gaze darted between the archway and the shadows of the forest beyond. Their usual sarcasm was absent now, replaced by a nervous energy that made their movements jittery. Their satchel hung heavily at their side, the leather worn and frayed, and they fidgeted with the strap, their fingers twitching as though searching for something to hold onto.

"Is it safe?" Anira asked softly, her voice barely breaking the stillness.

Ashric didn't look back. "Safe enough," he said, though the tension in his tone belied his words.

"That's not exactly comforting," Kael muttered, their voice tight.

"It's not supposed to be," Ashric replied, stepping under the archway. The light from the symbols brightened briefly as he passed through, flaring like a spark before fading again. He paused on the other side, his gaze sweeping the forest beyond.

Anira hesitated, her hand brushing against the pendant at her chest. The warmth of the Rose steadied her, its faint pulse grounding her as she took a deep breath and followed. The air beneath the archway was cooler, carrying with it a strange metallic tang that clung to the back of her throat. She felt the magic ripple over her skin as she stepped through, its touch fleeting but distinct, like the brush of a feather against her arm.

The clearing on the other side was darker, the trees pressing in closer, their gnarled branches reaching out like claws. The ground was uneven, littered with jagged rocks and patches of moss that gleamed faintly in the dim light. The path ahead was narrow, barely more than a suggestion carved into the earth, and it twisted sharply out of sight, disappearing into the shadows.

Kael emerged last, their knife gripped tightly in one hand as they cast a wary glance back toward the forest behind them. "I hate this place," they muttered, their voice low but audible in the oppressive quiet. "It feels... wrong."

Anira didn't disagree. The air here was heavier, the silence thicker, as though the world itself was holding its breath. The faint rustling of leaves in the distance was barely perceptible, but it sent a shiver down her spine all the same. She couldn't shake the feeling that something was watching them, hidden just beyond the edge of the trees.

"We keep moving," Ashric said, his voice breaking through the tension. He adjusted the grip on his sword, his movements fluid and practiced as he stepped onto the path ahead. "The guide marks should lead us out of this."

"If they don't?" Kael asked, their tone laced with forced bravado.

"Then we improvise," Ashric replied, his tone clipped but not unkind.

They fell into a tense rhythm, their steps careful and deliberate as they followed the faint path through the forest. The trees seemed to grow taller the farther they went, their trunks thick and knotted, their roots curling up from the ground like the limbs of some sleeping giant. The faint light that filtered through the canopy above was dim and uneven, casting jagged shadows that danced with every movement.

Anira's gaze lingered on the marks that appeared sporadically along the path, etched into the trunks of trees or carved into stones. Each mark pulsed faintly, their glow barely perceptible in the gloom, but they were enough to guide their way. She couldn't help but wonder who had left them, and how long ago. The magic felt ancient, older than the waystations they had found, and its presence was both reassuring and unnerving.

The silence stretched, broken only by the soft crunch of their footsteps and the occasional rustle of leaves. Anira's thoughts churned as they walked, the weight of the Rose at her chest a constant reminder of the burden she carried. She glanced at Ashric, his broad shoulders tense and unyielding as he led the way. He moved with a confidence that seemed unshakable, but she knew better. She had seen the cracks beneath his armor, the weight he carried silently, and it made her chest ache in a way she couldn't quite name.

"Do you ever wonder who built all this?" she asked, her voice breaking the quiet.

Ashric glanced back at her briefly, his expression thoughtful. "Sometimes," he said. "But wondering won't change what's ahead."

"Still," Kael interjected, their voice softer now, "it's strange, isn't it? All these marks, all this magic—someone had to leave it. Someone had to know we'd come this way."

Ashric didn't respond immediately, his focus returning to the path ahead. "Whoever they were," he said finally, "they're long gone. All that matters now is that it works."

Anira nodded, though the unease in her chest didn't fade. The path ahead seemed to stretch endlessly into the darkness, and she couldn't shake the feeling that whatever waited at the end would demand more from them than they were prepared to give.

The forest grew denser with every step, the gnarled roots curling upward like skeletal fingers trying to snag their boots. The path twisted sharply, disappearing behind massive trunks that seemed to lean in closer as if listening. The faint light filtering through the canopy above faded into near darkness, and the air grew heavier, filled with the damp scent of moss, decaying leaves, and something acrid that Anira couldn't place.

The guide marks continued, but they were fainter now, their glow flickering like the dying light of a distant star. Each one they passed felt more tenuous, like the magic binding this path together was fraying with time or use—or both.

Ashric moved with practiced precision, his sword always within reach, his every step deliberate. Anira followed closely, her dagger gripped in her hand, her nerves taut with the oppressive weight of the forest. Behind her, Kael's uneven footsteps betrayed their anxiety, the occasional muttered curse escaping them as they stumbled over hidden roots and loose stones.

"This place hates us," Kael grumbled, their voice breaking the silence. "I can feel it."

"It's a forest," Ashric said flatly, though his gaze remained fixed on the path ahead. "It doesn't feel anything."

"You say that," Kael replied, their tone tight, "but I'd bet every coin I don't have that it wants us dead."

Anira suppressed a faint smile despite the tension. "Let's just focus on getting out of here," she said, glancing back at Kael. "If you're right, we don't want to give it any more reasons."

Kael snorted, though it lacked their usual bravado. "Trust me, I'm already on my best behavior."

The path dipped sharply, the incline steep and uneven. Anira's breath caught as she slipped on a patch of slick moss, her feet sliding out from under her. Ashric was there instantly, his arm steadying her as she caught herself on a nearby tree.

"Careful," he said, his voice low but firm.

"I've got it," she said quickly, though her pulse was racing. She could feel the strength in his grip, the steadiness that belied the sharp edges of his demeanor. It was infuriating and comforting all at once.

His gaze lingered on her for a moment longer before he released her arm and stepped ahead. "Stay close," he said over his shoulder, his tone softer now.

They continued in silence, the air growing colder with every step. The faint rustling of leaves that had accompanied them earlier faded entirely, replaced by a suffocating stillness. Even the sound of their footsteps seemed muted, swallowed by the oppressive weight of the forest.

Anira couldn't shake the feeling that they were being watched. The shadows between the trees seemed to shift and ripple, though whenever she turned her head, there was nothing there. She felt the Rose at her chest pulse faintly, its warmth stronger now, as though it, too, sensed the unseen eyes.

"Do you feel that?" she asked, her voice barely more than a whisper.

Ashric didn't respond immediately, but she saw the slight tightening of his jaw, the way his shoulders tensed. "Yes," he said finally. "We're not alone."

Kael let out a sharp breath, their knife trembling in their grip. "Fantastic. Any guesses on what it is this time?"

"Doesn't matter," Ashric said, his voice low and even. "We stay focused and keep moving."

The path ahead twisted sharply again, opening into a small clearing. The ground here was uneven, littered with stones and patches of pale grass that glowed faintly in the dim light. At the center of the clearing stood a tree unlike any they had seen before. Its bark was dark and smooth, almost black, and its massive trunk twisted upward in spirals, its branches spreading out like veins. Strange, faintly glowing symbols were carved into the bark, their light flickering like embers.

"What is that?" Kael asked, their voice trembling with equal parts awe and fear.

"It's not a guide mark," Ashric said, his gaze narrowing as he approached the tree. "But it's magic."

Anira stepped closer, her breath catching as the warmth of the Rose surged against her chest. The symbols on the tree seemed to respond, their glow intensifying as she neared, and she felt the faint hum of power radiating from the trunk.

"It feels... alive," she said softly, her fingers hovering just above the bark.

"Don't touch it," Ashric said sharply, his voice breaking through her daze. "We don't know what it does."

She pulled her hand back quickly, her heart racing. "What do you think it is?"

Ashric shook his head, his eyes scanning the clearing. "It's a waypoint of some kind, but not one I've ever seen. Whatever it is, it's tied to the marks we've been following."

Kael stepped closer, their usual wariness tempered by curiosity. "It's beautiful," they muttered. "In a creepy, might-kill-us kind of way."

Ashric shot them a warning look. "Stay back. We don't know if it's safe."

Before anyone could respond, the tree pulsed with light, the symbols glowing brighter as a faint, resonant hum filled the clearing. Anira stumbled back, her hand flying to the pendant at her chest as the warmth of the Rose flared to near-burning intensity.

The ground beneath their feet trembled, a low vibration that sent loose stones skittering across the clearing. The hum grew louder, deeper, resonating in her chest like a heartbeat as the tree's symbols began to shift and ripple, their shapes twisting like liquid.

"What's happening?" Kael asked, their voice rising with panic.

"I don't know," Ashric said, his sword in hand, his stance defensive. "But we're about to find out."

Anira felt the Rose pulse again, its warmth spreading through her like fire, and she realized with growing dread that whatever was happening, it was tied to her. The tree's symbols seemed to reach for her, their glow intensifying as the hum became a deafening roar.

Then, with a blinding flash of light, everything went still.

The hum stopped. The trembling ceased. The clearing was silent once more.

And the tree was gone.

The clearing was swallowed by silence, thick and oppressive, as if the forest itself held its breath. The Rose, pulsing faintly against Anira's chest, emitted a sound that was neither heard nor entirely felt—a low resonance that seemed to vibrate in her bones, like the thrum of distant thunder trapped beneath the earth. It was an ancient rhythm, both familiar and foreign, whispering secrets she couldn't quite grasp.

She staggered back a step, her hand instinctively clutching the pendant. The resonance shifted, deepening into a melodic hum that coursed through her body, reverberating in time with her heartbeat. It wasn't music, not exactly, but something primal and raw, as though the very essence of the world had been caught in the pendant's glow.

Ashric turned sharply, his gaze narrowing on her. "What's happening?" he demanded, his voice cutting through the air like steel. The sound from the Rose swelled again, echoing in waves that seemed to ripple through the clearing, stirring the shadows at its edges.

"It's reacting to something," Anira said, her voice trembling. The vibration grew sharper, like the keen edge of a blade scraping against stone, setting her teeth on edge. The world around her blurred, and the Rose's sound intensified into a steady pulse, growing faster, urgent, as if warning her of what was to come.

And then, it stopped—sudden and complete, leaving the clearing plunged into silence once more.

The silence that followed was deafening, thick and unnatural, as though the forest had been stripped of all sound. Anira stood frozen, her chest rising and falling with shallow breaths as she clutched the Rose. Its warmth remained, but the pulsing sound that had filled the clearing was gone, replaced by an eerie stillness that set her every nerve on edge.

Ashric's voice broke the silence, low and sharp. "Whatever it did, it wasn't just for show." He scanned the clearing, his sword held steady, the faint light catching on its edge. "Stay close."

Kael edged nearer, their knife trembling in their hand. "I don't like this," they muttered, their voice barely audible. "It feels like we just rang some kind of bell."

"We might have," Ashric said grimly, his gaze fixed on the space where the tree had stood moments before. The grass and earth there were undisturbed, as if the massive, ancient thing had never existed, but the faint scent of ash lingered in the air—a bitter, metallic tang that clawed at the back of Anira's throat.

She took a cautious step forward, her eyes fixed on the empty space. "The marks were tied to it," she said softly, more to herself than the others. "It was part of the path."

"Then why is it gone?" Kael hissed, their eyes darting to the shadows at the edge of the clearing. "What kind of magic just... disappears like that?"

"Magic that isn't meant to linger," Ashric replied, his voice taut. "Or magic that's waiting for something."

A chill swept through Anira, and she forced herself to breathe deeply. The Rose stirred faintly against her chest, its warmth steady but subdued, as though resting after its earlier burst of power. She looked up at Ashric, her voice steady despite the fear coiling in her gut. "What now?"

He didn't answer immediately. His eyes remained locked on the treeline, his body tense and coiled, ready to strike at the first hint of movement. When he finally spoke, his voice was low, measured. "We follow the path. Whatever that tree was, it's gone now. But the marks haven't stopped."

Anira followed his gaze, her eyes searching the clearing. Sure enough, a faint guide mark glimmered on a tree just beyond the edge of the clearing, its light flickering like a fading candle. The sight was both a relief and a warning—it meant the path continued, but also that they hadn't yet escaped whatever force had drawn them here.

Kael groaned softly, rubbing the back of their neck. "Right. Follow the creepy disappearing magic into the even creepier forest. Great plan."

"Do you have a better one?" Ashric asked, his tone razor-sharp.

Kael held up their hands in mock surrender. "Not complaining. Just... mentally preparing for the inevitable doom."

Anira shot Kael a faint smile, though her heart felt heavy. "We'll make it," she said, more to herself than anyone else.

Ashric motioned for them to move, his sword leading the way as they stepped back onto the narrow path. The forest seemed darker now, the shadows thicker and more oppressive, as though the very trees were closing in around them. The air grew colder with every step, carrying with it a faint whisper that sent chills racing down Anira's spine.

She glanced at Ashric, her voice low. "Do you hear that?"

"Yes," he replied, his tone flat but laced with tension. "Keep moving."

The whispering grew louder, a soft, insistent murmur that seemed to come from every direction. It wasn't words, not exactly, but a sound that felt purposeful, as though the forest itself was speaking in a language just beyond comprehension.

Kael's voice trembled as they quickened their pace. "What are they saying? Do you hear them too?"

"Don't listen," Ashric said sharply, his voice cutting through the murmurs. "Focus on the path. Nothing else."

Anira forced her gaze forward, her hand tightening around her dagger. The guide marks appeared more frequently now, their glow steady and bright against the encroaching darkness. Each one felt like a lifeline, pulling them forward through the suffocating gloom.

The path twisted sharply again, and as they rounded the bend, the forest opened into another clearing. This one was different, larger, and filled with crumbling stone ruins that jutted out of the earth like jagged teeth. The air here was colder still, the whispers falling silent as they stepped into the space.

Ashric halted abruptly, his eyes narrowing as he took in the ruins. "Stay sharp," he said, his voice low. "We're not alone."

Anira felt it too—the presence, heavy and oppressive, that clung to the air like a shroud. Her breath hitched as she scanned the clearing, her eyes darting between the broken walls and crumbling pillars that cast long, jagged shadows across the ground.

"What is this place?" Kael whispered, their voice barely audible.

"A crossroads," Ashric replied, his gaze fixed on the largest of the ruins—a jagged archway that stood at the far end of the clearing, its surface etched with glowing symbols that pulsed faintly in the dark.

Anira stepped closer to him, her voice steady despite the fear clawing at her throat. "What does it mean?"

"It means we have a choice," Ashric said, his tone grim. "And whatever we choose, it's going to cost us."

The ruins loomed ahead, stark and ominous against the backdrop of the darkened forest. The jagged archway at the far end of the clearing seemed to call to them, its faintly glowing symbols pulsing in an uneven rhythm that reminded Anira of a heartbeat—uneven, irregular, as though the magic itself was struggling to stay alive.

Ashric stepped forward first, his sword held low but ready, his sharp gaze sweeping the clearing for movement. The air was heavy, thick with an unnatural stillness that made every sound—every breath, every step—feel deafening. Anira followed closely, her fingers brushing against the Rose at her chest as its warmth pulsed faintly against her skin. It was a steady reminder of the power she carried and the cost it might demand.

Kael lingered behind them, their movements hesitant, their knife clutched tightly in their hand. "I don't like this," they muttered, their voice barely more than a whisper. "It feels like we're walking into a trap."

"We probably are," Ashric said without looking back, his tone flat. "But we don't have a choice."

The words hung in the air, heavy and undeniable. The archway stood like a sentinel at the far end of the ruins, its surface etched with symbols that glowed faintly, casting uneven light across the broken stones and scattered debris. Anira couldn't shake the feeling that the symbols were watching them, their glow shifting slightly with every step closer.

The whispers began again, soft at first, like the rustling of leaves in a windless forest. Anira froze, her breath catching as the sound grew louder, more insistent, wrapping around them like an unseen presence. It wasn't words—not in any language she knew—but it carried a weight, a meaning that pressed against her mind like a shadow she couldn't escape.

"Do you hear that?" Kael whispered, their voice trembling.

"Yes," Ashric said sharply. "Keep moving."

Anira swallowed hard, forcing her legs to move even as every instinct screamed at her to turn and run. The Rose at her chest grew warmer, its pulse quickening as they approached the archway. She could feel the power radiating from it now, strong and wild, like a storm barely contained within its crumbling frame.

As they reached the base of the archway, Ashric held up a hand, motioning for them to stop. His gaze was locked on the glowing symbols, his expression grim. "Something's guarding this," he said, his voice low. "The magic here isn't just old—it's alive."

Anira shivered, her fingers tightening around her dagger. "What do you mean, alive?"

"It's waiting for us," Ashric replied, his gaze never leaving the archway. "And it's going to test us."

Kael let out a shaky laugh, though it lacked any humor. "A test? Great. Because everything else has been so easy."

Ashric ignored them, stepping closer to the archway. The symbols flared brighter as he approached, their light casting jagged shadows across the ground. The air around the archway seemed to hum, vibrating faintly with a sound that wasn't quite audible, but still pressed against their ears like a distant echo.

Anira felt the Rose burn hotter against her skin, its pulse quickening as Ashric reached out, his hand hovering just above the surface of the archway. "Are you sure about this?" she asked, her voice trembling.

"No," he said simply, and then he pressed his hand against the symbols.

The reaction was instant. The symbols flared to life, their light blinding as the hum became a roar, a deafening sound that shook the ground beneath their feet. The air around them crackled with energy, sharp and electric, and Anira stumbled back, her hand flying to the pendant at her chest as its warmth surged into a near-burning heat.

The archway shifted, its jagged edges shimmering as the space within it began to warp. The air inside twisted and rippled, distorting like a reflection in water, until it formed a swirling void of shadow and light. The whispers grew louder, overlapping and echoing in an unrelenting cacophony that pressed against their minds, their meanings just out of reach.

"Through the archway," Ashric shouted over the noise, his voice cutting through the chaos. "Now!"

Anira hesitated for only a moment before following, her legs carrying her forward despite the fear clawing at her chest. The void within the archway pulsed, its shadows writhing like living things as she stepped closer. The warmth of the Rose surged again, steadying her, and she took a deep breath before plunging through.

The sensation was immediate and overwhelming. The moment she passed through the archway, the air seemed to shift, heavy and suffocating, as though she had stepped into another world entirely. The light from the symbols faded, replaced by a cold, unnatural glow that illuminated the space around them.

It was a corridor—long and narrow, with walls of smooth black stone that pulsed faintly with light, like veins carrying molten fire. The floor beneath her feet was uneven, a patchwork of jagged stone and darkened earth, and the air was filled with the faint scent of ash and something metallic.

Ashric was already ahead, his sword raised, his gaze scanning the corridor with practiced precision. Kael stumbled through a moment later, their eyes wide as they took in the alien landscape.

"What is this place?" Kael whispered, their voice trembling.

"I don't know," Ashric said, his voice tight. "But it's not where we were."

Anira glanced back at the archway, her heart sinking as she realized it had vanished, leaving only smooth stone behind. The whispers were gone, replaced by a deep, resonant hum that seemed to come from the very walls around them.

"We're trapped," she said, her voice barely audible.

"No," Ashric said firmly, his gaze hard. "We're moving forward."

And with that, he began down the corridor, his steps deliberate, his sword ready. Anira followed, her hand clutching the pendant at her chest, the warmth of the Rose the only thing keeping her grounded as they ventured deeper into the unknown.

The corridor seemed to stretch endlessly, its dark stone walls pulsing faintly as though alive. Each step Anira took echoed unnaturally, the sound bouncing back to her as if the space were tighter than it appeared. The hum that filled the air wasn't a noise exactly but a vibration that crawled over her skin, setting her every nerve on edge.

Ashric led the way, his sword a gleaming point of light in the dim, oppressive glow. His steps were measured and deliberate, but his body was tense, his shoulders set as though he expected an attack at any moment. Anira followed closely, her hand resting on the hilt of her dagger. Kael trailed behind, their breathing sharp and uneven, each exhale carrying a faint muttered curse.

The air was cold—colder than it should have been—and carried a sharp metallic tang that made Anira's stomach churn. She felt the warmth of the Rose pulsing faintly against her chest, steady but subdued, as though it was holding something back.

"What is this place?" Kael asked, their voice barely above a whisper. "It feels like it shouldn't exist."

"It's a trap," Ashric said bluntly, his voice low but steady. "And we're walking straight into it."

"Comforting," Kael muttered, their fingers twitching against the knife they held.

Anira swallowed hard, her gaze darting to the walls. The faint veins of light that ran through the stone shifted and pulsed, their rhythm uneven. They seemed to pulse in time with the Rose's warmth, like a connection she couldn't yet understand. She felt as though the walls were watching them, the faint hum growing louder with each step.

The corridor suddenly widened, opening into a cavernous space that swallowed them in shadow. The ceiling arched high above, disappearing into darkness, while the floor beneath their feet smoothed out into polished stone that gleamed faintly in the dim light. Pillars lined the walls, their surfaces etched with symbols that glowed faintly, casting twisted shadows across the room.

In the center of the chamber was a pedestal, a low, jagged structure that seemed carved from the same black stone as the walls. It pulsed faintly with light, a slow, rhythmic throb that filled the room with an almost imperceptible vibration. Something rested atop it, a faint silhouette that shimmered in and out of view as though caught between worlds.

"Stay back," Ashric said sharply, holding up a hand. His voice echoed in the chamber, the sound carrying an unnatural weight that made Anira flinch.

Kael froze, their eyes locked on the pedestal. "What is that?" they whispered.

"Nothing good," Ashric muttered, his gaze narrowing.

Anira stepped forward despite herself, her chest tightening as the warmth of the Rose surged against her skin. The pendant seemed to pull her forward, its pulse aligning with the rhythm of the pedestal's light. Her fingers tightened around its edges, the heat almost unbearable.

"It's calling to me," she said softly, her voice trembling. "I think it's tied to the Rose."

Ashric stepped in front of her, his sword raised. "That doesn't mean it's safe."

The hum in the air grew louder, sharper, like the tuning of a distant instrument. Anira's breath caught as the shadows in the room began to shift, curling and writhing along the walls like living things. The glow from the symbols on the pillars grew brighter, casting jagged lines of light that flickered and danced like fire.

"Do you see that?" Kael hissed, their voice trembling. "The shadows—"

"I see it," Ashric said, his tone clipped. "Keep your weapon ready."

The shadows moved faster now, circling the edges of the room as the hum reached a near-deafening pitch. Anira's pulse raced as she stared at the pedestal, her instincts warring with her fear. The object on top of it shimmered again, its form sharpening briefly into something that looked almost like a key—long, slender, and carved from black stone.

Before she could speak, the shadows surged inward, coalescing into a mass that writhed and twisted like smoke caught in a storm. The air grew colder, the metallic tang growing stronger, and the room was filled with a sound that wasn't a growl or a roar but something deeper—something ancient and unrelenting.

"Move!" Ashric shouted, grabbing her arm and pulling her back as the shadow mass surged toward them. His sword slashed through the air, the blade glinting with a faint glow as it struck the darkness. The mass recoiled, shrieking in a soundless cry that vibrated in their skulls.

Anira stumbled, her back hitting one of the pillars as she struggled to catch her breath. The shadows shifted, their form breaking apart and reforming as they circled the pedestal, blocking the way forward.

"What is that thing?" Kael shouted, their knife clutched tightly in their shaking hand.

"Something that doesn't want us here," Ashric growled, his sword at the ready. He glanced at Anira, his gaze sharp. "Whatever that thing on the pedestal is, it's connected to the Rose. You're the only one who can get it."

Anira's heart pounded, her breath coming in shallow gasps as she stared at the writhing shadows. The Rose burned against her chest, its pulse steady and insistent, like a command she couldn't ignore.

"Go!" Ashric barked, his voice cutting through her hesitation. "We'll hold it off."

Kael's eyes widened. "Hold it off? You're joking, right?"

"Not the time," Ashric snapped, lunging forward as the shadows surged toward them again. His blade cut through the darkness, each strike sending ripples of light through the room that momentarily pushed the shadows back.

Anira didn't think—she couldn't. She forced herself forward, her feet pounding against the stone floor as she sprinted toward the pedestal. The shadows lunged at her, cold and sharp, but she dodged, the warmth of the Rose guiding her like a beacon. She reached the pedestal, her hand trembling as she reached for the object atop it.

The moment Anira's fingers closed around the key, a blinding surge of light exploded from the pedestal, washing over the chamber like a tidal wave. The pulse of energy was sharp, almost alive, and it drove into her chest like a hammer, momentarily stealing her breath. The Rose at her chest burned, its heat spreading outward, filling her veins with liquid fire. The warmth wasn't painful—it was something deeper, more overwhelming, as though the very essence of the magic had merged with her own.

The shadows shrieked, a soundless cry that vibrated through the chamber like a tremor. They writhed and twisted, their dark forms unraveling in the wake of the light. For a moment, it seemed as though the magic of the Rose was consuming them, reducing the writhing mass into nothing more than faint tendrils of smoke.

But then the light began to falter.

Anira staggered back from the pedestal, the key clutched tightly in her hand. The light dimmed, the pulsing glow from the walls and pillars flickering like a dying flame. The shadows surged again, regathering themselves into a mass of coiled darkness that seemed more solid, more deliberate.

Ashric lunged forward, his sword a blur of steel as it cut through the edge of the shadow. The creature shrieked again, recoiling, but only for a moment. It shifted, reforming into a serpentine figure with glowing eyes like molten silver. Its gaze fixed on Anira, and the air grew heavy with a palpable malice.

"Anira!" Ashric's voice was sharp, cutting through the haze of fear that gripped her. "Move! Don't stand there!"

She stumbled away from the pedestal, clutching the key as though it were her only lifeline. The warmth of the Rose pulsed against her chest, its rhythm quick and insistent, but it offered no further surge of magic, no guidance on what to do next.

Kael darted forward, their knife slashing at a tendril of shadow that lunged toward Anira. "Whatever that thing is, it's not backing down!" they shouted, their voice strained. "Do you have a plan, or are we just improvising?"

Ashric drove his sword into the core of the shadow mass, the blade glowing faintly as it made contact. "We don't stop," he growled, his voice low and fierce. "Anira, that key—if it's tied to the Rose, it has to do something. Figure it out!"

Her breath hitched, panic clawing at her chest. She turned the key over in her hand, its surface smooth and cold despite the heat of the magic that had poured from it moments before. The black stone glinted faintly, and the intricate carvings etched into it shimmered with a faint light, pulsing in time with the Rose.

The shadows struck again, their tendrils darting toward her. She threw herself to the side, hitting the ground hard as the cold, oily darkness swept past her. Kael yanked her to her feet, their grip firm but trembling. "No pressure or anything," they muttered, shoving her forward. "But figure it out now!"

Anira's gaze darted to the far side of the chamber, where another archway stood, its surface etched with symbols that mirrored those on the key. It pulsed faintly, almost in time with the rhythm of the Rose, and she realized with sudden clarity that the key wasn't just a tool—it was a gate.

"There!" she shouted, pointing toward the archway. "It's a door. The key—"

"Then use it!" Ashric barked, his sword slicing through another tendril of shadow. The creature recoiled, its form flickering as though struggling to maintain itself. "We'll hold it off!"

Anira didn't hesitate. She sprinted toward the archway, her legs burning as she dodged the grasping tendrils of shadow that lunged at her. The ground beneath her feet seemed to ripple, the stone trembling as though the chamber itself was alive and reacting to the battle.

She reached the archway, her breath coming in ragged gasps as she held the key up. The symbols on its surface flared to life, their light weaving through the air like threads of gold, connecting with the markings on the arch. The air shimmered, and a deep, resonant sound filled the chamber, vibrating through her chest.

Behind her, the shadow mass let out a deafening shriek, its form twisting and breaking apart as it surged toward her in one last desperate attack.

"Anira, now!" Ashric shouted, his voice cutting through the chaos.

She slammed the key into the center of the archway, the carvings on its surface aligning perfectly with the symbols etched into the stone. The moment it connected, the archway erupted with light, a blinding, golden surge that enveloped her completely. The air twisted, the chamber fading into nothingness as she was pulled forward, the light swallowing her whole.

For a moment, there was only silence—complete and consuming, like the world itself had been erased.

Then, the ground solidified beneath her feet, and the air returned, sharp and cold. She opened her eyes, her breath catching as she took in her surroundings. The chamber was gone, replaced by a vast expanse of open sky and rolling hills bathed in silver light. The air was fresh, carrying the scent of grass and earth, and the oppressive weight of the shadows was gone.

Ashric and Kael appeared beside her, their forms flickering briefly as though pulled through a veil. They stumbled forward, their faces pale and their eyes wide as they took in the unfamiliar landscape.

"Where... are we?" Kael asked, their voice barely above a whisper.

Ashric sheathed his sword, his expression hard as he scanned the horizon. "Somewhere else," he said simply. "Somewhere we weren't meant to find."

Anira clutched the key in her hand, its warmth fading as the Rose pulsed faintly against her chest. Whatever they had escaped, it wasn't over. This was only the beginning

The silver light bathed the rolling hills, casting long shadows that stretched like tendrils across the unfamiliar landscape. The air was sharp and cool, tinged with the faint scent of damp earth and something metallic that lingered at the edge of perception. The oppressive darkness of the chamber was gone, but the tension in Anira's chest remained, coiled tightly like a spring ready to snap.

Ashric stepped forward, his boots crunching softly against the dewy grass. His hand rested on the hilt of his sword, and his sharp blue eyes scanned the horizon with a hunter's precision. The rolling hills stretched endlessly, punctuated by jagged stone formations that jutted from the ground like broken teeth. Far in the distance, faint shadows danced along the edges of what looked like a dense forest, its canopy dense and shifting unnaturally.

"Wherever we are," Ashric said, his voice low, "we didn't leave the danger behind."

Kael groaned, collapsing to sit on a nearby stone. They ran a hand through their hair, their knife still clutched tightly in their other hand. "Great. A magical death maze turned into... whatever this is." They gestured vaguely at the eerie expanse. "Are we ever going to end up somewhere normal?"

Anira didn't respond immediately. She was still clutching the key, its surface cool now, its light extinguished. The Rose at her chest pulsed faintly, a steady rhythm that felt more subdued than before, as though it, too, was catching its breath. She stared down at the object in her hand, the intricate carvings etched into the black stone still faintly glowing.

"It brought us here for a reason," she said finally, her voice quiet but resolute. "The key, the Rose—this place is connected to them. To all of it."

Ashric turned to her, his gaze hard but not unkind. "Do you feel it?" he asked. "The pull?"

Anira nodded, her fingers brushing against the pendant at her chest. "It's faint, but it's there. Like... a thread leading somewhere."

Kael raised an eyebrow, their tone biting despite their obvious unease. "A thread leading where, exactly? Another trap? Another shadow monster? Because if that's the plan, I vote we turn around."

"We can't," Ashric said flatly. He motioned behind them, where the archway had been moments ago. In its place was nothing but empty air, the jagged stones and hills blending seamlessly into the horizon. "The way back is gone."

Kael muttered a string of curses under their breath, rising to their feet with a scowl. "Of course it is. Why wouldn't it be?"

Anira glanced toward the distant forest, her stomach tightening. The shadows beneath the canopy seemed to ripple, shifting in ways that defied explanation. It was as if the forest itself was alive, watching them, waiting for their next move. The pull of the Rose was stronger now, drawing her gaze toward the trees.

"We have to go there," she said, pointing toward the forest.

Kael paled. "You're joking, right? That place looks like it wants to eat us."

"Do you have a better idea?" Ashric asked, his tone sharp but laced with exhaustion. "We can't stay here. We're too exposed."

Kael threw up their hands in exasperation. "Fine. Let's walk into the creepy forest. What's the worst that could happen?"

Anira stepped forward, the key still clutched tightly in her hand as she followed the faint pull of the Rose. The grass was slick beneath her boots, the dampness seeping through the soles, but she pressed on, the tension in her chest growing with every step.

Ashric fell into step beside her, his movements quiet and deliberate. "If the Rose is leading you, trust it," he said, his voice low. "But don't ignore your instincts. If something feels wrong, it probably is."

She nodded, her jaw tightening. "I know."

Kael trailed behind them, muttering under their breath as they cast nervous glances at the horizon. The silence of the landscape was oppressive, broken only by the occasional whistle of wind that carried with it a faint, haunting sound—like whispers just out of earshot.

As they approached the forest, the pull of the Rose grew stronger, its pulse quickening against her chest. The shadows beneath the trees seemed to deepen, their movements more pronounced now, like figures shifting just beyond the edge of sight. Anira felt her breath catch, her hand tightening around the key as unease settled over her like a heavy cloak.

Ashric stopped abruptly, his hand raised in a silent command for them to halt. His gaze was fixed on the treeline, his body coiled like a spring. "Do you see that?" he asked, his voice barely above a whisper.

Anira squinted, her eyes scanning the dense shadows. At first, she saw nothing but the shifting darkness. Then, faintly, she caught movement—small, deliberate flickers of light that wove through the trees like fireflies, their glow cold and unnatural.

"What are they?" Kael whispered, their voice trembling.

"Not fireflies," Ashric muttered, his tone grim. He unsheathed his sword, the blade catching the faint light of the horizon. "Stay close. And whatever happens, don't let them touch you."

The lights grew brighter as they approached, their movements erratic and unsettling. Anira's heart raced as she stepped closer to Ashric, her fingers brushing against the dagger at her side. The pull of the Rose was almost unbearable now, urging her forward, toward the forest, toward the lights.

"Why does it feel like we're being led into something?" Kael asked, their voice rising with panic.

"Because we are," Ashric said, his voice sharp. He glanced at Anira, his gaze steady despite the tension in his jaw. "Are you ready?"

She nodded, though her hands trembled. "As ready as I'll ever be."

The three of them stepped into the forest, the darkness swallowing them whole. The lights danced around them, their cold glow casting jagged shadows across the trees. The air grew colder, the metallic tang sharper, and the whispers began again—soft and insistent, threading through the silence like a melody she couldn't understand.

Anira gripped the key tightly, her breath coming in short, shallow gasps as the Rose pulsed faster. The lights closed in, their glow growing brighter, and she felt the weight of the forest press down on her, suffocating and unrelenting.

And then, one of the lights stopped directly in front of her, hovering in the air like a frozen flame.

It spoke.

The light hovered before Anira, cold and unearthly. It wasn't fire—it was something sharper, its edges flickering like shattered glass caught in a pale, otherworldly glow. It pulsed faintly, a rhythm that mirrored the frantic beat of her heart. The whispers grew louder now, blending into a low hum that seemed to vibrate in her chest.

Ashric stepped closer, his sword raised, the blade trembling slightly in his grip. "Don't move," he said, his voice low and tight. "It's watching you."

Anira's breath hitched, her fingers tightening around the key. The light drifted closer, circling her slowly, its glow casting sharp shadows on her face. It was curious, almost deliberate, as though it were studying her. She could feel the warmth of the Rose intensify, its pulse matching the glow of the light, as though the two were locked in some silent communication.

"What does it want?" Kael whispered, their voice trembling. They stood frozen a few steps behind, their knife clutched tightly in both hands.

"I don't know," Anira murmured, her voice barely audible. "But it's not... attacking."

The light flared suddenly, bright and blinding, forcing her to shield her eyes. The hum in the air rose to a deafening pitch, and Anira staggered, her knees buckling beneath the weight of the sound. The Rose burned hot against her chest, its warmth searing, as though urging her to act.

"Anira!" Ashric's voice cut through the chaos, sharp and commanding. "Do something!"

She didn't know what to do—didn't know how—but the Rose seemed to. Its heat surged through her, spreading from her chest to her fingertips, and the key in her hand began to glow, its intricate carvings flaring to life with golden light.

The hovering light pulsed in response, its rhythm quickening, almost frantic. It stopped moving, hanging motionless before her, and then it spoke—not in words, but in a voice that echoed in her mind, deep and resonant, carrying the weight of something ancient and powerful.

"The gatekeeper," it intoned, its voice reverberating through her skull. "You carry the key. Will you pass?"

Anira's throat tightened, her chest heaving as she tried to form words. The Rose pulsed again, steady and insistent, and she realized the question wasn't rhetorical. The light was waiting for her answer.

"What does it mean?" Kael hissed, their wide eyes darting between the light and Anira. "Pass? Pass what?"

"It's a trial," Ashric said grimly, his gaze locked on the hovering light. "The Rose... it's testing her."

Anira swallowed hard, her hand trembling as she held the glowing key in front of her. "I'll pass," she said, her voice steady despite the fear clawing at her. "I have to."

The light flared brighter, the air around it crackling with energy. The hum deepened, the vibration coursing through the ground, through the air, through her, and the forest itself seemed to hold its breath.

"Then step forward," the voice said, low and echoing. "And face the cost."

The light vanished in an instant, leaving the forest in utter darkness. The hum stopped, replaced by a deafening silence that pressed against Anira's ears. She stood frozen, her pulse thundering in her chest as the Rose flared one last time, its warmth fading into a steady, quiet thrum.

Ashric stepped to her side, his expression hard but his eyes betraying a flicker of concern. "Are you sure about this?"

She nodded, her grip on the key tightening. "I don't think we have a choice."

Kael let out a shaky breath, their voice barely a whisper. "We never do, do we?"

Ahead, the path through the forest shifted. The trees bent inward, their branches curling like claws, forming a tunnel of shadow and faint light. At its end, a faint glow flickered—a distant beacon that pulsed in time with the Rose.

Ashric raised his sword, his jaw tight. "Whatever's waiting for us, it won't be friendly."

Anira stepped forward, her resolve firm despite the tremor in her legs. The forest seemed to press in closer with every step, the oppressive darkness growing heavier, more tangible. The faint glow ahead grew brighter, sharper, beckoning them deeper into the unknown.

Behind her, Kael whispered, almost to themselves, "This is a terrible idea."

Anira didn't look back. She kept moving, the key in her hand, the Rose at her chest, the weight of its magic pulling her toward whatever lay ahead.

The forest grew darker still, the whispers returning, faint but insistent, as though the shadows themselves were alive, speaking secrets they weren't meant to hear.

And then, as the tunnel opened into a wide expanse of blinding light, the whispers stopped.

And the screaming began.

The Screaming Light

The light was blinding, a searing white that burned away the oppressive shadows of the forest. Anira stumbled to a halt, shielding her eyes with one hand while the other gripped the key so tightly her knuckles turned white. The sound was deafening—not a scream made by any living thing, but a discordant wail that pierced through her mind, raw and unrelenting, as if the world itself was in pain.

Ashric grabbed her arm, steadying her. His sword was already raised, his sharp gaze scanning the space ahead. "Stay close," he barked, his voice barely audible over the wail. "We don't know what's waiting."

Kael staggered behind them, their face pale and eyes wide as they clutched their knife. "What is that?" they shouted, their voice cracking with panic. "What's making that sound?"

"I don't think it's a what," Anira said, her voice trembling as she forced herself to lower her hand and squint into the light. "I think it's the place."

The forest was gone, swallowed by the searing brightness that stretched in all directions. The ground beneath their feet was smooth and glassy, its surface reflecting the light in fractured patterns that shimmered and shifted like water. The air was heavy, thick with a metallic tang that coated the back of Anira's throat, making it hard to breathe.

And at the center of it all, rising from the ground like a jagged wound in the earth, was a massive spire of dark stone. It pulsed faintly, its surface etched with glowing red veins that pulsed in time with the wail. The closer Anira looked, the more the veins seemed to shift, twisting and writhing like living things trapped beneath the stone.

"This feels wrong," Kael muttered, their voice barely audible over the relentless scream. "Like... we're not supposed to be here."

Anira couldn't disagree. The Rose at her chest burned hotter now, its pulse quick and frantic, matching the rhythm of the spire. The key in her hand glowed faintly, its carvings shimmering with golden light, but it offered no answers, no guidance.

Ashric stepped forward, his every movement deliberate. "This is the trial," he said, his voice low but steady. "Whatever this place is, it's reacting to the Rose—and to you." He glanced at Anira, his eyes hard. "Be ready."

"For what?" she asked, her voice trembling. "What are we supposed to do?"

Ashric didn't answer. His focus was on the spire, his posture tense and coiled, ready to strike. The wailing grew louder as they approached, the sound drilling into Anira's skull until it was almost unbearable. Her steps faltered, her legs trembling beneath her.

And then, as they drew closer, the wailing stopped.

The sudden silence was deafening, thick and oppressive, pressing against Anira's ears like a weight. She staggered, her breath coming in short gasps as the echo of the wail faded from her mind. The spire pulsed once, its red veins flaring brightly, and then it began to shift.

The ground beneath their feet trembled, a low rumble vibrating through the glassy surface. The spire cracked, dark shards splintering from its surface and falling to the ground with sharp, echoing crashes. From the cracks emerged something that made Anira's blood run cold—dark, writhing tendrils that moved like smoke and shadow, coiling and twisting as they reached toward the sky.

Kael let out a strangled gasp, stumbling back. "No, no, no. This isn't—this can't—"

"Stay calm!" Ashric snapped, his sword flashing as he stepped in front of them. The tendrils didn't stop, their movements erratic but deliberate, as though searching for something—or someone.

Anira felt the Rose pulse again, its warmth spreading through her like a command. The key in her hand flared brighter, its golden light cutting through the oppressive glow of the spire. She stepped forward, her voice steady despite the fear clawing at her chest.

"It's me," she said, her gaze fixed on the writhing mass of shadow. "It's reacting to me."

Ashric shot her a sharp look. "Then don't get too close."

"I don't think we have a choice," she replied, her voice trembling. "The Rose brought us here for a reason."

Kael's hand shot out, gripping her arm. "You don't have to do this. We can find another way—"

"There isn't another way," she said firmly, pulling free of their grip. Her eyes met Ashric's, and in his gaze, she saw the understanding she needed. He nodded once, his expression grim, and stepped aside.

Anira approached the spire, the key glowing brighter with every step. The tendrils shifted toward her, their movements slower now, almost hesitant, as though they were waiting. The Rose burned hot against her chest, its pulse quickening until it matched the frantic rhythm of her heart.

She reached the base of the spire and held the key aloft. The tendrils froze, their writhing movements stilled as they coiled tightly around the jagged surface of the stone. The veins on the spire flared, a brilliant crimson light that pulsed outward in waves, and the ground beneath her feet shuddered.

The silence shattered.

With a sound like shattering glass, the spire erupted in light and shadow, the tendrils breaking free and spiraling into the air. Anira was thrown backward, her body hitting the ground hard as the key was torn from her grasp, its golden light vanishing into the chaos.

And then, from the heart of the spire, a figure emerged.

It wasn't human—not entirely. Its form was tall and lithe, wreathed in shadow and light, its edges shifting and rippling as though it existed in two worlds at once. Its eyes burned with the same crimson light as the spire, and when it spoke, its voice echoed with a terrible resonance that shook the ground.

"You have awakened the path," it said, its gaze fixed on Anira. "But the cost has only begun.

Anira scrambled backward, her palms scraping against the cold, glassy ground as the towering figure stepped free of the shattered spire. Its form was impossible to pin down, shifting like smoke caught in a gale, its edges flickering with bursts of crimson light. The air around it warped, bending and twisting with a weight that pressed against her chest like a vice.

Ashric stepped between Anira and the figure, his sword raised. The sharp edge gleamed faintly in the unnatural glow, but the trembling in his knuckles betrayed the tension in his body. "Stay back," he barked at the creature, though the command sounded hollow against the raw power emanating from it.

The figure tilted its head, its crimson eyes locking onto Ashric. "You raise steel against me?" Its voice was deep, resonant, and layered with echoes that seemed to come from every direction. It wasn't angry, nor amused—just curious. "Your weapon is a whisper in the storm. Do not tempt me."

Ashric didn't lower his sword, his stance unwavering. "You've already tempted us by bringing us here."

The figure's eyes flicked to Anira, the glow in them intensifying. "I did not bring you," it said, its tone carrying an air of finality. "The Rose did. It chose her. It demanded this awakening."

Kael, still crouched near the edge of the clearing, let out a sharp, nervous laugh. "Awakening? What the hell does that mean? Because so far, all it's done is try to kill us!"

The figure didn't spare Kael a glance, its focus wholly on Anira. "It means the trial has begun. And with it, the cost will be extracted."

Anira forced herself to her feet, her knees trembling beneath her. The warmth of the Rose pulsed faintly now, steady but muted, as though it were recovering from the burst of magic that had brought them here. She swallowed hard, her voice steady despite the fear crawling up her throat. "What cost?"

The figure moved closer, each step sending faint ripples through the ground. It stopped a few paces away, towering over her, and though its features were blurred by the shifting shadows, she felt the intensity of its gaze like a physical weight.

"You carry the Rose," it said, its voice softer now but no less powerful. "Its power is not freely given. Every choice you make with it carries a price. Every step you take will demand more."

Anira's fingers brushed the pendant at her chest, the faint warmth grounding her as she met the creature's gaze. "Why me?" she asked, her voice barely above a whisper. "Why did it choose me?"

The figure was silent for a long moment, its shifting form almost still. Then it said, "Because you are willing to pay."

Her breath hitched, her chest tightening. "Pay what?"

"Everything," the figure said simply. Its eyes flared brighter, and the ground beneath them shuddered. "The path ahead is not for the faint of heart. The Rose has set its sights on you, and it will not stop until you have fulfilled its purpose."

Ashric took a step forward, his voice sharp. "And what is that purpose? If you're going to put her through this, at least tell us what the end of this road is."

The figure turned its burning gaze on Ashric, and the weight of it made him falter, though he didn't lower his blade. "The end of this road is freedom—or ruin. She will decide."

"Decide what?" Anira demanded, her voice rising with frustration. "You're speaking in riddles, and I—"

The figure raised a hand, and the air shifted violently, cutting her off mid-sentence. "I speak only what you need to hear," it said, its tone edged with finality. "The path is yours to walk, and the choices are yours to make. But heed this: the shadows will follow you now. You have awakened them, and they will not rest until they have claimed what they seek."

The shadows that had burst from the spire swirled around the figure, curling and twisting like smoke caught in a storm. Its form began to dissolve, the crimson light fading as it stepped back into the fractured remains of the spire.

"Wait!" Anira called, her voice echoing in the stillness. "You can't just leave us here without—"

"You have all you need," the figure said, its voice resonating through the air as it vanished completely. "The rest is up to you."

The clearing fell silent once more, the oppressive weight of the figure's presence lifting. The spire's remains pulsed faintly, the red veins dimming until they disappeared entirely. The ground beneath Anira's feet was still now, smooth and unyielding, as if nothing had happened.

Kael let out a shaky breath, their voice trembling as they broke the silence. "Did anyone else hear the part where the shadows are going to hunt us now? Because I feel like we just stepped into a nightmare."

Ashric sheathed his sword, his movements deliberate and slow. "We've been in a nightmare," he said grimly. "This is just another layer."

Anira stared at the space where the figure had vanished, her chest tight and her mind racing. The Rose pulsed faintly against her skin, its warmth steady, but she felt the weight of its presence more acutely now. Whatever the figure had awakened, whatever it had meant by a trial, she knew one thing for certain.

Their journey was far from over.

"We need to move," Ashric said, his voice cutting through the heavy silence. He motioned toward the far edge of the clearing, where the faint outline of another path wound into the horizon. "Whatever that thing meant, the shadows won't wait. We need to stay ahead of them."

Anira nodded, slipping the key into her belt as she followed him. The pull of the Rose was still there, faint but insistent, leading them forward into the unknown. Kael trailed behind, their steps hesitant but steady.

As they crossed the clearing and stepped onto the new path, Anira couldn't shake the feeling of unseen eyes watching them. The air grew colder, heavier, and the forest ahead seemed darker, more foreboding.

Whatever trial the Rose had awakened, it had only just begun.

The path wound into the horizon like a scar carved into the earth, dark and jagged. The trees flanking the clearing were gnarled and twisted, their branches clawing at the sky as if in agony, their shadows stretching long and uneven across the glassy ground. The air hung heavy, oppressive, laced with a faint, metallic tang that clung to Anira's tongue and throat. It wasn't just the taste of the place—it was the taste of fear, ancient and unyielding, carried on the slow, unnatural wind that barely stirred her hair.

She tightened her grip on the key, its edges cool and smooth against her palm. It felt lighter now, its earlier glow extinguished, but its presence still pressed against her consciousness, insistent and unrelenting. The Rose pulsed faintly against her chest, its warmth steady but subdued, a stark contrast to the icy chill that seemed to radiate from the darkened path ahead.

Ashric led them forward, his boots crunching softly against the uneven ground. His movements were purposeful, every step deliberate, his sharp eyes darting between the looming trees and the horizon, where the path seemed to disappear into shadow. His sword remained unsheathed, the blade gleaming faintly in the dim, uneven light. He was a man carved from stone—hard, unyielding, every motion purposeful—but even stone could crack, and Anira saw it in the tightness of his jaw, the tension in his shoulders.

Behind her, Kael followed, their footsteps uneven as they stumbled over the rough terrain. They muttered under their breath, faint, sharp curses that barely carried above the suffocating quiet. Their usual bravado was gone, replaced by a nervous energy that clung to them like a second skin. Every few paces, they glanced over their shoulder, their eyes darting between the darkened treetops as though expecting the shadows themselves to strike.

"You feel it, don't you?" Kael whispered, their voice hoarse, barely audible. "The air—it's too heavy. Like it's watching us."

Anira didn't answer immediately. She felt it too—the weight pressing down on her chest, the faint vibration beneath her feet, the sense of something just out of sight, lurking in the dark. She swallowed hard, forcing herself to keep moving. The warmth of the Rose steadied her, but it was a fragile comfort, like a single flame in a storm.

"It's not just the air," Ashric said quietly, his voice cutting through the tension. "It's the land itself. Everything here is alive—and it knows we're here."

Kael let out a shaky laugh, the sound hollow. "Fantastic. Just what we needed. More things trying to kill us."

Anira glanced at Ashric, her voice trembling despite her best efforts. "Do you think the figure was telling the truth? About the shadows?"

He didn't look at her, his focus fixed on the path ahead. "Yes," he said simply. "But they were already hunting us. This just makes it official."

Kael cursed again, louder this time, their frustration and fear bubbling over. "And what does that mean for us? That we're bait now? That this trial thing is just... us running until we can't anymore?"

"It means we keep moving," Ashric said sharply, his tone leaving no room for argument. "We don't stop, and we don't waste time feeling sorry for ourselves. That's what gets people killed."

Kael muttered something under their breath, but they didn't argue further. The silence that followed was thick, the kind that wrapped itself around Anira's chest and made every breath feel heavier, slower. The path beneath their feet shifted subtly, the once-glassy surface giving way to uneven stone that crunched loudly with every step. The sound seemed to echo unnaturally, bouncing off the twisted trees as if amplified by the oppressive stillness.

The further they walked, the darker the world became. The faint silver light that had illuminated the clearing faded behind them, replaced by a murky gloom that swallowed everything outside the path. The shadows grew deeper, more solid, and Anira could swear they moved—slithering just at the edges of her vision, curling and twisting like smoke. Every now and then, a faint rustle would break the silence, sharp and sudden, and she would spin toward it, her dagger ready, but there was never anything there.

The air grew colder, the metallic tang sharpening until it burned the back of her throat. Her fingers trembled as she adjusted her grip on the key, its smooth surface feeling heavier now, as though it carried the weight of the choice she had made. The Rose pulsed again, its warmth flaring briefly, but the sensation only heightened her unease. It wasn't comfort—it was a warning.

"Something's wrong," she said softly, her voice barely more than a breath. "It's... closer now."

Ashric stopped abruptly, holding up a hand to silence them. The tension in his posture was palpable, his sword raised as he scanned the path ahead. The shadows pressed in tighter, their movements more erratic, and the rustling grew louder, closer, until it seemed to be coming from all sides.

"Get ready," Ashric said, his voice low and steady. "We're not alone."

Kael's knife trembled in their grip, their face pale as they stepped closer to Anira. "Not alone? What do you mean, not alone? We're in the middle of nowhere—"

The rustling stopped.

The silence that followed was deafening, a void that seemed to stretch endlessly, wrapping around them like a suffocating shroud. The shadows on the edges of the path grew still, frozen in place, and for one brief, terrible moment, the world itself seemed to hold its breath.

Then, from the darkness ahead, came a sound—a low, guttural growl that resonated deep in Anira's chest, raw and primal. It wasn't like the wail from the spire or the whispers in the forest. This was something alive, something hunting, and the sheer weight of its presence made her blood run cold.

Ashric stepped forward, his blade gleaming in the faint light. "Stay close," he said, his voice taut with controlled urgency. "And don't stop moving."

The growl came again, louder now, and the shadows ahead began to shift, twisting and coiling as something massive moved within them. Anira's breath caught as two faint glimmers of light appeared in the dark—silver, sharp, and unblinking, like the eyes of a predator catching the moonlight.

And then, it stepped into view.

The creature emerged from the shadows, its form twisting and unnatural, as if the darkness itself had given birth to it. Its body was massive, covered in a slick, obsidian-like sheen that reflected faint flashes of crimson light from veins that pulsed just beneath its surface. The air seemed to grow colder as it stepped closer, its movements deliberate and fluid, with a grace that belied its size. Its silver eyes locked onto Anira, unblinking and filled with a cruel intelligence.

Anira's breath hitched, her dagger trembling in her hand. The Rose at her chest pulsed violently now, a frantic rhythm that she could feel in her teeth and bones, as if it were screaming for her to act. But what could she do against something like this?

Ashric stepped in front of her, his broad shoulders blocking her view for just a moment. His sword gleamed faintly in the murky light, and his voice, though low, carried a firm command. "Stay behind me. I'll deal with it."

"I'm not hiding," Anira shot back, her voice sharper than she intended. "We're in this together."

Ashric turned his head slightly, his sharp blue eyes meeting hers. Even in the dim light, the intensity in them made her pulse quicken. "Together doesn't mean you die trying to play hero," he said, his voice dropping to a near growl. "You're the one it's after. If you die, this ends."

"I'm not planning to die," she snapped, her grip tightening on her dagger. "And you don't get to decide who does the saving."

The creature growled again, a deep, guttural sound that rattled the stones beneath their feet. It stepped closer, its movements slow and deliberate, as if savoring the fear that rippled through the air. Its silver eyes flicked to Ashric, then back to Anira, and it lowered its head slightly, the sharp edges of its form blurring as shadows curled around it like smoke.

"Focus," Ashric said, his voice breaking through the tension between them. "It's sizing us up. If you're going to fight, then fight smart."

Anira forced herself to breathe, the warmth of the Rose grounding her as she steadied her trembling hand. She wasn't sure if it was the creature or Ashric's unwavering intensity that had her heart racing, but she couldn't let either distract her now. "Fine," she said, her tone softer but no less determined. "But if we're doing this, we do it together."

"Always," Ashric replied, the word slipping out before he could stop it. For a brief moment, his eyes softened, a flicker of something unguarded passing between them. Then he turned back to the creature, his sword raising as his focus hardened once more. "Stay close. Don't make me regret letting you."

The creature lunged.

It moved faster than Anira expected, its massive form closing the distance between them in an instant. Ashric was already moving, his sword flashing as he drove it upward in a clean, deliberate arc. The blade connected with the creature's shoulder, a spray of inky black liquid bursting from the wound, but it didn't stop. It let out a roar, its silver eyes flashing as it swiped at him with a clawed limb.

Ashric ducked, his movements quick and fluid, and he drove his shoulder into the creature's side, shoving it back just enough to regain his footing. "Anira, now!" he shouted, his voice rough.

She didn't hesitate. The Rose pulsed violently as she lunged forward, her dagger aimed at the glowing veins that pulsed beneath the creature's slick skin. Her blade struck true, sinking into the soft, yielding surface just below its chest. The creature roared again, this time with a sound that was almost a scream, and it thrashed wildly, its movements erratic and dangerous.

"Fall back!" Ashric barked, grabbing her arm and pulling her away before the creature's claws could connect. His grip was firm but not harsh, his fingers lingering on her wrist for just a moment longer than necessary. "Are you trying to get yourself killed?"

"I'm trying to help," she snapped, her breath coming in short, sharp gasps as the adrenaline coursed through her. "You can't do this alone."

He turned to her, his eyes blazing with frustration and something else—something warmer, deeper, that made her stomach twist in a way that had nothing to do with fear. "You don't know when to quit, do you?"

"Not when it comes to keeping us alive," she shot back, her chin lifting defiantly.

Ashric's lips quirked into a faint smirk, though the tension in his expression didn't fade. "Good. Because I don't quit either."

The creature roared again, its form flickering as the shadows surrounding it grew darker, more solid. It lunged toward them once more, its massive limbs crashing against the ground with enough force to send tremors through the air.

"Stay behind me," Ashric said again, his voice low and urgent. "I'll distract it. You find a way to end this."

Anira hesitated, her instincts screaming at her to argue, but she caught the look in his eyes—a look that said he wasn't asking. Her chest tightened, but she nodded, her fingers brushing the Rose as its warmth surged against her chest.

"Don't do anything stupid," she said, her voice softer now.

"Too late for that," he replied, his smirk returning for just a moment before he turned and charged toward the creature.

Anira watched him go, her heart pounding as she gripped her dagger and focused on the Rose. The warmth spread through her like fire, steadying her, sharpening her focus. Whatever this creature was, it wasn't invincible. And she wasn't going to let it stop them—not now.

She just had to find its weakness before Ashric ran out of time.

The air seemed to shatter as Ashric charged the creature, the ground beneath his boots crunching with every step. The beast roared in response, a sound that rippled through the unnatural quiet of the forest, thick and full of rage. Its silver eyes flared brighter, tracking his every move as it braced itself, its massive limbs digging into the glassy ground like anchors.

Anira could only watch for a moment, her breath catching as Ashric moved like a force of nature, his sword flashing in arcs of gleaming steel. He was unrelenting, each strike precise and deliberate, his movements honed to a deadly rhythm. The beast lashed out, its claws scraping against the blade, sending sparks into the dim, murky light. The sheer weight of its attacks forced Ashric back with every blow, but he held his ground, his jaw clenched and his focus razor-sharp.

Anira forced herself to tear her gaze away from him. She couldn't let herself be distracted, not when the Rose burned so fiercely against her chest, its pulse quick and desperate, urging her to act. The creature wasn't invincible—she knew that now. Its wounds bled an inky, viscous liquid that hissed and smoked as it hit the ground, eating away at the stone like acid. It wasn't invulnerable, but it was relentless, and Ashric couldn't hold it forever.

Her eyes scanned the battlefield, the oppressive gloom pressing down on her as the forest loomed like a twisted labyrinth of shadow and malice. The jagged trees leaned inward, their clawed branches seeming to reach for her, their bark gleaming with faint, oily streaks that pulsed in time with the creature's veins. The air was thick with the metallic tang of blood and magic, sharp and suffocating, and every breath she took felt like swallowing broken glass.

Then she saw it.

Near the base of the creature's massive body, where the writhing veins pulsed brightest, was a faint glow—golden and flickering, almost hidden beneath the shifting shadows that clung to its form. The Rose flared hotter as her gaze locked onto it, its warmth spreading through her chest like wildfire, and she knew, with a bone-deep certainty, that this was its weakness. The key, the Rose, and the creature—they were all tied to this single point.

She took a step forward, her grip tightening on her dagger, and her voice broke the tense air. "Ashric! Its chest—there's something there. It's exposed!"

Ashric didn't turn, his focus still locked on the beast as he dodged another sweeping blow. "Then aim for it!" he shouted, his voice rough with exertion. "I'll keep it busy!"

Anira nodded, swallowing the lump of fear that threatened to choke her. She broke into a run, her feet pounding against the uneven ground as she circled the creature, her heart racing in time with the frantic pulse of the Rose. The shadows seemed to writhe around her, reaching for her with clawed tendrils that brushed against her skin like ice, but she didn't stop. She couldn't.

The creature reared back, its massive form blotting out what little light the forest offered. It lunged at Ashric with a deafening roar, its claws slashing through the air. He sidestepped the attack with practiced precision, his sword driving into its flank with a wet, sickening sound. The beast howled, its silver eyes narrowing in rage, and it twisted toward him, leaving its glowing chest momentarily exposed.

Anira didn't hesitate. She surged forward, the Rose burning like fire against her skin as she raised her dagger. The golden glow at the creature's chest flared brighter as she approached, and she could feel the magic pulling her closer, urging her on.

The beast sensed her too late. It turned with a snarl, its massive head snapping toward her, but Ashric was faster. He lunged, his sword slashing across its face, forcing it back with a bellow of pain. The distraction gave Anira the opening she needed.

With a cry, she drove the dagger into the glowing point at its chest. The blade sank deep, meeting little resistance, and the creature froze, its body stiffening as a deafening roar tore from its throat. The shadows surrounding it convulsed, twisting and writhing in violent arcs as the light at its chest flared to a blinding intensity.

Anira stumbled back, her breath coming in ragged gasps as the Rose pulsed wildly against her chest. The ground trembled beneath her feet, cracks splintering outward from the creature's body as its form began to collapse, its edges dissolving into streams of black smoke.

Ashric was at her side in an instant, his hand steadying her as she struggled to stay upright. "You did it," he said, his voice low and strained. His gaze met hers, his sharp blue eyes filled with something she couldn't quite name—relief, admiration, and a faint, fleeting warmth that made her chest tighten.

"I couldn't have done it without you," she said, her voice trembling but firm. Her hand brushed against his as she steadied herself, and for a moment, she forgot the shadows, the danger, the oppressive weight of the forest. All she saw was him.

His lips twitched into the faintest of smiles, a flicker of dry humor breaking through the tension. "You could've warned me you'd turn this into a competition."

"Would you have fought harder?" she asked, the faintest hint of a smile tugging at her lips.

"Maybe," he said, his tone light, though his eyes betrayed a deeper truth. "But you seem to handle the impossible well enough on your own."

Before she could reply, the ground beneath them shuddered violently. The cracks spreading from the creature's remains widened, black smoke billowing upward in spiraling tendrils that clawed at the sky. The Rose flared again, its warmth steadying her as she looked toward the dissipating creature.

The glow from its chest faded completely, and as the last of its massive form dissolved into smoke, the forest seemed to sigh, the oppressive weight lifting just slightly. But the shadows didn't retreat. They lingered, curling at the edges of the path, darker and heavier than before.

Ashric's expression hardened, his sword still in his hand. "It's not over," he said, his voice grim.

Anira nodded, gripping her dagger as she stared into the shifting shadows ahead. The Rose pulsed faintly now, its light subdued, but the pull it exerted on her chest was stronger than ever, leading her toward the dark, twisted path that stretched into the horizon.

"Then we keep going," she said, her voice resolute, though her heart still raced with lingering fear. "We've come too far to stop now."

Ashric's gaze lingered on her for a moment, his expression softening just slightly. "Just try not to get yourself killed," he said, his voice low. "I'd hate to lose my favorite competitor."

Anira smiled faintly, despite the dread pooling in her chest. "I'll do my best."

Together, they turned toward the darkness, the path stretching out before them like a wound, raw and unyielding. The forest loomed, its shadows watching, waiting, as the pull of the Rose guided them deeper into the unknown.

The darkness ahead seemed alive, a wall of shifting shadows that pulsed and curled like smoke. The air grew colder the closer Anira and Ashric moved toward the path, the unnatural chill cutting through her clothing and settling in her bones. The weight of the Rose pressed against her chest like an anchor, its faint warmth the only reminder of what had just transpired. Behind them, the clearing where the creature had fallen was silent, its jagged scars etched into the glassy ground like the remnants of a violent dream.

Kael stumbled to catch up, their breath coming in sharp gasps. "You call that a victory?" they said, their voice tinged with lingering panic. "Because I'm not feeling the celebration."

"Do you ever stop complaining?" Ashric shot back, his voice low and sharp. His sword remained in his hand, its faint gleam a steadying presence in the oppressive gloom.

"Only when I'm not about to be killed by shadow monsters," Kael muttered, their hand tightening around their knife. "Which, let's face it, isn't often these days."

"Enough," Anira said, her voice firm. The tension in her shoulders hadn't lessened, her body still taut from the encounter. She glanced at both of them, her gaze settling briefly on Ashric. His sharp profile was illuminated faintly by the glow of the Rose, the lines of his jaw tight and unyielding. "We need to focus."

Ashric nodded, his attention turning back to the path ahead. "It's only going to get worse from here."

Kael groaned softly, shaking their head. "That's what I was afraid of."

The path twisted before them, its jagged edges barely visible beneath the writhing shadows that clung to it like mist. The trees on either side were more twisted now, their limbs gnarled and blackened, with bark that seemed to glisten unnaturally in the faint light. Their roots stretched across the ground like tendrils, reaching toward the path as though drawn to the energy pulsing from the Rose.

Anira felt it too—a pull that was stronger now, more insistent, as though the Rose itself was guiding her steps. The warmth against her chest had grown sharper, its pulse quickening as they moved forward. Each step felt heavier, her legs trembling with the weight of the unseen force that pressed against her.

"Do you feel that?" she asked, her voice barely above a whisper.

Ashric nodded. "It's the Rose," he said, his voice steady. "It's pulling you toward something."

"Something worse," Kael muttered, their gaze darting nervously to the shadows. "It always is."

They continued in tense silence, the only sound the faint crunch of their footsteps against the uneven ground. The oppressive darkness seemed to close in around them, the air growing thicker with every step. The shadows at the edge of the path shifted, their movements deliberate, like figures watching from just beyond the veil of light.

Anira's heart raced as her hand brushed against the hilt of her dagger. The Rose pulsed again, harder this time, and she froze mid-step, her breath catching in her throat. "Wait," she said, holding up a hand.

Ashric stopped immediately, his sword raised. "What is it?"

"I don't know," she said, her voice trembling. "Something's... here."

Kael let out a nervous laugh, their eyes darting to the shadows. "Yeah, no kidding. The whole forest is watching us."

"No," Anira said, shaking her head. The warmth of the Rose surged suddenly, its pulse frantic, and her stomach twisted with a deep, primal fear. "It's closer."

The ground beneath their feet shuddered, a faint tremor that sent cracks splintering through the stone. The shadows ahead of them convulsed, twisting and writhing into shapes that seemed almost human, though their forms were jagged and incomplete. A low, guttural sound filled the air, vibrating in Anira's chest like a distant growl.

Ashric stepped in front of her, his blade gleaming as he scanned the shifting figures. "Get ready," he said, his voice calm but edged with tension. "They're not going to let us pass."

Kael cursed under their breath, their knife trembling in their hand. "I knew it. I knew it wasn't over."

Anira tightened her grip on her dagger, her eyes fixed on the shadowy forms. They moved slowly at first, their limbs stretching and bending unnaturally, like smoke caught in a violent wind. But as the tremor beneath their feet grew stronger, the figures solidified, their movements becoming deliberate and predatory.

The Rose flared again, its heat spreading through her chest, and she felt the key at her belt grow warmer, its surface beginning to glow faintly. The golden light cut through the gloom, casting jagged shadows across the ground, and the creatures hissed in response, their silver eyes narrowing.

"It's the light," Anira said, her voice quick and breathless. "They don't like it."

"Then make it brighter," Ashric said, his tone sharp. He glanced back at her, his gaze locking onto hers with a fierce intensity. "Whatever the Rose is telling you to do—do it."

Her fingers brushed against the key, the metal warm and pulsing in time with the Rose. The shadows surged forward, their movements faster now, more coordinated, and Anira's heart thundered in her chest as the first of them lunged toward Ashric.

He met it head-on, his blade slicing through the creature's dark form with a sharp, fluid motion. The shadow screamed, its voice high and piercing, as it dissolved into black smoke. But more followed, their forms writhing as they closed in around them.

"Anira!" Ashric shouted, his voice cutting through the chaos. "Now!"

She didn't hesitate. The warmth of the Rose surged through her as she raised the key, its golden glow flaring brighter. The shadows recoiled, hissing and shrieking as the light burned against them, their forms dissolving into smoke with each flare.

But the light wasn't enough to stop them all. For every shadow that fell, another surged forward, their movements growing faster, more desperate. The ground beneath her feet trembled violently now, and the weight of the Rose pressed against her like a physical force.

"I need more time!" she shouted, her voice trembling.

Ashric fought his way to her side, his blade dripping with the inky residue of the shadows. His hand brushed against hers briefly, steadying her, and the heat of his presence chased away some of the cold that had seeped into her bones. "You don't have time," he said, his voice low and urgent. "Do it now, or we're not getting out of here."

Her gaze locked with his, and for a moment, the chaos around them seemed to fade. His eyes burned with a fierce determination, but there was something else there too—something softer, unspoken, that sent a jolt through her chest.

"I won't let them take you," he said, his voice rough but steady. "Not here. Not ever."

The words grounded her, and the Rose burned brighter in response, its warmth spreading through her like fire. She nodded, her grip tightening on the key as its glow flared to blinding intensity.

And then, with a single, desperate motion, she drove it into the ground.

The moment the key struck the ground, the world seemed to crack open.

A wave of blinding golden light erupted from the impact, spreading outward in a furious cascade that devoured the darkness around them. The air vibrated with a deep, resonant hum that shook Anira to her core, its power pulsing through her veins like molten fire. The shadows recoiled, their forms twisting and writhing as the light tore into them, shredding their jagged shapes into formless black mist.

The ground beneath her feet shuddered violently, the cracks spreading outward like a spiderweb, glowing faintly with the same golden light. Anira fell to her knees, her breath coming in short, ragged gasps as the heat of the Rose surged against her chest. The power coursing through her felt infinite, unrelenting, and it was as if the forest itself was reacting, groaning under the weight of the magic unleashed.

Ashric was by her side in an instant, his hand gripping her arm as he pulled her upright. His sharp blue eyes burned with urgency, his breath misting in the cold air. "Anira! What did you do?"

"I—I don't know," she stammered, her voice trembling. The Rose pulsed again, harder now, as though it were alive and furious, demanding more from her.

The shadows screamed, their hissing cries piercing the air like shards of glass. They writhed and flailed against the light, their forms disintegrating piece by piece, but for every one that fell, more seemed to emerge from the shifting darkness beyond the path. The forest around them twisted, the gnarled trees bending and contorting as though trying to tear free of their roots.

"They're not stopping!" Kael shouted from behind them, their voice high and panicked. They stood with their back against a tree, their knife clutched tightly in their hand, their face pale. "What is this place trying to do—kill us or bury us alive?"

Anira's gaze darted to the ground where the key still glowed, its golden light spilling into the fractures that now radiated out like veins. The Rose burned hotter, its pulse frantic, and she realized with a sickening twist in her gut that it wasn't done yet.

"It's opening something," she said, her voice barely audible over the chaos. "The Rose—it's drawing them here, and the key—it's—"

Her words were cut off as the ground beneath her split open with a deafening crack, a jagged fissure tearing through the path. From the depths of the earth came a rush of searing heat and crimson light, and with it, a voice—not a whisper, not a scream, but something ancient and guttural, its tones vibrating in her bones.

"You have called me."

The voice wasn't human. It wasn't anything she could describe. It carried the weight of countless centuries, deep and terrible, a force of nature that had been awakened from a long, restless slumber. The light from the fissure flared brighter, illuminating the twisted forest with an eerie, unholy glow.

Ashric stepped in front of her, his sword raised, his stance unyielding despite the raw power emanating from the ground. "What is it?" he demanded, his voice rough. "What's coming?"

Anira couldn't answer. Her legs felt frozen, her body trembling under the weight of the energy surging around them. The Rose pulsed again, its warmth unbearable, and she clutched at it instinctively, her fingers brushing the smooth surface of the pendant.

The fissure widened, and from its depths rose a figure cloaked in shadow and flame. Its form was indistinct, its edges flickering like smoke, but its presence was suffocating, filling the air with a heat that pressed against Anira's chest. Its eyes burned crimson, twin orbs of molten fire that locked onto her with unrelenting intensity.

"You who bear the Rose," it said, its voice a low, resonant rumble that carried across the forest. "You have awakened the gate. Do you know what you have done?"

Anira opened her mouth to speak, but no sound came out. Her chest heaved, her breath shallow, and the words tangled in her throat like thorns. The figure stepped closer, the ground trembling beneath its weight, and the shadows at its feet writhed like living things.

Ashric took a step forward, his blade glinting in the crimson light. "If you're here for her," he said, his voice sharp and unyielding, "you'll have to go through me."

The figure tilted its head, the flames in its eyes flaring brighter. "Bold," it said, almost amused. "But futile. I am not your enemy, mortal. Not yet."

Kael let out a nervous laugh, their voice strained. "Not yet? That's... comforting."

The figure ignored them, its gaze fixed solely on Anira. "You have begun a chain that cannot be undone," it said, its voice softer now but no less terrible. "The Rose has chosen you as its bearer. The power you have called forth will demand more than you know. Are you prepared to pay its price?"

Anira's voice returned in a whisper, trembling but resolute. "What price?"

The figure's eyes burned brighter, and the ground beneath them trembled again. "Everything," it said. "The Rose demands everything."

Ashric's hand brushed against her arm, grounding her, and she turned to him, her breath catching at the intensity in his gaze. "We'll face it together," he said, his voice low but steady. "Whatever it takes."

Her chest tightened at his words, a flicker of warmth breaking through the fear. "You're sure about that?" she asked, her voice soft.

"Always," he replied, his tone carrying a certainty that sent a jolt through her heart.

The figure watched them in silence, its form shifting like fire caught in a storm. "You have made your choice," it said. "But know this—there will be no mercy on this path. The shadows will follow, and the light you carry will burn brighter... and fiercer."

Anira straightened, her hand tightening around the pendant as she met the figure's gaze. The Rose pulsed once more, its warmth steadying her, and she nodded. "We'll survive," she said, her voice stronger now. "We'll pay the price."

The figure inclined its head slightly, a gesture that felt more like acknowledgment than approval. Then, as suddenly as it had appeared, it dissolved into shadow and flame, sinking back into the fissure as the light dimmed and the ground sealed itself once more.

The forest fell silent, the oppressive weight lifting slightly, though the air remained thick with tension. Anira turned to Ashric, her chest still heaving as her pulse began to slow. His gaze lingered on her, sharp and searching, and for a moment, the chaos of the moment seemed to fade, leaving only the two of them standing in the dim light.

"You're reckless," he said finally, his tone soft but edged with something she couldn't quite place. "But you're stronger than I gave you credit for."

She offered a faint, tired smile. "And you're annoyingly good at being right."

His lips quirked into a faint smirk, but his eyes stayed serious. "This isn't over.

Whatever you started—it's going to get worse."

"I know," she said, her voice steady despite the weight of the truth. "But we'll survive. Together."

"Together," he echoed, his voice low, as they turned toward the darkened path ahead, the shadows still waiting.

The forest remained still, too still, as the fissure sealed itself and the crimson light faded into a faint, sickly glow at the edges of the path. The oppressive weight in the air hadn't gone, only shifted, like the lingering hum of a storm that hadn't fully passed. The shadows beyond the trees twisted and curled, but they held back, as if whatever had risen from the depths had left a mark even they feared to cross.

Anira adjusted the pendant at her chest, the Rose warm against her skin but quiet now, its pulse subdued to a faint rhythm. Her hand still trembled, the ghostly weight of the key lingering on her palm even though it was now safely tucked at her belt. The figure's words rang in her ears: The shadows will follow. The light will burn brighter.

And fiercer.

Ashric stayed at her side, his sword still unsheathed, the faint, jagged line of his jaw set in grim focus. He glanced at her briefly, his blue eyes sharp with tension. "Are you alright?" he asked, his voice low, edged with something softer beneath the hard exterior.

She nodded, though the truth felt more complicated. "I think so," she said, her voice quiet. "But that thing—whatever it was—it knew me. It knew the Rose."

"It knows a lot more than it said," he replied, scanning the treetops as if expecting the shadows to descend at any moment. "And I doubt it's the last time we'll see it."

Kael's voice broke through the silence, unsteady but laced with their usual sarcasm. "Oh, great. Because one encounter with a flaming nightmare wasn't enough. Let's invite it back for tea and a knife fight."

Ashric shot them a glare but said nothing, and Kael, to their credit, fell silent again, though their hands fidgeted nervously at their sides.

The path ahead seemed to pulse faintly, the golden cracks left by the key's power still visible beneath the darkened ground. They stretched forward like veins, leading deeper into the forest where the shadows grew thicker, more suffocating. Anira could feel the pull again, faint but insistent, urging her forward even as her instincts screamed at her to stop, to turn back, to run.

"We keep moving," Ashric said, his voice cutting through the tension. He pointed down the path with his sword, its blade catching the faint light of the glowing cracks. "Whatever this is leading us to, it's not waiting."

Anira hesitated, her hand brushing the pendant again. "What if it's leading us into something worse?"

Ashric turned to her, his expression calm but unyielding. "Then we face it," he said simply. "We've come too far to stop now."

She swallowed hard, her chest tightening at the weight of his words. There was no reassurance in his tone, no false promises that things would get easier. But there was conviction, solid and unshakeable, and it steadied her in a way she hadn't expected.

Kael muttered something under their breath and moved closer to the group. "If we die out here, I'm haunting you both," they said, pointing a finger at Ashric and Anira in turn. "Just so you know."

"Noted," Ashric said dryly, his lips twitching in the faintest hint of a smirk. "Now keep up."

They pressed on, the tension growing thicker with every step. The trees loomed larger now, their branches arching overhead in a tangled, suffocating canopy that blotted out what little light remained. The air felt heavier, colder, and the faint metallic tang that lingered in the back of Anira's throat sharpened, biting at her tongue like copper.

The cracks in the ground continued to pulse faintly, their light flickering in uneven patterns that felt alive, like a heartbeat struggling to steady itself. Anira couldn't shake the feeling that the ground beneath her feet was fragile, that with one wrong step, the earth would shatter beneath them again.

"Do you feel that?" she asked, breaking the silence.

"Feel what?" Kael asked, their voice tense.

"The ground," she said, her voice barely above a whisper. "It feels... unstable."

Ashric slowed, his steps deliberate as he scanned the path ahead. "It's not the ground," he said, his tone grim. "It's the magic. Whatever you released with the key—it's still here. It's following us."

Anira's breath caught, and she looked back over her shoulder. The shadows beyond the path remained still, but she could feel them watching, their presence a constant weight on her spine. The pull of the Rose grew stronger, sharper, and she clenched her fists, her nails biting into her palms.

"It's not just the magic," she said. "It's something else. Something waiting."

Ashric didn't reply immediately. His gaze lingered on her, searching, before he nodded. "Then we don't stop."

They continued, the forest pressing in closer, the shadows darker, deeper. The faint glow of the cracks was their only guide, casting long, jagged shadows that twisted unnaturally across the uneven ground. The air grew colder still, and Anira's breath came in faint puffs of mist, each one dissipating almost instantly in the chill.

Then the path shifted.

It was subtle at first—a faint ripple beneath their feet, like a wave rolling through the earth. But as they stepped farther, the ground began to tremble, the cracks flaring brighter with each shudder. The hum that had lingered in the air grew louder, resonating in Anira's chest like a drumbeat, quickening with every step.

"What now?" Kael asked, their voice rising in panic. "Please tell me this is just the earth... burping or something."

Anira stopped, her heart racing as the Rose flared hot against her chest. The glow of the cracks surged, blinding for a moment, and then dimmed, leaving the path shrouded in near-total darkness. A faint sound rose from the distance, low and guttural, like a growl that carried on the wind.

Ashric froze, his hand tightening on his sword. "That's not the ground," he said, his voice a razor-sharp whisper. "Get ready."

The growl grew louder, closer, and Anira felt the first tremor of fear crawl up her spine. She drew her dagger, the weight of it steady in her hand, and forced herself to focus. The pull of the Rose was insistent now, almost frantic, and the warmth spread through her like fire, burning away the cold.

The shadows ahead shifted, twisting and curling as something massive moved within them. Silver eyes glinted in the darkness, unblinking and predatory, and Anira's breath caught in her throat.

They weren't alone anymore.

The silver eyes in the shadows multiplied, one pair splitting into two, then four, then more until the darkness ahead teemed with glinting, predatory gazes. The guttural growl deepened, a rumble that seemed to emanate from the earth itself, vibrating through the soles of Anira's boots. The shadows ahead rippled like a living tide, and the chill in the air grew sharper, cutting through her resolve like a blade.

Ashric moved closer to Anira, his sword raised, his sharp gaze scanning the writhing mass ahead. "This isn't like the last one," he said, his voice low and urgent. "They're organized."

Kael let out a nervous laugh that carried no humor. "Organized shadow monsters. That's just fantastic."

The Rose flared suddenly, its warmth burning against Anira's chest. The cracks beneath their feet glowed brighter in response, pulsing in frantic, uneven rhythms that matched her racing heartbeat. She felt it then—not just a pull, but a presence, something vast and consuming pressing against the edges of her mind.

"They're not just shadows," she whispered, her voice trembling. "There's something else. Something controlling them."

The growl stopped.

The silence that followed was worse, heavier, as if the air itself had been sucked from the forest. The silver eyes stared unblinking, the shadows motionless now, coiled like a predator ready to strike. Anira's breath hitched as the Rose burned hotter, and she felt the weight of its power pressing down on her like a storm about to break.

Then the voice came.

"You should not have come."

It wasn't a roar or a growl. It was a voice, low and resonant, layered with echoes that carried through the oppressive quiet like the toll of a bell. It came from the shadows, yet it seemed to pierce directly into Anira's mind, its words carrying a weight that made her knees tremble.

Ashric stepped in front of her, his sword gleaming in the faint light. "Show yourself," he demanded, his voice steady despite the tension in his posture. "If you want a fight, you'll get one."

A faint laugh rippled through the darkness, cold and sharp. "Fight?" the voice said, dripping with mockery. "You think this is a battle you can win?"

The shadows shifted again, parting like a curtain to reveal a figure stepping forward. At first, it seemed like one of the shadow creatures—tall, lean, and wreathed in twisting darkness. But as it stepped into the faint light of the cracks, its form solidified, and Anira's breath caught in her throat.

It was human.

Or at least, it had been once.

The figure was tall and angular, its skin pale and stretched tight over sharp, unyielding features. Dark veins, glowing faintly with the same crimson light as the fissure they had left behind, twisted up its neck and into its face, where two silver eyes burned with cold fire. Its hair was long and dark, falling in wild strands around its shoulders, and its lips curved into a cruel, knowing smile.

But it wasn't the figure's appearance that made Anira freeze—it was its presence. The weight of it pressed against her like the crushing tide of the sea, and she felt the Rose burn hotter in response, its pulse growing frantic.

"You wear the Rose," the figure said, its gaze locking onto her with unnerving intensity. "You are the key."

Ashric stepped forward, his sword raised. "Stay back," he warned, his voice sharp. "Whoever—or whatever—you are, you'll have to go through me to get to her."

The figure tilted its head, its smile widening. "You think I want to harm her?" it asked, its voice calm and mocking. "No, mortal. I want her to understand."

"Understand what?" Anira asked, her voice shaking as she gripped her dagger tighter. The warmth of the Rose felt like fire now, unbearable, and she fought to keep her footing under the crushing weight of the figure's presence.

"Who you are," it said simply. Its silver eyes gleamed brighter, and it took another step forward, its movements slow and deliberate. "What you are."

Anira opened her mouth to respond, but the words tangled in her throat as the Rose pulsed violently, sending a searing wave of heat through her chest. Her vision blurred, and the world around her seemed to tilt, the forest dissolving into a swirl of shadows and light.

In the chaos, a memory surfaced—not hers, but vivid and overwhelming.

She saw a figure standing in a room bathed in golden light, holding the Rose in their hand. Their face was obscured, but their presence was familiar, achingly so, and they spoke words she couldn't hear. The light around them flared, and the vision shattered into darkness.

Anira gasped, her knees buckling as she stumbled forward. Ashric caught her, his grip steadying her as she struggled to stay upright. "Anira!" he said, his voice sharp with concern. "What's wrong?"

"I... I saw something," she whispered, her voice barely audible. "A memory. But it wasn't mine."

The figure laughed again, the sound cutting through the tension like a blade. "The Rose shows only truth," it said, its gaze never leaving hers. "And the truth is that you were chosen long before you ever held it."

Anira's stomach twisted, her chest tightening under the weight of the words. "What are you talking about?" she demanded, her voice trembling. "What truth?"

The figure stepped closer, its smile fading into something colder, more calculating. "You are more than its bearer," it said. "You are its maker."

The words struck her like a blow, stealing the breath from her lungs. She shook her head, her heart pounding in her chest. "That's not possible," she said, her voice breaking. "I don't even—"

"You will remember," the figure interrupted, its voice growing softer, almost tender. "The Rose will make sure of it."

Before she could respond, the figure raised a hand, and the shadows surged forward, swallowing it whole. The silver eyes lingered for a moment longer, gleaming in the darkness, before vanishing completely, leaving the forest in suffocating silence.

Ashric's hand on her arm steadied her, his sharp gaze fixed on her face. "What did it mean?" he asked, his voice low. "Maker?"

Anira shook her head, her chest tight. "I don't know," she whispered, her voice trembling. "But if it's true... then I've been lying to myself this whole time."

And, somewhere deep inside, she felt it: a terrible, undeniable truth stirring, waiting to come to light.

Anira stood frozen, her breathing shallow, as the suffocating silence of the forest closed in around them. The figure's words echoed in her mind, heavy and unrelenting: You are its maker.

Her legs felt weak, as though the weight of those words had stolen her strength. Ashric's hand remained firm on her arm, steadying her. His sharp blue eyes searched hers, hard but filled with an unspoken concern. "Anira," he said softly, his voice cutting through the tense quiet. "Whatever that thing said, it's trying to mess with your head. Don't let it."

She swallowed hard, her throat dry. "What if it wasn't lying?" she asked, her voice barely above a whisper. "What if—"

Kael's nervous laughter broke through her thoughts, sharp and unsteady. "Alright, alright, time out," they said, raising a hand like a reluctant referee. "We're not seriously believing that shadow-thing, are we? 'Maker'? That doesn't even make sense."

Anira turned to them, her fingers brushing the Rose at her chest. Its warmth was subdued now, a faint, steady pulse that felt almost accusatory. "It feels... right," she said reluctantly. "When it said it, the Rose—it responded. I felt it."

Kael shook their head, taking a step back. "You felt it? What does that even mean? Are you saying you made some ancient magic pendant and then forgot about it? That's insane."

"Maybe it is," Ashric interjected, his tone sharp as his gaze shifted to the darkened path ahead. "But whatever the truth is, we're not going to figure it out standing here waiting for something else to attack."

The tension between them was palpable, but his words were enough to break the moment. Anira took a deep breath, forcing herself to push the questions aside—for now. She tightened her grip on the dagger in her hand and nodded. "You're right. We have to move."

Ashric gave a curt nod, his sword still drawn as he stepped forward, his focus shifting back to the path. The faint glow of the cracks in the ground had dimmed, their light barely illuminating the jagged, uneven terrain that stretched ahead. The shadows beyond the trees remained still, but the weight of their presence lingered, pressing down on her like an unseen force.

Kael fell in line behind her, muttering under their breath. "I swear, if another nightmare-monster shows up, I'm just lying down and letting it take me."

"No, you won't," Ashric said, his tone matter-of-fact. "You're too stubborn to give up that easily."

Kael opened their mouth to retort but stopped, their expression softening for a moment. "I hate it when you're right."

The group pressed on, the path narrowing as it twisted deeper into the forest. The gnarled trees grew denser, their blackened bark glistening in the faint, flickering light. The air was colder here, biting at Anira's skin and carrying a faint, acrid scent that made her stomach twist. Every step felt heavier, the pull of the Rose growing stronger, sharper, as though it were dragging her toward something she couldn't yet see.

Ashric slowed suddenly, raising a hand to signal them to stop. Anira froze, her heart pounding as her eyes scanned the darkness ahead. The silence was thick, broken only by the faint rustle of leaves in the windless air.

"What is it?" she whispered, her voice barely audible.

"Something's wrong," Ashric said, his voice low and tense. "The path—look."

Anira followed his gaze, and her stomach lurched. The cracks in the ground, which had been their guide through the forest, abruptly ended. The golden light that had pulsed faintly beneath their feet disappeared into a jagged break in the earth, where the path fell away into an expanse of darkness that seemed to stretch endlessly below.

Kael let out a sharp exhale. "Oh, that's fantastic. Just fantastic. A bottomless pit. What now?"

Ashric ignored them, stepping closer to the edge of the chasm. He peered down into the abyss, his expression unreadable. "It's not a pit," he said after a moment. "It's something else."

Anira joined him, her breath catching as she looked down. The darkness below wasn't empty—it pulsed faintly, shifting like liquid shadow, and she could see faint shapes moving within it, their forms indistinct but terrifyingly large.

"Is it alive?" she asked, her voice trembling.

"Alive, or something worse," Ashric replied grimly. He turned to her, his expression serious. "The Rose is pulling you toward this. Whatever's down there, it's part of why we're here."

Kael groaned. "Oh, great. You're saying we have to go in there? That's what you're saying, isn't it?"

Anira's stomach churned as she stared into the abyss, her hand clutching the Rose. The pendant pulsed again, harder this time, and she felt the pull intensify, dragging her toward the edge. She took a step back, her legs trembling.

"I don't know if we have a choice," she said softly. "It's not letting me stop."

Ashric studied her for a moment, his gaze unwavering. "Then we find a way down," he said, his voice calm but firm. "And we face whatever's waiting."

Kael shook their head, their expression a mix of fear and frustration. "You two are insane."

"Maybe," Ashric said, his lips twitching into a faint, humorless smile. "But that's why we're still alive."

Without waiting for a response, he turned and began scanning the edge of the chasm, his sharp gaze searching for a path. Anira followed, the Rose pulsing steadily against her chest as the pull grew stronger, more insistent. The darkness below seemed to shift in response, the faint shapes within it moving closer, their presence sending a shiver down her spine.

They were being watched. And whatever waited below wasn't just another trial. It was something far worse.

The chasm stretched endlessly before them, a jagged wound in the earth filled with shifting shadows that pulsed and writhed like living things. The faint shapes below moved with purpose now, their edges indistinct but undeniably menacing. The air was heavier here, thick with a metallic tang that clung to the back of Anira's throat, making each breath feel labored and shallow. It wasn't just the scent—it was the weight of the place, oppressive and wrong, pressing down on her like unseen hands.

Ashric's boots scraped against the edge of the chasm as he moved along it, his sword still in hand, his every step measured and deliberate. His sharp blue eyes scanned the abyss, his face set in a hard, unreadable mask. "There's no bridge," he said, his voice low but carrying over the stillness. "No path. Whatever's pulling you, it wants us to go down."

Kael let out a bitter laugh, their voice tinged with panic. "Go down? Into that? You've got to be kidding."

"We've come this far," Ashric said, his tone flat. "There's no turning back."

"No turning back," Kael muttered, shaking their head. "Of course not. That would make too much sense."

Anira stood at the edge of the chasm, her hand brushing against the Rose at her chest. Its warmth was unbearable now, its pulse steady and strong, like a heartbeat that wasn't hers. The pull was undeniable, dragging her closer to the edge with every passing moment. She could feel the shadows below, their movements syncing with the rhythm of the Rose, as if they were connected, responding to its presence.

"It's not just pulling us down," she said, her voice trembling. "It's… calling them."

Ashric turned sharply, his gaze snapping to hers. "What do you mean?"

"The shadows," she said, gesturing toward the writhing mass below. "They're moving closer. They feel the Rose. They're waiting for me to—"

A sudden tremor cut her off, the ground beneath their feet shuddering violently. Anira staggered, her arms flailing as she fought to keep her balance. The edges of the chasm cracked and splintered, thin fissures spreading out like veins in glass. The shadows below roared to life, their movements frantic and frenzied, and the air was filled with a low, guttural hum that seemed to vibrate through her bones.

"Move back!" Ashric shouted, grabbing her arm and pulling her away from the edge just as the ground gave way beneath her. A section of the path crumbled, falling into the abyss with a deafening crash. The shadows below surged upward, clawing at the falling debris, their formless limbs twisting and reaching.

Anira's chest heaved as she stumbled back, her heart racing. "It's collapsing!" she cried. "The whole thing is falling apart!"

Ashric's grip on her arm tightened, his jaw clenched. "Then we jump," he said, his voice calm despite the chaos.

Kael's eyes widened. "Jump? Are you insane? Into that?"

"There's no time!" Ashric barked. He turned to Anira, his gaze piercing. "The Rose brought us here for a reason. Trust it."

Anira stared at him, her mind racing. The Rose pulsed violently now, its warmth spreading through her like fire, and she knew he was right. The pull was stronger than ever, and whatever waited below, she couldn't deny it any longer.

She nodded, swallowing her fear. "Together?"

"Together," he said firmly, his eyes steady.

Kael groaned, their face pale as they clutched their knife. "I hate this plan. I hate both of you."

Without another word, Ashric grabbed Anira's hand, and the three of them stepped to the edge. The chasm seemed to pulse in response, its depths alive with shadow and crimson light. Anira's heart pounded as she looked down, the abyss yawning before her like the mouth of a beast.

And then they jumped.

The fall was immediate, the air rushing past her in a deafening roar. The darkness swallowed them whole, the world above disappearing in an instant. The Rose burned against her chest, its pulse syncing with the rhythmic movements of the shadows that surged around them. For a moment, she felt weightless, her body suspended in the void, and then the world shifted.

The ground rose up to meet them, but it wasn't the jagged, glassy stone they had left behind. It was soft, pliable, yet it shuddered beneath her as if alive. Anira landed hard, the breath knocked from her lungs, and she gasped, her fingers clawing at the surface beneath her. It felt like flesh—warm and damp, pulsing faintly under her touch.

She scrambled to her feet, her legs trembling as she took in her surroundings. They were no longer in the forest. The chasm had led them to a vast, cavernous space bathed in faint red light that seemed to emanate from the walls themselves. The ground beneath them was uneven and slick, its surface covered in twisting, vein-like patterns that glowed faintly.

Kael groaned as they rose shakily to their feet, their knife still clutched tightly in their hand. "Where... are we?" they asked, their voice trembling. "This isn't... this isn't natural."

"It's alive," Ashric said, his voice grim as he scanned the space. His sword was already drawn, his posture tense. "The whole place—it's a living thing."

Anira shuddered, her gaze drawn to the faint veins on the walls. They pulsed in time with the Rose, their glow steady and rhythmic, and she felt the pull again, leading her deeper into the cavern. The air here was heavier, thick with the scent of blood and decay, and the low hum that filled the space vibrated in her chest like a heartbeat.

"It's waiting for me," she said softly, her voice trembling. "Whatever's here—it knows I've come."

Ashric stepped closer, his presence steadying her as he rested a hand on her shoulder. "Then we face it," he said, his voice low and certain. "Whatever it is, we end this."

Anira nodded, her chest tight as she clutched the Rose. The warmth of it spread through her like fire, burning away the fear that threatened to overwhelm her. She took a deep breath, her resolve hardening as she stepped forward into the crimson-lit abyss.

The shadows shifted around them, and the hum deepened. The cavern seemed to breathe, its walls contracting and expanding in slow, rhythmic waves, and as they moved deeper, the faint outline of a massive structure loomed ahead.

It wasn't natural. It wasn't safe.

But it was waiting.

The cavern walls pulsed faintly, the crimson veins casting an eerie glow that flickered against their faces as they walked deeper into the abyss. Each step seemed to echo, the sound swallowed almost instantly by the oppressive weight of the space. The air was thick with humidity, clinging to Anira's skin and making her breath feel heavier with each passing moment. The Rose burned steady and warm against her chest, its pulse grounding her, though her thoughts churned in a whirlwind of fear, determination, and something she hadn't expected: distraction.

Ashric moved ahead of her, his broad shoulders tense beneath his armor, his sword gleaming faintly in the dim light. He was always composed, always sharp, but now, there was something different about the way he carried himself. The set of his jaw was harder, the focus in his blue eyes more intense, and every movement was precise, deliberate. It was as though the weight of their situation had carved away the last vestiges of the walls he'd so carefully maintained.

She hated that her thoughts strayed in the face of danger, hated that her attention lingered longer than it should on the way his hair clung to his damp skin, the faint sheen of sweat on his neck catching the crimson light.

There was something about him—about the raw, unrelenting way he approached the world—that ignited something deep in her chest, something she hadn't felt in years.

Her gaze dropped to his hands, rough and calloused, the kind that told stories of countless battles. She remembered the way they'd steadied her earlier, firm and unwavering, his touch burning through her panic like a beacon. It had been fleeting, but even now, she could feel the ghost of his grip, the memory of his fingers brushing hers.

A flush crept up her neck, unbidden, and she swallowed hard, tearing her eyes away. This wasn't the time—it couldn't be the time—but her thoughts betrayed her, spinning out against her better judgment.

What would it feel like, she wondered, to let that armor fall away? To know the man beneath the stoic mask he wore so well? He was frustrating, infuriating even, but there was something about him that made her feel steadier, sharper. It wasn't just his strength—it was the way he never hesitated, never faltered when the world around them crumbled. It was the way he looked at her, his gaze steady and unyielding, as if he could see the parts of her she was still too afraid to face.

Her pulse quickened, heat spreading through her chest, and for a moment, she hated the Rose for its warmth, hated it for amplifying the ache that twisted inside her. She forced herself to look away, her cheeks burning as she tightened her grip on her dagger. Focus, she told herself, but the word felt hollow, the tension inside her a storm that refused to be calmed.

Ashric turned suddenly, his gaze locking onto hers as if he'd felt the weight of her thoughts. His sharp eyes softened for a fleeting moment, and his voice, low and steady, broke through the fog in her mind. "You alright?"

She nodded quickly, too quickly, her breath catching in her throat. "Yeah," she said, her voice rougher than she intended. "Just... thinking."

His brow arched faintly, a glimmer of dry humor breaking through the tension. "About the shadows or something worse?"

You, her mind betrayed her, but she pushed the thought down, hard, and forced a faint smile. "Both."

His lips quirked into a brief smirk, and he stepped closer, his presence warm and steady. "You think too much," he said softly, his tone carrying a faint edge of amusement. "Out here, instincts matter more than thoughts."

Her heart hammered in her chest, and she couldn't help the way her gaze flicked to his mouth for the briefest moment before she snapped it away. "I'll keep that in mind," she said, her voice barely above a whisper.

He nodded, his smirk fading as the weight of the cavern seemed to press down on them again. "Good. We'll get through this—one way or another."

With that, he turned back to the path ahead, leaving Anira to wrestle with the storm in her chest, the heat that refused to fade. She took a deep breath, steadying herself as the Rose pulsed faintly against her skin. There was no room for distraction here, no room for the tangled mess of feelings she couldn't quite name. But even as she moved forward, her thoughts lingered, her gaze trailing after him against her better judgment.

And the pull of the Rose felt sharper, as if it, too, recognized the fire she tried so desperately to smother.

The cavern seemed endless, a labyrinth of pulsating crimson light and twisting shadows that pressed in on them like a living, breathing thing. The further they walked, the heavier the air grew, thick with the scent of damp earth and decay, and the faint hum that filled the space vibrated through Anira's chest like an unwelcome heartbeat.

She kept her focus forward, but it was a fragile kind of focus, one that fractured at the edges every time her gaze drifted to Ashric. He moved ahead of her, his shoulders set and his sword gripped tightly in his hand. His every step was deliberate, purposeful, as though he could will the path ahead to make sense through sheer determination alone. The tension in his posture matched the tension in the air, but there was something else there, too—something she couldn't quite name.

She hated how aware of him she was, how the weight of her own thoughts felt like an anchor dragging her deeper into dangerous waters. His presence, steady and unyielding, was like a storm on the horizon, pulling at something buried deep inside her. It wasn't just admiration—though there was plenty of that, more than she'd ever admit—it was the quiet ache of something unspoken, something she couldn't afford to feel.

She caught herself staring again and snapped her gaze away, her cheeks burning despite the cold. Get it together, she thought, gripping the hilt of her dagger so tightly that her knuckles ached. You don't have time for this.

But the thought rang hollow, and she hated herself for the way her chest tightened every time she caught the faintest flicker of warmth in his eyes when he looked at her, like he could see the weight she carried and knew it because he carried it, too.

As if sensing her thoughts, Ashric slowed his pace and glanced back at her. His sharp blue eyes met hers, their intensity cutting through the shadows like a blade. "You're quiet," he said, his voice low and steady. "More than usual."

Anira stiffened, forcing herself to meet his gaze. "Just thinking," she said quickly, the words too sharp, too rushed. She cleared her throat, trying to steady herself. "About what's ahead."

He studied her for a moment, his expression unreadable. Then, faintly, his lips twitched into the ghost of a smile, though it didn't quite reach his eyes. "You think too much."

"You've mentioned that," she replied, her tone clipped, though it lacked any real bite.

He turned away again, but not before she caught it—a flicker of something in his expression, something that mirrored the turmoil she'd been trying so hard to hide. It was fleeting, almost imperceptible, but it was there. For the briefest moment, he looked at her the way she felt—conflicted, uncertain, but unable to look away.

The realization hit her like a jolt, and she bit the inside of her cheek, her heart pounding as she struggled to keep her expression neutral. No, she thought, a quiet, desperate plea to herself. Don't start imagining things. He's just focused. That's all this is.

But the way his shoulders tensed when he looked away, the way his jaw tightened as if he was fighting something he wouldn't let himself feel—it didn't feel imagined.

Kael's voice broke the silence, sharp and brittle. "I don't know about you two, but I'd really like to not die in a giant fleshy cave. Can we focus on the horrors waiting to kill us instead of... whatever this is?"

Ashric shot Kael a sharp look, his jaw tightening further, and Anira seized the distraction, forcing herself to move past him and take the lead. Her steps were quick, her chest tight with a storm of emotions she couldn't name, didn't want to name. The Rose pulsed faintly against her chest, its warmth a mocking reminder of the fire that refused to be extinguished.

They pressed on in silence, the weight of the cavern closing in around them. Anira kept her eyes forward, refusing to glance back, but she could feel Ashric's presence like a shadow at her back, steady and constant, and it only made the ache worse. She didn't dare let herself hope that he felt the same pull, didn't dare let herself think about the way his hand had lingered on hers when he'd pulled her back from the edge, or the way his voice softened every time he spoke her name.

But as they reached a fork in the cavern, the shadows shifting and writhing around them, she caught him looking at her again. His expression was unreadable, his blue eyes sharp and searching, but there was something there, buried deep beneath the surface—something that made her heart race and her chest tighten.

He looked away first, his grip tightening on his sword, and when he spoke, his voice was calm, measured. "We need to move quickly. Whatever's ahead, it's waiting for us."

Anira nodded, her throat dry, and forced herself to take the lead. She couldn't let herself think about him now, couldn't let herself fall into the trap of wanting something she could never have. But as they walked deeper into the crimson-lit abyss, the pull of the Rose steady against her chest, she couldn't shake the lingering thought that, for all his composure, Ashric might be fighting the same battle.

And that terrified her almost as much as the shadows waiting ahead.

The Crimson Maw

The cavern narrowed as they pressed deeper, the walls closing in like a throat swallowing them whole. The air was heavier now, damp and stifling, and each breath Anira took tasted of iron and decay. The veins of crimson light that pulsed along the walls grew brighter, their glow casting long, jagged shadows that danced and writhed with each flicker. The sound of their footsteps echoed unevenly, swallowed almost instantly by the oppressive hum that had become an ever-present weight around them.

Ashric walked close behind her, his presence a constant reminder of the tension that had simmered between them since the chasm. She could feel the heat of him, steady and grounding, but it only served to fray her nerves further. The memory of his fleeting glances, the brief moments where his gaze lingered just a little too long, burned in her mind like embers she couldn't extinguish.

Kael broke the silence, their voice sharp and brittle. "I know we're all trying to be brave here, but does anyone else feel like this place is alive? Because I swear the walls just... moved."

"They are," Ashric said without looking back. His tone was clipped, his focus fixed on the narrowing path ahead. "The entire cavern—it's reacting to us."

Kael muttered a curse under their breath. "Fantastic. Living, breathing death traps. My favorite."

Anira kept her eyes forward, though the weight of the Rose at her chest was a constant distraction. Its pulse was stronger now, quick and insistent, pulling her toward the darkness ahead like an invisible tether. The further they walked, the sharper the pull became, until it was almost unbearable, a force that tugged at her very soul.

"It's getting stronger," she said softly, her voice trembling. "The Rose—it's leading us."

"Leading us where?" Kael asked, their voice rising with unease. "To the mouth of whatever nightmare monster it's been feeding this whole time?"

"Quiet," Ashric said sharply. His sword was already in his hand, its blade gleaming faintly in the crimson light. His posture was tense, every muscle coiled, as though he expected the shadows to attack at any moment. "There's something ahead."

Anira felt it too—the oppressive weight that filled the air, a presence that seemed to thrum in the very walls around them. The shadows ahead were darker, denser, and the pulsing crimson light was brighter now, casting the path in a sickly glow that made her skin crawl.

They rounded a sharp bend, and the cavern opened into a vast chamber. The ceiling arched high above, disappearing into the darkness, while the floor sloped downward in uneven steps that glistened with an oily sheen. At the center of the chamber stood an enormous structure, its shape jagged and unnatural, like a spire carved from black glass and wrapped in twisting veins of crimson light. The hum that had filled the air was louder now, vibrating in Anira's chest like a second heartbeat.

Kael stopped short, their eyes wide. "What... what is that?"

Ashric didn't answer, his gaze locked on the spire as he stepped forward, his movements slow and deliberate. Anira followed, her chest tightening as the Rose flared against her skin, its pulse quick and frantic.

"It's connected to the Rose," she said, her voice barely audible. "I can feel it."

As they approached, the spire seemed to come alive. The crimson veins along its surface pulsed brighter, and a low, guttural sound echoed through the chamber, vibrating through the stone beneath their feet. Anira froze, her breath catching as the ground shuddered, sending cracks splintering outward from the base of the spire.

Ashric held out an arm, stopping her from moving closer. "Stay back," he said, his voice low. "We don't know what it's capable of."

The hum deepened, and the spire began to shift, its jagged edges twisting and writhing as though it were alive. The crimson veins pulsed faster, and the sound grew louder, sharper, until it felt as though the very air was tearing apart.

And then, with a deafening crack, the spire split open.

Anira stumbled back, her heart racing as the structure tore itself apart, revealing a seething mass of shadow and light within. It pulsed and twisted, its form constantly shifting, and from its center emerged a figure—tall, lean, and cloaked in darkness that seemed to consume the light around it. Its eyes burned crimson, and its voice, low and resonant, echoed through the chamber.

"Bearer of the Rose," it said, its gaze locking onto Anira. "You have come."

The weight of its presence pressed down on her, stealing the breath from her lungs. Her knees trembled, and the Rose burned hotter, its pulse matching the rhythm of the crimson veins that pulsed across the cavern.

Ashric stepped in front of her, his sword raised. "Who are you?" he demanded, his voice steady despite the tension in his posture. "What do you want?"

The figure's gaze shifted to him, and for a moment, the shadows around it seemed to curl tighter, as if it were amused. "What I want is not your concern, mortal," it said, its tone cold. "But you stand in my way, and that is a mistake."

Anira felt a surge of heat from the Rose, and the pull intensified, drawing her forward despite the fear clawing at her chest. "It's me you want," she said, her voice trembling but steady. "I'm the one the Rose chose."

The figure's burning gaze returned to her, and its voice softened, though it lost none of its weight. "You are more than its bearer," it said. "You are its vessel. Its purpose. Its end."

The words struck her like a blow, and she stumbled back, her breath coming in sharp gasps. "What are you talking about?" she demanded, her voice rising with panic. "What does that mean?"

The figure's form shifted, the shadows around it twisting and writhing like smoke caught in a storm. "It means you were chosen long before you ever touched it," it said. "And now, you will face the cost."

The chamber shuddered violently, and the shadows surged toward them, their forms coiling and twisting as they closed in. Ashric grabbed Anira's arm, pulling her back, his sword flashing as he prepared to fight.

"Anira," he said, his voice low but fierce. "Whatever this thing is, we'll face it together. Do you understand me?"

She met his gaze, her heart pounding as the weight of his words settled over her. There was no hesitation in his eyes, no doubt. For a moment, the storm inside her quieted, and she nodded, her grip tightening on her dagger.

"Together," she said, her voice trembling but resolute.

And then the shadows attacked.

The shadows moved with an unnatural speed, their twisting forms surging toward them like a living tide. The air grew colder, the metallic tang thickening into a stifling miasma that clung to Anira's skin and burned at her throat. The Rose flared hot against her chest, its pulse pounding in time with the rhythm of the crimson veins that pulsed along the cavern walls.

Ashric didn't hesitate. With a sharp, precise motion, he stepped in front of her and swung his sword in a wide arc. The blade gleamed faintly in the crimson light as it sliced through the nearest shadow, tearing it apart in a burst of dark mist. The creature let out a piercing shriek as it dissolved, but its absence was quickly replaced by two more, their coiling forms circling him like wolves hunting prey.

"Stay behind me!" he barked, his voice cutting through the chaos.

Anira barely heard him over the roar of her own heartbeat. Her grip tightened on her dagger as the pull of the Rose grew stronger, dragging her forward against the instinctual fear that clawed at her chest. The shadows weren't just moving toward them—they were moving toward her. Their forms shifted and stretched, their indistinct edges writhing like smoke, but their intent was clear. They weren't attacking blindly; they were being drawn.

"Anira!" Kael's voice snapped her out of her trance, sharp and panicked. "Do something! They're closing in!"

She tore her gaze from the writhing mass of shadows and forced herself to focus. The Rose's pulse burned in her chest, filling her with a heat that felt almost alive, and she knew, with a terrible certainty, that it wasn't just a weapon—it was a key. Whatever power had been sealed here, the Rose had unlocked it. But now it demanded something more.

Ashric cut down another shadow, his blade moving with ruthless precision, but the effort was beginning to show. His breaths were quick, his movements sharper, less measured, as the sheer number of creatures began to overwhelm him. "Anira," he called, his voice strained. "Whatever the Rose is pulling you toward, do it now."

Her chest tightened at the raw urgency in his voice, and she turned her attention to the towering spire at the center of the chamber. The shadows seemed to flow from it, their movements synchronized with the pulsing veins that snaked across its surface. The figure that had emerged from the spire watched her, its burning crimson eyes fixed on her with unrelenting intensity.

"You feel it, don't you?" the figure said, its voice a low, resonant rumble that seemed to vibrate through her bones. "The power. The truth. The choice."

Anira clenched her fists, her knuckles white as the Rose pulsed violently against her chest. The figure was right—she did feel it. The pull was unbearable now, an invisible force dragging her toward the spire even as her mind screamed for her to run. But running wasn't an option anymore.

She took a step forward, her legs trembling beneath her, and the shadows surged in response, their forms writhing with a renewed frenzy. Ashric lunged toward her, his blade cutting through one of the creatures before it could reach her, but the others pressed closer, their movements growing more deliberate.

"Anira, wait!" he shouted, his voice raw. "We don't know what's waiting for you!"

"I have to," she said, her voice trembling but resolute. Her gaze met his, and for a moment, she saw the flicker of something behind the sharp lines of his expression—fear, not for himself, but for her.

His jaw tightened, and he gave a sharp nod, stepping closer to her side. "Then I'm not letting you go alone."

"You don't have to do this—" she started, but he cut her off.

"Yes, I do."

His words were low but fierce, carrying a weight that made her chest tighten. He didn't look at her as he turned back toward the oncoming shadows, his blade already moving, but his presence was steadying in a way she hadn't expected. She swallowed hard, forcing herself to push aside the storm of emotions that threatened to consume her.

"Kael!" Ashric shouted, his voice sharp. "Cover her! Don't let anything through!"

Kael groaned, but they moved quickly, their knife flashing as they joined the fight, their sharp, panicked motions a stark contrast to Ashric's brutal efficiency. "If we survive this," Kael muttered, dodging a swipe from one of the creatures, "I'm demanding a raise in whatever imaginary salary you think I'm earning."

The figure at the spire tilted its head, its gaze locked onto Anira. "The light will consume you," it said, its tone almost mocking. "And the darkness will not release its hold. Are you ready to bear the cost?"

She didn't answer, couldn't answer. Her legs moved on their own, carrying her toward the spire, toward the writhing shadows and pulsing light that called to her like a beacon. The heat of the Rose spread through her chest, filling her veins with a fire that burned brighter with every step.

The shadows surged toward her, their forms coiling and snapping like living smoke, but Ashric was there, his blade flashing as he cut them down with ruthless precision. His movements were quick, almost desperate, as though he knew what was at stake. Each strike was a promise—a silent vow to keep her safe, no matter the cost.

"Go!" he shouted, his voice raw with effort. "Don't stop!"

Anira forced herself forward, the spire looming above her, its crimson veins pulsing in time with the Rose. The figure's gaze followed her, its burning eyes unrelenting, and the weight of its presence pressed against her like a physical force. The shadows clawed at her, their forms snapping at her heels, but she didn't stop.

As she reached the base of the spire, the Rose flared, its light blinding as it surged through her. The warmth was unbearable now, searing and all-consuming, and she cried out as the energy within it poured into her, demanding to be unleashed.

Her hand closed around the surface of the spire, and the world erupted in light.

The moment Anira's hand touched the surface of the spire, a searing pulse of energy exploded outward. The crimson veins that twisted along its surface flared with a blinding light, brighter and fiercer than anything she'd ever seen, bathing the chamber in a violent cascade of red and gold. The shadows that had surged toward her froze mid-attack, their forms writhing and curling in agony as the light tore through them, reducing their jagged shapes to shreds of flickering mist.

Anira cried out as the heat of the Rose poured through her chest, its power flowing into her like molten fire. It wasn't pain, not exactly, but an overwhelming force that filled every inch of her, threatening to consume her entirely. Her knees buckled, and she clung to the spire for support, her breath coming in sharp, shallow gasps.

The surface beneath her fingers wasn't smooth—it was alive. The spire pulsed beneath her grip, its texture warm and slick, like the skin of some massive, ancient creature. The veins that snaked across it writhed and twisted, responding to the touch of her hand, and the hum that had filled the air deepened into a low, resonant growl that seemed to come from the heart of the cavern itself.

"Anira!" Ashric's voice cut through the chaos, sharp and urgent.

She turned her head, her vision blurring as the heat of the Rose burned brighter. He was fighting his way toward her, his sword a blur of motion as he cut through the remaining shadows with brutal efficiency. His face was slick with sweat, his jaw tight with effort, but his focus was unrelenting. For a fleeting moment, their eyes met, and in the storm of light and shadow, she felt the weight of his gaze like a lifeline.

"Hold on!" he shouted, his voice raw. "You're almost there!"

The spire responded to the Rose, its pulsing light quickening to match the frantic rhythm in her chest. The energy surged again, and Anira let out a sharp gasp as the heat spread through her arms and into the spire, igniting its veins with an intensity that made the cavern tremble. The ground beneath her feet cracked, the fractures glowing with the same blinding light, and the low growl deepened into a roar that shook the air.

The figure in the shadows emerged again, its tall, lean form cloaked in writhing darkness that seemed to writhe and recoil against the light. Its crimson eyes burned brighter, its expression sharp with something that might have been rage—or amusement.

"You think you can control it," it said, its voice cutting through the roar of the spire. "You think you can master the light and survive the dark. But the Rose will take everything from you, vessel."

Anira gritted her teeth, her body trembling under the weight of the energy coursing through her. "I didn't choose this," she said, her voice strained but defiant. "But I'll finish it."

The figure tilted its head, its smile widening. "Such conviction," it said. "Let us see how far it carries you."

The shadows surged toward her, faster and more ferocious than before, their jagged forms slicing through the air. Ashric was there in an instant, his blade flashing as he intercepted the attack, his movements sharp and deliberate. One of the creatures lunged toward Anira, its claws outstretched, but Ashric drove his sword into its core with a roar, sending it shrieking into the void.

"I told you to keep going!" he shouted, his voice raw with urgency. He turned, his expression fierce as he cut down another shadow. "Don't stop now!"

Anira's breath hitched as she turned her focus back to the spire. The Rose pulsed again, its rhythm frantic, and she felt the pull of its energy guiding her, urging her deeper. Her fingers tightened against the surface of the spire, and she forced herself to lean closer, letting the heat of the Rose flow through her and into the veins that coiled beneath her touch.

The light around her exploded again, a searing wave of gold and red that filled the chamber and sent the shadows reeling. The figure hissed, its form flickering and shifting as the light tore at it, but it didn't retreat. Instead, it stepped forward, its burning eyes locked onto Anira with unrelenting intensity.

"You cannot win," it said, its voice resonating through the cavern. "The Rose will consume you. The light will betray you."

Anira clenched her jaw, her heart racing as the heat of the Rose flared once more. "Then let it try," she said, her voice trembling but fierce.

With a final surge of energy, she drove her hand deeper into the spire, her fingers curling around its pulsing veins. The light intensified, brighter and fiercer than anything she could have imagined, and the chamber erupted into chaos. The shadows shrieked, their forms unraveling as the light consumed them, and the ground beneath her feet shuddered violently.

Ashric's voice cut through the noise, sharp and desperate. "Anira!"

Her gaze darted to him, her chest tightening as she saw him fighting his way through the onslaught. His movements were slower now, his strikes heavier, but his focus was unwavering. The faint flicker of fear in his eyes wasn't for himself—it was for her.

The figure in the shadows lunged toward him, its form twisting into something massive and serpentine. Ashric turned to face it, his blade raised, but before it could strike, the light from the spire surged again, blinding and all-encompassing.

The world tilted, and Anira felt herself falling, the heat of the Rose consuming her as the cavern dissolved into searing white. She reached for Ashric instinctively, her fingers brushing the air where he had stood, and then there was nothing but the roar of light and the sound of her own heartbeat thundering in her ears.

And silence.

The silence was deafening, pressing against Anira's ears like a heavy shroud. She couldn't tell if her heart was still racing or if the thundering in her chest was just an echo of the light's roar. Slowly, the blinding white began to fade, replaced by a dull crimson glow that seeped into her vision like blood pooling beneath her eyelids.

She was lying on something cold and unyielding, though the ground beneath her pulsed faintly, a rhythmic vibration that felt disturbingly alive. Her fingers twitched, brushing against the rough texture of the stone—or flesh?—beneath her. It was slick and warm, and the sensation sent a shiver crawling up her spine.

Her thoughts were fragmented, scattered like shards of glass. Where was she? Where were the others? The last thing she remembered was the spire erupting, the shadows screaming, and Ashric's voice cutting through the chaos as the light consumed everything.

"Anira," a voice called, rough but steady, breaking through the fog in her mind.

Her head snapped up, her vision still blurred, and she blinked rapidly to focus. The glow of the Rose at her chest was faint now, its once-persistent pulse barely a whisper against her skin. She saw a figure moving toward her, shadowed by the dim crimson light.

"Ashric?" she whispered, her voice hoarse.

He knelt beside her, his sharp blue eyes scanning her face, his expression hard but tinged with relief. There was blood streaked across his jaw, dried and smeared like war paint, and the edges of his cloak were scorched. He looked as though he'd just survived a battle, but his presence was steady, grounding.

"You're alive," he said, his voice low. The words weren't a question, but a statement, filled with a quiet intensity that made her chest tighten.

"Barely," she murmured, forcing herself to sit up. Her body protested with every movement, her muscles aching and her head pounding. "What happened?"

Ashric's gaze flicked toward the spire—or what remained of it. The towering structure was fractured, its jagged edges glowing faintly with the remnants of the Rose's power. The shadows that had poured from it were gone, but the air was still heavy, thick with the scent of iron and decay.

"You happened," he said simply, his tone unreadable. "The Rose—it unleashed something. You tore that thing apart, but whatever it was... it's not gone. Not completely."

Her stomach twisted at his words, and she looked away, her fingers brushing against the pendant at her chest. The Rose was quiet now, its warmth barely noticeable, but she could still feel its presence, heavy and unrelenting.

"What about Kael?" she asked suddenly, her voice sharp with worry.

Ashric nodded toward the far side of the chamber. "They're fine. Shaken, but fine."

Anira followed his gaze and spotted Kael leaning against a jagged outcrop of stone, their knife still clutched tightly in their hand. Their face was pale, their chest heaving with shallow breaths, but they were alive. Relief flooded her, and she let out a breath she hadn't realized she was holding.

"Good," she said softly. "That's... good."

Ashric's hand brushed her arm, a brief but grounding touch, and her breath hitched at the sudden, unguarded tenderness in the gesture. She looked at him, and for a fleeting moment, the tension between them shifted, unspoken words hanging in the air.

"Don't scare me like that again," he said, his voice low but firm. His eyes held hers, and there was something raw in his expression—something she wasn't sure she could face right now.

"I didn't mean to," she replied softly, her voice trembling. She swallowed hard, forcing herself to look away. "I didn't know what would happen."

"You still threw yourself into it," he said, his tone softening but his gaze unwavering. "You always do."

She couldn't respond, couldn't find the words to explain the storm of emotions twisting inside her. Instead, she pushed herself to her feet, her legs shaking beneath her as the cavern seemed to tilt around her.

The remnants of the spire loomed ahead, its fractured surface glowing faintly with veins of crimson light. It was smaller now, diminished, but its presence was no less foreboding. The ground beneath it was cracked and uneven, and the faint hum that had filled the chamber before was gone, replaced by an eerie stillness.

"We need to move," Anira said, her voice steadier than she felt. "Whatever's left of this place, it's not safe."

Ashric stood beside her, his sword still in hand, his posture tense. "It hasn't been safe since we got here."

Kael staggered toward them, their steps uneven but determined. "If it wasn't clear already," they said, their voice shaky but laced with sarcasm, "I officially hate this place."

Anira managed a faint smile, though it felt fragile. "Join the club."

The three of them turned toward the far side of the chamber, where a narrow passageway wound into the shadows. The path ahead was darker now, the crimson light dimming as if the cavern itself was retreating, but the pull of the Rose was still there, faint but steady, guiding her forward.

As they stepped into the passage, the oppressive weight of the cavern seemed to settle over them once more, pressing against Anira's chest like a living thing. The quiet wasn't comforting—it was suffocating, filled with the unspoken promise of what lay ahead.

And yet, as Ashric fell into step beside her, his presence steady and unyielding, Anira felt a flicker of something she hadn't expected—hope. It was fragile, barely more than a whisper, but it was there, keeping her grounded even as the darkness closed in around them.

She didn't look at him, couldn't let herself risk what she might see in his eyes. But as their shoulders brushed briefly in the narrow corridor, she caught the faintest shift in his expression, a flicker of something raw and unguarded.

And for the first time in what felt like forever, she let herself believe that they might survive this—together.

The corridor narrowed as they moved deeper, the walls closing in until the three of them were forced to walk single file. The air was thicker here, heavy with an almost tangible weight that clung to Anira's skin and made her every breath feel labored. The faint glow of the crimson veins that lined the walls pulsed faintly, casting flickering shadows that seemed to shift and curl at the edges of her vision.

Anira kept her focus forward, her hand brushing against the Rose at her chest. Its warmth was subdued now, steady but muted, yet she could still feel the pull, urging her onward into the oppressive dark. Each step felt heavier than the last, the silence around them broken only by the faint scrape of their boots against the uneven ground and the occasional muttered curse from Kael.

Ashric walked just behind her, his presence steady and unrelenting. She could feel his gaze on her, not in the way of someone distracted, but of someone deeply attuned to everything around them. He was a soldier through and through, his instincts honed to protect and defend, and yet there was something more in the way he watched her—something unspoken that lingered between them like a breath held too long.

When they reached a wider stretch of the corridor, Anira paused, pressing her palm against the wall for support. The Rose flared briefly, its pulse quickening, and she let out a shaky breath, her fingers brushing over its surface.

"Are you alright?" Ashric's voice came from behind her, low and steady, breaking through the heavy silence.

She turned to find him standing a few steps away, his sword still drawn and his expression carefully guarded. But his eyes—sharp, piercing blue—betrayed a flicker of something softer, something she wasn't sure she wanted to name.

"I'm fine," she said quickly, though her voice wavered. She straightened, forcing herself to meet his gaze. "The Rose... it's just pulling harder now. It's close."

Ashric stepped closer, his boots crunching softly against the ground. He stopped just shy of her, his presence filling the narrow space between them, and for a moment, the tension in the air shifted. His eyes scanned her face, his expression hard and unreadable, but there was an intensity there that made her pulse quicken, even as the weight of the Rose pressed harder against her chest.

"You've been carrying this thing like it's yours to bear alone," he said quietly, his voice low but firm. "You don't have to."

Her throat tightened, and she looked away, her hand tightening on the hilt of her dagger. "It's not about what I have to do," she said softly. "It's what I can't let go of. If I don't carry it, who will?"

His silence was heavy, but when she glanced back at him, his gaze hadn't left her. The lines of his face, sharp and unyielding, softened just slightly, and for the briefest moment, the mask he wore cracked.

"If it takes you," he said, his voice barely above a whisper, "what's left for the rest of us?"

The words hit her like a blow, stealing the breath from her lungs. There was no anger in his tone, no accusation—just a raw, quiet conviction that cut through the chaos in her mind like a blade. She opened her mouth to respond, but the words tangled in her throat.

He stepped closer still, his gaze locked on hers, and the air between them seemed to still. The shadows on the walls, the pulsing crimson light, even the distant hum of the cavern—all of it faded, leaving only the sound of her own heartbeat pounding in her ears.

"You've got a way of making people want to follow you," he said, his lips twitching into the faintest hint of a smile. "Even when it means walking straight into hell."

Anira's chest tightened, and for a moment, she couldn't look away from him. The steady warmth of the Rose pulsed faintly between them, and she could feel the weight of his gaze like a physical thing, pressing against her in ways she wasn't ready to name.

But then, just as quickly as the moment came, Ashric stepped back, his expression hardening once more. He turned his attention to the darkened path ahead, his grip tightening on his sword. "We need to keep moving," he said, his voice sharp and clipped. "Whatever's waiting for us isn't going to wait much longer."

Anira nodded, swallowing hard as she forced herself to turn away. Her thoughts were a tangled storm, but she pushed them down, burying them beneath the weight of the Rose's pull and the danger that lay ahead.

Ashric's steps were steady as he moved forward, but she caught the faintest shift in his posture, the tension in his shoulders that hadn't been there before. He didn't look at her again, but she could feel it—the same unspoken storm she carried mirrored in his movements, in the way he gripped his sword like it was the only thing holding him together.

Anira clenched her fists, her chest tight as she followed him into the shadows, the pull of the Rose guiding her forward. There was no room for distractions here, no room for the fire that burned in the spaces between their words. But even as the crimson light flickered and the corridor grew darker, she couldn't shake the lingering heat of his gaze, or the quiet, unyielding certainty that he would stand beside her—no matter how far they fell.

The path twisted and narrowed again, forcing them into a tight line as the crimson glow along the walls dimmed further, casting the corridor into a murky half-light. The air was suffocating now, heavy with the scent of iron and something acrid, something that clung to Anira's throat and made her stomach churn. The hum of the Rose had deepened, vibrating in her chest like a second heartbeat, and its pull was sharper, more insistent, like a hand gripping her and dragging her forward.

She pressed on, her footsteps slow and deliberate, her fingers brushing the dagger at her side. Ashric followed closely behind, his presence a steadying weight at her back. She didn't have to turn to know he was watching her again; she could feel the heat of his gaze, sharp and unyielding, yet carrying a quiet intensity that set her nerves on edge.

It wasn't fear—not exactly. It was something deeper, more dangerous. Something she wasn't sure she could contain much longer.

The corridor opened suddenly into a small chamber, the ceiling low and arched, the walls lined with jagged veins of glowing crimson that pulsed unevenly. The light reflected off the slick, uneven ground, casting strange patterns that shifted and writhed like living things. Anira stopped at the threshold, her breath catching as the pull of the Rose intensified, burning hot against her chest.

"We're close," she said softly, her voice trembling despite her best efforts.

Ashric stepped beside her, his sword still in hand, his expression hard but focused. His gaze swept the chamber, taking in every corner, every shadow, before settling back on her. "Are you sure?"

She nodded, swallowing hard. "I can feel it. Whatever it's pulling me toward, it's here."

Kael stumbled in behind them, their knife clutched tightly in one hand. "Great," they muttered, their voice sharp with nerves. "Let's just hope it's not another 'unleash the shadows' situation, because I'm running out of creative ways to not die."

Ashric didn't respond. His focus remained on Anira, his sharp blue eyes scanning her face as though searching for some sign of weakness—or resolve. She felt the weight of his gaze like a physical thing, pressing against her, making it harder to breathe.

"You're burning up," he said, his voice low and rough. "The Rose... it's taking too much."

"I'm fine," she said quickly, though the heat in her chest was almost unbearable. She took a step forward, toward the center of the chamber, but his hand shot out, gripping her arm and pulling her back.

"Don't rush in blind," he said sharply. "We don't know what's waiting."

The touch was meant to steady her, but it sent a jolt through her that made her breath hitch. His hand was rough and calloused, warm despite the chill in the air, and his grip lingered a moment too long. She turned to him, her pulse racing as their eyes met, and the world seemed to narrow, the crimson light fading into the background.

"Ashric," she began, her voice barely a whisper, but she didn't know what else to say. The words tangled in her throat, caught somewhere between desperation and something she didn't dare name.

His gaze was unrelenting, his jaw tight, and for a moment, the mask he wore cracked. There was something raw in his expression, something that mirrored the storm inside her, and it stole the breath from her lungs.

"Anira," he said, her name rough on his tongue, filled with a quiet urgency that made her knees tremble. "You don't have to do this alone."

She couldn't look away from him, couldn't stop the heat rising in her chest, but the words came before she could stop them. "I'm not alone," she said softly. "You're here."

Something shifted in his gaze, and his grip on her arm tightened, not enough to hurt, but enough to hold her steady. His free hand twitched, as though he wanted to reach for her but stopped himself at the last moment. The tension between them was unbearable, a taut string pulled to its breaking point, and she could feel the air crackling with the unspoken words that hung between them.

His lips parted, his breath brushing against her skin, and for one reckless, fleeting moment, she thought he might close the distance between them, might let the fire in his eyes consume the silence.

But then, just as quickly, he stepped back, his jaw tightening as the mask fell back into place. His hand dropped from her arm, and the cold air rushed in where his warmth had been.

"This isn't the time," he said, his voice rough and clipped, as though he were fighting to regain control. He turned away, his grip tightening on his sword. "We need to focus. Whatever's here, it's not going to wait for us to figure this out."

Anira's chest ached, her heart pounding as she tried to steady herself. She forced a nod, her fingers brushing against the Rose at her chest as its pulse steadied her. "You're right," she said, though her voice shook. "Let's move."

Kael cleared their throat, their voice cutting through the thick tension like a blade. "Hate to break up the moment, but if you two are done being cryptic and broody, can we deal with the fact that this whole place feels like it's about to eat us?"

Anira forced a faint, humorless smile, turning her attention back to the chamber. The pull of the Rose was stronger now, sharper, and she stepped forward with a quiet resolve that masked the storm in her chest.

Ashric followed, his steps steady but deliberate, his expression unreadable. But as their shoulders brushed in the narrow space, she caught the faintest flicker of something in his gaze, something raw and unguarded that sent a shiver through her.

It was a fleeting moment, gone before she could fully grasp it, but it left her breathless all the same. Whatever was waiting for them in the depths of this place, it wouldn't break her. She wouldn't let it.

And neither, she knew, would he.

The chamber's oppressive air grew heavier as they stepped further inside, the light from the crimson veins pulsing erratically, as though the cavern itself were alive and struggling to breathe. The hum in the air intensified, vibrating through Anira's chest and spreading out in waves that made her fingers tremble. The pull of the Rose was sharper now, a constant force that dragged her toward the chamber's center, where the ground dipped into a shallow depression that glowed faintly with a swirling, otherworldly light.

Anira's steps slowed as they approached the depression, her gaze fixed on the shimmering pool of light at its core. It wasn't liquid—not entirely. The surface shifted like water, but the edges curled with dark tendrils that snapped and coiled like smoke caught in a violent wind. The sight of it sent a shiver crawling up her spine, but she couldn't look away. The Rose burned hotter against her chest, its pulse syncing with the shifting waves of light, and she knew, with a bone-deep certainty, that this was what it had been pulling her toward.

"What is that?" Kael asked, their voice sharp with unease. They hung back near the edge of the chamber, their knife clutched tightly in one hand. "Because if the answer is 'our doom,' I'd like to suggest we turn around."

Ashric didn't respond immediately. His sharp blue eyes were fixed on the pool, his jaw tight and his posture coiled with tension. His sword was still in his hand, the faint crimson light gleaming off its blade as though it were hungry for whatever waited in the swirling depths. Finally, he spoke, his voice low and deliberate. "It's a source."

Anira turned to him, her brow furrowing. "A source of what?"

"Power," he said simply, his gaze never leaving the pool. "Old, buried, and dangerous."

Kael muttered a curse, shaking their head. "Of course it's dangerous. Nothing in this nightmare is not dangerous."

Anira ignored them, her focus shifting back to the pool. The pull of the Rose was unbearable now, a relentless force that dragged her closer with every beat of her heart. She clenched her fists, her nails biting into her palms, but it wasn't enough to stop her feet from moving forward.

"Anira," Ashric said sharply, stepping in front of her and blocking her path. His presence was solid, a barrier between her and the swirling light. "Don't."

"I have to," she said, her voice trembling but steady. "This is why the Rose brought me here. If I don't... whatever's left of this place won't let us leave."

Ashric's jaw tightened, his sword lowering slightly as his free hand hovered near her arm. His gaze locked onto hers, hard and unyielding, but there was something else there too—something raw and desperate. "We'll find another way," he said, his voice low but fierce. "You don't have to sacrifice yourself for this."

Her chest tightened at his words, and she shook her head, her throat dry. "It's not about sacrifice," she said softly. "It's about finishing what I started."

"And if it takes you?" he asked, his voice rising slightly, his tone edged with something close to anger. "What happens then?"

Anira swallowed hard, the weight of his words settling over her like a stone. She could see the storm in his eyes, the way his grip on his sword tightened as though he wanted to fight whatever was pulling her toward the pool—but there was no fighting this. The Rose had made its choice.

She reached out, her fingers brushing against his wrist. The touch was light, fleeting, but it was enough to steady her, to anchor her in the chaos. "I don't know what happens," she said, her voice barely above a whisper. "But I do know that if I don't do this, none of us are walking out of here."

Ashric's lips pressed into a thin line, and for a moment, she thought he might argue. But then his shoulders sagged slightly, and he stepped aside, his gaze flicking toward the pool with a mix of anger and resignation.

"Just... don't be reckless," he said, his voice rough. "You're too stubborn to let something like this beat you."

Anira managed a faint smile, though it didn't quite reach her eyes. "I'll try."

As she stepped closer to the pool, the heat of the Rose grew almost unbearable, and her breath came in shallow gasps. The swirling light at the pool's center pulsed in time with its rhythm, and the dark tendrils coiling at the edges seemed to reach for her, beckoning her closer. The hum in the air deepened, becoming a low, resonant growl that vibrated through her bones.

She stopped at the edge, her fingers brushing against the pendant at her chest. The light reflected in the swirling depths was hypnotic, drawing her in with a force she couldn't resist. She glanced back at Ashric, her heart tightening at the way he stood tense and ready, his sharp eyes fixed on her as though willing her to survive this.

I'll come back, she wanted to say, but the words caught in her throat. Instead, she turned back to the pool, her hand tightening on the Rose.

The moment her foot crossed the threshold, the world erupted.

A wave of searing heat and blinding light surged outward, enveloping her in a force so powerful it knocked her off her feet. The sound was deafening, a roar that filled her ears and swallowed her thoughts, and for a moment, the world dissolved into chaos. She felt the pull of the Rose intensify, dragging her into the depths of the light, and she let out a sharp gasp as the ground disappeared beneath her.

And then there was nothing—just the endless swirl of light and shadow, pulling her deeper into the unknown.

Far beyond the crimson-lit cavern, in a realm of shifting shadows and jagged obsidian, the Shadowborn stirred.

The air in their domain was thick and heavy, laced with the scent of burning ash and decay. The void-like space pulsed with an eerie rhythm, resonating with the faint echoes of a power that had been disturbed—an ancient energy that whispered through the darkness like a beckoning call.

A massive figure stepped forward, its form cloaked in coiling shadows that writhed and twisted as though alive. Its glowing silver eyes pierced the gloom, sharp and predatory. It stood on the edge of a jagged precipice overlooking a sea of black mist, where smaller forms—half-formed, shifting creatures—moved restlessly, their movements jerky and deliberate.

"They have awakened it," the figure said, its voice deep and resonant, reverberating through the space. Its tone carried no emotion, only the weight of certainty.

Another figure emerged from the shadows, smaller but no less imposing, its body slick with an oily sheen that reflected the faint, pulsing glow of the realm. Its voice was sharp, a hiss that sliced through the suffocating silence. "The bearer stumbles closer to the truth. She carries the Rose, but she does not yet understand its cost."

The first figure turned slightly, its silver eyes narrowing. "She will. The Rose reveals all in time. Her resistance will fade."

"And the guardian?" the smaller one asked, venom dripping from its tone. "The one who shields her? He is persistent."

The larger figure's form shifted, the shadows around it curling and twisting in agitation. "He is mortal. Mortals are predictable. He will break, like all the rest."

The shadows beneath them convulsed, writhing upward in jagged arcs that licked at the air like flames. The faint echo of the Rose's power rippled through the void again, and the first figure raised a hand, silencing the lesser creatures.

"She is drawing closer," it said, its voice low and contemplative. "Prepare the way. They will not escape this time."

With a single, deliberate motion, the figure stepped into the mist, its form dissolving into the shadows. The others followed, their movements silent but purposeful, leaving the void empty once more—except for the pulsing rhythm of something vast and ancient waiting to be unleashed.

The light in the cavern began to fade, the blinding radiance receding into a faint, flickering glow. Ashric pushed himself up from where he'd been thrown against the jagged wall, his chest heaving as he scanned the chamber. His sword was still in his hand, its blade chipped but steady, and his sharp blue eyes darted toward the center of the room.

"Anira!" he called, his voice rough and strained.

Kael groaned from somewhere nearby, their voice muffled but laced with their usual sarcasm. "Could you not scream? My head is still spinning."

Ashric ignored them, his gaze locking on the faint silhouette near the center of the chamber. Anira was there, standing unsteadily, her figure bathed in the residual glow of the Rose. The swirling pool of light had dimmed now, its edges curling inward like a dying flame, but it still pulsed faintly, mirroring the rhythm of the veins that snaked along the walls.

"Anira," Ashric said again, softer this time as he moved toward her. His boots crunched against the fractured ground, each step deliberate and measured, and his grip on his sword remained tight.

She turned to him slowly, her face pale and her eyes wide with something he couldn't quite place—fear, awe, or both. The Rose at her chest glowed faintly, its warmth visible even from where he stood, and the air around her seemed to hum with the remnants of its power.

"I... I'm fine," she said, her voice trembling. She placed a hand over the pendant as though trying to contain its energy. "It's quiet now. For the moment."

"What happened?" Ashric asked, stopping just short of her. His gaze swept over her, sharp and searching. "The light—it consumed everything."

Anira shook her head, her fingers tightening around the Rose. "I don't know. It... pulled me in, showed me flashes of something. Shadows, fire, a voice. It's like it's trying to tell me something, but I can't—" She broke off, her voice catching as she turned away, her shoulders tense.

Ashric reached out, his hand brushing her arm. The touch was brief, but it steadied her, and when she turned back to him, there was a flicker of something familiar in her eyes—determination.

"Whatever it's doing," she said, her voice steadier now, "it's not finished. There's more."

"Of course there's more," Kael muttered as they approached, rubbing their temples. "There's always more. Let me guess—we've awakened some ancient nightmare, and now it's going to hunt us down because that's just our luck."

Ashric shot Kael a sharp look, but it lacked its usual edge. He turned back to Anira, his expression softening just slightly. "We'll deal with it," he said, his voice low but firm. "One step at a time."

She nodded, her fingers brushing the Rose again as its warmth pulsed faintly against her skin. The cavern was quiet now, the oppressive hum replaced by a tense, fragile silence. But as Anira met Ashric's gaze, she felt a flicker of something she hadn't expected—hope, fragile and fleeting but real.

"Let's move," she said softly, her voice carrying a quiet resolve. "We've lingered here too long."

Ashric nodded, falling into step beside her as they turned toward the narrow passage leading out of the chamber. Kael followed reluctantly, muttering under their breath about "doom and glowing jewelry," but their steps were quick and steady.

The shadows beyond the corridor seemed heavier now, darker and more deliberate, as though they were watching, waiting. Anira felt the pull of the Rose steadying her steps, even as the weight of what lay ahead pressed against her like a storm on the horizon.

The journey wasn't over—not even close. And whatever awaited them in the darkness, they would face it together.

The narrow passage stretched out before them, jagged and dark, the crimson veins along the walls dimming with every step. The oppressive silence had returned, wrapping around them like a shroud, and each footfall echoed faintly, swallowed almost instantly by the shadows. The faint pulse of the Rose was the only sound Anira could hear clearly, its rhythm steady but subdued, like a whisper in the dark.

Ashric walked beside her, his sword still drawn, his sharp blue eyes scanning the corridor for any sign of movement. The tension in his posture was palpable, his every step deliberate, as though he expected the shadows themselves to attack. His presence was steadying, a reminder that no matter how suffocating the darkness became, she wasn't alone.

Kael followed a few steps behind, their knife clutched tightly in their hand. They muttered under their breath, their voice low and sharp, though it was unclear whether they were cursing the situation or trying to keep their own nerves in check.

"Do you feel that?" Anira asked softly, breaking the silence. Her voice sounded too loud in the stillness, and she winced at how it echoed faintly.

Ashric glanced at her, his brow furrowing. "Feel what?"

"The air," she said, her fingers brushing the Rose at her chest. "It's... heavier. Like it's pushing back."

Kael let out a nervous laugh, their footsteps faltering. "Great. Now even the air wants to kill us. Fantastic."

Ashric didn't respond immediately. His gaze lingered on Anira for a moment longer than necessary, searching her face as though trying to gauge her strength. Then he turned back to the corridor, his grip tightening on his sword. "Stay close," he said, his voice low but firm. "We're being watched."

The words sent a shiver down Anira's spine, and she glanced over her shoulder instinctively. The shadows at the edges of the passage seemed to twist and curl, though it was impossible to tell if they were truly moving or if her mind was playing tricks on her. She tightened her grip on her dagger, her knuckles white, and forced herself to keep walking.

As they moved deeper into the corridor, the passage began to widen, the walls pulling back to reveal another chamber. This one was smaller than the last, its ceiling lower and the crimson veins along the walls brighter, pulsing in slow, rhythmic waves. The air here was colder, biting at her skin, and the metallic tang in the back of her throat was sharper, almost choking.

At the center of the chamber stood an archway, carved from the same jagged black stone as the spire in the previous room. Its edges were lined with intricate markings that glowed faintly with a pale, silvery light, and the space within the arch shimmered like the surface of a still pond, rippling faintly as though touched by an invisible wind.

"What is that?" Kael asked, their voice tinged with equal parts awe and dread. "Is it… a portal?"

Anira stepped closer, the pull of the Rose growing stronger as she neared the archway.

The pendant at her chest burned hotter, its warmth spreading through her chest and down her arms, and she clenched her fists against the overwhelming sensation.

"It's connected to the Rose," she said, her voice trembling. "It's… calling me."

Ashric's hand shot out, gripping her arm before she could step any closer. His touch was firm but not harsh, his fingers steadying her as her legs threatened to give out beneath the weight of the pull. "Don't," he said sharply. "Not yet."

She turned to him, her breath catching at the intensity in his gaze. His blue eyes burned with a fierce determination, but there was something else there too—something softer, unspoken, that sent a jolt through her chest.

"I have to," she said softly, though her voice wavered. "It's why we're here."

"You don't even know what's on the other side," he said, his voice low but edged with frustration. "This thing—it's tied to the Rose, to whatever's hunting you. It's a trap."

"Maybe," she admitted, her fingers brushing the Rose. "But if it is, it's one I have to spring."

Ashric's jaw tightened, and for a moment, the mask of control he always wore slipped. His hand lingered on her arm, his grip firm but not unkind, and the tension in his expression softened into something raw, something vulnerable.

"You don't have to do this alone," he said, his voice barely above a whisper. "Let me go with you."

Her chest tightened at his words, and she hated how much she wanted to say yes. But the pull of the Rose was sharp and insistent, and she knew, with a terrible certainty, that this was her burden to bear.

"You can't," she said, her voice trembling. "It's pulling me—not you. If you follow, it might destroy you."

Ashric's grip on her arm tightened briefly, and she saw the storm in his eyes, the unspoken battle he was waging against himself. For a moment, it looked as though he might argue, might push past the boundaries she'd set. But then he stepped back, his hand falling to his side, and the storm in his expression hardened into resolve.

"Then I'll be here," he said, his voice steady but quiet. "If you come back broken, I'll pick up the pieces."

Anira swallowed hard, the weight of his words settling over her like a shroud. She nodded, her throat too tight to speak, and turned toward the archway. The shimmering surface within it rippled as she approached, and the warmth of the Rose burned hotter, urging her forward.

Kael's voice broke the tense silence, sharp and nervous. "This is a terrible idea, just so we're clear. But, uh, good luck."

Anira managed a faint smile, though it felt fragile. "Thanks."

She stepped toward the archway, the light rippling as her hand brushed its surface. The warmth of the Rose flared, and the world around her dissolved into a blinding flash of silver and crimson light. For a moment, there was nothing but the roar of her own heartbeat and the sensation of being pulled forward, deeper into the unknown.

The silence pressed in on Anira like a weight, heavy and suffocating. Her breath echoed faintly in the stillness, the sound swallowed almost immediately by the void around her. For a moment, she wasn't sure if she was standing, falling, or floating—only that the warmth of the Rose at her chest had flared to an unbearable heat before dimming into a faint, steady pulse.

Then, slowly, the world began to take shape.

Shadows flickered at the edges of her vision, curling and writhing like smoke. The air here was cold, biting and sharp, with a faint metallic tang that clung to her tongue. The ground beneath her feet was solid but uneven, the texture rough and jagged like raw stone. She couldn't see much beyond the faint glow of the Rose, its light casting long, shifting shadows that danced along the walls of what appeared to be another chamber—this one vast and cavernous, with a ceiling that disappeared into the darkness above.

Anira took a step forward, her boots scraping against the rough ground, and the sound echoed faintly in the stillness. The pull of the Rose was stronger now, sharper, guiding her deeper into the chamber, though the path ahead was shrouded in shadow.

"Where… am I?" she whispered, her voice trembling.

The answer came not in words but in the low, resonant hum that filled the space around her. It wasn't the same as the hum she'd felt in the previous chambers—this one was deeper, more deliberate, vibrating through her bones like the toll of a distant bell. The shadows shifted in response, curling inward as though drawn toward the Rose, and she felt a cold, creeping presence brush against her mind.

"You have come."

The voice was low and guttural, layered with echoes that seemed to come from every direction at once. It wasn't the voice of the figure from before—it was something older, darker, and infinitely more dangerous.

Anira's chest tightened, and she gripped the hilt of her dagger instinctively. "Who's there?" she demanded, her voice firmer than she felt.

The shadows coiled and twisted, drawing closer to the edges of the Rose's light, but they didn't attack. Instead, the presence grew stronger, pressing against her mind like the weight of an unseen hand.

"Bearer of the Rose," the voice said, its tone heavy with disdain. "Do you think you can wield its power without consequence? Do you think you can walk this path and remain unbroken?"

Anira's pulse quickened, but she forced herself to stand her ground, her fingers tightening around her dagger. "I didn't choose this," she said, her voice trembling but defiant. "But I'll finish it. Whatever this is—whatever you are—you won't stop me."

The presence recoiled slightly, the shadows curling away from the Rose's light as its warmth flared briefly. The hum deepened, resonating through the chamber, and the voice grew quieter, almost amused.

"Such resolve," it said. "But the Rose will demand more from you than you can give. You will see."

Before she could respond, the shadows withdrew, dissipating into the darkness, and the hum faded into silence. The pull of the Rose surged again, dragging her forward, and she took a shaky step into the darkness, the faint light guiding her path.

The silence was broken suddenly by the sound of her name, sharp and urgent. "Anira!"

She spun around, her breath catching as she saw Ashric standing at the edge of the chamber, his sword drawn and his expression hard. His sharp blue eyes scanned the space, locking onto her with a mixture of relief and frustration. Behind him, Kael stumbled into view, their knife clutched tightly in one hand.

"You made it through," she said, her voice trembling with relief.

Ashric stepped closer, his jaw tight. "Barely. That thing nearly closed behind us. What happened here?"

She shook her head, the weight of the encounter pressing heavily on her. "Something... spoke to me. It knows about the Rose. It said... it said it would break me."

Kael let out a nervous laugh, their voice sharp and brittle. "Well, that's not ominous at all."

Ashric ignored them, his gaze fixed on Anira. He stepped closer, his presence steadying her, though the tension in his expression hadn't lessened. "Whatever it is, it's wrong," he said, his voice low but fierce. "You're stronger than it thinks."

Anira opened her mouth to respond, but the words caught in her throat. The pull of the Rose surged again, and she stumbled forward, catching herself against Ashric's arm. His grip steadied her instantly, his hand firm but not harsh, and for a moment, their eyes met, the unspoken weight of everything between them hanging in the air.

"We're not done here," she said finally, her voice soft but resolute. "It's not over."

"No," Ashric agreed, his voice steady. "But we'll finish it—together."

Anira nodded, forcing herself to straighten as the pull of the Rose dragged her attention back to the path ahead. The faint glow of its light illuminated another narrow passage, its edges lined with jagged, pulsing veins of crimson.

"Let's move," she said, her voice carrying a quiet determination.

Ashric fell into step beside her, his sword at the ready, and Kael followed reluctantly, muttering under their breath about "cursed jewelry and doomed adventures." The shadows at the edges of the chamber seemed to watch them, waiting, but Anira kept her focus on the path ahead.

The journey was far from over, and the darkness would only grow deeper. But for now, the flicker of light from the Rose and the steady presence of her companions gave her the strength to keep moving forward.

The Echo of Shadows

The narrow passage pressed in around them, the jagged walls lined with veins of crimson that pulsed faintly, casting an eerie, shifting light across their faces. The air here was colder than before, sharp and biting, and every breath Anira took felt heavier, as though the very atmosphere conspired to drag her down. The hum that had filled the previous chambers was gone now, replaced by a brittle silence that seemed to stretch endlessly.

Ashric moved ahead of her, his sword drawn, his steps deliberate and quiet. He scanned the passage with sharp, unrelenting focus, his sharp blue eyes flicking to every shadow, every shift of light. Behind them, Kael followed, their knife in hand, though their grip was less steady, their shoulders tense with nervous energy.

The Rose's pull was relentless, dragging at Anira's chest with every step, its faint warmth a constant reminder of its presence. The pendant's light flickered in sync with the pulsing veins on the walls, as though it were responding to something deep within the passage. The sensation was both unsettling and undeniable, and Anira clenched her fists to keep herself grounded.

"Does anyone else feel like we're walking into a trap?" Kael asked, their voice breaking the silence. It was a nervous mutter, but it carried through the tight space like a shout. "Or is it just me?"

"It's not just you," Ashric said, his tone clipped. His gaze didn't leave the path ahead, his grip on his sword tightening. "But it's too late to turn back."

"Wonderful," Kael muttered, their voice dripping with sarcasm. "Love that for us."

Anira didn't respond. Her focus was locked on the pull of the Rose, its steady pulse a beacon that guided her deeper into the passage. The further they walked, the more she felt the weight of something vast and ancient pressing down on her, a presence that seemed to linger just beyond the edges of the light.

The passage began to widen, the walls pulling back to reveal a larger chamber. It was circular, the ground uneven and lined with jagged cracks that glowed faintly with crimson light. The ceiling stretched high above, disappearing into darkness, and the air was thick with a metallic tang that stung her throat.

At the center of the chamber stood an obelisk of black stone, its surface etched with intricate runes that pulsed with a pale, silvery light. The markings glimmered faintly, shifting and writhing as though alive, and the hum of energy emanating from it vibrated through the ground, making the cracks along the floor ripple like water.

"What is that?" Kael asked, their voice barely above a whisper. They took a hesitant step forward, their eyes fixed on the obelisk. "Because it looks like something we shouldn't be messing with."

"It's a ward," Ashric said, his voice low and grim. "Old magic. It's sealing something—or protecting it."

"Protecting it from what?" Anira asked, her gaze locked on the obelisk. The Rose burned hotter now, its pulse quickening as the pull dragged her closer to the center of the chamber. She took a step forward, her hand brushing the pendant as though to steady it.

Ashric's hand shot out, grabbing her arm before she could get too close. His grip was firm, his gaze sharp. "Be careful," he said, his voice edged with warning. "This thing wasn't meant to be touched."

She turned to him, her chest tightening at the intensity in his expression. His fingers lingered on her arm, grounding her, but there was something else in his gaze—something unspoken, filled with a mix of frustration and concern.

"I have to," she said softly, though her voice trembled. "The Rose—it's pulling me toward it."

"That doesn't mean you should follow blindly," he said, his tone hard but not unkind.

"Whatever's tied to that thing—it's dangerous."

Kael snorted from behind them, their voice sharp with sarcasm. "You mean like everything else we've run into so far? Dangerous is kind of our theme."

Ashric ignored them, his focus locked on Anira. His grip on her arm loosened slightly, though he didn't let go entirely. "If you're going to touch it, at least let me shield you."

"I don't need shielding," she said, though her voice lacked conviction.

His lips twitched into the faintest hint of a smirk, though his eyes stayed serious. "Humor me."

Anira nodded reluctantly, her heart pounding as she turned back to the obelisk. The energy emanating from it was stronger now, pulsing in waves that resonated through the chamber. The markings along its surface shifted and writhed, and the air around it seemed to shimmer with an unnatural light.

She stepped closer, her hand trembling as she reached out toward the smooth, dark surface. The moment her fingers brushed against it, a surge of energy shot through her, burning hot and searing cold all at once. She gasped, stumbling back as the Rose flared against her chest, its light bright and blinding.

The obelisk responded instantly. The markings along its surface blazed with silvery light, and a deep, resonant hum filled the chamber, vibrating through the ground and the walls. The cracks beneath their feet began to widen, glowing brighter as tendrils of shadow seeped out, curling and twisting toward the obelisk like living things.

"Anira!" Ashric shouted, his voice cutting through the chaos. He stepped forward, his sword raised, as the shadows surged toward them. "What did you do?"

"I don't know!" she shouted back, her voice trembling. The Rose burned hotter, its pulse quick and frantic, and she clutched it instinctively as the tendrils coiled closer.

The shadows moved faster now, their forms twisting and writhing as they reached for her, their edges jagged and sharp. Ashric stepped in front of her, his blade slashing through the nearest tendril, which dissolved into dark mist with a shriek. Kael darted to her side, their knife flashing as they cut down another.

"We need to get out of here!" Kael yelled, their voice high with panic. "This whole place is falling apart!"

The chamber shuddered violently, the walls groaning as chunks of stone fell from the ceiling. The light from the obelisk flared brighter, and the tendrils of shadow multiplied, their movements growing more deliberate, more coordinated.

Anira forced herself to move, her chest heaving as the pull of the Rose dragged her closer to the obelisk. She could feel its energy surging through her, overwhelming and unrelenting, but she couldn't stop. The tendrils lunged for her again, but Ashric was there, his blade a blur as he cut them down with brutal efficiency.

"Anira, now!" he shouted, his voice raw with urgency. "Do whatever you're going to do, or we're not getting out of here!"

She nodded, her hand trembling as she reached for the obelisk again. This time, she didn't hesitate. Her fingers closed around the smooth, dark surface, and the energy surged through her, blinding and all-consuming.

The world dissolved into light and shadow, and everything went silent.

The world around Anira flickered and shifted, the blinding light from the obelisk receding into a dim, surreal glow. The chamber she had been standing in moments before was gone, replaced by a vast expanse of shifting shadows and glimmering light. The ground beneath her feet was uneven, rippling like liquid stone, and the air was thick with a metallic tang that made her stomach churn.

The Rose at her chest burned steadily, its warmth a sharp contrast to the biting cold of this strange place. Its pulse matched the rhythm of her heartbeat, grounding her as the oppressive weight of the shadows pressed down on her from all sides.

"Anira!" Ashric's voice echoed sharply, cutting through the eerie silence. She turned, relief flooding her as she saw him just a few paces behind her. His sword was drawn, its blade glinting faintly in the shifting light, and his sharp blue eyes scanned the space around them, hard and calculating.

Kael stumbled into view a moment later, their expression pale and tight with panic. "Where—where are we?" they asked, their voice trembling. They clutched their knife tightly, their knuckles white as they glanced nervously at the shadows curling at the edges of the space.

"I don't know," Anira said, her voice trembling despite her best efforts to sound steady. She turned back toward the horizon—or what passed for it here. The shadows stretched endlessly, broken only by the faint glimmers of light that pulsed in slow, deliberate patterns. "But the Rose... it brought us here for a reason."

"That's comforting," Kael muttered, their voice dripping with sarcasm. "Dragged into another death trap because of your cursed jewelry. Love that for us."

Ashric ignored Kael's remark, his focus locked on Anira. "Do you feel it?" he asked, his voice low. "The presence—it's here."

Anira nodded, her chest tightening as she felt the weight of the presence that lingered just beyond the edges of the light. It was the same cold, creeping sensation that had pressed against her mind in the previous chamber, but here it was stronger, more deliberate. She could feel it watching them, its attention fixed on her like a predator stalking its prey.

"We're not alone," she said softly, her voice barely above a whisper.

The words had barely left her lips when the shadows began to move.

They surged inward, coiling and twisting like smoke caught in a violent wind. The glimmers of light scattered across the horizon flared brighter, illuminating the writhing mass of darkness as it closed in on them. The hum of the Rose deepened, vibrating through Anira's chest, and she felt the pull intensify, dragging her toward the heart of the shifting shadows.

Ashric stepped in front of her, his sword raised, his stance unyielding. "Stay close," he said, his voice sharp and commanding. "Whatever this thing is, it's not going to let us pass without a fight."

Kael let out a nervous laugh, their grip on their knife tightening. "Fight what, exactly? The shadows? They don't exactly have faces we can stab."

The shadows surged again, faster now, and from their depths emerged a figure—a towering, jagged silhouette wreathed in darkness. Its form was indistinct, its edges shifting and flickering, but its presence was suffocating, filling the space with a crushing weight that made it hard to breathe.

"Bearer of the Rose," the figure said, its voice low and resonant, vibrating through the air. "You have come far, but your journey ends here. The light you carry will falter. The shadows will claim you."

Anira's breath hitched, and she took an involuntary step back, her fingers clutching the Rose at her chest. The pendant flared in response, its light pushing back against the darkness, but the figure didn't retreat. Instead, it raised a hand—if the jagged, shifting appendage could be called that—and the shadows around it surged forward.

Ashric moved instantly, his sword cutting through the first wave of shadows with precise, brutal efficiency. The creatures dissolved into mist with piercing shrieks, but more took their place, their movements faster and more coordinated. Kael darted to Anira's side, their knife flashing as they slashed at one of the shadows that lunged toward her.

"Anira!" Ashric shouted, his voice sharp. "Whatever the Rose is pulling you toward, do it now!"

She nodded, her heart pounding as she took a shaky step forward. The pull of the Rose was overwhelming now, its heat spreading through her chest and into her limbs, guiding her toward the towering figure at the center of the shadows. The pendant's light flared brighter with each step, pushing back the darkness, but the figure didn't falter. Instead, it raised both hands, and the shadows around it surged upward, forming jagged, spiked shapes that arched toward the ceiling before slamming down into the ground with a deafening crash.

The impact sent shockwaves rippling through the ground, throwing Anira off balance. She stumbled, but Ashric was there in an instant, his hand steadying her as he pulled her back to her feet.

"Go," he said, his voice low but fierce. "I'll hold them off."

Her chest tightened at his words, and for a moment, she hesitated, her gaze locking onto his. The unspoken weight of everything between them hung heavy in the air, but there was no time to address it, no time to say what couldn't be said.

"Be careful," she said, her voice trembling.

He nodded, his grip on her arm lingering for just a moment before he turned back to the fight, his sword raised. "Always."

Kael shouted something unintelligible as another wave of shadows surged toward them, their movements faster and more violent. Anira forced herself to turn away, her focus locking onto the figure at the heart of the darkness. The Rose burned hotter, its light flaring in sync with the pulsing rhythm of the glimmers around them, and she knew this was it—the final step.

She moved forward, the shadows parting before her as the light of the Rose pushed them back. The towering figure didn't retreat, its burning silver eyes fixed on her with an intensity that sent a shiver through her. Its voice echoed again, colder now, laced with anger.

"The light will destroy you, vessel. The Rose demands all. You will not survive."

Anira clenched her fists, her resolve hardening. "Then let it take what it must," she said, her voice trembling but defiant. "I won't stop."

She reached out, her hand trembling as it closed around the jagged surface of the figure's shadowy form. The Rose flared brighter than ever, its light consuming everything, and the world around her erupted into chaos.

The explosion of light from the Rose spread outward, consuming the towering figure in a blaze of gold and crimson. Anira staggered back, her breath coming in sharp, shallow gasps as the energy surged through her. The shadows shrieked and writhed, their forms dissolving into wisps of mist that disappeared into the dark. For a fleeting moment, she thought they had won, that the power of the Rose had done what it was meant to do.

But then the light flickered—and faltered.

The shadows surged back, not as fragmented tendrils but as a solid, unified mass, coiling together until they formed a singular, monstrous shape. The towering figure emerged from the darkness once more, its form sharper and more defined, no longer a formless silhouette but something painfully familiar. Its body was cloaked in jagged armor of living shadow, its edges glinting with the same faint crimson that pulsed from the veins on the walls. Its face—pale and angular, with burning silver eyes—sent a shiver of recognition through Anira.

It wasn't just any shadow. It was hers.

"Impossible," she whispered, her voice trembling. "That's not—it can't be."

The figure's lips curled into a cruel smile, its voice low and mocking. "Why so surprised, vessel? Did you think the Rose's power came without a cost?"

Ashric stepped between them, his sword raised. "What are you?" he demanded, his voice hard and unyielding. "What have you done to her?"

The shadow's smile widened, and it tilted its head, its burning gaze fixed on Anira. "I am what she was, what she could still become," it said. "I am the reflection the Rose does not show. Every choice, every fear, every failure—given form."

Anira's chest tightened as the weight of its words settled over her. The Rose pulsed against her chest, its warmth flickering erratically, and she clutched it tightly, as though holding it could steady her. "You're lying," she said, though her voice wavered. "This is just another trick."

The shadow laughed, a sound that echoed through the chamber like shattering glass. "Am I? The Rose feeds on more than light. It takes what you are, what you could be, and turns it into fuel. You thought you were its bearer, but you are its source."

Ashric's gaze flicked to Anira, his expression hard but edged with concern. "Don't listen to it," he said firmly. "Whatever this thing is, it's trying to break you."

"I don't need to break her," the shadow said, its voice sharp with amusement. "She's already fractured. All I have to do is wait."

Anira's breath hitched, her chest tight as the shadows around the figure began to writhe again, stretching outward in jagged arcs. The ground beneath her feet shuddered, and the Rose flared once more, its light clashing with the crimson glow that pulsed through the chamber. The figure stepped closer, its movements slow and deliberate, and the air grew colder, heavier, until it felt as though the very space around them was collapsing.

"I'm not fractured," Anira said, her voice trembling but fierce. She stepped forward, clutching the Rose as its light flared brighter, pushing back against the oppressive darkness. "And you don't get to decide who I become."

The figure paused, its silver eyes narrowing. For the first time, its smile faltered, replaced by something harder, more calculating. "We shall see," it said softly, its voice low and resonant. "The light burns bright, but the shadows never fade."

With a sudden, violent motion, the figure raised its hand, and the shadows surged forward in a wave, crashing toward Anira and her companions like a tidal force. Ashric moved instantly, his sword flashing as he cut through the first tendrils, his movements sharp and precise. Kael shouted something unintelligible as they lunged to Anira's side, their knife slashing at the writhing shadows.

The Rose burned hotter, its light flaring in a desperate attempt to hold the darkness at bay. Anira clenched her fists, her breath coming in sharp gasps as the weight of the energy coursing through her threatened to overwhelm her. She could feel the shadow's presence pressing against her mind, cold and relentless, and for a moment, she wavered.

Then Ashric's voice cut through the chaos, sharp and commanding. "Anira! Focus! You're stronger than it is—don't let it take you!"

She met his gaze, her chest tightening at the intensity in his eyes. His expression was fierce, unyielding, but there was something else there too—something raw and unspoken, filled with a quiet urgency that steadied her in a way she couldn't explain.

"I won't," she said, her voice trembling but resolute. "Not now. Not ever."

She raised the Rose, its light flaring brighter than before, and the shadows recoiled, their jagged forms dissolving into mist. The figure let out a low growl, its silver eyes burning with anger, and it stepped back, its form flickering as though struggling to hold its shape.

"This isn't over, vessel," it said, its voice low and dangerous. "You can't outrun the shadow within. You can only delay the inevitable."

With that, the figure dissolved into the darkness, its form scattering into the shadows that lingered at the edges of the chamber. The oppressive weight in the air lifted slightly, though the tension remained, and Anira's chest heaved as she lowered the Rose, its light dimming to a faint, steady glow.

Ashric stepped to her side, his sword still in hand, his gaze scanning the chamber for any sign of movement. "Are you alright?" he asked, his voice low but filled with concern.

Anira nodded, though her hands trembled as she clutched the Rose. "I'm fine," she said softly. "But it's not gone. Not really."

Kael let out a shaky laugh, their voice tinged with nervous energy. "Nothing ever is with us, is it?"

Ashric's gaze lingered on Anira for a moment longer before he turned back to the path ahead. "Then we keep moving," he said, his tone sharp. "Whatever's waiting for us, we face it together."

Anira nodded, her resolve hardening as she followed him. The shadows still lingered, watching and waiting, but for now, the path was clear.

And for the first time, she felt the faintest flicker of hope that they might survive what lay ahead—if only they could hold onto the light.

The chamber remained unnervingly still after the shadow's retreat, the faint echoes of its mocking voice lingering in the air like a distant storm. The crimson veins along the walls dimmed, pulsing faintly, as though the cavern itself had retreated into uneasy silence. Anira's chest rose and fell in sharp, uneven breaths, her grip tight on the Rose as its faint warmth began to steady her.

Ashric took a step forward, his sharp blue eyes scanning the chamber for any sign of lingering danger. His sword was still drawn, its blade reflecting the faint, flickering light, and his posture remained tense, coiled like a spring ready to snap.

Kael broke the silence, their voice trembling but filled with an edge of sharp sarcasm. "So... that thing was you? Or, like, shadow-you? Because I've got to say, Anira, that was unsettling even for us."

Anira forced a shaky breath, her lips pressing into a thin line as she turned to face them. "It wasn't me," she said, though her voice wavered. "It was—something else. Something the Rose brought out."

"Brought out?" Kael raised an eyebrow, their knife still gripped tightly in their hand. "That doesn't exactly fill me with confidence. What else is the Rose hiding?"

Ashric cut them off with a sharp look, his voice calm but firm. "Whatever it was, it's gone for now. And if it comes back, we'll deal with it. Right now, we need to keep moving."

Anira nodded, though the shadow's words echoed in her mind, each one a weight pressing against her resolve: The light burns bright, but the shadows never fade. She couldn't shake the feeling that it wasn't entirely wrong. The Rose was changing her, pulling her toward something she couldn't fully understand—and something she wasn't sure she could control.

The three of them moved toward the far end of the chamber, where a narrow passage stretched into the shadows. The path ahead was darker than before, the faint light from the veins barely enough to illuminate the jagged ground beneath their feet. The air grew colder as they walked, carrying with it the faint metallic tang that clung to the back of Anira's throat.

Ashric walked beside her, his presence a steadying weight that helped her push back the creeping doubt. He didn't say anything, but the occasional glance in her direction spoke volumes. His sharp gaze was always searching, always assessing, and she knew he was watching for any sign that the shadow's influence might still linger.

Kael, however, had no such reservations about speaking. "This place just keeps getting worse," they muttered, their voice echoing faintly in the tight space. "First the living shadows, then the creepy light show, and now we're heading into a tunnel that might as well have a giant 'abandon all hope' sign above it."

"Keep your voice down," Ashric said sharply, his tone low. "We don't know what's ahead."

Kael rolled their eyes but fell silent, their grip on their knife tightening as they followed closely behind. The passage wound deeper into the cavern, its walls closing in until they were forced to walk in single file. The faint glow of the veins flickered with every step, casting shifting shadows that seemed to twist and curl at the edges of Anira's vision.

The Rose pulsed steadily against her chest, its warmth a small comfort in the suffocating darkness. But the pull had shifted—it was no longer the sharp, insistent force that had dragged her into the previous chambers. Now, it was subtle, almost hesitant, as though it were unsure of the path ahead.

"I don't like this," she murmured, her voice barely above a whisper. "It feels… different."

Ashric glanced back at her, his expression hard. "Different how?"

"The pull," she said, her fingers brushing against the pendant. "It's not as strong. It's like it's waiting for something."

Kael let out a nervous laugh. "Waiting for what? Because I don't think I can handle another surprise shadow-demon."

Anira didn't respond. The weight of the Rose pressed against her chest, its rhythm steady but muted, and the air around her felt heavier with every step. She could feel the tension building, a quiet hum beneath the surface that made her skin crawl.

The passage opened suddenly into another chamber, this one smaller and darker than the last. The air here was colder, biting against her skin, and the faint glow of the veins was dim and uneven. At the center of the chamber stood another structure—this one a circular platform carved from black stone, its surface etched with intricate runes that pulsed faintly with silvery light.

Anira stepped forward, her breath catching as the pull of the Rose intensified again, dragging her toward the platform. The warmth of the pendant flared against her chest, and the faint hum in the air deepened into a low, resonant vibration.

Ashric grabbed her arm, his grip firm but not harsh. "Wait," he said, his voice sharp. "This feels wrong."

"It's pulling me," she said, her voice trembling. "This is where it's been leading us."

"That doesn't mean it's safe," he said, his eyes narrowing. "We don't know what this thing does—or what it wants."

Kael stayed near the edge of the chamber, their gaze darting nervously between the platform and the shadows that clung to the walls. "I've got a bad feeling about this," they muttered. "Like, worse than usual."

Anira turned to Ashric, her chest tight as the pull of the Rose grew stronger, sharper. "I have to," she said, her voice barely above a whisper. "If I don't, we'll never get out of here."

His jaw tightened, and for a moment, she thought he might argue. But then he nodded, his grip on her arm loosening. "Just... be careful."

She stepped toward the platform, her heart pounding as the light from the Rose flared brighter, illuminating the runes that covered the stone. The hum deepened, vibrating through the air, and she could feel the energy radiating from the structure, powerful and ancient.

The moment her foot touched the platform, the runes erupted into light, and the ground beneath her shuddered violently. The chamber filled with a deafening roar as the shadows surged forward, coiling and twisting like a living storm.

And from the center of the platform, something began to emerge.

The roar was deafening, a sound that seemed to erupt not just from the chamber but from within the very marrow of Anira's bones. The platform beneath her feet vibrated violently, its surface trembling as if alive. The runes carved into the black stone blazed with an unearthly silver light, sharp and cold like the reflection of a blade under the moon. Every edge, every curve, every line of the ancient etchings seemed to writhe, as though rejecting the stillness of stone.

Anira steadied herself, her legs shaking, her boots slipping against the slick surface of the platform. The warmth of the Rose burned against her chest, its pulse hammering faster now, each beat resonating with the rhythmic tremor of the runes. She clutched the pendant tightly, as though anchoring herself to its power could stave off the oppressive force pressing against her from all sides.

The shadows around the chamber surged and coiled, thickening like smoke caught in an unseen wind. They licked at the edges of the platform, their jagged tendrils reaching with a hunger that seemed almost sentient. The light from the runes pushed back against them, casting harsh, shifting patterns against the chamber walls, but it was a tenuous fight, the darkness pressing harder with each passing moment.

From the center of the platform, the stone cracked with a sharp, echoing sound. A thin fissure ran along its surface, jagged and raw, splitting the delicate patterns of the runes. From within the fissure came a faint glow—dim at first, a pale, flickering light that pulsed like a heartbeat. It grew steadily, its glow climbing up through the stone, filling the air with a warmth that was both inviting and suffocating.

Ashric shouted something, his voice sharp and commanding, but the roar of the platform swallowed his words. He was moving, his sword drawn and his body tense, his sharp blue eyes fixed on the shadows surging toward the platform's edge. His blade caught the light, flashing in arcs as he slashed at the encroaching tendrils, each strike precise and deliberate. The mist-like shadows recoiled with every blow, hissing and writhing, but they did not retreat.

Kael, crouched near the chamber's entrance, looked pale and wide-eyed, their knife gripped tightly in their trembling hands. They muttered curses under their breath, their eyes darting between the shadows and Anira. "What the hell is that thing?" they shouted, though their voice cracked with barely masked panic.

Anira couldn't answer. The pull of the Rose was overwhelming now, dragging her closer to the fissure, its warmth turning to heat, and then to fire. The light spilling from the crack wasn't silver like the runes—it was red, deep and molten, like the last embers of a dying sun. It bled upward, spilling out in uneven, flickering waves that cast long, jagged shadows against the chamber walls.

And then the light shifted.

It was subtle at first—a flicker, a faint distortion in the glow—but it grew quickly, warping and twisting until the light seemed to take on a shape. It rose from the fissure, unfolding like smoke but denser, heavier. The shape stretched upward, its form jagged and unnatural, its edges shifting as though it couldn't quite hold itself together. It towered over the platform, its surface glinting faintly in the crimson light, and its eyes—if they could be called eyes—burned like embers, sharp and unrelenting.

It wasn't a shadow. It wasn't light. It was something caught between the two, something ancient and angry, something that radiated power so raw and unrestrained that Anira felt the breath catch in her throat.

The creature—or being—turned its gaze on her, its presence pressing against her like a physical weight. Its voice, when it spoke, was a low, guttural rumble, resonating through the chamber with a force that made her knees tremble.

"Bearer of the Rose," it said, its tone heavy and slow, like the grinding of stone against stone. "You have awakened what should have remained buried. Do you understand what you have done?"

Anira forced herself to stand tall, though her legs felt weak beneath her. Her fingers tightened around the Rose, the pendant flaring in response, its light pushing back against the creature's oppressive presence. "I don't know what I've done," she said, her voice trembling but resolute. "But I know it wasn't meant to end here. You're what's been waiting for me, aren't you?"

The creature's form twisted, its edges flickering as though caught in an unseen wind. Its burning gaze fixed on her, unyielding. "I am not your end, bearer. I am your mirror."

The words sent a jolt through her, cold and sharp, and for a moment, the warmth of the Rose felt distant, its light dimming slightly. "What does that mean?" she demanded, her voice rising. "What are you?"

The creature leaned closer, its form towering over her, and the light of the runes seemed to flicker and dim in its shadow. "You carry the light, but you cannot escape the shadow. One cannot exist without the other. You are both—and neither."

Anira's breath caught, her mind racing as the creature's words sank in. The shadows surged again, coiling around the platform's edge, their jagged tendrils snapping like whips. Ashric lunged forward, his blade flashing as he cut through the darkness, his movements sharp and relentless.

"Anira!" he shouted, his voice raw with urgency. "Whatever this is, end it! Now!"

The Rose pulsed sharply, its light flaring brighter than before, and Anira felt its warmth flood her chest, steadying her. She turned back to the creature, her grip tightening on the pendant.

"I don't care what you are," she said, her voice trembling but fierce. "You're not stopping me."

The creature's form flickered, its edges curling inward, and for the briefest moment, it smiled—a sharp, jagged expression that sent a shiver down her spine. "We shall see," it said softly.

And then the shadows surged forward, and the platform erupted in light.

The explosion of light was blinding, a force that surged from the Rose and the platform like a storm unleashed from the heavens. The chamber trembled violently, the ground beneath Anira's feet shuddering with enough force to send cracks splintering outward from the platform's base. The runes on the stone blazed with fierce, silvery light, their intricate patterns glowing so brightly they etched themselves into her vision.

The creature reeled back, its jagged form flickering and writhing as the light consumed the edges of its shadow. It let out a guttural roar, a sound that reverberated through the chamber like the toll of a monstrous bell. The shadows that had coiled at the edge of the platform surged upward, their tendrils lashing out in desperation, but the Rose's light flared brighter, forcing them to recoil and dissipate into mist.

Anira stood her ground, her chest heaving as the energy coursing through her intensified. The Rose burned hotter than ever, its warmth spreading through her veins like molten fire, and she could feel its power building, growing to something vast and uncontrollable. The air around her seemed to shimmer, heavy with heat and light, and every breath tasted of metal and ash.

"Anira!" Ashric's voice cut through the chaos, sharp and commanding. She turned her head, her vision blurring from the sheer intensity of the light. He was fighting his way toward her, his sword a blur of motion as he cut down the remaining shadows that darted toward the platform. His blue eyes locked onto hers, fierce and unrelenting, and for a moment, their gazes held.

"Don't stop!" he shouted, his voice raw. "You're winning—don't let it push you back!"

The creature roared again, its form flickering as the Rose's light burned away at its edges. Its crimson gaze snapped back to Anira, filled with a rage so palpable it made her chest tighten. "You think you understand the power you wield?" it hissed, its voice layered with echoes. "You think the light will save you? It will consume you just as surely as I would."

Anira gritted her teeth, her hands trembling as she tightened her grip on the Rose. Its light flared again, brighter and more intense, and she felt the pull of its energy reaching into the very core of her being. She could feel the weight of the creature's words pressing against her mind, heavy and cold, but she refused to falter.

"This isn't your world anymore," she said, her voice trembling but resolute. "It's mine. And I won't let you take it."

The creature lunged forward, its jagged form twisting and elongating, but the Rose responded before Anira could even move. Its light surged outward in a violent wave, slamming into the creature with a force that sent it sprawling backward. The shadows that clung to its form peeled away, disintegrating into the air like ash scattered by the wind.

The platform shuddered beneath Anira's feet, its runes blazing so brightly now that the light seemed to cut through the very fabric of the shadows in the chamber. The fissure at the center of the platform widened, glowing with an intense, molten red that pulsed in rhythm with the Rose. The air around her grew heavier, the heat suffocating, and she stumbled slightly, her knees buckling as the energy threatened to overwhelm her.

"Anira, move!" Kael shouted from somewhere behind her, their voice high and frantic. "That thing—whatever it is—it's not going to stop!"

She forced herself to steady, her breath ragged as she faced the creature again. Its form was barely holding together now, its jagged edges flickering and fading with each pulse of the Rose's light. But its eyes remained sharp, burning with a fierce, unrelenting hatred.

"You will burn with it, bearer," it snarled, its voice dripping with venom. "The light you trust will be your undoing."

"Not today," Anira said, her voice low but filled with a quiet determination.

She raised the Rose, its light flaring one final time, and the energy within it surged outward in a blinding, all-encompassing wave. The light tore through the chamber, consuming the creature and the shadows with a force that felt like the very essence of the sun unleashed. The creature let out a final, agonized roar as its form dissolved, scattering into the light and leaving nothing behind but the faint echo of its voice.

The chamber fell silent.

The light from the Rose dimmed slowly, its warmth receding as the energy faded, leaving only the faint, steady pulse of its glow. Anira sank to her knees, her chest heaving as exhaustion washed over her. The platform beneath her feet was cracked and scorched, its runes now faint and lifeless, and the oppressive weight of the shadows had vanished, leaving the air feeling strangely empty.

Ashric was at her side in an instant, his sword sheathed as he knelt beside her. His hands were steady as he gripped her shoulders, his sharp blue eyes scanning her face with an intensity that made her heart ache.

"Are you alright?" he asked, his voice low but filled with concern.

She nodded weakly, her breath still shaky. "I... think so."

Kael stumbled toward them, their expression pale and wide-eyed. "What the hell just happened?" they asked, their voice cracking. "Did we win? Is it over?"

Anira looked down at the Rose, its faint glow casting soft shadows across her hands. Its pull was gone now, replaced by a quiet, subdued warmth that felt almost reassuring. She glanced back at the chamber, its once-menacing shadows now replaced by a stillness that felt both alien and comforting.

"I think we did," she said softly, though her voice wavered. "At least for now."

Ashric's gaze lingered on her, his expression hard to read, but he didn't press her. Instead, he helped her to her feet, his grip steady as she swayed slightly. "Let's get out of here," he said firmly. "Before something else decides to wake up."

Anira nodded, her resolve steadying as she turned toward the faint light of the passage ahead. The journey wasn't over—not yet. But for the first time, the weight of the shadows no longer felt insurmountable. They had survived, and for now, that was enough.

The passage stretched ahead like the throat of some great beast, its jagged walls alive with faint veins of crimson light that pulsed slowly, as if measuring time by the beating of a monstrous heart. Anira's footsteps were uneven, her legs heavy with exhaustion, but the glow of the Rose, now subdued and steady, kept her moving forward. The air in the corridor was cool, the oppressive heat of the platform chamber now replaced by a brittle stillness that carried its own kind of weight.

Ashric walked beside her, his sword still in hand, his sharp blue eyes scanning every shadow for movement. His steps were deliberate, steady, and unrelenting, but Anira could see the tension in his posture, the way his free hand flexed and relaxed as though itching to grab her arm and hold her back.

Behind them, Kael trailed, their knife still clutched tightly, though their face was pale and their movements slower than usual. "Tell me we're actually getting closer to the end of this," they muttered, their voice rough. "Because I swear, if this corridor opens up into another 'surprise, it's death' room, I'm going to lose it."

Ashric shot a glance over his shoulder, his expression grim. "Keep your voice down," he said. "Whatever's left here doesn't need help finding us."

Kael let out a faint, humorless laugh but said nothing more.

Anira's chest tightened as she felt the pull of the Rose begin to shift again—not sharp or overwhelming, but subtle, like a faint whisper in the back of her mind. It wasn't dragging her forward this time; instead, it seemed to be... guiding her, nudging her steps as though urging her to move in a certain direction. She glanced down at the pendant, its glow faint but warm, and frowned.

"It's changing," she murmured, her voice barely above a whisper.

Ashric's gaze flicked to her. "What is?"

"The Rose," she said, her fingers brushing against the pendant. "It's not pulling me the way it was before. It's... quieter."

"Quieter is good," Kael muttered, though their voice was laced with doubt. "Quieter means it's not about to explode or summon another one of those shadow things."

"Or it's waiting for something worse," Ashric said bluntly, his grip tightening on his sword.

Anira glanced at him, her heart sinking at the hard edge in his tone. He wasn't wrong—nothing about this journey had suggested the Rose would lead them anywhere but deeper into danger. And yet, for the first time since they had entered this forsaken place, she felt the faintest flicker of something she hadn't dared to hope for: clarity.

The corridor began to widen, its jagged walls giving way to smooth, polished stone that gleamed faintly in the dim light. The air here was colder, sharper, and the metallic tang that had clung to the back of her throat grew stronger, filling her mouth with a taste like rusted iron. Ahead, the faint outline of an archway took shape, its edges lined with delicate, swirling patterns that seemed to shift and ripple like water.

The Rose's warmth flared slightly, its pulse quickening as they drew closer. Anira's steps slowed, her heart hammering in her chest as a low, resonant hum filled the air. It wasn't the oppressive hum of the earlier chambers—this was softer, almost melodic, like a song sung from a great distance.

"Do you hear that?" she asked, her voice trembling.

Ashric nodded, his expression hardening. "I hear it."

Kael frowned, their eyes narrowing as they stepped closer to the archway. "It's like... singing," they said slowly. "But not in a good way. Like the kind of singing that makes your skin crawl."

The hum deepened as they passed beneath the archway, spilling into a vast, circular chamber. The ceiling was high and vaulted, disappearing into darkness, while the walls were lined with intricate carvings that glowed faintly with shifting light. At the center of the room stood a pedestal, carved from the same dark stone as the platform in the previous chamber. It was simple, unadorned, and upon it rested a single object.

It was a mirror.

The surface of the mirror shimmered like liquid silver, its edges framed by twisting patterns of light and shadow that seemed to pulse in time with the hum that filled the chamber. The air around it felt heavier, thicker, and Anira's breath caught in her throat as the Rose's warmth flared again, dragging her attention to the object with an intensity that made her head spin.

"What is that?" Kael asked, their voice a mixture of awe and dread. "It looks like..."

"A gateway," Ashric said, his tone sharp. He stepped forward, his sword raised as he scanned the room for any sign of movement. "Or a trap."

Anira didn't respond. She couldn't. Her focus was locked on the mirror, its surface shifting and rippling as though alive. The Rose burned hotter, its pulse hammering against her chest, and she felt its pull intensify, not dragging her forward this time but urging her to look closer.

"Anira," Ashric said, his voice cutting through the haze. "Don't—"

"It's calling me," she said softly, her voice trembling. She took a step forward, her hand brushing the Rose as though to steady herself. "I think... I think this is what it's been leading me to."

Ashric moved to block her, his expression hard. "We don't know what that thing does," he said sharply. "For all we know, it's another trap."

"It's not a trap," Anira said, though her voice wavered. "It's something else. Something... important."

Kael let out a nervous laugh, their eyes darting between Anira and the mirror. "Important like what? Because last time the Rose wanted something, it nearly killed all of us."

Anira ignored them, her focus locked on the mirror as she stepped closer. The hum deepened, resonating through her chest, and the surface of the mirror rippled like water touched by a breeze. Her reflection wavered, shifting and distorting, and for a moment, she thought she saw something else—something dark and jagged, with burning silver eyes.

She froze, her breath catching as the image flickered and faded. The Rose's warmth flared again, its pulse steadying her, and she took another step forward.

"Anira," Ashric said, his voice low and urgent. "Don't do this."

She glanced back at him, her chest tightening at the storm in his eyes. For a moment, she hesitated, the weight of his gaze pulling at her, grounding her. But the pull of the Rose was stronger, its presence sharp and insistent, and she knew there was no turning back.

"I have to," she said softly, her voice trembling. "It's the only way forward."

With that, she reached out, her fingers brushing against the shimmering surface of the mirror.

The world dissolved into light and shadow.

The moment Anira's fingers touched the shimmering surface of the mirror, the chamber exploded in light. It surged outward like a tidal wave, golden and crimson threads twisting together in a storm of blinding intensity. Ashric threw his arm in front of his face, shielding his eyes from the searing brilliance, but his body instinctively moved toward her. Always toward her.

The light pulsed and swirled around Anira, her silhouette at its center. She stood motionless, her hand still pressed against the mirror, her head tilted upward as if caught in a trance. The Rose around her neck glowed fiercely, its light pulsing in perfect harmony with the mirror's, the rhythm so precise it was as though they were one.

Ashric's heart clenched at the sight, the raw intensity of her vulnerability pulling him forward even as the oppressive force of the light pushed him back. His sword was useless here—he knew that—but the weight of it in his hand steadied him. It gave him a focus, something to anchor him against the chaos that raged through the chamber.

"Anira!" he shouted, his voice raw. The sound was swallowed by the roaring light, but he pushed forward anyway, every step a fight against the invisible barrier that seemed determined to keep him away from her.

Kael's voice rang out behind him, sharp and panicked. "Ashric, don't! You'll get yourself killed!"

He ignored them, his jaw tightening as he forced his way closer to the platform where Anira stood. His movements were deliberate, each step driven by a force greater than duty, though he would never admit it to anyone—not even himself. Protecting her was his mission, his oath, but it had become more than that. It was a need that had burrowed deep into his bones, a quiet but undeniable truth that he couldn't shake no matter how hard he tried.

Ashric reached the base of the platform, his boots skidding against the cracked stone as the light intensified, the heat rolling over him in waves. Anira stood just ahead of him, her face serene despite the chaos swirling around her. The Rose's glow bathed her in an otherworldly light, casting delicate shadows across her features, and for a fleeting moment, he was struck by how impossibly fragile she looked.

And yet, she was anything but fragile.

She was strong in ways he could never be, carrying the weight of the Rose and the darkness it had awakened without faltering. She bore it with a quiet, unyielding determination that both awed and infuriated him. She didn't need his protection—she had proven that time and time again—but he would give it to her anyway. Because if he didn't, who would?

He stepped closer, his free hand reaching out as though to steady her, though he knew the gesture was futile. The light around her was unrelenting, its energy surging in waves that pushed him back even as he fought to stay upright. He could feel the heat on his skin, the hum of power vibrating through his chest, but none of it mattered. All that mattered was her.

"Anira," he said, his voice low and strained. "You don't have to do this alone."

Her head turned slightly, her eyes meeting his for the briefest moment. Her gaze was distant, as though she were looking through him rather than at him, but the faint flicker of recognition in her expression was enough to make his chest tighten. She didn't speak, didn't move, but he could see the tension in her posture, the faint trembling of her hand as it pressed against the mirror's surface.

And he knew, in that moment, that she was afraid.

The realization hit him like a blow, sharper than any blade. She had carried so much—too much—and she had done it all without complaint, without asking for help. But now, in the midst of this impossible storm of light and shadow, her strength was faltering.

Ashric's grip on his sword tightened, his knuckles white. He wanted to pull her away, to drag her back to safety, to tell her that she didn't have to face this alone. But he couldn't. This was her burden, her fight, and all he could do was stand beside her, ready to catch her if she fell.

The light around Anira flared again, brighter and more intense, and Ashric instinctively raised his sword, as though he could shield her from whatever force the mirror was unleashing. The heat was unbearable now, searing against his skin, but he didn't move. His entire body ached with the effort of staying upright, but the thought of stepping back—of leaving her unprotected—was unthinkable.

He clenched his jaw, his gaze locked on her as the light reached a blinding crescendo. "You're stronger than this," he murmured, his voice low but fierce, meant only for her. "You always have been."

Kael shouted something from the far side of the chamber, their voice muffled by the roaring light, but Ashric didn't turn. His focus was entirely on Anira, on the faint tremor in her frame, on the way the Rose's glow pulsed faster and faster, as though building toward something.

And then, without warning, the light collapsed inward, folding in on itself with a deafening roar. The chamber plunged into darkness, the sudden absence of light leaving Ashric momentarily blind. His heart pounded as he staggered forward, his arms outstretched, searching for her in the suffocating black.

"Anira!" he called, his voice hoarse.

For a moment, there was no response, just the deafening silence of the void. Then, faint and trembling, he heard her voice.

"Ashric... I'm here."

Relief surged through him, sharp and overwhelming, and he moved toward the sound of her voice. When his vision finally adjusted, he saw her slumped on the platform, her hand still clutching the Rose, its faint glow casting a soft, golden light across her face. She looked exhausted, her breathing shallow, but she was alive.

Ashric dropped to his knees beside her, his sword clattering to the ground as he reached for her. His hands hovered for a moment, unsure, before finally settling on her shoulders, steadying her. "You're alright," he said softly, his voice rough with emotion. "You're alright."

Anira looked up at him, her eyes filled with exhaustion but also something softer, something that made his chest tighten. "Thank you," she whispered, her voice barely audible.

He swallowed hard, his grip on her shoulders tightening slightly. "I'm not going anywhere," he said quietly. And he meant it. Whatever came next, whatever trials they faced, he would be there—because protecting her was more than duty now. It was everything.

The oppressive stillness of the chamber lingered as Ashric crouched beside Anira, his hand steady on her shoulder. Her breathing was shallow, but the faint rise and fall of her chest assured him she was alive. The Rose, cradled in her trembling hands, still glowed softly, its light fragile yet determined. The mirror, now dim and inert, reflected only the faint flickers of the crimson veins along the walls.

Kael stumbled closer, their knife clinking against their belt as they leaned against the jagged edge of the platform. Their face was pale, their expression wide-eyed and frantic. "What... what just happened?" they asked, their voice shaky. "Because from where I'm standing, that looked like she was about to blow herself to pieces."

Ashric shot them a sharp look, his jaw tightening. "She didn't."

Kael raised their hands in mock surrender, their fingers trembling. "Yeah, I see that now, Captain Obvious. But the room's still here, and she's... still glowing." Their gaze flicked to the Rose, wariness written across their face. "So, what did it do? Did it... finish?"

Anira stirred, her head tilting slightly toward Ashric. Her voice was faint, barely a whisper, but it carried the weight of something profound. "It wasn't just a gateway," she said. "It was... showing me something."

Ashric leaned closer, his expression hard but attentive. "Showing you what?"

Anira's eyes flickered open, the golden light of the Rose reflected in their depths. "A memory," she said, her voice trembling. "Not mine. It was the Rose's. It... remembers everything."

Kael groaned, dragging a hand down their face. "Fantastic. The creepy glowing thing has memories now. Because that's exactly what we needed."

Anira ignored the comment, her gaze distant as she clutched the pendant tightly.

"It wasn't just memories. It was a warning. A way forward... and a cost."

Ashric's frown deepened, and he shifted slightly to block her from Kael's nervous pacing. "What cost?" he asked, his tone low and firm.

Her fingers tightened around the Rose, and she closed her eyes, her breath hitching. "The shadows aren't just following us," she said, her voice barely above a whisper. "They're feeding. Growing stronger. The further we go, the more they take from the Rose—and from me."

Ashric's grip on her shoulder tightened slightly, his chest tightening at the admission. He had suspected the toll the Rose was taking on her, but hearing it confirmed was like a blade to the gut. "Then we stop them," he said, his voice hard with resolve. "We find where they're coming from, and we end it."

"It's not that simple," Anira said, her gaze snapping to his. There was a sharpness in her voice, but it was tinged with fear. "The Rose can't hold them forever. It's why they're chasing us—because the closer we get to the source, the weaker the barrier becomes."

Kael let out a low whistle, their nervous energy spilling over into frantic movement. "So, let me get this straight. The shadow-things are feeding on us, the Rose is the only thing keeping them at bay, and the thing keeping them at bay is also running out of steam? That about sum it up?"

"Roughly," Anira said, her voice tight.

Kael muttered a string of curses under their breath before slumping against the wall. "Great. Just great. So, what now? We let the Rose burn itself out and hope for the best?"

"No," Ashric said sharply. His voice cut through the tension like a blade, his expression hard and unyielding. He turned to Anira, his gaze steady. "What did the memory show you? What's the way forward?"

Anira hesitated, her lips pressing into a thin line. The warmth of the Rose flared faintly, as if urging her to speak, and she finally exhaled. "There's a place," she said. "A final chamber, deeper than this one. The source of the shadows is there, but so is... something else."

"What else?" Ashric pressed.

Her gaze dropped to the Rose, its soft glow casting shifting patterns across her hands. "A way to stop them," she said. "But it requires..."

She trailed off, her throat tightening as the weight of the realization settled over her. She looked up at Ashric, her voice barely audible. "It requires a sacrifice."

Ashric's chest tightened, but his expression didn't waver. "What kind of sacrifice?"

Anira hesitated, her eyes searching his for something she couldn't name. "It didn't show me everything," she admitted. "But I felt it. Whatever's waiting for us there, it won't let us leave unchanged."

Kael let out a bitter laugh, their voice sharp with frustration. "Unchanged? We've been changed six times over since we got here! What's one more?"

Ashric ignored them, his focus locked on Anira. "If that's what it takes, we'll face it," he said firmly. "But you're not doing it alone."

Her breath hitched at his words, and for a moment, she couldn't look away from him. The raw intensity in his gaze was unrelenting, but there was something else there too—something unspoken, hidden behind the sharp lines of his expression. It was a promise, fierce and unwavering, and it sent a shiver through her.

"You don't have to protect me," she said softly, though her voice wavered.

"I know," Ashric said simply. "But I will anyway."

Anira swallowed hard, her fingers brushing against the Rose as its light flared again, steadier now. The path ahead was dark and uncertain, but for the first time, she felt the faintest flicker of hope. They weren't finished yet—not by a long shot—but they were still standing. Together.

"Then let's keep moving," she said, her voice stronger now.

Ashric nodded, his hand falling to the hilt of his sword as he turned toward the passage leading out of the chamber. Kael muttered another curse but followed, their knife still clutched tightly. Anira took a steadying breath, the warmth of the Rose grounding her, and stepped forward into the shadows, her companions at her side.

The journey was far from over, but they would face it together. And whatever waited for them in the depths, they would find a way to survive—no matter the cost.

The narrow corridor leading out of the chamber was suffused with a quiet tension, the oppressive hum of the Rose and the distant whispers of shadows creating an almost suffocating atmosphere. Anira led the way, her steps steady despite the weight of the pendant that pulsed faintly against her chest. The dim, crimson glow from the veins along the walls barely lit the path ahead, leaving the group enveloped in half-darkness, the flicker of the Rose's light their only guide.

Ashric stayed close beside her, his sword held at the ready, his sharp blue eyes constantly scanning the darkness for any signs of movement. He walked with the quiet precision of someone who understood the gravity of every step, his focus unrelenting. The tension in his jaw betrayed his thoughts, though he kept them locked behind his stony demeanor. It was better that way, he told himself—better to keep his mind sharp, his emotions tempered.

Kael trailed a few paces behind, their knife still gripped tightly in their hand. They muttered to themselves occasionally, their words half-lost to the oppressive quiet, but the nervous edge in their tone betrayed their own fears. "This place better have a way out," they whispered, their voice carrying through the corridor. "Because if we're heading deeper into this mess, I'm starting to rethink my life choices."

"Quiet," Ashric snapped, his tone sharper than usual. His gaze flicked back to Kael, his expression dark. "You'll attract attention."

Kael huffed but fell silent, their steps growing quieter.

The corridor began to widen, its jagged walls giving way to smoother stone that gleamed faintly in the Rose's light. The metallic tang in the air thickened, clinging to Anira's throat and filling her lungs with every breath. The pull of the Rose was growing stronger now—not sharp and urgent, as it had been before, but deeper, heavier, as though urging her onward with quiet insistence.

"We're close," she said softly, her voice carrying just enough to reach Ashric.

He glanced at her, his brow furrowed. "Close to what?"

"The next step," she said, her tone distant. "Whatever's waiting for us... it's ahead."

As they stepped into another chamber, the air shifted, carrying with it an oppressive weight that pressed down on their shoulders. The space was vast and circular, the ceiling vanishing into darkness high above. The walls were lined with intricate carvings, their patterns swirling and twisting like the veins of a great, ancient heart. At the center of the room stood another platform, larger than the last, its surface covered in jagged cracks that pulsed with faint, silvery light.

The light from the Rose flared, illuminating the room in warm, shifting hues, and Anira felt the pull intensify, dragging her attention to the platform. The pendant burned hot against her skin, its rhythm quickening, and she took a hesitant step forward.

"Wait," Ashric said, his voice low but commanding. He moved to her side, his hand hovering near her arm, though he didn't touch her. "This feels wrong."

"It always does," she said, her voice trembling slightly. "But we don't have a choice. This is where it's leading us."

Kael stepped closer, their gaze darting nervously around the room. "Anyone else feel like we just walked into a trap?"

"It's not a trap," Anira said, though her voice wavered. "It's... something else."

Ashric's eyes narrowed as he scanned the room, his grip on his sword tightening. "We're not alone."

Anira froze, her breath catching as the faint sound of movement reached her ears. It was subtle, barely more than a whisper, but it sent a shiver crawling up her spine. The shadows at the edges of the chamber seemed to shift, curling and twisting like smoke, and the silvery cracks in the platform began to glow brighter, their rhythm syncing with the pulse of the Rose.

"Whatever's coming," Ashric said, his voice low, "we're not running."

Anira turned to him, her chest tightening at the fierce resolve in his expression. His gaze locked onto hers, steady and unwavering, and for a moment, the weight of everything they faced seemed to fade. He didn't need to say it—she could see it in his eyes. He wasn't going to let anything happen to her. Not while he still stood.

The air in the chamber grew colder, the oppressive weight pressing harder against them. The shadows moved faster now, surging toward the platform in twisting, jagged arcs. The light of the Rose flared in response, its warmth flooding through Anira's chest as it pushed back against the darkness.

Kael let out a nervous laugh, their grip on their knife tightening. "Here we go again."

The first tendril of shadow lashed out, sharp and deliberate, and Ashric moved instantly, his blade cutting through the darkness with precise, brutal efficiency. The tendril dissolved into mist with a shriek, but more surged forward, their jagged forms coiling toward the platform.

"Stay behind me," Ashric said sharply, his sword flashing as he intercepted another tendril. His movements were fluid and unrelenting, each strike carrying the weight of his resolve.

Anira clutched the Rose tightly, its light growing brighter as the pull intensified. She stepped toward the platform, her breath trembling as the energy coursing through her built to a fever pitch. The shadows recoiled from the light, their forms writhing and twisting, but they didn't retreat.

"Anira!" Ashric called, his voice raw with urgency. "Whatever you're going to do, do it now!"

She nodded, her resolve hardening as she reached the base of the platform. The Rose's light flared, its warmth flooding her senses, and she placed her hand against the cracked stone, feeling the pulse of energy beneath her palm. The silvery light from the cracks surged upward, filling the chamber with blinding brilliance.

The shadows let out a collective roar, their forms unraveling as the light consumed them, and the chamber trembled violently. The air was filled with a deafening hum, the sound vibrating through Anira's chest as the energy from the platform and the Rose merged into one.

And then, with a final, blinding surge of light, everything went silent.

Beneath the Shroud

The silence was absolute, heavy and suffocating, like the world itself had been swallowed by the void. Anira blinked against the lingering brilliance that still burned in her vision, her breath shallow and uneven as she tried to reorient herself. Her fingers trembled where they rested against the cracked surface of the platform, the warmth of the Rose fading to a faint, steady glow that barely illuminated the space around her.

The chamber felt different now. The oppressive weight of the shadows was gone, replaced by a brittle stillness that pressed against her chest like a held breath. The faint hum of the Rose, once a constant companion, had quieted, its rhythm subdued and almost hesitant.

"Anira," Ashric's voice broke the silence, low and edged with urgency.

She turned, her vision slowly adjusting to the dim light. He was standing a few feet away, his sword still in hand, his sharp blue eyes scanning the room for any lingering threat. His face was drawn, a faint sheen of sweat glistening along his brow, but his focus was entirely on her.

"I'm here," she said, her voice trembling. She straightened, her legs unsteady beneath her, and forced herself to meet his gaze. "I'm... fine."

Kael's voice came next, sharp and incredulous. "Fine? Fine? Are you kidding me?" They stepped closer, their knife still clutched tightly, though their hand shook. "You just lit up like a damned star and nearly got all of us killed. What part of that is fine?"

Anira didn't respond, her attention shifting to the platform beneath her. The jagged cracks that had pulsed with silvery light were dull now, their glow extinguished, but the faint warmth that lingered beneath her palm suggested that whatever power had been housed here wasn't entirely gone. She glanced at the Rose, its soft golden light casting faint patterns across her hands, and felt the pull of its energy, weaker now but still present.

"It did something," she said softly, her gaze distant. "I don't know what, but... it worked."

Ashric stepped to her side, his presence steadying. "What worked?" he asked, his voice low but firm. "What did you see?"

Anira hesitated, her fingers brushing against the Rose. The memory of the mirror's vision was vivid in her mind—the shadows coiling, the blinding light, the weight of a choice that felt inevitable. But even now, she couldn't put it into words. It was too vast, too fragmented.

"It showed me... a path," she said finally. "A way to end this. But it didn't show me how."

Ashric's jaw tightened, his expression unreadable. "So we're still guessing."

"Not guessing," she said, her voice gaining strength. "Following. The Rose knows where it's leading us."

Kael let out a bitter laugh, their eyes narrowing. "Great. So we're trusting the creepy glowing rock again. Because that's worked so well for us so far."

Ashric shot them a sharp look. "Enough, Kael."

They raised their hands in mock surrender but muttered under their breath as they moved to the edge of the chamber, their gaze darting toward the shadowy passage ahead. "Just saying, I hope this magical death trap of hers knows how to find the exit."

Anira ignored them, her focus shifting to Ashric. "The shadows are weaker now," she said. "I can feel it. The Rose pushed them back."

"For how long?" he asked, his voice quiet but weighted.

"I don't know," she admitted. "But if we keep moving, we can find the source and end this."

He nodded slowly, his sharp gaze lingering on her face. "Then we keep moving."

Anira took a steadying breath, the warmth of the Rose grounding her, and turned toward the passage. The air was colder here, the metallic tang fainter but still present, and the faint glow of the crimson veins along the walls cast shifting patterns across the jagged stone. The path ahead was dark, the light from the Rose barely reaching the edges, but she didn't falter.

Ashric stayed close beside her, his sword ready, his presence steady and unyielding. Kael followed a few paces behind, their footsteps lighter now, though their muttered curses suggested they were still less than thrilled about the journey ahead.

As they descended deeper into the shadows, the quiet stretched, heavy and oppressive. The faint hum of the Rose returned, soft and rhythmic, and Anira felt its pull again, subtle but insistent. The path wound downward, the air growing colder with every step, and the light of the veins began to dim, their faint glow flickering like dying embers.

"What's down here?" Kael asked, their voice breaking the silence. "Because if it's more shadows, I'm going to lose it."

Anira glanced back at them, her expression unreadable. "Whatever it is," she said softly, "it's waiting for us."

Kael muttered another curse, their hand tightening on their knife. "That's what I was afraid of."

The passage opened suddenly into another chamber, smaller than the last but no less foreboding. The walls were lined with jagged carvings, their patterns sharp and chaotic, as though etched by an unsteady hand. The air was colder here, biting against Anira's skin, and the faint metallic tang was stronger, almost choking.

At the center of the chamber stood a single pedestal, its surface smooth and polished, but empty. The faint glow of the Rose intensified, its warmth flaring against Anira's chest, and she stepped forward, her breath catching as the energy coursing through her grew stronger.

"What is this?" Ashric asked, his voice low.

"I don't know," she said, her gaze locked on the pedestal. "But it's connected to the Rose. I can feel it."

Kael approached cautiously, their eyes narrowing as they scanned the room. "So... what's supposed to happen here? Because it looks like another one of those 'touch it and hope for the best' moments."

Ashric's hand hovered near Anira's arm, his tension palpable. "Anira," he said, his voice sharp. "Be careful."

She nodded, her chest tight as she reached out toward the pedestal. The moment her fingers brushed its surface, the room shuddered violently, the carvings on the walls flaring with crimson light. The air grew heavier, the metallic tang almost unbearable, and the faint hum of the Rose deepened into a low, resonant vibration.

Anira's breath caught as the light from the Rose flared, illuminating the chamber in a blinding flash. The pedestal beneath her hand grew warm, its surface vibrating, and she felt a sharp pull in her chest, dragging her toward something vast and unseen.

And then, from the darkness, a voice spoke—low, guttural, and impossibly ancient.

"Bearer of the Rose. You have come far. But the end is not yet written."

The room plunged into darkness, and everything went still.

The chamber was plunged into absolute darkness, thick and heavy, swallowing sound and space like a living thing. Anira could feel the weight of it pressing against her skin, a suffocating force that sent shivers down her spine. The Rose pulsed steadily against her chest, its faint golden glow the only thing keeping the void from consuming her completely.

Ashric's presence beside her was a tether, a sharp contrast to the abyss they now faced. His grip on her wrist was firm but not forceful, his body positioned slightly in front of her, protective even now. She felt the heat of him through the cold, the steady rhythm of his breathing, and it anchored her against the creeping dread curling at the edges of her mind.

Kael's voice was barely above a whisper. "Did... did anyone else hear that?"

The voice. That impossible voice that had slithered from the dark, wrapping around her name like a curse.

"Bearer of the Rose. You have come far. But the end is not yet written."

It wasn't a threat. It wasn't a welcome. It was something deeper, something ancient, like the whisper of time itself pressing against the edges of reality.

"Yes," Anira said, her voice steadier than she felt. "I heard it."

The darkness didn't lift, but the walls of the chamber flickered to life with a sickly, crimson light. Veins of black stone split open, bleeding eerie illumination across the space, revealing the pedestal now empty in the center of the room. The carvings lining the walls twisted and shifted, reforming into shapes that seemed to pulse and breathe, like something had been waiting, watching, beneath the surface all along.

And then, the voice spoke again—low and resonant, layered with echoes of things she did not want to see.

"You stand on the threshold of eternity. The choice has been made. The path will unfold."

The air crackled. The stone beneath their feet trembled.

And then the shadows came.

They poured from the walls like liquid void, curling and twisting into forms that barely resembled anything human. Their shapes flickered and stuttered, moving in unnatural ways, bending and stretching like marionettes with broken strings. Their eyes—if they could be called that—were pits of glowing silver, cold and merciless.

Kael cursed violently, stepping back against the pedestal, their knife useless against things that were more air than substance. "Tell me we're not fighting those things."

Ashric didn't hesitate. His sword was already drawn, the steel flashing in the crimson light. "Stay behind me."

But the shadows didn't attack. They loomed, shifting and seething, filling the chamber with a presence so thick it was almost physical.

Anira swallowed hard, forcing herself to breathe. The Rose burned against her chest, its warmth surging outward, pushing back the oppressive cold that threatened to claw into her bones.

"They're waiting," she realized aloud.

Ashric shot her a sharp glance. "For what?"

The answer came before she could speak.

The pedestal, once dark, flared to life, its surface splitting open in jagged, spiraling patterns. Light, impossibly bright and yet suffused with an underlying darkness, surged upward, and from within the stone, something rose.

A figure.

Not a shadow. Not entirely human. Something else.

It emerged from the pedestal as though it had always been waiting there, sealed in stone and time. A cloak of midnight billowed around it, woven from something that absorbed the light rather than reflected it. Its hands—pale and long-fingered—were empty, but the power surrounding it was undeniable. Its face was hidden behind an intricate mask, its silver surface etched with symbols that burned and twisted, shifting even as Anira tried to focus on them.

She couldn't breathe.

The shadows knelt.

Not in fear. Not in reverence.

In recognition.

Ashric's grip tightened on his sword, his entire body tense, coiled like a blade ready to strike. "Who are you?" he demanded.

The figure turned its head slightly, as if considering him. And then, it spoke.

"The first and the last. The keeper of the undone. The architect of what will be."

Its voice was neither male nor female, neither young nor old. It was the weight of eternity pressed into syllables, and it sent ice through Anira's veins.

The Rose trembled against her chest, its warmth now laced with something else—resistance.

The figure turned its masked face toward her.

"Bearer. You have come to claim what is yours."

A cold, creeping realization settled into her bones.

This wasn't just the source of the shadows.

It was the origin.

The force behind the Rose. The thing that had always been watching.

The thing that had been waiting for her.

Ashric shifted, placing himself more firmly between Anira and the figure. His stance was deliberate, his sword held in warning rather than outright attack. "She didn't come here for you," he said, his voice steady, dangerous. "We're here to end this."

The figure tilted its head slightly, as if amused.

"You misunderstand. There is nothing to end. There is only the becoming."

The Rose flared, its light slamming outward in a pulse of heat.

The figure didn't flinch.

Anira felt it then. The choice.

It sat between them, invisible and vast, pressing against her ribs like a second heartbeat. This was what the Rose had shown her in the mirror, what it had been leading her toward all along.

She could take the power. Accept it. Become the thing the Rose had always meant her to be.

Or she could fight it.

Refuse it.

But at what cost?

Ashric's hand brushed against her arm, grounding her. She turned, locking eyes with him, and the weight in his gaze nearly undid her. He wasn't just looking at her—he was seeing her. The fear. The burden. The impossible choice laid at her feet.

And beneath it, something raw, something unspoken that had always been there.

"You're not alone," he said, his voice barely more than a whisper.

The figure took a slow step forward.

"Choose, Bearer."

The chamber trembled.

The shadows stirred.

The Rose pulsed.

And Anira took a breath.

The choice was hers.

And the world would never be the same.

The chamber trembled with unseen power, the very air thickening until every breath felt like a struggle, as though the space itself resisted the presence of mortals. The masked figure stood motionless, its midnight cloak shifting despite the absence of wind, the silver etchings on its mask twisting, reforming symbols Anira did not recognize but could feel in the marrow of her bones.

The shadows remained kneeling, their bodies flickering at the edges like flame caught in a windstorm, waiting.

Waiting for her.

The Rose burned hotter against her chest, its pulse hammering like a second heart, its golden glow battling against the oppressive darkness pressing in on all sides. The pull of it was unlike anything she had felt before—not a gentle guiding force, not an urgent command, but a demand.

She felt the presence of the choice settle into her bones, thick and unrelenting.

Take it.

Accept the power.

Become what the Rose had been waiting for.

Her fingers curled around the pendant, nails biting into her palm. It was too much—too heavy, too vast. The weight of it made her dizzy, the magnitude of what she was about to do pressing against her skull like a storm gathering at the edges of her mind.

Ashric's voice cut through the suffocating quiet, sharp and grounding.

"Anira," he said, stepping closer, his hand hovering near her arm but not touching. His eyes burned with something fierce, something desperate. "Whatever this is, you don't have to face it alone."

She turned toward him, her breath catching at the intensity in his gaze. He was tense, his sword gripped so tightly that his knuckles had gone white. He was ready to fight for her—to die for her if it came to that.

It nearly broke her.

But she wasn't sure if even Ashric could stand against this.

The masked figure tilted its head slightly, its voice low and resonant.

"He is not part of this."

A ripple of force blasted outward from its form, slamming into Ashric like an invisible wave. He staggered, cursing as he dug his heels into the stone, barely keeping himself upright.

Kael wasn't so lucky. They were flung backward, crashing into the far wall with a sharp, pained grunt before crumpling to the ground.

Ashric recovered instantly, his sword raised in an instant, his stance coiled with lethal intent. "Don't touch her," he snarled.

The figure ignored him entirely.

It stepped forward, slow and deliberate, its silver mask gleaming in the dim light.

"The Rose has chosen you, Bearer. You cannot deny what you are."

Anira's pulse pounded in her ears, her fingers tightening around the pendant. "And what am I?" she demanded, her voice shaking with fury. "Tell me what you want from me!"

The figure's head tilted slightly, considering.

"To become."

The words sent a shock through her system, a weight that settled into her ribs like iron. She understood what it meant, even if it hadn't explained. She could feel it in the depths of her being. The Rose had never been an object. It had never been a tool.

It had been waiting.

For her.

Anira stumbled back a step, her breath catching in her throat. "No," she whispered, shaking her head. "I won't."

The figure did not move, but the shadows around them did.

They surged forward, faster than before, no longer kneeling. No longer waiting.

Ashric barely had time to react before the first tendril lashed out toward Anira. He moved instinctively, his blade cutting through the darkness with ruthless precision, his body between her and the oncoming storm. The strike sent the shadow reeling back, dissolving into mist, but more came—many more.

Kael groaned from where they had landed but managed to push themselves up, shaking their head violently. "Oh, screw this," they growled, unsheathing their knife and lunging forward. They weren't graceful, but they were fast, their blade flashing as they slashed at the shadows closing in from the left.

Ashric barely spared them a glance before turning to Anira, urgency burning in his expression. "You have to make a choice, now!"

Her heart pounded, her breath ragged as she turned back to the masked figure.

It stood perfectly still in the chaos, untouched, unbothered. Waiting.

She could take it. The Rose would answer her call. She could end this, right now, if she just let it happen.

The thought terrified her.

Because she didn't know if she would survive it.

Or if she would still be her once it was over.

A shadow lunged toward her, faster than the others, its jagged form slicing through the air with deadly intent. She had no time to react.

But Ashric did.

He moved in a blur, intercepting the creature mid-strike. His sword cut through it with a flash of steel, but the moment his blade made contact, the shadow exploded into black mist, slamming into him with enough force to send him staggering backward.

Anira's breath caught in her throat. "Ashric!"

He dropped to a knee, his free hand bracing against the stone as he sucked in a sharp breath. The veins along his arms had darkened, black tendrils slithering up beneath his skin like an infection. His body shuddered violently, his breaths ragged and uneven.

The shadows had touched him.

Anira didn't think. She moved.

She dropped to his side, her hands reaching for him instinctively, but he gritted his teeth and forced himself upright before she could steady him. His grip on his sword was still strong, but his fingers trembled.

"I'm fine," he rasped.

She shook her head, fear rising in her throat. "You're not."

His gaze met hers, and for the first time, she saw it—fear. Not for himself.

For her.

"I can fight it," he said, his voice tight, raw.

But she knew what he wasn't saying.

Not forever.

Not unless she ended this.

The masked figure spoke again, its voice colder this time.

"You waste time. Choose."

Anira's hands curled into fists, rage rising in her chest like wildfire. The shadows, the

Rose, the figure, the choice—it was all pressing in, closing around her, demanding an answer.

But there was only one choice she could make.

She turned to Ashric, her breath uneven. "Stay with me."

His expression hardened, his free hand reaching for her arm, gripping it tightly. "I will."

She nodded once.

Then, with the last of her hesitation burning away, she turned back to the masked figure—back to the endless, impossible power waiting to claim her.

And she stepped forward.

The chamber exploded in light and darkness.

The explosion of light and darkness sent shockwaves rippling through the chamber, warping the very air around them. The force knocked Anira off her feet, her vision consumed by a blinding gold flare as the Rose unleashed its power in a violent, unrestrained surge. Shadows screeched in agony, their forms twisting and convulsing as the wave of energy blasted outward, disintegrating the closest ones in an instant. But the others—the stronger ones—did not fall. They reformed, growing sharper, more jagged, their eyes burning silver in the flickering chaos.

The masked figure did not move.

Anira gasped as her back struck the cold stone, her lungs seizing against the thick, choking air. The very fabric of the chamber felt stretched, tearing at the edges as if something monstrous was clawing its way into existence. The light of the Rose flared wildly, erratic and desperate, fighting against the darkness even as it seemed to bleed into it.

Footsteps. Fast. Desperate.

Ashric was already moving, his silhouette cutting through the fractured light. He reached her before she could rise, gripping her wrist and pulling her up with force. His eyes were wild, fever-bright, and in the dim glow she could see the black veins creeping up his arm from where the shadow had touched him, pulsing like something alive beneath his skin.

He barely seemed to notice.

"You need to end this now," he snarled over the howling void. "Before it—"

A new force slammed into them.

Not physical. Not tangible.

A pull.

Anira's stomach lurched as her body was yanked forward, dragged toward the pedestal, toward the thing that had risen from it. The masked figure remained still, its silver etchings shifting in slow, unnatural spirals. It did not need to move. The force did its bidding for it.

Ashric's grip tightened painfully around her wrist, his muscles flexing as he fought against whatever unseen force had taken hold. He would not let go. But his breath hitched, his strength faltering for the first time since she had met him.

Kael screamed from somewhere in the dark. "Anira! What the hell is it doing?!"

The shadows converged, their tendrils coiling into something massive—not a figure, not a beast, but something worse. Something unfinished. It loomed at the chamber's edges, stretching beyond sight, its form flickering like a mirage caught between existence and something else entirely. Its presence was suffocating, not of this world, never meant to be seen.

A terrible, keening wail rose from its depths.

Anira felt the weight of it slam into her mind, an ancient, unbearable sorrow, laced with something hungry, something endless. Her vision blurred. Her limbs turned cold. For a moment, she thought her body might unravel like the shadows themselves, pulled apart strand by strand, unmade into the void.

Then Ashric's voice cut through the storm.

"Anira!" His grip did not loosen. "Look at me!"

Her head snapped toward him, gasping, drowning in the weight of whatever was trying to take hold. His face was set in raw, desperate defiance. The veins along his neck pulsed black now, spreading outward in thick, twisting roots, but still—he did not let go.

He had always been steady. Always unyielding.

She could not lose him.

With the last shred of strength she had, Anira ripped herself free from the pull and turned toward the masked figure. The Rose burned hotter, scalding against her skin, searing through every nerve as it demanded she use it. The choice. The sacrifice.

The power.

The figure finally moved.

It raised a single hand.

The chamber buckled.

Anira's knees gave out. Her vision swam. The darkness itself bled from the walls, rushing toward her in great, writhing tendrils, all of them aimed for her chest—for the Rose.

Ashric moved before she could.

His body collided with hers, knocking her aside just as the shadows struck.

The sound that left him was not a scream—it was something guttural, broken, a sharp inhale before the impact ripped through him. The tendrils did not lash at him the way they had before. They dug in.

Anira felt the moment his body locked, his breath stalling as the shadows coiled tight around his limbs, around his chest, dragging him back—toward the masked figure, toward the source.

She screamed his name.

Kael's curses rang from somewhere beyond the chaos, but they were lost in the roar of the void. The Rose surged again, angry now, its light blinding, pushing back against the tendrils before they could finish their work.

The masked figure tilted its head.

It did not speak.

It only watched.

And Anira understood.

This wasn't a punishment.

This was payment.

The choice had always been hers.

She had stepped forward. She had denied the power. She had fought the transformation.

And now, it would take something else.

"No." The word was barely more than a whisper.

The shadows pulled Ashric further, his body convulsing as the black veins pulsed harder, spreading too fast, too deep. He turned his head toward her, his face tight with pain.

But his eyes—they were still his.

"No!" Anira surged forward, grasping at his hand, at his armor, but the pull was too strong. The Rose's warmth flared wildly, its glow flickering, uncertain, teetering between breaking and something else.

She felt it again.

The offer.

Take it. Take the power. Save him.

Ashric's fingers twitched against hers, tightening—whether in warning or in goodbye, she didn't know.

Her vision blurred.

Kael's voice rang out again, frantic, cursing.

The shadows swallowed the light.

The masked figure lowered its hand.

And Ashric—vanished into the dark.

The world fractured in an instant. One breath, Ashric was there, his grip firm, his body tense, his presence a constant, unshakable force in the chaos. The next, he was gone.

Ripped from her grasp. Swallowed whole. Unmade.

The silence that followed was worse than the roar of battle. It was hollow. Gaping. The kind of silence that came when the soul recognized a loss too deep to name.

Anira fell forward, her knees slamming hard against the cold stone. Her breath came in ragged gasps, her fingers clawing at the empty space where he had been. The Rose was still pulsing against her chest, frantic and erratic, but it no longer burned—it was cold. Distant. As if a part of its fire had been taken along with him.

"No," she whispered. "No, no, no, no—NO!"

Her scream shattered the quiet, raw and furious, laced with something deeper, something breaking inside of her. Kael was moving, stumbling toward her, but they were distant—too far, too removed from the black void that had just devoured Ashric.

The masked figure remained standing, motionless as ever.

Watching.

Waiting.

The darkness had accepted its sacrifice. The bargain had been made.

The edges of Anira's vision blurred, her breath coming in ragged, disbelieving gasps. It wasn't real. It couldn't be real. He had been right there. She had held onto him.

And she had let him go.

A sharp hand yanked at her shoulder, pulling her back, forcing her to focus.

"Anira—snap out of it!" Kael's voice was raw, desperate, shaken in a way that rarely surfaced. "Move! We don't have time to lose it right now!"

She turned toward them slowly, her mind barely processing the way their chest heaved, the blood smeared across their temple, the way their fingers shook against her arm. Kael never looked afraid—not like this.

And that's when she realized.

The shadows had stopped moving.

They had won.

For now.

The figure did not speak. It did not move. But Anira felt its gaze settle on her, its weight pressing down against the fracture inside her chest like a blade against an open wound.

It had taken Ashric. And she could feel the silent warning.

It could take more.

She was shaking. Violently. Her fingers curled into her palm, her nails digging into flesh until she felt the sting of blood.

Her heartbeat was a war drum.

She wanted to burn this place to the ground.

But not yet.

Not yet.

Kael, panting, still gripping her arm, met her eyes and gave the smallest shake of their head.

Not now. Survive now. Burn it later.

Anira swallowed hard, barely able to keep herself from shaking apart at the seams, but nodded.

The Rose—traitorous, hollow thing—still pulsed against her chest. It had led her here. It had chosen her. And now, it had given her the one thing she never would have sacrificed.

Her grief curled tight inside her ribs, raw and smoldering.

It would pay for this.

The whole damned thing would pay.

She forced herself to rise. To move. Kael steadied her for only a second before following her lead, keeping a watchful eye on the silent, motionless figure that had stolen their friend.

They stepped away from the platform.

One step. Then another.

The shadows did not move.

They did not need to.

The weight of their loss followed them out of the chamber, trailing behind them like something alive.

Anira kept her back straight. She kept walking. She did not look over her shoulder.

But deep inside the hollow void where her grief festered, there was something else.

Faint.

Distant.

But there.

A presence. A pull. A whisper.

Not dead.

Not gone.

Not yet.

The tunnel stretched endlessly before them, winding downward in a slow, suffocating descent. The air was thick, oppressive, pressing against Anira's lungs as if the very walls were closing in around her. The faint, flickering veins of crimson light pulsed in the stone, breathing like something alive, like something watching. It made her skin crawl, but not as much as the silence.

A silence too heavy.

Too hollow.

Too wrong.

Her limbs moved on instinct alone, every step mechanical, every breath shallow. The weight of absence pressed against her like chains, wrapping around her ribs, digging into her bones. Her fingers clenched, curling into fists so tight her nails bit into the flesh of her palms, but she welcomed the pain. It was real. It was something solid.

Unlike him.

Unlike Ashric.

Gone.

The word lodged itself like a knife beneath her ribs, twisting with every step, cutting deeper, sinking into the spaces he had left behind.

She had let him go.

She had failed.

Her jaw tightened, the pressure in her throat threatening to choke her, but she refused to let it break her. If she broke now, if she let even a sliver of that grief slip through the cracks—she might not come back from it.

Kael moved beside her, quiet. Hesitant. Unsteady.

It was wrong.

They were always talking, always muttering something sarcastic under their breath, always rolling their eyes at the impossible horror they were trudging through. But now—

Nothing.

No dry remark.

No jab about how they were all going to die down here.

Just silence.

And Kael never let silence sit this long unless they were afraid of what might slip out if they spoke.

The tunnel pulsed again, the veins of light flickering, stretching in uneven patterns through the rock like the roots of some ancient thing buried deep beneath the surface. The walls seemed to lean inward, warping as the dim glow cast their elongated shadows ahead of them. Their own twisted silhouettes loomed before them, wavering with every step, looking more like shades than living people.

Shades.

Like Ashric had become.

Anira swallowed hard, her chest aching.

He had always been beside her. Through every battle. Through every narrow escape. Through every impossible moment that should have killed them both but somehow didn't.

And now—

She turned her head slightly, the habit so ingrained in her bones she did it without thinking, without truly expecting—

Empty space.

No sharp blue eyes scanning ahead for threats.

No steady, unwavering form just ahead of her, always keeping to her left.

No weight at her side, always a step ahead when danger was near.

Nothing.

Just the tunnel.

Just the cold.

Just the silence.

Her stomach twisted, something raw and violent coiling in the pit of her gut.

She hadn't even—

Her steps faltered, her balance wavering.

She hadn't even gotten to say anything.

Not goodbye.

Not I'm sorry.

Not Don't go.

Not *Come back.*

Her legs wavered, her knees nearly giving way.

A sharp inhale from Kael. A misstep. Their boots scraped against the stone, hesitating before they adjusted their pace to match hers.

"Hey."

Their voice was softer than she had ever heard it.

She didn't respond.

Kael stepped closer, hovering at her side, not touching but close enough that their presence was something solid in the emptiness, something real.

"You—" They hesitated, exhaled sharply, tried again. "You can break down later. But not now. You can't. Not yet." Their voice shook, just barely. "We can't lose both of you."

Anira closed her eyes for the briefest moment, exhaling through her nose.

Kael was right.

She kept walking.

Her hands still curled into fists. The cold weight of the Rose still pressed against her chest, no longer burning, no longer guiding—just there, a hollow, useless thing that had taken just as much as it had ever given.

She kept walking.

She did not look back.

The tunnel deepened, the shadows thickening around them.

A distant sound rumbled ahead—low, guttural, the grinding of stone against stone, something shifting in the darkness, waiting.

Waiting for them.

The horrors of this place were not finished with them yet.

The shadows had taken Ashric.

But they had not taken her.

And whatever had done this—whatever had stolen him, whatever had dared to make her choose—

It would pay.

The tunnel narrowed, the air thick and sour, stale with the breath of something long buried. Their footsteps were the only sound, soft and uneven against the stone. No voices. No wasted breath. No distractions. Only the dull echo of boots scraping against rock, moving forward, because stopping wasn't an option.

Anira's hands ached. She hadn't realized how tightly she'd been clenching them, how her nails had bitten into her palms deep enough to break skin. She flexed her fingers, blood smeared and stiff against her skin, but the pain was dull. Distant. She didn't care. It was something to hold on to.

Kael walked beside her, their face drawn, their movements rigid, shoulders hunched like they were expecting something to reach from the dark and take them next. They weren't talking anymore. That scared her more than anything. They always had something to say. A snide remark. A well-placed curse. A joke made too soon. But now? Just silence. Just the sound of breathing, of boots against the ground, of the weight of everything pressing down on them like a closing fist.

She could still feel him.

The empty space where Ashric should be was too loud, too large, a shape in the dark carved out of nothing. He had always been beside her, his steady presence like the hum of a blade, waiting, watching, keeping the edges of the world sharp. Now, there was only absence. A hollow space carved between her ribs. He had been there—just there. And then he wasn't.

She hadn't said anything.

Not goodbye. Not hold on. Not please, please stay.

Her jaw tightened, and she forced the thought away. It would consume her if she let it. She couldn't afford that. Not here. Not now.

The tunnel twisted, the stone walls growing slick with something thick and dark, a wet sheen that shimmered in the faint, pulsing veins of crimson light overhead. The walls pulsed, slow and uneven, like something was alive just beneath the surface, something breathing, waiting, listening.

A groan of shifting rock rumbled through the tunnel, deep and distant. The whole place felt unstable. Like the earth had been hollowed out from the inside, leaving only a shell. A tomb waiting to be sealed.

Anira kept walking.

The Rose was useless now. Cold against her chest, its glow dulled to nothing, its pulse faint, hesitant. Cowardly. It had taken from her, drained from her, led her to the edge of something she had no name for and demanded a price she hadn't been ready to pay. And she had paid it anyway.

But she had nothing left to give.

Another sharp inhale from Kael, and then a word. "There."

They barely spoke above a whisper, but Anira followed their gaze to where the tunnel widened ahead, opening into something deeper, vaster. A cavern. The air shifted as they drew closer, the scent of old blood and scorched stone thick in her nostrils, coating the back of her throat.

She didn't stop walking.

She didn't hesitate.

She didn't care what waited for them.

Because she was going to burn this place down to the bones.

She was going to find what had taken him.

And she was going to end it.

No matter what it cost her next.

The Abyss Unleashed

The cavern stretched before them like the ribcage of something long dead, the jagged arches overhead curling inward, as if the earth itself had been twisted around this place, trapping it, keeping it from escaping. The air was thick, heavy with the scent of decay and something older, something wrong.

Anira stepped forward, her pulse hammering in her ears, her breath sharp, shallow. The ground beneath her boots was uneven, slick with a dark sheen that glistened in the crimson light pulsing from the walls. It was wet. Not water. Not blood. Something thicker. Something that moved when she wasn't looking.

Kael was beside her, their blade tight in their grip, their posture stiff, coiled. They weren't joking anymore. Their usual nerves had hardened into something sharper, something ready. They didn't look at her. They didn't need to.

They knew what this was.

It was the end.

Or the beginning of something worse.

Anira inhaled, slow and deliberate, forcing herself to ignore the gnawing ache in her chest, the empty space where Ashric should have been. The hollow place in her ribs burned, raw and ragged, but she had no room for grief now. Only rage. Only purpose.

Something stirred in the dark ahead.

The shadows rippled.

A breath—not hers. Not Kael's. Something else.

Then another.

Then many.

Low, shuddering inhales, crawling out of the depths, filling the cavern with the whisper of something waking up.

The walls shifted.

The ground trembled.

And then, they came.

The first shadow peeled itself from the wall, its form still half-liquid, stretching and twisting like something unraveling from a nightmare. It had no eyes. No face. Just a gaping maw of jagged nothingness, a hollow void in the shape of something once human, its limbs too long, its fingers ending in hooked claws that scraped against the stone as it moved.

The second followed. Then the third. Then too many to count.

They flooded from the edges of the cavern, slithering forward in an unnatural tide, their bodies flickering between solid and smoke, their movements jerky, unfinished.

Anira's fingers curled around the Rose, even though she knew it wouldn't help her. It was dead weight now, a useless relic, its glow nothing but a dim, failing ember.

She didn't need it.

She still had her blade.

She still had her rage.

Kael let out a shaky breath. "Tell me we have a plan."

Anira exhaled. Cold. Focused. Unbreakable.

"We kill them all."

Kael let out a humorless laugh. "Alright. That's a plan."

The first creature lunged.

Anira moved before she had time to think. Her blade met flesh—or what should have been flesh—but the thing didn't bleed. It splintered, breaking apart in jagged shards of darkness that melted into mist before reforming, faster, angrier.

A clawed hand swiped toward her chest.

She ducked. Moved. Spun.

Kael was already in motion beside her, their knife flashing silver as they dodged the first strike, slipping past the second, burying their blade into the place where the creature's ribs should have been. It shrieked, a sound that wasn't quite a scream, more like the tearing of something that wasn't meant to exist.

More were coming.

Too many.

They were surrounded before they even had a chance to run.

Anira gritted her teeth, her grip tightening on her sword.

Let them come.

She wasn't afraid.

Not anymore.

Not after what they had already taken from her.

This was it.

The last fight.

And she would burn this place down to the bones before she let it take anything else.

The creatures pressed in, circling like wolves sensing the slow bleed of their prey. Their jagged limbs twitched, stretching impossibly, their bodies flickering between form and void. The space between Anira and Kael shrank with every passing second, the tide of shadows tightening around them.

Anira's breath came hard and fast, but her hands were steady. The weight of her sword was familiar, solid, an anchor in the sea of horror that threatened to drag them both under.

The first one lunged.

She moved on instinct, twisting to the side as its hooked claws scraped through empty air where her throat had been a second before. Her blade was already coming down, cleaving into the creature's shoulder. It splintered, not like flesh, not like bone, but like glass cracking under pressure. The thing recoiled, its body flickering, its form unraveling at the edges before snapping back together, the wound already sealing itself.

They didn't bleed.

They didn't die.

Kael had noticed too. "Oh, that's just great!" they snarled, kicking one of the creatures back. "Any ideas that don't involve stabbing the unkillable?"

Anira's grip tightened on the hilt of her blade. Think. Think fast. The Rose wasn't burning the way it had before. It had given all it had to the masked figure. It had given all it had to—

To Ashric.

Her pulse jumped, her body reacting before her mind could catch up. She slashed low, forcing back the creature closest to her, her thoughts racing through the storm of battle.

Ashric had been taken. But not like this. Not like these creatures.

The shadows had pulled him under, but they hadn't consumed him.

Hadn't unmade him.

Because they couldn't.

He had fought them. He had resisted. Even as they swallowed him whole, even as they dragged him into whatever abyss they had been waiting in.

The masked figure had taken him, but it had never said forever.

The thought slammed into her like a hammer.

She could get him back.

She would.

But first—

They had to survive.

Another creature lunged, and this time she was ready.

She sidestepped, her blade catching the thing mid-strike. It splintered like before, but now she watched—not just the wound, but what lay beneath the cracks.

And there—deep inside the shattering void—something else flickered.

Not shadow.

Not empty.

A core.

A pulse of light so faint it was barely visible, hidden beneath layers of smoke and wrongness.

A weakness.

"Kael!" Anira shouted, twisting her blade against the creature's shifting form. "There's something inside them!"

Kael ducked as one of the creatures slashed too close to their shoulder. "Inside them?" they gasped. "You wanna be a little more specific while we're actively dying?"

Anira gritted her teeth. She had seen it. A flicker. A light. And if there was light—

Then there was a way to break them.

"Their cores!" she shouted, her voice ragged. "They can be killed—we just have to get to whatever's inside them!"

Kael swore under their breath but didn't hesitate. They pivoted, darting past one of the creatures, their knife a quick, flashing arc. They drove the blade deep, past the shifting, writhing exterior of the thing, aiming not at the surface but beneath it.

The result was instantaneous.

The creature froze, its limbs locking, its body shuddering as a low, warping groan tore from its shifting form. And then, just like that—

It collapsed.

Shattered.

Dissolved into mist and nothingness.

Kael's breath came fast. "Holy shit."

Anira didn't give them time to celebrate. "Again!"

The battlefield had changed.

They could win.

And if these things had cores—if they had something buried inside them that could be reached, cut free—

Then so did Ashric.

Her grip on the Rose tightened. The cold metal pressed against her palm, the once-burning warmth now no more than a faint ember. But it wasn't dead. It wasn't gone.

Just like he wasn't.

She would get him back.

She just had to carve through the darkness first.

The battle tore at the edges of reality, shadows shattering and reforming, limbs twisting in unnatural angles, mouths opening where none should be. Anira moved through it all, her mind a storm of focus, her blade carving paths through the writhing tide of darkness.

The creatures could be killed. She had seen it.

And if they could be killed—if there was something inside them, buried beneath the layers of void and corruption—then Ashric wasn't gone.

Not yet.

Her pulse pounded in her ears, a sharp contrast to the eerie silence of the creatures as they fell. There were no death cries, no final wails. Just unraveling, just dissolving, like the last wisps of a nightmare fading with the morning light.

Kael was still at her side, their knife flashing quick and lethal, their breathing ragged but controlled. "I don't know how many more of these things I can take down before I start losing my mind," they huffed, slicing through another creature's core. "It's like fighting smoke and teeth."

Anira didn't respond. Her mind was on something else—someone else.

The masked figure had taken Ashric, pulled him into the abyss, into the depths of whatever lay beyond the edges of this forsaken place. But it hadn't killed him. He hadn't become one of them.

Which meant there was time.

She pivoted, cutting through another creature, watching—waiting—for the flicker of something more, something alive beneath the surface of the void. The Rose pulsed weakly against her chest, its warmth barely there, like the faintest heartbeat in a sea of silence.

And then—

A whisper.

Not a voice. Not a sound.

A presence.

Faint. Distant.

But there.

She gasped, nearly losing her footing as the sensation hit her like a cold wind rushing through the cracks of a broken door.

Kael caught her elbow, eyes wild. "What? What's wrong?"

She barely heard them. Her gaze darted to the edges of the battlefield, to the dark void that still pulsed and breathed at the edges of the cavern.

It was pulling at her.

No.

Not at her.

At him.

"Ashric." The name left her lips as more instinct than thought.

Kael swore, following her gaze. "You felt something, didn't you?"

Anira nodded, her breath sharp, her chest tight. "He's not gone. I know it."

Kael cursed again, shaking their head. "That's great and all, but unless you've got a rescue plan that doesn't involve you hurling yourself into the literal abyss, I suggest we survive first."

Another shadow lunged. Anira ducked, her blade flashing, cutting deep. The thing split, its core flickering for half a breath before shattering completely.

She was running out of time.

Then, the air shifted.

A pulse—deep and slow.

Like a second heartbeat.

Anira felt it.

Not her own.

Not Kael's.

Something else.

Something familiar.

Her breath hitched.

Ashric.

She turned, scanning the battlefield, scanning the endless dark, and then—

A shape.

At first, it was just another shadow, another piece of the void, but then—

A step.

Unsteady. Weak.

Another.

And then, out of the black, he emerged.

Ashric.

His silhouette wavered at the edges, flickering, like the darkness still had him, still held onto him, but he was there.

His blade hung in his grasp, loose but not forgotten. His head was bowed, his breath slow, ragged, like he had been drowning in something endless and had only just broken the surface.

And his eyes—

Still his.

Not silver. Not void.

His.

But the shadows weren't letting him go so easily.

They curled around him, clawing at his edges, trying to pull him back.

Kael saw him at the same time Anira did. "Holy—he's—he's alive!"

The relief barely had time to settle before reality snapped back into place.

They had to get to him.

They had to hold the line.

Anira tightened her grip on her blade. The battle wasn't over.

It was only just beginning.

Ashric staggered forward. His body wavered at the edges, flickering like a candle caught in a breath of wind, like something unfinished, something not yet whole. He looked like a man stepping from a dream he hadn't chosen, from a place too deep, too dark, where the air had no weight and time did not exist. His breath was slow, uneven, a thing stolen back from the void itself.

The shadows still clung to him. They curled at his limbs, at his back, twisting and grasping like unseen hands, trying to pull him under again. They didn't want to let him go. He wasn't theirs to return.

But he walked anyway.

One step. Then another.

His sword hung in his hand, loose, forgotten. His shoulders were tight, like something heavy had settled there. Like the weight of whatever he had seen hadn't left him, would never leave him. His head was still bowed, his face hidden beneath the shadow of his own return.

And his eyes—

Still his.

Not silver. Not void.

But haunted.

Anira's breath caught. Her pulse ached against her ribs. For one long, trembling second, she could do nothing but stare, her thoughts a broken, frantic mess of disbelief and something else—something worse.

He was alive.

No, not yet.

Not fully.

The void still had him. It still pulled. He was caught between here and there, between life and something else entirely. The darkness was holding him, even now.

Kael saw him too. Their breath hitched, sharp and uneven. "Holy—he's—he's alive."

The words tasted wrong. Too soon. Too uncertain.

Anira moved before she thought.

The battlefield didn't matter anymore. The creatures pressing in didn't matter. The exhaustion in her limbs, the ache in her chest, the blood dried on her fingers—it didn't matter.

She took a step. Then another.

The ground shook beneath her boots, but she didn't stop.

Because he wasn't back yet. Not fully.

And if she didn't reach him, if she didn't pull him free—

He never would be.

The shadows tightened around him. The void sensed her coming.

It fought.

So she ran.

The ground beneath her boots trembled as if something ancient had stirred from its slumber, something vast and cruel and waiting. The shadows knew she was coming. They felt her now, sensed the way her pulse hammered, how her breath tore through her lungs like a blade. But she didn't stop.

She ran.

Not away. Not from them.

Toward him.

Ashric still wavered, flickering between existence and the void that still clung to him, trying to drag him back. The darkness wrapped around his limbs like oil, like chains, a thing with no shape and yet all shapes at once. It coiled in his ribs, in the curve of his throat, latching on with the same sick hunger that had tried to take her the moment she touched the Rose.

She had chosen.

Now it wanted him.

Not yet, she thought fiercely. Not today. Not like this.

The creatures were still moving, still swarming around the battlefield, but they were shifting now. They had changed. No longer lunging for her, no longer circling like beasts waiting for their prey to fall. They had turned, all of them, toward him.

Because they knew.

He was caught between.

And the void devoured what did not belong.

Kael cursed beside her, panting, their boots skidding against the slick stone. "Anira—what the hell is happening? He's—"

"I don't know," she bit out, her grip tightening on the hilt of her sword. "But we have to reach him. Now."

The words barely left her lips before the creatures moved again.

Not toward her.

Not toward Kael.

Toward Ashric.

A tidal wave of black limbs and jagged, shifting forms lunged for him, their claws slicing through the thick air, their hollow mouths opening wide as if to swallow him whole.

Anira threw herself forward.

She didn't hesitate. Didn't think. Didn't let the fear creep in. She couldn't.

Her blade found the first creature mid-strike, slashing deep into its shifting ribs. The thing shrieked, a noise that made her skull vibrate, but she didn't stop. She twisted, slashing again, carving through it, searching—reaching—for the flicker of light inside, the core, the only thing that could end them.

Kael was beside her, moving fast, their knife flashing in quick, lethal arcs, carving through the things before they could reach Ashric.

But there were too many.

Anira's breath was ragged now, her limbs aching, her pulse hammering against her ribs as she cut and cut and cut. She carved her way through the storm of shadows, desperate, furious, her body burning from the effort—

But they weren't fast enough.

Ashric staggered.

The shadows tightened around him, their jagged tendrils coiling around his chest, around his throat, pulling him deeper, dragging him down. His sword dropped from his fingers, clattering against the stone. His knees buckled, his body folding like something losing its grip on reality.

Anira felt it.

The moment he started slipping away.

Her heart lurched.

No.

Not like this.

Not like this.

She moved before she knew what she was doing.

She threw herself at him.

The moment her fingers wrapped around his wrist, the world shattered.

The shadows fought her grip, coiling tighter, twisting around him like a thousand hands, yanking him back, deeper, away.

But she held on.

She would not let go.

The Rose flared against her chest, searing hot, burning like a dying sun.

She pulled.

Harder.

Harder.

She gritted her teeth, her whole body trembling, her muscles screaming, her soul stretching—

And then, like a breath finally released, the void snapped.

The darkness recoiled, ripping away from Ashric in a violent, wailing shriek.

He gasped, alive, his body lurching forward, into her.

She caught him.

His weight crashed into her, sending them both to the ground, his breath ragged against her shoulder, his body shaking like he had been somewhere else entirely.

The battlefield went still.

The creatures had stopped moving.

The masked figure was gone.

The Rose pulsed against her chest. Once. Twice.

Then—silence.

Ashric shuddered in her arms, his breath uneven, his fingers weakly clutching at her arm like he wasn't sure if he was real.

She swallowed, her throat raw, her hands tightening around him, proving he was here. That he had made it back. That she had brought him back.

His voice was rough when he finally spoke, low and rasping against her ear.

"...You owe me for that."

A sharp, broken laugh tore from her throat before she could stop it. She pressed her forehead against his shoulder, squeezing her eyes shut as the relief cracked through the exhaustion, too deep, too raw, too much.

"You idiot," she whispered. "You absolute idiot."

He let out a weak huff, shifting against her, but didn't try to move away.

Kael exhaled somewhere behind them. "I hate both of you," they muttered, breathless and half-hysterical. "I hate all of this. I'm quitting. The moment we get out of here. I'm done. I'm—"

They paused.

Then, softer.

"...Holy shit. You actually pulled him back."

Anira opened her eyes, tilting her head slightly to glance at them.

Kael was staring. Not at her. Not at Ashric.

At the battlefield.

At the shadows.

They were dissolving.

Not in the way they had before. Not with violence, not with shrieks of rage and fury.

They were fading.

Drifting apart, slipping into nothingness, into what they had always been—remnants of something that should have died long ago.

Ashric shifted in her arms, pulling in a slow, shaky breath.

"…It's over," he murmured.

She wasn't sure if he meant the battle. Or the war.

Or something else entirely.

She swallowed hard, her fingers still curled into his jacket, her heart still hammering in her chest.

"No," she said softly.

She wasn't sure what had just happened. What she had just done.

But she knew one thing.

This wasn't over.

Not by a long shot.

This was just the beginning.

The cavern was still now. The battle had ended, but its echoes lingered, seared into the stone, into their bodies, into their bones. The shadows had retreated, fading into nothingness, slipping into the cracks of the world like mist swallowed by the wind. The air smelled of fire and ruin, of something ancient that had finally unraveled. The war here had ended.

But war never truly ends.

Anira was still holding him. Her fingers dug into his jacket, refusing to loosen, refusing to let go, as if she could anchor him here, keep him here, force him to stay in the world she still clung to. Her breathing was uneven, shallow and fast, the adrenaline refusing to release her.

She had him back.

But how close had she been to losing him forever?

Ashric stirred against her, his body solid and warm, and for the first time since the void had taken him, she felt his weight, his realness. He was here. The truth of it ached in her chest, a pain sharp enough to steal the air from her lungs.

She let out a breath, trembling, then whispered, "You idiot."

His voice was hoarse when he replied. "You keep saying that."

She pulled back just enough to look at him, her hands still fisted in his jacket, her heart hammering against her ribs. He was pale, the remnants of the void still clinging to him in the dark shadows beneath his eyes, the tremor in his fingers. But his eyes—gods, his eyes—were the same. His.

Not silver. Not empty.

She had brought him back.

And she didn't know how to deal with the way that felt like drowning.

Ashric studied her, his breath uneven, as if he were memorizing her just as frantically as she was memorizing him. His gaze flickered over her face, her hands still clutching his jacket, the tension in her shoulders that hadn't faded even though the battle was over.

He let out a slow exhale, then whispered, "You pulled me back."

She swallowed hard. "Of course, I did."

"You weren't supposed to," he said, something unreadable flickering in his gaze.

Her fingers curled tighter into the fabric of his coat. "Then you don't know me very well."

He let out a rough, tired laugh. "No," he admitted. "I do. That's the problem."

She felt the words before she could stop them. "You scared me."

His breath hitched. His hand lifted, slow and unsteady, and for a moment, she thought he was going to pull away. But instead, his fingers brushed her cheek, barely a touch, hesitant and uncertain, like he wasn't sure if he had the right.

She didn't pull away.

His thumb traced just beneath her eye, a quiet, unspoken acknowledgment of the weight still sitting there. "You scared me too," he murmured. "More than anything else ever has."

She exhaled, her forehead nearly pressing against his. "Don't do that again."

His lips twitched, the ghost of something teasing, something softer, something so terribly Ashric despite everything they had just survived. "No promises."

She let out a broken laugh, but it faded too quickly, swallowed by the silence, by the weight of everything that hadn't been said.

He was here.

She had him back.

But the war wasn't over. The shadows had lost this battle, but the war still loomed ahead. And for the first time, she realized how fragile everything was. How close she had come to losing him for good.

She couldn't take that.

She wouldn't.

Her fingers curled into his coat again, pulling him just the slightest bit closer, her breath unsteady but her resolve unwavering.

"I can't do this without you," she whispered. "I won't."

Ashric didn't flinch. He didn't try to step back.

"Then you won't have to," he murmured. "Not ever."

Her chest ached.

The shadows were gone now. The fight had ended. The cavern stood silent.

But the war was far from over.

For now, though—just for now—she let herself believe him.

The Weight of Survival

The cavern walls loomed around them, silent now, no longer shifting with the pulse of unnatural forces, no longer breathing with the weight of something watching from beyond. The battle had ended, but the air still felt wrong—charged, waiting, thick with the remnants of what had been.

Anira felt it too, the exhaustion curling into the edges of her limbs, seeping into her bones like rot settling in wood. The adrenaline had kept her upright, had kept her moving, but now, in the cold silence that followed, it began to slip away, leaving behind only the raw, aching truth.

She had won.

But the cost of that victory was still unknown.

Ashric was beside her, alive, his breath slow and steady but tinged with something deeper—something not yet settled. The void had touched him, had nearly taken him, and even now, even with the weight of him real and solid beside her, she wasn't sure if it had truly let him go.

Kael was pacing near the cavern entrance, arms crossed, face drawn, muttering half-formed curses under their breath. They had fought like hell, like someone with nothing left to lose, but now, in the wake of it all, their usual sharp-edged bravado was dull.

They were all different now.

No one walked out of something like this unchanged.

The Rose had gone quiet. The pendant rested against Anira's chest, cold, its once-burning warmth dimmed to a faint pulse, weak and uncertain, as if it, too, was unsure of what came next.

She pressed her fingers against it, expecting something—anything—but it remained silent.

For the first time since she had taken up this burden, it didn't feel like it was leading her anywhere.

And that terrified her.

Kael finally stopped pacing. "We need to move." Their voice was rough, tired, barely keeping hold of its usual snark. "We've been sitting here like easy targets long enough. Whatever the hell that thing was—it might be gone, but I don't trust this place. And I sure as hell don't trust that we're alone."

Anira exhaled, nodding. They weren't wrong.

She turned to Ashric, studying him, watching for any lingering sign that the shadows still clung to him, waiting to pull him back under. His face was pale, drawn, but his eyes were steady.

Still his.

"Can you walk?" she asked, her voice softer than she intended.

He gave her a look that was almost offended, then pushed himself upright. The movement was slow, deliberate, but he didn't stumble. He rolled his shoulders once, testing his balance, then nodded. "I'm fine."

She didn't believe him.

But she didn't argue.

Not now.

Kael let out a slow breath. "Then let's get the hell out of here."

They started toward the tunnel that led out, their steps quick, ready to leave this nightmare behind. But as Anira and Ashric followed, something made her stop.

A feeling.

A warning.

The weight of something unseen pressed against her skull, not like before—not a presence, not a voice, but a shift in the air, a whisper in the silence that made her blood run cold.

She turned, scanning the cavern one last time.

The battle was over.

The shadows had retreated.

The tunnel stretched ahead, rough-hewn and endless, a path carved by hands that no longer existed, leading them away from the ruin of what they had survived. Their boots scuffed against the stone, the only sound in the heavy silence, save for their breath—still sharp, still raw, still laced with the memory of the battle behind them.

Ashric walked beside her, close enough that she could feel the warmth of him, the steady presence of someone who had been torn from her grasp and given back. His arm still bore the remnants of the void's grasp, faint black lines etched beneath his skin, a mark of what had nearly been taken. But he was here. Real. And that was enough.

For now.

Anira exhaled slowly, pressing her fingers against the Rose where it rested at her chest, its pulse weak, like something weary from all it had endured. She understood the feeling.

Kael strode ahead, mumbling to themself, hands gesturing faintly as if already trying to piece together whatever disaster came next. It was a comforting sight—Kael plotting, preparing, never quite still, never quite quiet.

It left her alone with him.

With Ashric.

And the silence that settled between them.

Not the heavy, unspoken silence of grief.

Not the tight-lipped, battle-worn silence of what almost was.

But a silence made of something else.

Something undeniable.

Something that had been waiting far too long.

She turned her head slightly, glancing at him, her breath catching when she found him already watching her. Not just watching—studying, his sharp blue eyes tracing the curve of her face, the cut on her brow, the tension in her jaw that she hadn't even realized she still held.

"You're staring," she murmured, her voice softer than she meant.

Ashric didn't look away. "So are you."

She huffed, glancing forward, but the warmth creeping up her neck betrayed her.

"I thought I lost you." The words left her lips before she could stop them, unguarded, unfiltered. The admission felt like something she had carried too long, pressing against her ribs, desperate to escape.

"You didn't," he said, and it wasn't just a reassurance. It was a promise.

Her throat tightened. She turned to face him fully, her pulse hammering against her ribs in a way that had nothing to do with battle, nothing to do with fear.

The exhaustion was still there. The ache in her bones, the weight of survival, the unsteady ground of whatever came next. But here, in this moment, she felt something else curling through the exhaustion. A kind of relief so sharp it cut.

He was alive.

And so was she.

And they were here, standing in the wake of everything, still breathing, still whole—together.

Her gaze flickered to his lips.

It was a mistake.

Or maybe it wasn't.

Ashric let out a slow breath, his fingers curling at his sides before he reached for her, hesitant at first, like maybe she would step back.

She didn't.

She never would.

His fingers brushed her jaw, tilting her chin ever so slightly, his touch careful, deliberate. And then—gods, finally—he kissed her.

It wasn't soft.

It wasn't hesitant.

It was everything they had been holding back—every unspoken word, every moment they had stood too close, every time his hand had lingered a second longer than it should have. It was anger, it was fear, it was I almost lost you and I won't let that happen again. It was the promise of war still ahead of them, the fire of everything they hadn't said and never needed to say.

Anira curled her fingers into the fabric of his jacket, pulling him closer, sinking into the moment, letting it consume her the way battle never could. His grip tightened, one hand sliding against the small of her back, steady, unyielding, his. He kissed her like it was the only way to prove he was still here, like if he let go, he might slip between her fingers again.

He wasn't going anywhere.

She wouldn't let him.

A loud, exasperated groan broke through the quiet.

Kael.

"For the love of everything, could you two wait until we're not standing in a death tunnel to start making out?"

Ashric barely moved, though his lips did twitch against hers. "Not now, Kael."

"Oh no, now," Kael shot back, arms crossed, head tilting dramatically as they regarded the two of them. "Because I have been waiting for this. You think I didn't see this coming? First moment I met you two , I said to myself, 'Yep, that one's gonna die for her, and that one's gonna get pissed about it and bring him back.' And look where we are."

Anira's forehead dropped against Ashric's chest, hiding the laugh that threatened to spill out, still breathless, still caught in the moment she hadn't let go of yet.

Ashric exhaled slowly, his arm tightening briefly around her before he pulled back just enough to look at Kael, deadpan. "And you let us go through all of that without warning us?"

Kael threw their hands up. "Oh, I tried to warn you. But noooo, you two love to be tragic. What's romance without a little life-threatening peril, right?"

Anira shook her head, biting back a smile. "Kael—"

"Nope," Kael said, turning on their heel. "Nope, not listening, nope, don't want to hear it, I am leaving you two here to stew in your feelings." They started walking ahead, muttering, "If either of you so much as sighs wistfully, I swear, I will throw myself into the next void we find."

Anira closed her eyes, taking one slow breath, trying to collect herself.

Ashric was still watching her when she opened them.

And despite everything—despite the exhaustion, the battle, the war still looming ahead—she smiled.

She had survived.

He had survived.

And for the first time in a long time, something inside her felt light.

They walked in silence, the three of them moving through the narrowing tunnel, leaving the battlefield and its horrors behind. The air shifted the further they went, losing its unnatural weight, its bitter metallic tang, its lingering scent of ruin. The Rose was quiet now, cold against Anira's chest, no longer pulling her forward, no longer burning in warning.

But something else had taken its place.

The knowledge that this wasn't over.

That the shadows had not lost.

They had only retreated.

Kael muttered something under their breath, kicking a loose stone ahead of them, their voice still carrying that sharp edge of humor, but it was forced. The truth sat between them, unspoken. Survival felt temporary. Like a brief inhale before the weight of everything crashed down again.

Anira stole a glance at Ashric.

He caught her looking.

He didn't speak, but the shift in his gaze told her he felt it too.

They stepped into the open air.

The tunnel spat them out into a vast, barren landscape, the sky overhead a stretch of deep twilight, the stars barely visible through the thick, shifting clouds. The wind was sharp and cold, pulling at their coats, their hair, wrapping around them like unseen hands whispering of what had been lost.

And what was coming next.

Kael exhaled loudly. "Right. We survived. Again. You know, I think we need a new strategy because almost dying this often is really starting to feel like a personality trait."

Anira huffed, shaking her head. "Maybe we should start taking bets on which of us nearly dies next."

Kael's grin was immediate. "Oh, I'm putting my money on him." They jerked a thumb toward Ashric. "He's way too noble for his own good."

Ashric sighed, dragging a hand through his hair. "You could bet on the two of you learning to stay out of danger."

Kael snorted. "Now, where's the fun in that?"

Anira let the banter wash over her, let the humor pull at the frayed edges of her exhaustion. It was a moment of normalcy—a brief flicker of what used to be.

But something still felt wrong.

The wind carried a sound—so faint, so distant she almost convinced herself she had imagined it.

But then—

A tremor rolled beneath their feet.

Subtle. Barely there. But unmistakable.

Kael stopped mid-step. "Uh. Did anyone else feel that?"

Ashric's hand was already on his sword. "Yes."

Anira turned slowly, scanning the dark horizon, her breath catching in her throat.

The ground was shifting.

The stars above—the sky itself—wavered.

And then—

A sound.

A low, resonant hum.

Familiar.

But deeper. Stronger.

The Rose had stopped guiding her.

Because something else had awakened.

A shadow rippled in the far distance, massive, shifting, rising.

Not a creature.

Not an army.

Something worse.

Something ancient.

Something that had been waiting.

Anira's pulse hammered against her ribs.

Kael took an unsteady step back. "I, um. I really don't like that."

Ashric's gaze darkened, his jaw tight. "Neither do I."

The hum grew louder.

The wind picked up, whipping at their coats, their hair, carrying with it a whisper—low, broken, a voice not meant for mortal ears.

Anira swallowed hard, her fingers curling around the cold weight of the Rose.

The battle was over.

The war had just begun.

And they were already running out of time.

A Personal Thank You

Dear Reader,

Out of all the books out there, you chose this one. And for that, I am truly grateful.

Time is precious, and the fact that you spent some of yours with this story means the world to me. Whether it made you think, feel, escape, or simply pass the time, I hope it left something with you—something that lingers in your mind, if only for a little while.

Writers tell stories because we believe in their power to connect us, even across distances. And though I may not know you personally, I do know this: without readers like you, stories would have nowhere to go. So, thank you for giving this one a place to land.

If you enjoyed the book, I'd love to hear your thoughts. Reviews, recommendations, and even just a message saying you liked it. That would mean more than you might think. And if this isn't goodbye forever, if our paths cross again in another story—I'll be honored to have you back.

With gratitude,

Everett Vale